I'M HERE TO KILL YOU

I'M HERE TO KILL YOU

SMOKE JENSEN AND THE TAMING OF THE WEST

WILLIAM W. JOHNSTONE

AND J.A. JOHNSTONE

PINNACLE BOOKS
Kensington Publishing Corp.
kensingtonbooks.com

THE JENSEN FAMILY
FIRST FAMILY OF THE AMERICAN FRONTIER

Smoke Jensen—*The Mountain Man*
The youngest of three children and orphaned as a young boy, Smoke Jensen is considered one of the fastest draws in the West. His quest to tame the lawless West has become the stuff of legend. Smoke owns the Sugarloaf Ranch in Colorado. Married to Sally Jensen, father to Denise ("Denny") and Louis.

Preacher—*The First Mountain Man*
Though not a blood relative, grizzled frontiersman Preacher became a father figure to the young Smoke Jensen, teaching him how to survive in the brutal, often deadly Rocky Mountains. Fought the battles that forged his destiny. Armed with a long gun, Preacher is as fierce as the land itself.

Matt Jensen—*The Last Mountain Man*
Orphaned but taken in by Smoke Jensen, Matt Jensen has become like a younger brother to Smoke and even took the Jensen name. And like Smoke, Matt has carved out his destiny on the American frontier. He lives by the gun and surrenders to no man.

Luke Jensen—*Bounty Hunter*
Mountain Man Smoke Jensen's long-lost brother, Luke Jensen, is scarred by war and a dead shot—the right qualities to be a bounty hunter. And he's cunning, and fierce enough, to bring down the deadliest outlaws of his day.

Ace Jensen and Chance Jensen—*Those Jensen Boys!*
The untold story of Smoke Jensen's long-lost nephews, Ace
and Chance, a pair of young-gun twins as reckless and wild
as the frontier itself . . . Their father is Luke Jensen, thought
killed in the Civil War. Their uncle Smoke Jensen is one
of the fiercest gunfighters the West has ever known. It's no
surprise that the inseparable Ace and Chance Jensen have a
knack for taking risks—even if they have to blast their way
out of them.

CONTENTS

BRUTAL NIGHT
OF THE MOUNTAIN MAN

CHAPTER 1

El Paso County, Texas

The Eagle Shire Ranch was second in size only to the King Ranch in Southwest Texas. Silas Atwood, owner of Eagle Shire, had been ruthless in building his ranch. He began the process by buying, from the bank, the mortgage paper on many of the smaller adjacent ranches. If a blizzard or drought or some other calamity would happen to cause the smaller ranchers to miss payments, Atwood was merciless in foreclosing on them immediately. In this way he continued to expand his already large holdings.

Bo Willis, Tony Clinton, Abe Creech, and Danny Reed rode for Atwood, though they couldn't exactly be called cowboys since their positions for the ranch called for a set of skills that were different from those required by working cowboys. Atwood called such men his "special cadre." At the moment, Willis and the others were at Glen Creek, a year-round stream that supplied water for this part of the county. They were near the spillway where, even now, water was pooling into a widening lake behind gate number one. Closing the gate stopped the creek from flowing onto the Double Nickel Ranch. A medium-size ranch, the Double Nickel had, so far, managed to survive blizzards and droughts.

Bo Willis took a leak against an ocotillo cactus, aiming at a sunning frog as he did so. He laughed when the creature, caught in the stream, hopped away. Buttoning his pants, he walked back over to the others.

"See anything yet?" Willis asked.

Clinton spit a wad of tobacco before he answered. "Nope," he said. "I'm not sure anyone will be here."

"Oh, someone will be here all right. Either Dumey or some of his men," Willis said. "They're goin' to want to know what happened to the stream."

Reed laughed. "When they find out, I don't reckon Dumey is goin' to be all that happy about it."

"Yeah, well he can bitch all he wants, Mr. Atwood has a court order allowin' us to close the gate, so there's nothing he can do about it. Nothing legal, that is. That means that if he, or any of his men, show up, it can only be to cause us trouble. And remember, when they do arrive, they will be trespassing, which means we have every right to shoot them down."

"Hey, Bo," Creech said. "Looks like we've got company comin'."

Creech pointed out three riders.

"All right, you fellas stay out of sight," Willis said. "Have your rifles loaded and ready. When I give the signal, shoot 'em."

"Shoot at them?" Reed asked.

"No, shoot them," Willis said. "You got a problem with that? 'Cause if you do, it may just be that you'll need to find another place to work."

"No, I ain't got no problem with that," Reed insisted. "I just wanted to be sure that's what Mr. Atwood wanted, is all."

"He give us fifty dollars apiece to come out here 'n do just that," Willis said. "I don't intend to go back 'n tell 'im the job didn't get done. So if you ain't got it in you, just go on back now, 'n I'll take your fifty dollars."

"Like hell you will," Reed said. "You just give me the word, then step out of the way so they don't none of them fall on you."

Clinton and Creech laughed at Reed's comment.

"Go on, then, 'n get out of sight," Willis ordered.

Clinton, Creech, and Reed got out of sight behind an outcropping of rocks. Willis walked out to the middle of the road and stood, waiting until the three riders came close enough for him to identify them. One of them was Gus Dumey, son of the owner of the Double Nickel. The other two were Paul Burke, who was the foreman of the Double Nickel, and a man named Poke, who was one of the Double Nickel riders. Poke was the only name Willis knew him by.

"That's far enough!" Willis called out, holding his hand up to stop the riders. "You three men are trespassing on Eagle Shire Ranch property."

"Is that you, Willis?" Burke asked.

"Yeah. What are you three doin' here, Burke?"

"Our crick has run dry," Burke said. "We're tryin' to find out why."

"It's run dry 'cause we closed the gate," Willis said.

"What?" Dumey shouted. "Why the hell did Atwood do that?"

"It ain't Mr. Atwood's doin'," Willis replied. "Judge Boykin ordered it shut down so as to divert some water to the other ranches because of the drought."

"There aren't any other ranches serviced by Glen Creek except Eagle Shire and the Double Nickel," Dumey said angrily. "And there isn't a drought."

"Well, then, if their ain't no drought, you got no need for the crik, do you?" Willis said with a smug smile.

Dumey started toward the gate.

"Where do you think you're a-goin'?" Willis asked.

"I aim to open that gate," Dumey replied.

Willis looked toward the concealed men and nodded. Shots rang out and Dumey, Burke, and Poke all three went down as a cloud of gunsmoke drifted up over the rocks.

Clinton and the others came out then. "Dead?" Clinton asked.

"Yeah," Willis replied.

"Let's get 'em throwed over their saddles, then take 'em into Marshal Witherspoon. Mr. Atwood wants this done all legal-like."

Big Rock, Colorado

Smoke Jensen and Cal Wood were standing in the crowd of some fifty or so spectators, watching the horseshoe-pitching contest. They were here to support their friend Pearlie, who was representing Big Rock in the Eagle County championship match. Pearlie was defending his position as county champion, but he was facing stiff competition this time from Jim Wyatt, who represented Red Cliff.

The two men were tied, and Wyatt, who was up, held the shoe under his chin, studied the pit at the far end, then made his toss. His shoe hit the stake and lay there, in contact with the stake.

"Good toss, Wyatt," someone called.

"Yeah? Watch this one."

Wyatt threw his second shoe. There was a loud clang as the horseshoe hit the iron stake, then fell. The judge made a quick examination of the shoe, then called back, "The ends are all the way through. It's a ringer."

"That gives Wyatt twenty-one points, Pearlie," someone shouted. "Looks to me like you ain't a-goin' to be the horseshoe-throwin' champion of Eagle County no more."

The man who called out was Beans Evans, one of the wagon drivers for Big Rock Freighters.

"Don't count 'im out yet, Beans," Cal said. "He's got two more throws."

"He ain't hit a ringer in the last ten tosses," Beans replied. "He ain't likely to do it now."

Pearlie threw the shoe. It hit the stake and then whirled around. Pearlie held his breath until it dropped.

"It spun off," Wyatt said.

"No, it didn't," the judge replied, examining the shoe. "Mr. Wyatt's ringer is canceled, and there is zero score for either man."

"You're at nineteen points, Pearlie. Another ringer is all you need."

"I bet you five dollars he don't get it," Beans said.

"Now, Beans, I know you don't really want to bet that much," Smoke said. "Suppose we just bet a beer on it."

Beans laughed. "Yeah," he said. "I was gettin' a little carried away there, wasn't I? All right, I'll bet you a beer."

Sugarloaf Ranch

Sally Jensen was sitting on Eagle Watch, the high escarpment that guarded the north end of the ranch. She had found this place shortly after she and Smoke were married, and she came here quite often to enjoy the view. From here she could see the house, a large two-story edifice, white, with a porch that ran all the way across the front. It had turrets at each of the front corners, the windows of which now shined gold in the reflected sunlight. Also in the compound were several other structures, including the bunkhouse, cook's shack, cowboy dining hall, barn, granary, and other out-buildings.

Now was bluebell season, and at her insistence some of the meadow was left free of any livestock so she could enjoy the tulip-shaped blooms and their rich color from deep blue, to almost purple. Although Sally had grown up in New England, she was now living the life of her dreams; married to the man she loved.

Smoke Jensen's reputation reached far beyond the Colorado state lines, far beyond the West. He was someone whose reputation as a rancher, and as a courageous champion of others, was the stuff of heroes, and indeed, there had already been many books written about him.

Even as such thoughts played across her mind, she looked down onto Jensen Pike and smiled at the sight of three approaching riders. They were, she knew, Smoke, Pearlie, and Cal. Pearlie and Cal were their two top ranch hands, but they were much more than that. The two young men had been with them for a long time, having come to the ranch when they were relatively young. As a result, Smoke and Sally looked at them more as if they were members of the family than just employees.

Sally mounted her horse, then rode back down the trail to meet them, arriving back at the house at about the same time Smoke, Pearlie, and Cal did.

"I made some bear sign," Sally said. "I figured they would be good as consolation in case you lost, or as a celebration in case you won. Which was it?"

Pearlie reached down into his saddlebag, then, with a big smile, pulled out a brass cup.

"We'll be celebratin'," he said, holding the cup up so she could see it.

"My," Sally replied. "I do believe that one is even prettier than the other three."

"It is, isn't it?"

"They all look just alike," Cal said.

Smoke laughed. "I believe you have just been subjected to a bit of Sally's sarcasm."

Eagle Shire Ranch, El Paso County

There were two separate bunkhouses on the Eagle Shire Ranch. The larger of the two bunkhouses was for the men who were actually cowboys, men who rode the range, kept the fences repaired, pulled cattle out of mud holes, and maintained the wagons and equipment. The smaller bunkhouse was for Silas Atwood's cadre of gunmen. It was because Silas Atwood was so successful that he justified the presence of his own personal army of gunmen. He suggested that a man of his wealth and prominence was always in danger of being attacked.

The working cowboys weren't jealous of the special cadre. In fact, honestly they gave the gunmen little thought.

"They have their job, we have ours," is the way Miner Cobb, the foreman of the ranch, explained it. Because of the decreasing number of area ranches, the working cowboys of Eagle Shire were just thankful for the job.

Steady employment was not the norm for the cowboys working at any of the few remaining ranches. It was not only that none of the other ranchers had the economic clout as Silas Atwood, it was that many of the smaller ranches that had started the year under the ownership of one man had changed hands when they found the challenge of trying to survive in the shadow of a huge ranch, like the Eagle Shire, to be more difficult than they could handle.

Some sold out to Atwood on his first offer. They were the lucky ones. Those who insisted that they could survive sometimes found that their source of water was compromised, or mysterious fires burned away their grass. Also, because Atwood owned so much land, he had the smaller ranches blocked so that passage in and out of town was possible only by paying high toll fees. Most gave up, and abandoned their ranches with only what they could carry with them.

It wasn't just the ranchers who were having to deal with Atwood, several of the businessmen of the town of Etholen found their livelihood threatened as well.

"Do you know anything about the old feudal system of England?" Atwood once asked. "Men who owned large areas of land, and who controlled the village, became members of the peerage. We don't have peerage here, but I intend to have as much power as any duke in the realm."

Atwood already controlled the law in Etholen, not only the marshal and his deputy but the city council and the circuit judge as well. It was Atwood's control of the law that allowed him to bring in the bodies of Gus Dumey, Paul Burke, and Poke without having to face any consequences.

The only official in town that Atwood did not control was Mayor Joe Cravens. But he intended to take care of that in the next election.

CHAPTER 2

The most popular saloon in town was the Pretty Girl and Happy Cowboy Saloon. If he could gain control of that saloon, Atwood felt that it would give him influence over much of the rest of the town. The Pretty Girl and Happy Cowboy Saloon was enjoying a peaceful Saturday afternoon. There was a friendly card game going on at one of the tables, and the teases, touches, and flirtatious laughter of the girls who gave the saloon its name were in play all through the room. The owner of the saloon, Kate Abernathy, was sitting at a table with Mayor Joe Cravens and Allen Blanton, the editor and publisher of the *Etholen Standard*.

Rusty Abernathy, Kate's son, was playing the piano, his music adding to the ambience of afternoon. Unlike the pianos in most saloons, this wasn't an upright . . . this was a Steinway Grand Piano, and, unlike most saloon piano players, Rusty had natural talent, great skill, and classical training. It was relatively rare when he played classical music, but even when he played the saloon classic songs, such as "The Old Chisholm Trail," "The Cowboy's Lament," or "I Ride an Old Paint," he offered a melodic poignancy that made the musical experience in the Pretty Girl and Happy Cowboy to be quite unique.

"Atwood said that young Dumey, Burke, and Poke

came out there to tear down the gate, and when they were challenged, they opened fire," Mayor Cravens said. "They said they were killed in self-defense."

"You don't believe that, do you, Joe?" Blanton asked.

"Not for a minute. But Witherspoon believed it. And so did Judge Boykin, so that's the end of it."

"I don't think that Witherspoon or Boykin believe it any more than we do. They're both in Atwood's pocket. You know that," Blanton said.

"Yes, well, it doesn't matter whether Boykin absolved Willis and the others out of belief or graft, he's made his ruling, and there's nothing we can do about it."

"You're the mayor," Kate said.

"I can't do a thing without the backing of the city council, and Atwood controls them as much as he does Witherspoon and Boykin."

"Maybe you can't do anything, but I've got the newspaper and freedom of the press," Blanton said. "And I intend to use it."

"You're a good man, Allen," Mayor Cravens said.

"Thank you. And, speaking of the paper, I've got some advertising copy I have to set, so, if you two will excuse me."

"I'll come with you," Mayor Cravens said.

The two men stood, then turned toward Kate. "Kate, my dear," Cravens said, taking her hand and lifting it to his lips. "It has been a pleasure visiting with you. You are like a long, cool drink of water in the midst of a blazing desert."

"Damn!" Blanton said. "And here I am supposed to be the one with a facility for words."

Kate laughed. "You gentlemen make my day."

Silas Atwood never went anywhere without at least two of his gunmen. Tonight, when he rode into town, he took Jeb

Calley and Tony Clinton with him. He never hired anyone unless he knew quite a bit about them. Calley had deserted the army and robbed a stagecoach up in Wyoming, before drifting down to Texas. Clinton was wanted for murder back in Arkansas. The fact that Atwood knew so much about the men he hired for his special cadre helped him exercise control over them.

Kate saw Atwood and his two men come into her saloon, and she braced herself because she knew that Atwood was going to come to her table to talk to her. She also knew what he was going to talk about, because the subject came up every time Atwood came in. The Pretty Girl and Happy Cowboy Saloon was more than a mere saloon. It was almost like a country club, so that even women of the town could come in without being scandalized. The Pretty Girls of the saloon were just that, pretty girls who acted as hostesses and who provided the cowboy customers with what, for most of them, was their only opportunity to ever have a pleasant conversation with a woman.

Because of the popularity of the Pretty Girl and Happy Cowboy Saloon, Atwood had made it a point to try to buy it. He wanted to control the entire town, and it was his belief that control of the Pretty Girl and Happy Cowboy would give him enough of a presence, and influence over the town, that he would be able to realize his ambition.

As she expected, Atwood, leaving his two bodyguards standing at the bar, came over to Kate's table.

"You may as well sell out to me, Kate," Atwood said. "You must know that no decent woman would ever own a saloon. I have made you a very generous offer."

"I appreciate the offer, Mr. Atwood. But my late husband opened this saloon, and I intend to manage it for as long as there is breath in my body."

"I'm sorry to hear you say that. I fear that you may find that remark to be most prophetic."

"Prophetic. What do you mean by that?"

"Let's just leave it at that, shall we?"

Atwood got up to leave, but on his way out, he stopped to say something to a man who was standing at the end of the bar that was nearest the door. As Atwood left the saloon, Clinton left with him, but Calley stayed behind.

Kate was sure Atwood had ordered him to stay behind, but why? After Atwood left, Calley looked directly at her, and with that glance, Kate was certain that their brief conversation had had something to do with her.

For a few moments after Atwood left, Calley continued to stand at the bar, then he shouted over to Rusty, "Hey you! Play 'Wait for the Wagon'!"

Rusty held up his hand, nodded, then played the song Calley requested. After he completed the song, he started another one.

"Play 'Wait for the Wagon'!" Calley called again.

Rusty chuckled, waved, and continued with what he was playing.

"Play 'Wait for the Wagon'!" Calley shouted.

Rusty nodded again, then hurried through the song he was playing. "Mr. Calley, do you really want to hear it again?" he asked.

"Yeah," Calley replied.

"All right, here it is again."

Rusty played the song through to the end, even adding a few of his own flourishes. Then, he started another song.

"Hey, you! Play 'Wait for the Wagon'!" Calley demanded.

Rusty continued with the song he was playing.

"I told you to play 'Wait for the Wagon'!"

Rusty stopped in the middle of his song and turned around to face his heckler. "Mr. Calley, I have played that song for you, twice. There are other people who have asked that I play something for them, and I'm going to honor their requests. After that, I will play your song again, but that will be the last time tonight."

"If you don't commence a' playin' that song by the time I count to ten, I'm goin' to draw my gun and shoot you dead," Calley said menacingly.

There were fifteen other people witnessing the event, counting the customers, plus Kate and the "girls" who worked for her. One of the fifteen was Deputy Tim Calhoun, but he couldn't exactly be called a witness, since he was sitting at a table in the back of the room, too drunk to be aware of what was going on. At Calley's words, all conversation came to a halt as they looked at the drama that was playing out before them.

"Mr. Calley, surely you don't mean that," the bartender said.

"Peterson, you got that scattergun under the bar?"

When Peterson didn't answer, Calley drew his pistol and pointed it at the bartender.

"I asked you a question. Do you still have that scattergun under the bar?"

"Yeah," Peterson replied quietly.

"Pull that gun out by the barrel 'n lay it up on the bar," Calley ordered.

With shaking hands, Peterson reached down under the bar, then came up with his hands wrapped around the two barrels of the double-barreled, twelve-gauge, Greener shotgun. He put the gun on the bar.

"Good for you," Calley said. Then, with a grin that could only be described as malevolent, he turned back to Rusty.

"Piano player, you ain't started playin' yet," Calley said.

"I've no intention of playing 'Wait for the Wagon' again," Rusty said resolutely.

"Then I aim to commence a' countin', 'n if you ain't a' playin' that song by the time I get to ten, I'm goin' to shoot you," Calley said. "One!"

Rusty stood up, then moved out from behind the piano bench. "Mr. Calley, I wish you wouldn't do this," he said.

"Deputy Calhoun, do something, please!" Kate said, calling back to the deputy marshal, whose head was on the table in front of him.

"Ha!" Calley said. "You think that drunk's goin' to be able to do anything?" He added to the count. "Two."

"Mr. Calley, as I am sure you are fully aware, I'm not a gunman," Rusty said. "Perhaps you have noticed, by now, that I'm not even wearing a pistol. I don't think you want to shoot an unarmed man, do you?"

"You," Calley said, pointing to one of the other customers. "Take your pistol over there, 'n lay it on the bench beside 'im." Calley laughed, though there was little humor in his laugh. "He's right, I don't want to shoot an unarmed man, 'n when I kill 'im, I don't want no one to say I wasn't bein' fair."

"That ain't fair, Calley," the customer said. "Like Rusty said, he ain't no gunfighter. Hell, all he does is play the piano and help his ma around the place."

"Take your pistol over there 'n lay it on the bench beside 'im like I told you to, or use it yourself," Calley said menacingly.

"You got no call to make me do that," the customer said.

"Either do what I told you to do, or draw your gun when I get to three." Calley smiled, an evil smile. "And mayhaps you mighta noticed, I'm already up to two."

"All right, all right!" the customer said, holding his hands out in front of him. "I'll do it!"

"Walk over there, take your gun out just real slow like, 'n put it on the bench alongside of 'im, then get out of the way. I wouldn't want you to maybe get yourself shot when I kill the piano player here."

Under Calley's watchful eye, the customer walked over

to the bench. "I'm sorry, Rusty," the customer said. "But you can see how it is. What else could I do?"

"That's all right, Doodle, I understand," Rusty replied.

Doodle pulled his pistol, put it on the piano bench, then stepped back up to the bar.

"Three," Calley said after Doodle stepped away.

Rusty felt a hollowness in the pit of his stomach, and his throat grew dry.

"Four."

Calley continued to count. When he got to seven, he interrupted the count for a moment.

"Boy, if you think I'm just foolin' you, then you got another think comin'. By the time I get to ten, I'm goin' to kill you. Onliest chance you got is to pick up that gun 'n try 'n beat me. You ain't goin' to beat me, but you can at least try. Eight."

"Calley, what you're a' doin' is murder, pure 'n simple!" one of the other customers said.

"I tell you what," Calley said to Rusty. "If that whore mama of your'n would be willin' to sell this place to Mr. Atwood, why maybe I wouldn't kill you."

"Wait a minute! Is that what this is all about?" Kate asked. "This is so I'll sell my place to Atwood? I saw Atwood talking to you just before he left. Did he put you up to this?"

Calley turned to look toward Kate. "Nah, he didn't say nothin' like that to me. But I know he wants to buy this place, so I figure, if I could talk you into it, why he might just be real thankful for me doin' 'im a favor like that."

Out of the corner of her eye, Kate saw Rusty moving his hand slowly but steadily toward the pistol that Doodle had put on the piano bench. She decided to keep Calley's attention as long as she could.

"You can tell Atwood for me that I have no intention of selling my place to him."

"Well now, that's pure-dee a shame, ain't it?" Calley said. "I guess I'm just goin' to have to continue with the countin'. Nine . . . ."

Suddenly the room was filled with the explosive sound of a gunshot. Blood squirted out from a bullet hole in Calley's temple, and he went down quickly, dead before he hit the floor.

Rusty stood there in shock, staring at the body of the man he had just shot. He was still holding the pistol, and he could smell the gunsmoke that curled up in a thin stream from the barrel.

"Damn!" Peterson said.

"Rusty!" Kate yelled, hurrying over to her son. She embraced him.

"I . . . I shot him, Mom," Rusty said, speaking the words in quiet awe. "I've never shot anybody before."

"You didn't have any choice, boy," Peterson said. "The son of a bitch was about to shoot you."

By now several people were coming into the saloon from the street, some drawn by the sound of the shot, and some because word of what had happened had already begun to spread.

One of those who came in was Marshal Witherspoon. He saw Rusty standing there holding the gun.

"Did you do this?" Witherspoon asked.

"Yes," Rusty answered.

Witherspoon walked over to take the gun. Rusty offered no resistance.

"You're under arrest for murder," he said.

CHAPTER 3

Judge Henry L. Boykin rapped his gavel on the bench of the Circuit Court of Etholen.

Rusty looked over at Emil Cates, his court-appointed defense counsel. Rusty could smell whiskey, and Cates was so drunk he could barely hold his head up. He groaned when he saw the makeup of the jury. He recognized Willis, Clark, Booker, Creech, Walker, Pardeen, and Clinton, all members of Atwood's special cadre.

"Mr. Cates, can't you do somethin' about the jury?" Rusty asked. "Seven of them ride for the Eagle Shire Ranch."

"But five of them are citizens of the town," Cates replied. "Four are members of the city council, plus the manager of the bank is on the jury. They are all outstanding citizens, and it would do no good to challenge."

"Atwood owns the bank, and everyone knows that he controls the city council."

"Court will now come to order," Judge Boykin said. "Are counsels for prosecution and defense present?"

"Prosecution is present," C.E. Felker said.

"Defense?"

"Present."

"I want another lawyer," Rusty said.

"Mr. Cates has been appointed to defend you," Boykin said.

"I don't need a court-appointed attorney. I've got enough money to hire my own lawyer. I'll get a lawyer from El Paso."

"You are out of order. This trial is about to commence. Prosecutor, you may make your case."

"Prosecution calls Marshal Witherspoon," Felker said.

After Witherspoon was sworn in, he told about coming into the saloon and seeing Jeb Calley's body lying on the floor. He also testified that he saw Rusty Abernathy holding a gun.

"Did you question the defendant?" Felker asked.

"Yes, I asked him if he killed Calley."

"What was his answer?"

"He said yeah, he did it."

"Your witness," Felker said.

"No questions," Cates replied.

"Wait a minute!" Rusty said. "What do you mean, no questions? I told him I did it in self-defense."

Boykin began banging his gavel on the bench. "You are out of order! Witness is dismissed."

"Your Honor, prosecution rests," Felker said.

"Mr. Cates, do you have any witnesses?"

"No witnesses, Your Honor."

"What do you mean, no witnesses?" Kate Abernathy screamed from the gallery. Her protest was joined by a dozen others, all of whom had come to testify on Rusty's behalf.

"Order!" Boykin shouted. "If there is one more outburst, I will have this court cleared." Boykin turned back to Cates who, at the moment, was drinking from a whiskey flask.

"Are you prepared to present a case for the defense?" Boykin asked.

Cates corked the bottle, wiped the back of his hand across his lips, then stood, shakily.

"Your Honor, the boy said he did it in self-defense." Cates burped. "Defense rests, Your Honor."

It came as no surprise that after a deliberation of less than two minutes, the jury returned a verdict of guilty. Boykin dismissed the jury, then pronounced sentence.

"It is the sentence of this court that the defendant be held in jail until Friday next, at which date, with the rising of the sun, he is to be hanged by the neck until dead."

"No!" Kate screamed.

"Court is adjourned."

Big Rock

Smoke, Pearlie, and Cal had left Smoke's ranch, Sugarloaf, earlier this morning, pushing a herd of one hundred cows to the railhead in town. Shortly after they left, Sally had gone into town as well, but she had gone in a buckboard so she could make some purchases. Her shopping complete, she was now on Red Cliff Road halfway back home. The road made a curve about fifty yards ahead, and, for just an instant, she thought she saw the shadow of a man cast upon the ground. She had not seen anyone ahead of her, and the fact that no man materialized after the shadow put her on the alert. The average person would have paid no attention to the shadow, but one thing she had learned in all the years she had been married to Smoke was to always be vigilant.

"I've made a lot of enemies in my life," Smoke told her. "And some of them would do anything they could to get at me. And anyone who knows me also knows that the thing I fear most is the idea that you might be hurt because of me."

Smoke had also taught Sally how to use a gun, and she was an excellent student. She once demonstrated her skill with a pistol by entering a shooting contest with a young woman by the name of Phoebe Ann Mosey. The two women matched each other shot for shot, thrilling the audience with their skills, until, at the very last shot, Miss Mosey put a bullet half an inch closer to the center bull's-eye than did Sally. It wasn't until then that Sally learned the professional name of her opponent. It was Annie Oakley.

Sally pulled her pistol from the holster and held it beside her.

As the buckboard rounded the curve, a man jumped out into the road in front of her. His action startled the team of horses, and they reared up, causing her to have to pull back on the reins to get them back under control.

Sally had not been surprised by the man's sudden appearance, nor was the fact that he was holding a pistol in his hand unexpected.

"Is this a holdup attempt?" Sally asked. "If so, I have very little money. As you can see by the bundles in the back I have been shopping, and I took only enough money for the purchases."

"Nah, this ain't no holdup," the man said. "You're Smoke Jensen's wife, ain't ya?"

"I'm proud to say that I am."

The man smiled, showing crooked, tobacco-stained teeth. "Then it don't matter none whether you've got 'ny money or not, 'cause that ain't what I'm after."

"What are you after?" Sally asked.

"I'm after some payback," the man said.

"Payback?"

"The name is Templeton. Adam Templeton. Does that name mean anythin' to you?"

"Would you be related to Deekus Templeton?"

"Yeah. What do you know about 'im?"

"I know that he took as hostage a very sweet young girl named Lucy Woodward, and held her for ransom."

"Yeah, he was my brother. I was in prison when your man killed him."

"Actually, it wasn't Smoke who killed him, it was a young man by the name of Malcolm Puddle."

"It don't make no never mind who it was, Jensen was there 'n as far as I'm concerned, it's the same thing as him killin' my brother."

"Why did you stop me?"

"Why, I thought you knew, missy. I plan to kill you. I figure me killin' you will get even with him."

"Will you allow me to step down from the buckboard before you shoot me?" Sally asked.

Templeton was surprised by Sally's strange reaction, not so much the question itself as the tone of her voice. She was showing absolutely no fear or nervousness.

"What do you want to climb down for?"

"I bought some material for a dress I'm going to make," Sally said, "and I wouldn't want to take a chance that I might bleed on it."

Templeton laughed. "You're one strange woman, do you know that? What the hell difference would it make to you whether you bleed on it or not? You ain't goin' to be makin' no damn dress, on account of because you're a-goin' to be dead."

"May I climb down?"

"Yeah, sure, go ahead."

Holding her pistol in the folds of her dress, Sally climbed down from the buckboard, then turned to face Templeton.

"Mr. Templeton, if you would put your gun away and ride off now, I won't kill you," Sally said. Again, the tone of her voice was conversational.

"What? Are you crazy? I'm the one holdin' the gun here. Now, say your prayers."

Suddenly, and totally unexpectedly, Sally raised her pistol and fired, the bullet plunging into Templeton's chest.

He got a look of total shock on his face, dropped his pistol, then, as his eyes rolled up in his head, collapsed onto the road.

Cautiously, Sally walked over to look down at him.

Templeton was dead

Leaving Templeton's body lying on the side of the road, Sally turned the buckboard around and went back to town. Stopping in front of the marshal's office, she went in to tell Marshal Monty Carson what had happened.

Unaware of Sally's adventure, Smoke, Pearlie, and Cal were pushing cows up the loading ramps into the four stock cars that were parked on a side-track, doing so at a rate of twenty-five animals per car.

"When will they be picked up?" Smoke asked. "I don't want them to be in these cars any longer than they have to be."

"The engine is already here," Gus Thomas said. "They'll be out of here by one this afternoon, 'n they'll be in Kansas City three days from now."

"Three days?"

Thomas chuckled. "Sure beats the old days of long cattle drives, don't it?"

"It does at that," Smoke said.

It took no more than half an hour to finish loading the cattle, then Smoke took Pearlie and Cal to lunch at Lamberts Café.

"Heads up!" someone shouted just as they stepped inside, and Pearlie reached up to grab a biscuit that came sailing through the air. *Tossed Biscuits* was a trademark of the café.

"Why, there's Sally," Smoke said. "I wonder what she's doing here."

"I hope there's nothing wrong," Pearlie said.

The three men joined her.

"I thought you were going back home," Smoke said.

"Something came up," Sally said. She told him about the encounter with Templeton on her way back.

"Where is he now? Templeton, I mean?" Smoke asked.

"I stopped by the marshal's office and Monty sent someone out to pick up the body."

"Smoke, before I go back to the ranch, I'd like to run down to the gunsmith shop," Pearlie said after lunch. "Seabaugh ordered a new pistol for me, 'n I'm pretty sure it's in by now."

"What did you get?" Cal asked.

"A Smith and Wesson Model Three," Pearlie said.

"Colt isn't good enough for you?"

"I like the Smith and Wesson," Pearlie said. "The way it breaks down, it's easier to load."

"I'll come with you," Cal said. "I need to buy a box of shells."

"And I've been wanting a new shotgun," Smoke said.

"You three go have your fun in the gun shop," Sally said. "I still have a buckboard full of purchases to unload. I'll see you when you get home."

CHAPTER 4

Etholen, Texas, Thursday night

"How does it feel, knowin' this is your last night on earth?" Witherspoon asked, standing just outside Rusty's cell.

Rusty glared at the marshal but said nothing.

"You ever seen anyone hang?" Witherspoon asked. "I have. Sometimes their eyes bulge out so far that you can just near 'bout pluck 'em out with your fingers. Well, wait until tomorrow mornin', 'n you'll see what I'm talkin' about. Oh, wait, you won't be able to see nothin', will you, 'cause it'll be your eyes that's all popped out like that."

Witherspoon laughed, a cackling laugh, then he walked back into the front of the office, just as Deputy Calhoun came in.

"Watch over him, Calhoun," Witherspoon said. "This is his last night, you know."

"Marshal, I ain't said nothin' 'bout this before, but do you think the boy really had a fair trial?"

"What difference does it make whether the trial was fair or not?" Witherspoon asked. "Truth is, there warn't really no need for a trial in the first place, seein' as he told me his own self that he was the one that kilt Calley."

"Yes, but everyone who saw it said the boy didn't have any choice."

"You were there," Witherspoon said. "What do you think?"

"I . . . uh . . . didn't actually see what happened," Calhoun replied.

"No, you didn't see it, 'cause you were drunk. I don't know why I keep you on as deputy anyway."

"You keep me on because no one but me will deputy for you, and the only reason I will is 'cause I can't get work nowhere else."

"Yeah, well, seein' as you was drunk, if I was you, I just wouldn't be makin' no more comments about the trial. Besides which, Kate will probably wind up sellin' the saloon to Atwood before she lets her boy hang, 'n then it'll all be over."

"If that's all it takes to save 'im, wonder why she ain't done it yet?" Calhoun asked.

"Maybe she thinks Atwood is bluffing, and she's going to play it out to the last minute," Witherspoon suggested.

As soon as Witherspoon left, Calhoun walked over to a window, pulled a flask of whiskey from behind the shutter, then sat at the desk.

Over in the Pretty Girl and Happy Cowboy Saloon, Cletus Murphy and Doodle Higgins, who were not only regular customers of the saloon but friends with Kate, were meeting with her back in the saloon office. Dolly was there as well.

"I told you Cletus and Doodle would be willing to do it."

"You don't have to do it, you know," Kate said. "Atwood has told me that if I would be willing to sell out to him, he would see to it that Rusty is set free. I've been waiting, hoping he was just running a bluff and would let Rusty out before he was actually hanged. That was no more of a trial than it was a church service, and if they actually did hang him, why it would be murder."

"Yes, ma'am, it would be murder," Cletus said. "But don't you think, for a moment, that Atwood ain't the kind of person who would murder someone. Remember what happened to young Gus Dumey and Burke and Poke. They was all three murdered, there ain't no doubt in my mind."

Kate nodded. "Yes, I believe you. That's why I'm going to tell Atwood that I'll sell out to him."

Doodle shook his head. "Ain't no need for you to do that. We'll have Rusty out of here and gone before mornin' ever rolls around."

"But it will be dangerous for you to do that . . . not only for you, but for Rusty as well."

"Calhoun will be watching him tonight," Cletus said. "Like as not, Calhoun is passed out drunk already."

Kate walked over to a cabinet, opened a door, and took out a box. "Here is one hundred dollars," she said, removing the money from the box. "This is all the cash I have on hand at the moment. Give this to him, and tell him I'll try and get more money to him later."

"Yes, ma'am," Doodle said, taking the money. "And don't you worry about a thing. Rusty will be long gone before anyone even misses him."

Five hours later, when the clock struck midnight, Calhoun didn't hear it. He also didn't notice when Cletus Murphy and Doodle Higgins came into the office. Doodle walked over to the desk.

"Asleep?" Cletus asked.

"Passed out drunk," Doodle answered.

Cletus reached up to take the ring of keys down, then,

while Doodle kept an eye on Calhoun, Cletus went into the back of the jail. As it turned out, Rusty was the only one incarcerated at the moment.

"Rusty!" Cletus said as he opened the cell door.

"Cletus?"

"Here's a hundred dollars," Cletus said, giving Rusty the money. "There is a saddled horse out back. Go on up to Rattlesnake Springs; I've got a brother that owns a bakery there. Give 'im this letter."

"I need to see Mom before I go."

"No, it would be better if you just got on out of town now. She knows about this. Where do you think the one hundred dollars came from? Just go on up to Rattlesnake Springs and wait. We'll get your ma up to see you in a few days, then you all can figure out what you want to do next."

Rattlesnake Springs, Texas

Francis Murphy not only helped Rusty find a room, he also gave him a job, telling all the locals that Rusty's name was Terry Cooper and that he was his cousin from Fort Worth.

Rusty had been there for four days when he looked up to see Cletus coming in through the front door of the bakery. Rusty's broad smile at seeing him faded when he saw the expression on his friend's face.

"Cletus, what is it? What happened?"

"It's your ma, Rusty."

"My mom? What's wrong? What happened?"

"She's in jail. They say if you don't come back within a month, they'll hang her in your place."

"Then I'm going back!"

"No, don't, your ma doesn't want that. She's afraid if you come back they might just hang both of you."

"Well I'm not going to just stand by and let her hang. Can't you break her out of jail the way you did me?"

"Witherspoon is being a lot more careful with her. Anyway, if I broke her out and she left town, Atwood would wind up with the saloon, and she could sign over the saloon to him and save her own life now. But she doesn't want to do that unless it is absolutely necessary."

"Well, she's going to have to do that," Rusty insisted. "Because I'll be damned if I'm going to let her hang."

"Do you have an Uncle Wes?" Cletus asked.

"Yeah," Rusty said. "I've never seen him, but I do have an Uncle Wes."

Cletus gave Rusty a piece of paper. "You ma said this is where you'll find him."

Sugarloaf Ranch

When Smoke, Pearlie, and Cal dismounted in front of the house, Sally stepped down from the front porch to meet them. There was a young man with her, younger even than Cal.

"Hello," Smoke said.

"Hi, yourself," Sally replied with a smile.

"Looks like you've got company, Smoke. Give me your reins, and I'll take Seven to the barn," Pearlie said.

"No, Pearlie, let Cal take care of the horses," Sally said. "You come on inside, too. This concerns you."

"This concerns me?" Pearlie replied with a confused look on his face. "How does it concern me? What is this about?"

"We'll talk about it inside," Sally said.

"Damn, Pearlie, have you done somethin' you don't want anyone to know about?" Cal asked.

"I've done lots of things I don't want anyone to know about," Pearlie replied as he turned over the reins of his horse to Cal. Smoke and Pearlie followed Sally and the young man into the house.

"Pearlie," Sally said when they went into the parlor. "This is Rusty Abernathy. He has come to see you."

"Do I know you?" Pearlie asked.

"No, but you know my mom."

"I know your mother? What do you mean, I know your mother? What is her name?"

"Her name is Abernathy now. But you would know her as Kate Fontaine."

"What?" Pearlie gasped. He sat down quickly. "Katie is your mother?"

"Yes, sir, she is. Hello, Uncle Wes."

Pearlie was silent for a long moment. "How did you know where to find me?" he asked.

"You came to Texas not too long ago to deliver some horses to Mr. Tom Byrd. Do you remember that?"

"Yes, I remember that," Pearlie said.

"Mom knew you were there, 'n she almost went to see you then. But she said you were in some trouble when you were real young, and she wasn't sure you would want to see her."

"She's right about that," Pearlie said. "Oh, not about me not wantin' to see her," he added quickly. "I mean she's right about me being in trouble when I was young. But it was more than *some* trouble, I was in a hell of a lot of trouble."

Cal came in then.

"Dooley said he'd take care of the horses," Cal said. "I thought I'd come in and see what was going on in case you needed me for something."

"We don't need you for anything, Cal," Sally said. "This concerns Pearlie."

"No, Miz Sally, please, let 'im stay," Pearlie said, lifting his hand. "I'm about to tell you all a story, and being as

Cal is my friend, he may as well hear it at the same time you and Rusty do. Smoke, you can listen, too, of course, but you already know the story. I told it to you a long time ago, back when I first come to work for you."

Smoke nodded. "Yes, I remember the story."

"I asked you then not to tell Miz Sally, 'cause I didn't want her thinkin' bad of me, but I guess she's pretty much made up her mind about me now, no matter what, so I figure I may as well tell it."

"Pearlie," Sally said. "I don't think there's anything you could tell me about your past that would change how I feel about you. You and Cal are both very special to me."

"Yes, ma'am, I know that, and I appreciate it more than I can say. But I guess this is as good a time as any to get this off my chest.

"My folks died when I was thirteen years old, and I got on as a cowboy, riding for the B Bar B brand. It was hard work, but I discovered then that I liked being a cowboy, and I became a pretty good hand, even if I do say so myself. I made a lot of really good friends with all the other cowboys at the B Bar B, and one night when I was fifteen, I went into town with some of the boys, and we went to a saloon."

"Pearlie, you were in a saloon when you were only fifteen?" Sally asked.

"Yes, ma'am, but you don't have to worry any about that, because the only thing I was drinking was lemonade. Only as things turned out, it would have been better if I had been drinking beer or whiskey, 'cause it was drinking the lemonade that started the trouble."

"I don't see how just drinking a glass of lemonade could start trouble," Sally said.

"Yes, ma'am, you wouldn't think so, would you?" Pearlie replied. "And if Miller had been a decent kind of man, why, there wouldn't have been any trouble."

"Someone named Miller gave you trouble just because you were drinking lemonade?"

"Yes, ma'am. Emmett Miller, his name was."

As Pearlie continued, he spoke with such feeling and such intensity that the story played out in front of the others as if they had been actual witnesses.

CHAPTER 5

Southwest Texas, several years earlier

There were four others who had come into town with Pearlie, whose real name was Wes Wesley Fontaine. The other four ordered beer, but Wes ordered a glass of lemonade.

"Ha, lemonade? You come into a man's bar and order lemonade?" one of the saloon patrons taunted.

"I like lemonade."

"That ain't much of a man's drink now, is it?"

Wes, realizing that the man was trying to pick a fight, didn't respond.

"What's a kid like you doin' comin' in here with the men? Ain't they someplace you could go to be with the other children to drink lemonade?"

"Why don't you back off and leave him alone, mister? He ain't botherin' you none," one of the other B Bar B riders said. "Wes is as good a worker as any rider we have."

"Yeah? Well tell me, has he been weaned yet? Or do you boys carry a sugar tit around for him?" the heckler taunted.

"Here's your lemonade, Wes."

"Thanks," Wes said.

"Tell me, kid, can you drink that without a nipple?"

Wes set his lemonade down and turned toward the cowboy who was riding him.

"What is your name, sir?"

"Well now, this kid called me sir. Maybe does have some manners after all. Or, maybe he thinks that if he's just real nice to me, I won't turn him over my knees and give him a spanking."

"My name is Wes. Wes Fontaine. You haven't told me your name, sir."

"His name is Miller," one of the other B Bar B riders said. "Emmett Miller."

"Well, Miller," Wes started.

"That would be *Mister* Miller to you, you snot-nosed little brat," Miller said, emphasizing the word "Mister."

"Mr. Miller, I'm going to ask you now, in the nicest possible way, to leave me alone."

Miller laughed. "You're asking me in the nicest possible way, are you? And if I don't leave you alone, what are you going to do?"

"It may be that I have to kill you," Wes replied in a quiet, matter-of-fact voice. "I don't want to, but if you don't leave me alone, it may come to that."

"What did you just say?" Miller shouted at him.

"I said that if you don't leave me alone, I'm going to kill you," Wes repeated. "But, in the nicest possible way, of course," he added with a sardonic grin.

"By God! I don't have to take that from no snot-nosed, big-mouthed kid!"

"No, you don't have to take it," Wes said. "You don't have to take it at all. All you have to do is shut up, go your way, and let me go mine. Then we can act as if none of this has even happened."

"No, by God, I ain't goin' my way!" Miller said, reaching for his gun even as he was shouting the words.

What neither Miller, nor even any of the other B Bar B

riders, realized was that Wes, knowing that he was younger than most of the others, had decided his best way of protecting himself would be with a gun. And because of that, he had been practicing with his draw for some time now. And though Miller started his draw first, Wes had his gun out and shooting before Miller was even able to bring his gun up to aim. Miller fell back on the saloon floor with a bullet in his chest.

"Son of a bitch!" one of the B Bar B riders said. "Who knew the kid was that good?"

Although he was good with a gun, this was the first time Wes had ever shot at another man, and now as he looked at the man he had just killed, lying on the floor, he felt a little nauseous.

"Mr. Poppell, I think I would like to have a whiskey," Wes said.

"You ever had yourself 'ny whiskey before, Wes?" one of the other B Bar B riders asked.

"No."

"Then take my word for it, you don't want none now, neither. Wait till you get a mite older afore you start on somethin' like that."

"Jimmy's right," one of the B Bar B riders said. "Folks that get started too early sometimes wind up as drunks, 'n you sure as hell don't want nothin' like that."

"I'll give you a whiskey if that's what you want, boy," Poppell said. "But I think you should listen to your friends and stick to lemonade."

"All right," Wes said. He picked up the lemonade Poppell had put in front of him earlier.

"What the hell's goin' on in here? I just heard a gunshot!" someone said, pushing in through the batwing doors. He was wearing a badge.

"Hello, Marshal Gibson, I was about to send for you," Poppell said.

Marshal Gibson had a bad reputation; some said he had been a cattle rustler before coming here. Others said that he had sold his gun to the highest bidder. Pinning on the badge had not made an honest man of him, because it was well known that he was selling protection to the honest businesses and taking a cut from the dishonest businesses. He stared down at Miller's body.

"Someone want to tell me what happened?" Gibson asked.

"Miller got hisself kilt," someone said.

"Hell, I can see that. What I want to know is, who done it?"

"I did," Wes said. He didn't look at the marshal. Instead, he stared into his glass of lemonade.

Gibson laughed out loud. "Are you kidding me? I'm askin' a serious question here. Now, who was it that kilt Miller?"

Wes turned toward the marshal. "I told you, Marshal, I killed him."

"The kid's tellin' you the truth," one of the other saloon patrons said.

"But he didn't have no choice, Marshal," the bartender put in quickly. "Miller kept ridin' the kid, for no good reason. Finally, the kid stood up to him, 'n when he did, Miller drawed on 'im."

"Are you tellin' me that Miller drawed first, but the kid kilt 'im anyway?"

"Yeah," Poppell said.

"I don't believe you."

"That's right, Marshal. Ever'thing Poppell is tellin' you is right," another patron said, and every one of the B Bar B riders said the same thing.

"So you kilt 'im, did you?" the marshal said, finally coming to the understanding that Miller had drawn first.

"Yes, sir. I didn't want to kill 'im, but he didn't leave me any choice."

"Get out of my county, kid," the marshal said.

"What?"

"You heard me. I said get out of my county."

"But I live here. Where would I go?"

"I don't give a damn where you go, just as long as you leave."

"Why?"

"Why? Because the last thing I need is some young punk who thinks he's a gunfighter."

"You heard everyone, Marshal. I didn't start this fight, Miller did. Anyhow I don't want to leave. Like I said, I live here, and I have a good job and good friends."

"You don't understand, do you, kid? I don't really give a damn whether you want to leave or not. I'm *orderin'* you to leave, and you ain't got no choice."

"Yes, sir, I do have the choice of leavin' 'cause the truth is, you've got no right to force me. I'm tellin' you right now, I don't have any intention of leavin'. So if you want to arrest me, why you just go right ahead. I'll come peacefully, then I'll take my chances with a trial."

"There ain't goin' to be no trial. With all these people testifyin' for you, you'd more'n likely get off, then you'd still be in my county, and I don't plan on that happenin'. So I'm going to tell you one more time, to get out of my county."

Wes shook his head. "I ain't goin'."

"You got no choice, boy. You either get out of my county now, or get ready to die."

"Wait a minute. You're plannin' to draw on me? Why? I haven't done anything wrong. You heard everyone in here tell you that I was in the right."

An evil smile spread across the marshal's face. "Boy, I don't know if it's your brain or your ears that ain't workin'. I told you to get out, 'n you're either goin' to do that, or I'm goin' to kill you right here, 'n right now."

At those words, everyone in the saloon stepped out of the way to give the two room. They hadn't done so with the first shooting, because it had happened too quickly, and by the time they realized there was going to be a shooting, it was too late. Not so now, as a shooting seemed inevitable.

"Marshal, I ain't leavin'," Wes said. "So if you're plannin' on shootin' me, I reckon you better just go ahead and try."

"You think you can beat me, do you?" the marshal asked.

"I reckon I can," Wes said. "I sure didn't plan on it goin' this far, but yeah, if it comes down to it, I can beat you."

With a triumphant smile, the marshal's hand dipped toward his pistol, but before he could clear leather, Wes had already drawn and fired. The marshal, with a surprised look on his face, went down.

Sugarloaf Ranch, the present

Pearlie stopped his story there and was quiet for a long moment, realizing that Sally, Cal, and Rusty were hanging on every word. Smoke was listening quietly as well, though he already knew the story.

"Do you understand what I'm saying?" Pearlie asked. "Within ten minutes' time I had killed two men, and one of the two men I killed was a lawman."

"I knew about the story because Mom heard it," Rusty said. "You left right after that, didn't you?"

"Yeah, I left right after that. I didn't have two dimes to rub together, but the other men took up a collection, and even the bartender and the soiled doves added to it. I left town with forty dollars, which, at the time, was the most money I had ever held in my hand at one time."

"You were older than fifteen when you came here," Sally said.

"Yes, well, I . . . uh . . . didn't come here right away,"

Pearlie said. "I wandered around for a while, and I did some things that I'd just as soon not talk about, things that I'm not very proud of."

"Mom has been wanting to write to you, to tell you that there was nobody looking for you anymore," Rusty said. "She was upset with herself for not coming to see you when you were at the Byrd Ranch. So after you left, she found out where you lived and was planning on maybe coming to see you sometime. That is, before this happened."

"Before what happened?" Pearlie asked.

Rusty took a deep breath, held it for a moment, then let it out in an audible sigh. "Well, like you, Uncle Wes, I killed someone. And, like you, it wasn't something I set out to do, it was self-defense."

Rusty explained how a man named Silas Atwood controlled most of El Paso County, and how he was now trying to take over the town of Etholen as well. He told of his encounter with Jeb Calley, and the subsequent jailbreak.

"Was anyone killed during the jailbreak?" Smoke asked.

"No, sir, there wasn't even anyone hurt. You see, they came by in the middle of the night and Calhoun, he's the deputy that was supposed to be watching me, was passed out drunk. All they had to do was take the cell keys down from where they were hanging on a nail alongside the calendar. They opened the cell door and let me out, just slick as a whistle."

Pearlie nodded. "It's good to have friends," he said.

"Yes, sir, friends, and relatives."

"By relatives, you mean me, don't you?" Pearlie asked.

"Yes, sir, I do mean relatives, and since you're the only relative that I have, I mean you. Uncle Wes, Mom is in jail now."

"Katie is in jail?" Pearlie asked, the expression on his

face showing his shock at the pronouncement. "Why on earth is Katie in jail?"

"Atwood blames her for helping me escape."

"Well, I wouldn't worry too much about her," Smoke said. "It'll be hard for him to make the case that she helped you escape."

Rusty shook his head. "You don't understand how crooked a judge Boykin really is. Mom has already been tried and found guilty of accessory to murder, and helping a condemned murderer to escape. Judge Boykin says he will keep her in jail for thirty days, though he also says he will set her free if I come back and turn myself in."

"Well, then all you have to do is stay away for thirty days, and they'll let her loose," Sally suggested with a bright smile.

"No, ma'am, it isn't like that. It isn't at all like that. What Atwood plans to do is hold her for thirty days, then hang her."

"Why, that is outrageous!"

"You said Atwood was going to hold her for thirty days," Smoke said. "Don't you mean this judge . . . Boykin that you're talking about, is the one who is going to hold her?"

"Boykin does exactly what Atwood tells him to do," Rusty said.

"What makes this Atwood person think he can get away with something like that?" Sally asked.

"He don't just think he can get away with it, Miz Sally, he knows he can get away with it. It's like I said, Atwood controls all of El Paso County, and a lot of Reeves and Presidio Counties as well. To be honest, I doubt if Atwood even wants me to come back. Because if they really do hang Mom, then he'll be able to buy up the saloon at a public auction."

"How many days has Katie been in jail, so far?" Pearlie asked.

"She's been in jail for over a week now, maybe even

a few days longer. As soon as I found out about it, I took a train and came up here to see you."

"That means we've only got three weeks left," Smoke said.

"We?" Rusty asked.

"Of course, we," Smoke replied. "You did come up here to ask for Pearlie's help, didn't you?"

"Yes, sir, but I didn't figure anyone other than Uncle Wes would get involved."

"Rusty, here is something you are going to learn about us," Cal said. "If one of us is involved, all of us are involved."

CHAPTER 6

After a two-day trip down from Big Rock, the train rolled into the station in Gomez, Texas, where they were told that the train would have a half-hour wait.

"Are you in any danger of being recognized here?" Pearlie asked his nephew.

Rusty shook his head. "I hardly think that anyone would know me here. Only way I could get recognized would be if I happened to run into someone from Etholen who was visiting, or if someone had come to Etholen and heard me play the piano."

"Play the piano?" Sally asked, perking up at that information.

"Yes, I play the piano in Mom's saloon. Anyway, I've never been here before, so I'm reasonably sure I won't be recognized by anyone."

"That's good to know. How are you fixed for money?" Pearlie asked his nephew.

"Oh, don't you worry about that, I'm in good shape," Rusty replied. "Mom and I have more'n five thousand dollars in the Etholen Bank."

"No, you don't," Smoke said.

"What do you mean, we don't? We sure do have money in that bank."

"Oh, you may have money there, all right," Smoke agreed. "But you aren't going to be able to get to it until this is all cleared up."

"How much do you have on you, right now?" Pearlie asked.

"About twelve dollars," Rusty said. "I had a hundred dollars when I left town, but I've used most of it up."

"Here's another hundred dollars," Pearlie said, pulling the money from his billfold and giving it to Rusty. "We've been talking it over and we've decided it would be better for you to stay here until we get this all settled."

"What do you mean you want me to stay here? That's my mom in jail in Etholen, and they're planning on hanging her if I don't show up."

"Yes, and if you show up now, they'll hang you *and* your mother, which means I'll be losing a sister I just found, and a nephew I never knew I had," Pearlie said. "And I'm not willing to do that, so I want you to listen to what I'm telling you. You are going to stay here, in Gomez, until we send for you."

Rusty shook his head. "No, I don't think you understand. Witherspoon is the marshal, and he's only got one deputy. But the real power, I told you, is Silas Atwood. Atwood has a whole bunch of hired guns working for him. That's how he keeps control of everything. You'll be badly outnumbered if you go in there, with just the three of you."

"Four of us," Sally said.

"Four of you? But, you're a woman."

Pearlie chuckled. "Damn, Miz Sally. Did you know you were a woman?"

Sally smiled. "I've been told that."

Smoke chuckled. "Rusty, don't you worry about Sally being a woman. That's never stopped her before."

Sally put her hand on Rusty's shoulder. "I know it's going to be hard on you, honey, but I've been around these three for a long time and I learned, a long time ago, to have faith in them. They will get things taken care of, and we will send for you."

"All right," Rusty agreed. "I'll wait here, but I'm going to be on pins and needles until I hear from you."

"I plan to visit Kate as soon as I arrive," Sally said. "I'll let her know that you are all right."

"Good, that'll take some of the worry away," Rusty said.

Sally smiled. "I expect she'll be surprised by a visit from a stranger."

"Oh, she knows who you are, Miz Sally. Don't forget, she'd been makin' plans to come up 'n see Uncle Wes ever since you all took them horses down to the Byrd Ranch. And she is the one that got word to me that I should come up and get Uncle Wes."

"Good, then I shouldn't have any trouble getting in to see her."

"Unless Marshal Witherspoon stops you," Rusty said. "You be careful of him. He's about the biggest crook there is."

"We'll be careful," Sally promised.

During the two-hour trip from Gomez to Etholen, Smoke, Sally, Pearlie, and Cal came up with a plan. Execution of the plan, however, would depend upon Kate's approval.

"What if Kate doesn't believe I'm who I say I am?" Sally said. "What if she thinks I don't even know Pearlie, that I'm working for Atwood?"

"Tell her that one night she and I went over to Mr. Rowe's farm and stole a watermelon," Pearlie said. "Then, Mr. Rowe came out of his house and shot at us with a shotgun, and I put myself in front of her, to protect her, so that I was the one who got hit."

"Oh, heavens, Pearlie! You were shot with a shotgun?"

Pearlie laughed. "Yeah. The shells had been loaded with

strips of rawhide, so it stung like the dickens when it hit me, but it didn't do much more than wound my pride."

"What happened to the watermelon?" Cal asked.

This time it was Sally who laughed. "Leave it to Cal to worry about the watermelon."

"I dropped it and it broke open," Pearlie said. "So, Kate and I just scooped the heart out, then ran."

Prior to leaving Big Rock, Smoke had made arrangements to lease a special stock car to be attached to their train. The purpose of the car was to provide transportation for the horses, and when the four of them reached Etholen, the job of taking care of the horses fell to Cal. Smoke, Sally, and Pearlie took the luggage to the Milner Hotel where they arranged for the rooms. Then, from the hotel, Sally went to the jail to visit with Kate, while Smoke and Pearlie went to the Pretty Girl and Happy Cowboy Saloon.

When Sally stepped into the jail, it smelled of cheap cigar smoke, and the origin of the smell was quickly and easily ascertained. A thin man, with what looked like a week's growth of scraggly whiskers, sat behind a desk with a lit cigar clenched between his teeth. He was dealing poker hands, but he was the only one playing since he was alone in the jail.

"Marshal Witherspoon?" Sally asked.

Sally had entered the room so quietly that she hadn't been seen, and when she spoke, the man behind the desk was visibly startled.

"Jesus, lady! Who the hell are you, and how did you get in here?"

"I opened the door and walked in," Sally replied. She

purposely omitted giving her name. "Are you Marshal Witherspoon?"

"Nah, I ain't the marshal. I'm Deputy Calhoun. What do you want?"

"I wish to visit one of your prisoners," Sally replied.

"One of 'em? Ha! We only got us one prisoner."

"That would be Mrs. Abernathy?"

"Yeah. You know Kate, do you?"

"You call her by her first name?"

"Ever'one does. Hell, she runs a saloon. Any woman that runs a saloon don't expect to be called by nothin' else. Are you one of her whores? 'Cause if you are, I ain't never seen you before."

"No."

"Then why do you want to see her?"

"We have a mutual acquaintance."

The deputy squinted his eyes. "Yeah? That mutual acquaintance wouldn't be her son now, would it? 'Cause, maybe you don't know nothin' 'bout it, but Rusty Abernathy, he's wanted for murder."

"No, Rusty Abernathy isn't the name of the person we share in common."

"Well, who is it then?" the deputy asked.

"Why would you need to know who it might be?"

"On account of 'cause I'm the law, 'n I got a right to know things like that. It's all a part of investigatin' 'n all, you know, so as we can find out where Rusty Abernathy is."

"The mutual acquaintance we share is her brother."

"Ha! Now I know you're lyin'. She ain't got no brother."

"Where was Kate born?" Sally asked.

"What? How do I know where she was born?"

"If you don't know where she was born, then you don't know everything about her, do you? She could have a brother, and you would know nothing at all about it."

Calhoun ran his hand through the scraggly growth of whiskers on his chin and stared at Sally for a long moment.

"You're wearin' a pistol."

"Oh, for heaven's sake, Deputy, you aren't afraid of a woman, are you?"

"All right," Calhoun finally agreed. "Let me have your pistol and you can go on back there; you can talk to her. But I plan to listen to everything you talk about."

"Well, you are certainly welcome to do that," Sally replied as she handed her pistol over, butt first. "We have no secrets."

When Sally stepped into the back of the jail, she saw a woman sitting on the edge of her bed.

"You got a visitor, Kate," Calhoun said.

"Who are you?" Kate asked, looking up in curiosity.

"Wes Fontaine sent me," Sally said.

Kate gasped. "Wes?"

"Yes."

"Say, Kate, do you know who this fella Wes Fontaine is?" Deputy Calhoun asked.

"Yes. Wes Fontaine is my brother."

"All right then, you wasn't lyin'. You two go ahead and talk, I'll just listen in."

"Wes wanted me to tell you about the new quilt I made for him," Sally said. "Which do you like, Cactus Wreath? Or Country Stable? Of course, I also like Sassy Sunflower. But then, Tile Tangle is nice, too."

At first, Kate was puzzled, then, when she saw the expression on the deputy's face, she realized what Sally was doing.

"Well, I've always liked Lilies of the Field. What sort of stitch are you using? Stitch in the Ditch, or Outline?"

"Stitch in the Ditch; I know it's more difficult, but it makes a much more beautiful quilt. Why I . . ."

"Is this all you two are going to talk about?" Calhoun asked with a sigh.

"Oh, but Deputy Calhoun, you should see the quilt. Why, if I say so myself, it's the most beautiful quilt I've ever made."

Calhoun shook his head in disgust. "There ain't no way I'm goin' to stay back here 'n listen to you two prattle on about quiltin' and such."

Calhoun left, then closed the door behind him so that the two women were alone in the back of the jail. They looked at each other and laughed.

"At first, I wasn't sure what you were talking about," Kate said. "That was a good way of getting rid of him. How is Wes doing?"

"He's doing just great. He got your message, and he's here, in town."

"What about . . ." Kate stopped in midsentence, then looked toward the door to make certain that the deputy wasn't listening. "Wait a minute. How do I know you are who you say you are? It could be that my message to Wes was intercepted, and you're somebody Atwood paid to pretend to know Wes. I think it would be better if we didn't talk."

"What happened when you and your brother tried to steal watermelons from Mr. Rowe?" Sally asked.

For a moment Kate was surprised by the question, then a broad smile spread across her face.

"Mr. Rowe had loaded some of his shotgun shells with bits of rawhide, and he shot Wes." She laughed. "There's absolutely no way you could possibly know that if Wes hadn't told you. You are who you say you are."

"I am indeed. And we are here to help you."

"Have you seen Rusty?"

"Yes, and he's fine," Sally said. "He's the one who told us about your problem."

"Oh, but, he isn't here, in town, is he? It's much too dangerous for him to be here."

"No, he is nearby, but he isn't here. We'll get you together when it is safe to do so."

"We?"

"My husband, Pearlie, Cal, and I."

"By Pearlie you mean . . ."

"Your brother," Sally said, answering before the question was completed. Sally reached through the bars, and Kate took her hand.

"Yes, I heard that he was calling himself Pearlie now."

"Just sit tight, and don't worry about a thing," Sally said. "We are going to get you out of this."

CHAPTER 7

"I'm told a lady owns this saloon. Is that true?" Smoke asked as he and Pearlie stepped up to the bar to order a drink. Smoke was well aware that it was true, but he asked the question so that he could measure the bartender's reaction.

"Yes, sir, and a fine lady she is, too," the bartender said as he drew two beers.

"Lady, hell? She ain't much more'n a whore," one of the drinkers at the other end of the bar said.

"That ain't true, 'n you know it, Pardeen. Miss Kate is not a whore," the bartender said.

"What do you mean, she's not a whore? She's got whores that works for her, don't she? That's the same thing. What she should do is sell this place to my boss."

"Why should she do that?" the bartender asked. "Miss Kate is a fine woman, and she treats all of us real good."

"Yeah? Well what are you goin' to do when they wind up hangin' her in place of her son, on account of he run away after he murdered Calley."

"Rusty didn't murder Calley. You forget, I was here, and I saw what happened. That shooting was self-defense, pure 'n simple," the bartender said.

"The hell it was. Calley warn't even a' lookin' at Abernathy when he got shot. I was on the jury, remember, 'n that's how come we found 'im guilty. 'N that's how come Judge Boykin sentenced him to hang."

"Hell, Pardeen, Calley was countin' out loud, 'n he told ever'one in the saloon that he was goin' to kill Rusty when he got to ten. He was already up to nine when Rusty shot 'im, 'n if Rusty hadn't of shot him, Calley damn sure would've shot Rusty," one of the other patrons said.

"Yeah, but Calley was lookin' away from Rusty when Rusty picked up that gun 'n kilt 'im."

"That doesn't matter. There is nobody who saw it who would say that the shooting wasn't justified," the bartender said.

"Yeah, well I seen it, 'n I was on the jury, 'n we said what he done was murder," Pardeen said.

"Wait a minute," Smoke said. "Are you telling me that you were a witness to the event, and yet you served on the jury?"

"Yeah," Pardeen said. "That's what I'm tellin' you."

"There was no one on that jury except men who Atwood either controls or men who ride for him. And none of them were real cowboys, either. They were all gunhands, same as Calley," the bartender said.

"It don't make no never mind now whether Rusty is guilty or not," Pardeen said. "He won't never be comin' back here. 'N if he don't come back, the whore that owns this place is goin' to get her neck stretched."

"Maybe common sense will prevail," the bartender said.

"If there was any common sense, she woulda sold this place to Atwood when she had the chance. Now, she's goin' to wind up dead, that no-count son of hers is gone to hell 'n back, 'n that means they won't be nobody left to own this place. What's goin' to happen is the marshal will wind up takin' it over, then he'll sell it to the highest bidder, 'n that'll be Atwood."

"I'll tell you this, Pardeen," the bartender said. "If Atwood does wind up owning this place, he'll have to get a new bartender, because I sure as hell won't work for him."

"No, and neither will any of the girls," a nearby bar girl said.

"Ha," Pardeen replied. "Bartenders are a dime a dozen, 'n whores are even cheaper. You won't have to quit, Atwood will more'n likely fire ever'one anyway. Why, I might wind up tendin' bar myself."

"Yeah, you'd make a fine bartender. You don't know scotch from bourbon," the bartender replied.

"What is your name, bartender?" Smoke asked.

"The name is Peterson. Ray Peterson."

"Mr. Peterson, I like a man who is loyal to his employer. You're a good man."

The bartender smiled. "Why, I thank you, sir," Peterson replied. "But when you have a boss like Miss Kate, it isn't hard to be loyal."

The scoffing sound Pardeen made may have been a laugh. "You beddin' her, Peterson?" he asked. "Is that why you takin' up for her like that?"

"You have a big mouth," Peterson said.

"You know what? I don't want you to quit. I want you to beg Atwood to let you stay on. I want to see him fire you."

"Mr. Pardeen, you keep talking about Atwood. Do you know him?" Smoke asked.

"Yeah, I know him. I work for him."

"You're a cowboy?"

"Cowboy?" Pardeen smiled. "Yeah, I'm a cowboy."

"He's no more a cowboy than I am," Peterson said. "He's one of Atwood's gunhands."

"I want you to take a message to Atwood," Smoke said.

"A message? What kind of message?"

"You can tell him that he is not going to buy this saloon."

"Oh? Who's going to buy it? You?"

"Nobody is going to buy it. It's going to stay in the hands of its current owner."

"Really? You bein' new here, maybe you don't know that Kate is in jail now, 'n she's more'n likely goin' to hang if her no-count son don't come back so's we can hang him."

"My sister isn't going to hang, and neither is my nephew. We aren't going to let that happen," Pearlie said.

"Your sister? Who the hell are you?"

"My name is Pearlie, and Katie is my sister."

Pardeen laughed. "Pearlie? What the hell kind of name is Pearlie?"

"It's my name," Pearlie said without any further explanation.

"And you're going to stop 'em from hanging, are you? Tell me . . . Pearlie, just how do you plan to stop that?"

"We're going to stop it by taking Atwood down. You might tell him that for us," Smoke said.

Pardeen turned to face Smoke and when he did so, Pearlie, recognizing the expression on Pardeen's face, stepped to one side.

"You're going to take Mr. Atwood down, are you?"

"Yes."

"It could be that I'll just take you down instead," Pardeen suggested.

"I wish you wouldn't do that," Smoke said.

"Yeah?" Pardeen said with an easy, confident grin on his face. "I'll just bet you do. Don't want to get shot, do you?"

"No, I don't want to have to kill you," Smoke replied. "I'd rather you stay alive so you can deliver my message to Atwood."

"You don't need to worry none about . . ." Pardeen didn't finish his sentence, and it was soon obvious that he had no intention of doing so, because the sentence was just a distraction. Pardeen snaked his gun from his holster in a lightning-swift move.

But Smoke was faster. Smoke intuitively knew that Pardeen was about to go for his gun, and even before Pardeen was able to bring his gun to bear, Smoke was pulling the trigger.

Pardeen pulled the trigger as well, but it was a reflexive action because as he went down with a bullet in his heart, the bullet from his gun punched a hole in the floor, in front of the bar.

There were a few gasps of surprise from some of the other patrons in the saloon, and they looked on in shock at the calmness the two men displayed as Smoke and Pearlie took their beers over to a table near the back wall, leaving Pardeen dead on the floor behind them.

"Who are those men?" someone asked.

"That one feller said he was Kate's brother, but I never heard her say nothin' 'bout havin' a brother. I don't have no idee who the other 'n is."

Smoke and Pearlie had chosen this particular table because its location meant that nobody could get behind them, and from here, both men could see everyone at the bar.

"Do you think that might shake Atwood up a bit?" Smoke asked.

"Yeah," Pearlie replied with a chuckle. "I think it might just do that."

Smoke noticed that a couple of the men who had been standing next to Pardeen when they first came in were now talking to one another in what could only be described as anxious whispers. They were joined by a third man.

"From the way those men are acting, keeping their conversation close and glancin' over here toward us, I wouldn't be surprised if they were plannin' somethin'," Pearlie said.

"I would say that is a good observation," Smoke replied.

Smoke and Pearlie continued to monitor the three men, though doing so without being too obvious.

After their brief conference the three men separated, one standing at either end of the bar, and one taking his place at the middle of the bar. Then, as one, they all three turned to look back toward the table occupied by Smoke and Pearlie.

"Here it comes," Smoke said quietly.

"Mister, you've just committed murder," one of the men said. "And until the marshal comes, we intend to keep you from running away."

Smoke took a swallow of his beer before he put the glass down. "I'm not planning on going anywhere," he said.

That wasn't the answer the man was expecting, so he blinked his eyes in surprise. Then he continued to tell Smoke and Pearlie what he was thinking, just as if they had asked him.

"What I'm a' thinkin' is, Mr. Atwood is more'n likely not goin' to be too pleased with you killin' one of his men like that."

"Do you mean you work for Atwood?" Smoke asked.

"Yeah, we do."

"Willis, if I were you, I'd leave that gentleman alone," Peterson said. "There's not a soul in this room who didn't see what happened, and we'll give Witherspoon an earful when he gets here."

"There ain't goin' to be no need for you to be a' tellin' Witherspoon anything," Willis said. "I expect by the time Witherspoon gets here this will all be over with."

"Pearlie, I do believe these three folks are getting ready to draw against us," Smoke said.

"Do you think so?" Pearlie replied.

"I don't know, but it seems to me like they're trying to get up their courage to give us a try."

Smoke and Pearlie were talking about the potential

life-or-death situation as calmly as if they were discussing whether or not it might rain. Their calmness in the face of this situation awed the patrons of the saloon and somewhat unnerved Willis and the two men with him.

But by then, Smoke and Pearlie had seen something that the three men hadn't seen. They had seen Cal come into the saloon just in time to take notice of the situation.

Pearlie smiled. "You know, I think it would be a big mistake for these men to draw on us," Pearlie said.

"Oh, don't be so hard on them, Pearlie. It's clear that Mr. Willis just hasn't thought this through. He doesn't realize that he could wind up getting himself, and his two friends, killed."

"What the hell are you two talkin' about?" Willis asked, his voice reflecting his growing nervousness. "If they's anyone that's likely to get kilt here, it's goin' to be you two. Maybe you didn't notice, but they's only two of you, and there's three of us."

Slipping his pistol from the holster and moving very quietly, and unnoticed, Cal stepped up behind the man who was standing at the end of the bar nearest the door. He brought his pistol down on the head of that man. Hearing him fall, Willis turned, only to see Cal holding a pistol in his hand.

"Now there are three of us, and two of you," Cal said.

"Now, Cal, it's not fair for you to be butting into this," Pearlie said as he brought his gun up. "We're the ones that loudmouthed son of a bitch has been picking on. That means I'm the one that gets to kill him. If you want to, you can kill the one that's down at the other end of the bar."

"Now wait a minute," Smoke said. "Cal already got his man. You can have the loudmouth if you want him, but I'll be killing the one at the other end of the bar."

Like Pearlie, Smoke had drawn his pistol during the distraction caused by Cal's dramatic entrance. He pointed it at the man at the other end of the bar, then cocked his pistol. As the hammer came back, the gear engaged the cylinder, making a loud clicking sound that filled the now silent room.

"What . . . what are we goin' to do, Willis?" the man standing at the opposite end of the bar asked. "My God! They're goin' to kill us! They're goin' to kill us, just like he did Pardeen." He held both his hands out in front of him as if, by that action, he could ward off any bullets. "No, no! Don't shoot me! Please don't!"

By now the man Cal had knocked out was coming to, and he groaned.

"Take off your pistol belts, and hand them to Mr. Peterson," Smoke said.

"What the hell! I ain't givin' up my pistol!" Willis said.

"Mr. Willis, you will either hand your pistol belt over to Mr. Peterson while you are alive, or I will kill you and give him the belt after you are dead," Pearlie said.

"You better do it, Willis, 'cause I ain't standin' with you!" the man at the far end of the bar said as, quickly, and with shaking hands, he removed his own belt.

"Booker! You cowardly son of a bitch!" Willis said, but even as he was talking, he joined the other two in taking off his pistol belt. Then the three men, after turning their belts over to Peterson, left the saloon.

"Damn!" someone said. "I never thought I would see any of Atwood's cutthroats be disarmed like that and run off with their tails tucked between their legs."

"If you two fellas want another drink, I'll be glad to buy it," another said.

"We're good," Smoke said. "But you can buy one for our friend. Step up to the bar, Cal, and tell Mr. Peterson what you'll have."

With a broad smile, Cal ordered a beer, then, saluting his

benefactor by raising the beer toward him, he joined Smoke and Pearlie at their table.

"I got the horses taken care of," he said.

"Good. Did you see Sally?" Smoke asked.

"Not since we separated at the depot."

CHAPTER 8

"You need to get over to the Pretty Girl Saloon. Some son of a bitch just kilt Pardeen!" Willis said. He and the others had come straight to the marshal's office after leaving the Pretty Girl and Happy Cowboy Saloon.

"What do you mean, someone kilt Pardeen? You mean he shot 'im in the back?" Calhoun replied.

"No, he faced Pardeen down."

"I didn't think anyone could beat Pardeen."

"This feller did," Booker said. "He's the fastest I've ever seen."

"Who was it?"

"He has some funny name like Stoke or Shoke or somethin' like that."

Sally and Kate, in back of the jail, were unaware of the conversation taking part out front.

"I must be going," Sally said. "But I don't want you to worry anymore. Smoke says that we will get you out of jail, and I learned, a long time ago, to trust him when he is determined to do a thing."

"Sally, thanks for coming. And please ask Wes to come visit me."

"I'll send him right over," Sally promised.

When Sally reached the front of the jail, she saw three men there with Deputy Calhoun.

"He took our guns," one of the men said.

"He didn't take 'em, Booker. You give 'em up to 'im."

"Then you should thank Mr. Booker," Sally said. "By giving up your guns like that, Smoke didn't have to kill you."

"Who the hell are you?" the loudmouthed one asked.

"She says she's a friend of Kate's brother," Calhoun said.

"I am Mrs. Smoke Jensen."

"Smoke! Yeah, that was the son of a bitch's name that kilt Pardeen! It was Smoke!"

"May I have my pistol back, Deputy?" Sally asked.

Calhoun opened the drawer, took out the gun, and handed it to Sally.

"Thank you," Sally replied. She turned to the loudmouth. "And your name, sir?" Sally asked.

"It's Willis."

Sally pointed her pistol at Willis.

"What the hell?" Willis cried out. "What are you doin'?"

"Mr. Willis, I would appreciate it if you didn't use such language around me. Especially about my husband. And I would appreciate an apology."

"Do somethin', Calhoun!" Willis said.

"What do you expect me to do?" Calhoun asked.

"Iffen we had our guns, she wouldn't be doing this," Willis said.

Sally cocked the pistol. "My apology?"

"I'm sorry!" Willis said desperately. "I'm sorry."

Sally smiled. "Your apology is accepted."

"If Witherspoon wants us, we'll be down at the Bull and Heifer," Willis said. "That is, unless you're plannin' on shootin' us," he added, looking back at Sally.

"No, as I said, your apology is accepted. You're free to go wherever you wish."

"Come on," Willis said to the others in a voice that could only be described as a growl.

Sally waited until the three men were gone before she slipped her pistol back into its holster.

"You probably shouldn'ta done that, Missy," Calhoun said. "It ain't good to have them boys as enemies."

"Well, I certainly wouldn't want them as friends," Sally replied.

Sally's response was unexpected, and after blinking in surprise, Calhoun laughed out loud. "I guess you have a point there," he said.

When Sally reached the saloon a couple of minutes later, she saw two men putting a body into the back of a wagon. The words WELCH UNDERTAKING SERVICE were painted on the side of the wagon.

As soon as Sally stepped into the saloon, she was met by Smoke.

"I hear I missed some excitement," Sally said.

"A little," Smoke said.

"A little? I did see someone being loaded into the back of an undertaker's wagon, didn't I? Tell me, Smoke, how can someone be a little dead?"

Smoke laughed. "Well, you've got me on that one, Sally, I'm not sure someone can be a little dead. Why don't you come join Pearlie, Cal, and me at the table?"

"I'd be glad to," Sally said.

"Mr. Peterson, a white wine if you please," Smoke called over to the bartender as he led Sally to the table.

"Yes, sir," Peterson said.

"Oh, Mr. Peterson, Kate said to tell you she is doing fine, and she thanks you for standing by her."

"You saw Kate?" Peterson asked, surprised at the comment.

"I did indeed."

Pearlie and Cal stood as Sally approached the table, then waited until Smoke pulled out a chair for her before they sat again.

One of the bar girls, having overheard Sally's comment to Peterson, approached the table.

"How is Miss Kate? Is she doing all right?" the girl asked.

"Yes. She doesn't enjoy being in jail, of course, but she is doing just fine, and of course, she is worried about all her friends here."

"Have you seen Rusty? I mean, if you have, you don't need to tell me where he is, or anything like that, I wouldn't want to put him in danger. I would just like to know if he is all right."

Sally reached up and put her hand on the girl's arm. "He's doing just fine, dear," she said with a warm smile.

"Oh!" the bar girl said with a happy smile. "Oh, that's wonderful to hear! I mean . . . uh . . . well, all the girls who work here will be real glad to hear that. If you go see Miss Kate again, would you tell her that Dolly asked about her?"

"I'll be glad to," Sally replied.

"Do you think they really intend to hang her if Rusty doesn't come back?" Dolly asked.

"I will guarantee you that you don't have to worry about that," Smoke said. "We will not let that happen."

"And if Atwood insists on it?" Dolly asked.

"We will stop it."

"But, how? Atwood has so many men who work for him. To say nothing of Marshal Witherspoon. And there are only three of you."

"There are four of us," Sally said.

"What do you mean, four?" Dolly asked.

Sally counted off, pointing her finger at Cal, Pearlie, and

Smoke. "One, two, three." She paused, then turned her finger to herself. "Four."

"Oh," Dolly said. "Oh, I didn't think . . . uh, that is, I mean you're a . . ."

"Yeah, I am," Sally said with a big smile.

"Did you have any trouble getting in to see Kate?" Pearlie asked after Dolly walked away.

"Not really," Sally said. "Oh, and Pearlie, Kate wants you to come see her."

"You mean now? She wants to see me now?"

"Yes."

A broad smile spread across Pearlie's face. "I'm glad to hear that. After all these years, and with me making no effort to get in touch with her, I wasn't sure she would ever want to see me again, even if I tried."

"You aren't the only one who feels guilty," Sally said. "She blames herself for not trying to find you."

"You mean Katie thinks it's all her fault?"

"Apparently so."

Pearlie laughed. "Good, I'll let her think that, and I'll make her apologize to me."

"Pearlie, don't you dare!" Sally said.

"I was just teasing. I have to confess, though, that I am a bit nervous about going to see her."

"Don't be. She's as sweet a person as you would ever want to meet. Please, go see her now. I promised I would send you over there as soon as I could."

"All right," Pearlie replied with an assenting nod. "I reckon I'll just go on over there now."

"You ain't goin' nowhere, mister!" a loud voice called out. "There ain't nobody goin' nowhere till I say they can!"

Looking toward the man who had spoken, Smoke saw a man standing just inside the batwing doors. He was wearing a star on a shirt that strained at the buttons.

"Witherspoon, you ain't got no case here. Pardeen drew first," one of the patrons said.

"Cletus is right," Peterson said. "Pardeen drew first."

"That's the way it happened, Marshal," Dolly said, and she was backed up by all the other girls in the saloon.

"We ain't goin' to let you do to this man what you done to Rusty," yet another patron said.

"We'll . . . we'll see about that," Witherspoon said, jabbing his finger toward everyone. "We'll just see about that," he repeated as he backed out of the saloon.

Witherspoon's departure was followed by a loud burst of laughter from the throats of everyone present.

Pearlie followed Witherspoon out the door, and a moment later someone came in and stepped up to the bar to say something to Peterson. Peterson nodded, then stepped around the bar and led the man over to the table where Smoke, Sally, and Cal were sitting, Pearlie having just vacated his seat.

"Mr. Jensen, this is Slim Pollard," Peterson said. "He rides for the Eagle Shire."

"Atwood?"

"Yes," Peterson said. "But Slim here is a good man, I've known him for some time. And he's one of the real cowboys, he's not one of Atwood's gunhands."

"What can I do for you, Pollard?" Smoke asked.

"I, uh, have come to pick up the guns for Willis 'n the two men that was with 'im," Pollard said.

"Where are those men now?" Smoke asked.

"They're down at the Bull 'n Heifer," Pollard said.

"They sent you after their guns, did they?"

"No, sir, I volunteered to come get 'em. I figured if they come for 'em, well, there could maybe be some more shootin'. But if I was to come 'n just ask for 'em real polite, there wouldn't be no more trouble."

"All right," Smoke said. "Mr. Peterson, give him the guns."

"I appreciate that," Pollard replied.

"Why don't you join us for a beer?" Smoke invited.

"Thank you!" Pollard said, this time with a broad smile.

Smoke held his hand out toward Sally. "This is my wife."

"Nice to meet you, ma'am," Pollard said.

"Tell me, Mr. Pollard," Smoke said after the beer was served. "If you are a good man, as Mr. Peterson says, and I don't doubt him, why are you riding for someone like Silas Atwood?"

"He's got cows and horses that need tendin'," Pollard replied. "And bein' as they're just dumb animals, they don't know what kind of man it is that owns them. Besides which, after Mr. Dumey left, the Double Nickel, which is the brand I used to ride for, wasn't no more, 'n I didn't have no job left. So when Miner Cobb offered to put me on, I took 'im up on it."

"Miner Cobb?"

"He's the foreman out at the Eagle Shire. 'N he's a good man, too, he ain't no gunhand like them others that Mr. Atwood has hired."

Smoke drummed his fingers on the table for a moment or two as he stared at Pollard.

"Mr. Pollard, for reasons that I'm not going to go into, actually for reasons I'm sure you already know, I plan to take Atwood down."

"Take him down? You mean you . . . you plan to kill 'im?" Pollard replied with a troubled expression on his face.

"It is not my intention to kill him," Smoke said. "When I say take him down, what I mean is, disengage him from his hold over this town."

Pollard shook his head. "He ain't never goin' to just willingly give that up."

"Fortunately, my plan does not depend upon a willing relinquishment of his position of power. But I will bring that about, with, or without, Atwood's willing acquiescence."

"Oh," Pollard said.

"Where will you stand on that issue, Mr. Pollard?" Smoke asked.

"Well, sir, I've been a cowhand, man, and boy now for more'n twenty years," Pollard replied. "And I've always believed that a cowboy owes some loyalty to the brand he's ridin' for."

"I can understand loyalty," Smoke said.

"On the other hand, I was loyal to Mr. Dumey, too, but when he give up 'n left his ranch, I didn't think twice 'bout ridin' for the man that run 'im off. If it comes right down to a battle between you 'n Mr. Atwood, I won't be fightin' ag'in you, 'n I don't think any of the regular Eagle Shire hands will, either. I expect that about the onliest ones you're goin' to have to worry about will be them boys that lives in the special bunkhouse."

"Special bunkhouse?"

"Yes, sir, that's what the rest of us call the place where the gunhands, folks like Willis, 'n Clark, 'n Booker, and such live. That was where Pardeen lived, too, till you shot 'im."

"I see."

Pollard snorted what might have been a laugh. "Pardeen, well, he sort of lorded over all of us regular cowboys. I'll be honest with you, Mr. Jensen, I don't expect any of us is goin' to be all too broke up over him gettin' kilt."

CHAPTER 9

When Pearlie stepped into the jail, there were two men inside and both were wearing a badge. One of the men was Marshal Witherspoon, who had just left the saloon.

"What the hell are you doing here?" the marshal asked. "Did you follow me?"

"No. Well, yes, I suppose I did, but not specifically. Marshal Witherspoon, my name is Pear . . . , uh, that is, Wes Fontaine. I'm here to see my sister."

"We ain't got nobody here by the name of Fontaine," Witherspoon said.

"Her married name is Abernathy. Kate Abernathy," Pearlie said.

"This here's the feller the woman mentioned when she was here a little while ago."

"Let me ask you something," Witherspoon said. "Were you in the saloon when Pardeen was shot?"

"Yes."

"Which one of you shot him?"

"What difference does it make who shot him? Pardeen drew first. You heard everyone in the saloon tell you that."

"I just want to know which one of you done it is all."

"Willis said it was the one named Smoke," Calhoun said.

"It was Smoke, but it could just as easily have been me, because if Pardeen had drawn on me like he did on Smoke, I would have shot him."

"Ha! You think you could've beaten Pardeen?"

"Yes."

"I doubt that. Pardeen was really good with a pistol."

"Is that so? Well, as it turns out, he wasn't good enough, was he?"

Pearlie's response quieted Witherspoon for a moment. "What's the purpose of your visit?" he asked.

"I told you, Katie is my sister. What other purpose would I need?"

The marshal stroked his chin for a moment, then he nodded. "All right. Shuck out of that gunbelt, 'n I'll let you go on back."

Pearlie unbuckled the gunbelt, then held it out toward Deputy Calhoun. The deputy took it, then pulled the pistol from the holster to examine it.

"What kind of pistol is this, anyway?"

"Smith and Wesson, Model Three."

"Don't think I've ever seen one like it."

"It's new. I don't have to tell you to be careful with it, do I?" Pearlie asked.

"No," Calhoun said as, self-consciously, he returned the pistol to its holster.

"Take 'im back there to see the whore," Witherspoon said.

Pearlie glared at Witherspoon but said nothing.

"What's the matter, Fontaine? You didn't know your sister was a whore?" Witherspoon asked with a chuckle.

"To be honest, Marshal, she ain't really a whore, 'n none of them girls that works for her is whores, neither," Calhoun said.

"Shut up, Calhoun. When I want your opinion, I'll ask for it," the marshal replied in a low, hissing voice.

When Pearlie reached the back of the jail, he stopped and stood there for just a moment, regarding the woman who was sitting on the bunk looking toward the window. He was able to remain unobserved because she had not yet noticed him.

Kate was five years older than Pearlie, and as he stood there, he recalled when he had last seen her. He was thirteen years old at the time.

"You ain't my mama," Wes said. "You ain't the boss of me."

"I'm your big sister, I have to look out for you," Kate said.

"You look out for yourself and I'll look out for myself," Wes said resolutely. "I'm goin' to go get me a job punchin' cattle."

"Wes, don't go," Kate pleaded. "You're too young."

"No, I ain't. I can ride as good as anyone."

"Please, don't go. You're not old enough, I'll be so worried about you."

That was the last time Wes had seen his older sister, but now, despite the passage of time, there was enough of a familiarity about her that he knew without question this was the sister he had left so long ago. He took a deep breath, then walked back to her cell.

"Hi, Katie," he said.

"Wes!" she said. She jumped up from the bed, then hurried over to the bars. "Oh, Wes!"

Her eyes filled with tears, and she stuck her hands through the bars to touch his face. "You have grown up so. What a fine-looking man you have become."

"Now, don't go embarrassing me first thing after we meet again," Pearlie said, though there was a smile in his voice as he spoke.

"There was a lady here, Sally Jensen, who said that you were in town. I was almost afraid to let myself believe her."

"You can believe it, 'cause here I am."

"She seems like an awfully nice lady."

"She's the nicest lady I've ever known. I know proper grammar, I've read books, good books, too, not just dime novels. Why, I can quote Shakespeare, did you know that? And you can even ask me a question about history. Miz Sally taught me."

"My brother, quoting Shakespeare. Who would have ever thought something like that?"

Pearlie assumed an affected position with hand over his heart, and the other arm extended. In a deep voice, he began to intone. "'*Tomorrow, and tomorrow, and tomorrow, creeps in this petty pace from day to day,*'" he broke his pose. "And it goes on from there."

Kate laughed. "You *can* quote Shakespeare. Oh, Wes, I'm so glad to see you. I have worried so about you over the years."

"Rusty said you knew I had come to Texas to deliver some horses to Mr. Byrd?" Pearlie asked. "How did you know that was me? I gave up the name, Wes Fontaine, a long time ago."

"One of the men you had ridden with at the B Bar B learned, somehow, that you were going by the name of Pearlie and that you were living in Colorado. Then, when I happened to be in San Vicente, I was told that there were some people who had brought some horses to Mr. Byrd. I saw you at dinner in the Marshal House, and I heard someone call you Pearlie. I studied you from the other side of the room and saw enough of the brother I thought I had lost that I just knew it was you. I almost walked up to you then."

"Oh, Katie, why didn't you?"

"I was afraid."

"Afraid of what?"

"It had been so many years since we had last seen one another. And when you left you were so adamant about being on your own. I don't know; I was afraid that you might reject me."

"I'm sorry. I suppose I can see why you might think something like that. I mean, I certainly gave you every cause to be a little scared of me."

"As I thought more about it, I realized I should have come out to the ranch to see you. But, when Mr. Byrd's daughter, Katrina, was killed, I didn't want to impose on his grief. It wasn't until much later that I approached Mr. Byrd to ask about you. He told me that you worked for Smoke Jensen on the Sugarloaf Ranch near Big Rock, Colorado.

"I knew then that you had made a good life for yourself, and I was pretty sure you didn't need a long-lost sister to show up and complicate things. So, I made a vow never to bother you. And I never would have if this hadn't come up. I sent a message for Rusty to find you, and I see that he did."

"Well, I can tell you right now that I'm glad he did. Katie, I'm sorry we haven't kept up," Pearlie said. "I should have; it was my responsibility to do so because I knew how to get ahold of you, but you had no idea how to find me." Pearlie chuckled. "That is, not until we delivered those horses to Mr. Byrd. As it turns out now, I'm glad you happened to be in San Vicente that day."

"I'm glad as well, because it led to our finally meeting. But, Wes, or would you rather I call you Pearlie?"

Pearlie chuckled. "I've been called Pearlie a lot longer

than I was ever called Wes, so if it's all the same to you, I think I would prefer to be called Pearlie."

Kate smiled. "All right, then, Pearlie it is. And, Pearlie, you did absolutely the right thing by not trying to get in touch with me. You have no idea how many times marshals and deputies questioned me about you when you first, uh, ran into trouble. And every time they came to see me I was able to tell them, truthfully, that I didn't have any idea where you were, or even who you were. Then, of course, I had never heard of anyone named Pearlie."

"Katie, it's important to me that you know those killings weren't my fault. Every witness in the saloon was willing to testify that both of them were in self-defense. But it's hard to make a case of self-defense when you kill a marshal."

"I know. Some of your friends from the B Bar B looked me up because they said they wanted me to know the truth about what happened. Our reunion, such as it is, has certainly been a long time in coming. I'm just sorry that, when we finally did meet again, it had to be like this, with me being in jail."

Pearlie smiled. "Don't worry about it, Katie. I can promise you that you won't be in here long. I know Rusty's story, too, and I know that he's no more guilty of murder than I was, so my friends and I are going to get both you and Rusty out of this mess."

"I appreciate your efforts, We . . . I mean Pearlie," Kate said with a wan smile. "But I don't see how you are going to be able to do that. It isn't just the marshal and the judge. The person who is really in charge is . . ."

"Silas Atwood," Pearlie said, interrupting her.

"Yes, and if you know about him, then you must know how many men he has working for him. He has his own private army."

Pearlie smiled. "He has one less now."

"What? What do you mean? Pearlie, you haven't killed someone on my account, have you?"

"It wasn't me, it was Smoke."

"Who?"

"Sally's husband. But don't worry about it, everyone in the saloon is willing to testify that Pardeen drew first."

"Pardeen? Pardeen is dead?"

"Yes."

"Oh. Well, I don't want to celebrate someone's death, but Pardeen was one of the worst of the lot. Does Atwood know about it yet?"

"He may know by now. As it turns out some of his other men were in there as well."

"That's unusual for so many of Atwood's people to be in there. Most of the time they can be found in the Bull and Heifer. They like the girls better there."

"What do you mean? The girls down at the Bull and Heifer can't possibly be prettier than the girls at your place."

Kate smiled. "It's not that they are prettier, it's that they will . . . uh, it's what they are willing to do."

"Oh," Pearlie said, understanding then what Kate was saying.

"Pearlie, be careful while you are here. Atwood is a very dangerous man."

"Don't you worry any about it, Katie," he said. "I've got a pretty good army with me, as well."

"You do?" Kate asked, surprised by Pearlie's comment. "How many men do you have with you?"

Again, Pearlie assumed the position of an actor on stage. "*'We few, we happy few, we band of brothers; for he to-day that sheds his blood with me shall be my brother; be he ne'er so vile. This day shall gentle his condition.'*"

"What?" Kate asked.

Pearlie laughed. "I told you that Miz Sally had taught me Shakespeare. That's from *King Henry the Fifth*. Anyway, all you need to know is that there are enough of us to get the job done. But the first thing we're going to do is make bail so we can get you out of this jail."

"Judge Boykin won't give you bail," Kate said. "He's as much one of Atwood's toadies as is the marshal."

"We'll get you out of here," Pearlie repeated. "And we'll do it legally. You don't worry any about Marshal Witherspoon, Judge Boykin, or even Silas Atwood. We have a few strings and connections we can pull ourselves, if we have to."

"Oh, how I pray that you are right. By the way, how are Mr. Peterson and the girls doing, back at the saloon? I know they must be worried about what is going to happen to them."

"They seem to be doing as well as can be expected, but they are more worried about you than they are about themselves. Peterson, Dolly, and the young women who work for you all send their greetings. Katie, you have some very loyal people there."

"Yes," Kate agreed. "They are good people, all of them. I want you to do something for me."

"All right."

"You haven't heard what it is I want you to do."

Pearlie reached in through the bars and took Kate's hand into his own. "It doesn't matter what it is. If you want me to do it, I'll do it."

"I have left Mr. Peterson in charge of the saloon. I know that Atwood is going to try again to take over the saloon. I want you to help Mr. Peterson hold on to it for me."

"Atwood is not going to get the saloon. I promise you, it will still be there for you when we get you out."

CHAPTER 10

When Pearlie walked back into the front of the jailhouse, Deputy Calhoun returned his holster and pistol to him.

"How is Miz Kate getting along back there?" Calhoun asked. There seemed to be a degree of actual concern in the deputy's question.

"She's doing all right. She'll be a lot better when I can get her out of here, though."

"Only way you're going to get her out of here is if that no-count boy of hers comes back so we can hang him instead of his whore mama," Marshal Witherspoon said.

Pearlie had just strapped his pistol belt back on and now, in a lightning-fast draw, he pulled his pistol and stuck the barrel into the marshal's mouth, doing so with such force that the front blade-sight cut Witherspoon's lip.

"Whug . . . whug arg yug doig?" Witherspoon mumbled, unable to say the words clearly because of the gun barrel in his mouth. His eyes were open wide in fright.

"You know, Marshal, I would take it just real neighborly of you if you wouldn't call my sister a whore anymore," Pearlie said. Even though he was jamming his pistol into the back of the marshal's throat, he spoke the words quietly, and calmly, which had the effect of making them much more frightening than if he had raised his voice in anger.

"I won't, I won't!" Witherspoon said, but because the barrel of the gun was in his mouth, the words came out, *"Ah wug, ah wug."*

Smiling, Pearlie returned his pistol to his holster. "I thought you might see things my way," he said.

"I could arrest you for armed assault against an officer of the law!" Witherspoon said as a little sliver of blood oozed from the cut on his lip.

"Could you?" Pearlie replied.

"I'll . . . I'll let it go this time," Witherspoon said.

"Well now, I appreciate that, Marshal. I'll just be going then. But you do take care now, you hear?"

Witherspoon watched Pearlie leave, then he took out his handkerchief and dabbed it against the small cut on his lip.

"You just stood there and did nothing," Witherspoon said.

"What would you have had me do, Marshal?" Calhoun asked. "He had the gun stuck in your mouth. I was afraid that if I did anything he would've blowed the back of your head off."

"Get out," Witherspoon said with an angry wave of his hand.

"Where do you want me to go?"

"I don't care where you go, as long as I don't have to look at you. Go somewhere and get drunk. That's what you do, ain't it?"

"Marshal, I was just lookin' out for you is all," Calhoun said.

Witherspoon held the handkerchief against his lip and glared at Calhoun, but he said nothing.

A few minutes later, Calhoun showed up in the Pretty Girl and Happy Cowboy Saloon. He saw Kate's brother talking to two other men and the woman who had visited

Kate earlier. He stared at them for just a moment, but he didn't approach their table.

"What can I get for you, Deputy?" Peterson asked, moving down the bar to stand in front of him. Peterson had a towel in his hand, and he made a swipe across the bar in front of Calhoun.

"Whiskey."

"I thought you said you were tryin' to quit. When you couldn't testify at Rusty's trial it was 'cause you were drunk 'n couldn't remember. Wouldn't you rather just have a beer?"

"Whiskey," Calhoun said again. "I need a drink."

Peterson shrugged his shoulders, then poured a shot. Calhoun tossed it down quickly, then pushed his glass out.

"Another one."

"Are you sure?"

"I want another one, damnit!" Calhoun said angrily.

Witherspoon had ridden out to Eagle Shire Ranch, and he was met by Atwood even before he dismounted.

"Willis told me Pardeen was killed today," Atwood said.

"Yes, sir, he was, by a man named Jensen. Smoke Jensen."

"Why didn't you arrest him?" Atwood asked angrily. "Pardeen was one of my best men, and this man killed him."

"It wouldn'ta done no good to arrest 'im," Witherspoon said. "Ever'one in the entire saloon said it was Pardeen that drawed first."

"Are you telling me that this man, Jensen, was able to outdraw Pardeen?"

"That's what ever'one in the saloon said."

"I don't believe it. Pardeen was the fastest gun of all my special cadre."

"Maybe so, but if I had arrested 'im, ever'one in the saloon would've testified that it was a fair fight."

"What difference does that make? They would've said the same thing about Kate's brat, too. We didn't let them testify."

"It's not the same thing," Witherspoon said. "Rusty Abernathy wasn't nothin' but a piano player, 'n he didn't have nobody that would be willin' to challenge us. But this here Jensen ain't alone. They's two others with 'im, and I figure that any one of them is ten times better than most men. I can't see them just standin' by 'n lettin' us do to another what we done to Rusty Abernathy."

Atwood stroked his Van Dyke beard for a moment. "Yes, well, it may wind up being better this way," he said. "Getting someone convicted and sentenced to hang doesn't always work out that well anyway, as we have recently seen. Perhaps it will be best for us to handle this in some other way."

"What other way? What are you talking about?"

"How do you fight a prairie fire?" Atwood asked.

"I don't know. I guess the best way is to set a back fire," Witherspoon said.

"Precisely. You fight fire with fire. Do you see what I mean?"

"Not exactly," Witherspoon replied, the expression on his face showing the confusion.

"You just let me worry about it."

Back in Etholen, Smoke and Pearlie were standing in front of the courthouse. They were able to find it, both by the flagpole and by the caisson-mounted thirty-two-pounder cannon that Peterson had told them to look for. Stacked up next to the gun were enough cannon balls to form a waist-high pyramid. A printed sign explained the display.

THIS CANNON

"OLD THUNDER"

WAS DONATED TO OUR TOWN
by the OFFICERS *and* MEN
of FORT QUITMAN

"Look at this," Pearlie said, running his hand over the smooth barrel of the artillery piece. "Do you think it would still fire?"

"I don't know why not," Smoke replied as he examined it more closely. "The touchhole hasn't been spiked."

They were to visit with Judge Henry L. Boykin, and after a moment of examining the gun, Smoke and Pearlie went into the building where they were directed to Judge Boykin's office.

"Smoke Jensen? I understand you are the man who killed Rufus Pardeen," Boykin said.

"I am."

"Have you come here to seek some sort of official dismissal? If you have, you are wasting your time, because I cannot issue a dismissal. However, you shouldn't worry about it, as there has been no charge filed. As far as I'm concerned, you are free to go."

"I'm not in the least worried about it," Smoke said. "I'm here for a different reason."

"And what would that be?"

As Smoke began to make an appeal for bail for Kate Abernathy, Boykin blew his nose, then stuck his handkerchief back into his pocket, doing so in such a way as to indicate his complete disdain for the idea.

"Are you a lawyer, Mr. Jensen?" Boykin asked.

"No, Your Honor, I am not a member of the bar."

"But you have read for the law?"

"No, Your Honor, I have not."

"Then tell me, Mr. Jensen, what right do you have to apply for bail for Miss Abernathy?"

"That would be Mrs. Abernathy, Your Honor. And she has designated me as her personal representative."

"Well, Mr. Jensen, whether you have been designated her personal representative or not, I'll tell you here and now, that I'm denying her bail."

"For what reason?"

"Reason? Reason, Mr. Jensen? I don't need a reason. I am the judge, and it is within my purview to grant or not to grant bail. In this particular case I choose not to grant bail, and no further justification for my action is required. I know you have only the most rudimentary knowledge of the law, Mr. Jensen, but do you understand that?"

Smoke smiled. "I do, Your Honor. And I thought you might deny her bail."

"If you thought that, then why did you even bother to apply?"

"I guess I just wanted to see if it was true what people say, that you are a fawning sycophant who jumps at Atwood's bark. I can see now that you are."

"How dare you, sir!" Boykin said angrily. "If you were in my court right now, I would hold you for contempt."

"Funny you would say that, Judge, because we don't need to be in a court for me to hold you in contempt."

"Mr. Jensen, as our business is complete, I am going to ask you to leave my chambers."

"All right, I'll go. I guess I'll just have to find another way to get Mrs. Abernathy out of jail."

Boykin's eyes narrowed, and he pointed a bony finger at Smoke. "You wouldn't be suggesting that you are going to try to break her out of jail, would you, Jensen?"

"Judge, if I decide to do that, there won't be any *trying* to it. I will succeed."

"I intend to instruct Marshal Witherspoon to keep his eye on you."

Smoke chuckled. "Oh, I expect he is already doing that. Yes, sir, I'm quite aware of the marshal's scrutiny."

When Smoke and Pearlie returned to the Pretty Girl and Happy Cowboy, they were met by Cal.

"Miz Sally is back there, by the piano," Cal said.

"Hey, Mr. Peterson, what's the story with that cannon?" Pearlie asked.

"Just like the sign says, Pearlie. When Fort Quitman shut down, they gave the cannon to the town."

"Will it still shoot?"

"I'll say it does. We fire it off every Fourth of July. It makes one hell of a racket."

Pearlie hurried on to join Smoke, Sally, and Cal.

"So he said no?" Sally was asking as Pearlie joined them.

"He said no, but I wasn't really expecting him to say anything else," Smoke said.

"I was talking to Mr. Peterson," Cal said. "He told me that Boykin is as crooked as a dog's hind leg. I'm not surprised he found Rusty guilty and won't grant bail to Miss Kate."

"Well, we won't worry about Rusty yet," Smoke said. "He's safe for the time being. It's Kate we need to get out of jail. We'll do it legally if we can. But if we can't get it done legally, we'll break her out. There's no way we're going to let them hang her."

"Yeah, well, we're probably going to have to break Katie out because there's no way we can do it legally if Boykin won't even grant bail," Pearlie said.

"There's a federal court in El Paso," Smoke said. "I'm

going to go over there and try to convince the federal judge to overturn Judge Boykin's ruling that put Kate in jail in the first place."

"How is a federal court going to help?" Pearlie asked. "They're holding Katie for accessory to murder, and murder is a state law."

"Going to the federal court was Sally's idea," Smoke said.

"Your idea?" Pearlie asked.

"Yes," Sally answered. "You are right, murder is a state law, but what they are doing here is a violation of the Fourteenth Amendment, which says that no state shall deprive any person of life, liberty, or property, without due process of law, nor deny to any person within its jurisdiction the equal protection of the laws. The incarceration of your sister, Kate, is in direct violation of that amendment, and that is all the justification a federal judge would need to order her immediate release."

"Yes, but even so, won't it just be our word against Boykin's word?" Pearlie asked.

"I suppose it will be," Smoke admitted. "But I've got to try."

"It need not be just our word against Boykin's word," Sally said. "Smoke, a moment ago, you said not to worry about Rusty yet. But if we can get Rusty's conviction overturned, that will automatically apply to Kate as well, wouldn't it?"

"Well, yes, I'm sure it would."

"I think we can get his conviction overturned under the same argument."

"How? I can see how your idea might work with Kate, she didn't get a trial."

"We can show that Rusty's rights to a fair trial were violated, so we can use the Fourteenth Amendment in appealing his case, as well."

"Do you have an idea how to do that?" Smoke asked.

"Yes, but we're going to have to talk to Mr. Peterson about it."

"I'll bring him over to the table," Cal offered.

A moment later Cal returned to the table with the bartender. "Yes, ma'am, Cal said you wanted to talk to me about somethin'?" Peterson asked.

"Mr. Peterson, you saw what happened in here the night Rusty killed Calley, didn't you?" Sally asked.

"Yes, ma'am, I saw every bit of it."

"Do you have a pen and paper?"

"A pen and paper? Well, I . . . wait a minute. Dolly does. She's always writing poetry and such."

"Would you ask her if she would bring paper and pen to me?"

"What have you got in mind, Sally?" Smoke asked.

Sally smiled. "I intend to validate the story we are going to tell him."

"We?"

"I'll be going with you," Sally said.

CHAPTER 11

"You wanted this, Miz Sally?" Dolly asked, bringing a pen and a few sheets of writing paper with her.

"Yes, Dolly, thank you," Sally replied. Sally looked up at Peterson.

"Now, Mr. Peterson, if you would please, tell us what happened that night, and be as accurate as you can."

Peterson began talking, and as he did so, Sally recorded his words. Peterson told the story in exact detail, chronicling how Calley had put a pistol on the piano stool, then began counting to ten, declaring that when he got to ten he was going to shoot.

"He looked away when he got to eight, 'n that's when Rusty grabbed the gun and shot him, just as he said 'nine.' But if he hadn't done that, Calley would have kilt him sure. You see, Calley had some reputation as a gunfighter and Rusty? Well, as far as I know there weren't nobody that ever even seen Rusty wearin' a gun at all. He didn't have no choice but to do what he done."

"That's true, Miz Sally," Dolly, who had been listening, said. "Calley would've killed poor Rusty, if Rusty hadn't taken the opportunity to shoot him when he had the chance."

"Then, when it come to the trial, Judge Boykin, he

wouldn't let anyone who actually saw what happened tell their story," Peterson said in conclusion.

"How many others were in the saloon that night?"

"Well, Dolly 'n the girls was all here. That makes five. 'N there was at least six or seven more that was here that seen what happened."

"We, who affix our signatures hereto this document, do affirm that the particulars as recorded above are true and accurate in every detail," Sally said aloud as she penned the validating statement.

"Now," she said. "Let's get as many of the witnesses to sign this as we can, then we'll take this document to see the federal judge in El Paso."

"Sally," Smoke said with a big smile. "That is positively brilliant!"

"I just wish we could get them notarized," Sally said.

"Oh, you can get it notarized all right, there's no problem with that. I can do it for you," Dolly said.

"You can? How?"

"I'm a notary public," she said with a broad smile.

"You?" Sally asked in surprise. "You are a notary public?"

"Yes, ma'am, I sure am. Miss Kate asked me to do it so I could notarize things for her."

"That's wonderful!" Sally said.

Within an hour, they had the signature of every witness but one.

"Who's missing?" Smoke asked.

"Deputy Calhoun was here," Peterson said. "But it won't do any good to get his signature."

"Well, even if he rebutted the testimony of the others, it would still be," she counted the names, "eleven to one."

"Oh, he wouldn't refute it," Peterson said. "He couldn't. He was passed out drunk that night and didn't see anything."

"Besides, he most likely wouldn't refute it anyway," Dolly said.

"Why not?"

"Deputy Calhoun is a good man, don't get me wrong. I mean he is Marshal Witherspoon's deputy 'n all, but he isn't a mean man like Witherspoon."

"That's true," Peterson said. "Calhoun's actually a pretty good man."

"Why does he stay on with him, then?"

"To be honest, I don't think Calhoun could get a job anywhere else. And Witherspoon keeps him on because he's a drunk and easy for Witherspoon to control," Peterson said.

"He didn't testify at Rusty's trial," Dolly said. "He coulda said that Rusty murdered Calley, but he told the judge he didn't see anything."

"Who did testify against Rusty?"

"The marshal did."

"But he wasn't even here, was he?"

"No, he wasn't. But that didn't stop him from testifying," Dolly said.

"Lying, you mean," Peterson added.

Eagle Shire Ranch

Silas Atwood lived on the Eagle Shire Ranch in an antebellum house, three and a half stories high, topped by a large cupola, with Corinthian columns across the front. It was an exact replica of Colonel Raymond Windsor's mansion, Windsor Hall, on Moss Point Plantation in Demopolis, Alabama. Atwood had grown up on Moss Point Plantation, the son of the white overseer. Atwood hadn't built the house to honor Colonel Windsor, but to prove to himself that he was just as good as Windsor was.

Windsor had not treated Atwood's father any differently than he had his slaves, nor had he treated Atwood any differently from the young blacks on the plantation. That's not to say that Atwood was mistreated, because Windsor had actually treated everyone well, but that wasn't the point. The point was, Atwood was white, and he felt as if he should have been treated better than the slaves.

Raymond Windsor had supported the Confederacy to the point that he raised and equipped a regiment of cavalrymen from his own funds. But before he left for the war, he converted half of his money, which was a considerable amount, into gold as a hedge against the Confederate dollar.

Atwood and his father had both joined the regiment, and his father had been killed at the Battle of Tupelo in July of 1864. Five months later, Colonel Windsor lay mortally wounded at the Battle of Franklin. He sent for Atwood, who he had recently promoted to lieutenant.

"Lieutenant Atwood," Windsor gasped. "I'm releasing you from the army now because I want you to take care of something for me. Return to Moss Point to look after my family. Wait until the war is over, and when everything has settled down, dig on the north side of the center silo. There, you will find the gold that I hid. Give it to my wife and children so that they aren't left destitute by this cruel war. And keep one thousand dollars for yourself."

"You are being very generous, Colonel," Atwood said.

"You have earned it, my boy. And if you do this for me, it will be money well spent. Do I have your word that you will do this?"

"You have my word, Colonel," Atwood promised.

Atwood returned to Moss Point, stayed for a few weeks, just long enough to earn Mrs. Windsor's trust, then, in the middle of the night, left with a horse and a pack mule. The pack mule was carrying one hundred fifty pounds of gold . . . or 2,175 troy ounces. At nineteen dollars and eighty cents a troy ounce, that came to just over forty-three thousand dollars.

When he arrived in Texas two months later, he was far from the closing battles of the war. And he was a rich man.

* * *

Now, more than twenty years later, Silas Atwood was much wealthier than he had been when he first arrived. At the moment he was sitting in a library, surrounded by books, none of which he had ever read, lighting a cigar and talking around puffs to Marshal Witherspoon and Judge Boykin.

"What do you know about these men who have come to town?" He puffed a few times until the end of the cigar glowed red, and his head was wreathed with aromatic smoke before he finished his question. "I am particularly interested in the one that killed Rufus Pardeen."

"That would be Smoke Jensen," Witherspoon replied.

"I was paying Pardeen more than any of my other special cadre because he had the reputation of being exceptionally good with a gun. This man, Jensen, did he beat him fair and square?"

"That's what all the witnesses in the saloon say," Witherspoon replied.

Atwood pulled the cigar from his mouth and examined the end of it. "One of the newcomers is Kate's brother, I understand?"

"Yes, and she is why they are here. Kate's brother, and Smoke Jensen, came to my office trying to get me to set bail for her."

"What did you tell them?"

"I said no, of course."

"Well, what with the shooting of Pardeen, and the humiliating and disarming of Willis and the two men who were with him, I'm sure that Kate's brother . . . what is his name?"

"Fontaine," Witherspoon replied. "Wes Fontaine, though he calls himself Pearlie nowadays."

"Pearlie," Atwood said. "Yes, Pearlie. Pearlie and Smoke, they with their colorful names, may feel that they have the upper hand for now. But when all is said and done, I'm sure Kate Abernathy's champions will give us no real difficulty."

"It may not be as easy as all that," Judge Boykin said.

"Why do you say that?"

"Apparently this man Jensen has earned somewhat of a reputation as a hero."

"A hero?" Atwood replied. "What do you mean, he's a hero?"

"When he came to visit me I thought that, perhaps, I had heard his name before, so I walked down to the newspaper office to look him up. There have been several articles written about his exploits, which have been notable enough to warrant syndication by the Associated Press. They've even written some books about him, I understand. He is quite well known in Colorado where it is said that there is no one who is faster, or more accurate, in the use of a pistol."

"Colorado?" Atwood removed his cigar and used it as he gestured. "Well, that may be. But he is in Texas now, and he is going to have to deal with me." The tone of Atwood's voice displayed his incredulity that anyone would dare challenge him.

"Yes, sir, he will have to deal with you, but he is already aware of your position here," Judge Boykin said. "He mentioned your name while we were in conversation."

Returning the cigar to his mouth, Atwood smiled around it. "He mentioned my name, you say? In what way was my name used?"

"He . . . uh . . . questioned the relationship I had with you, suggesting that you may have an undue degree of influence over any judicial decision I might make."

Atwood chuckled. "You mean he knows that I have you by the balls?"

Boykin cleared his throat in embarrassment. "Well, uh, I wouldn't exactly say that."

"How would you say it?"

"I would say that, uh, your interests and mine coincide."

"Yeah," Atwood said, chuckling again. "You might say that. And Jensen pointed that out to you, did he?"

"Yes."

"Well, it could be that this man, Jensen, isn't as dumb as I thought. But what I want to know is, why is he getting involved in the first place? What does he have to do with Kate Abernathy?"

"Wes Fontaine works for Smoke Jensen," Marshal Witherspoon said. "Apparently he and his sister haven't seen each other in many years."

"If they haven't seen each other in a long time, what do you suppose made him show up now?" Atwood said.

Witherspoon smiled. "Well, he showed up now because, somehow, he learned that she was in trouble. And, I suppose he feels guilty about not seeing her for all these years. Who knows why he's here? Whatever the reason he is here, he and Jensen are bound to make trouble for us."

"You say Fontaine works for Jensen?"

"Yes."

Atwood studied the end of his cigar for a moment. "Then that's how we'll handle it. If we get rid of Jensen, that will take care of Fontaine and the other man who is with them. To kill a snake, you cut off its head."

"Mr. Atwood, you aren't actually suggesting that we kill Jensen, are you?" Boykin asked. "That would be murder."

"Perhaps not," Atwood replied.

"What do you mean?"

"You did say that he is a well-known gunfighter, didn't you, Boykin?"

Upon hearing himself called by his last name, without the

honorific title "Judge," there was just a flicker of resentment, though Boykin covered it up well.

"Yes, I did say that."

"Well, there's your answer then. Someone who is that good with a gun is bound to have had some paper out on him at some time in his past. All you have to do is find the wanted poster."

"And if I can't find one?"

"Make one up," Atwood said easily.

"I'd rather not make one up. I'm sure you are right; I'm sure that someone with his propensity for violence is bound to have a wanted poster out on him somewhere."

"Just make certain that it is a poster that says 'dead or alive,'" Judge Boykin instructed.

CHAPTER 12

El Paso

When Smoke, Sally, and Pearlie arrived in El Paso, they saw that, unlike Etholen, which was a rather bucolic community, El Paso was quite a thriving city. There was a great deal of wagon and buggy traffic, and dozens and dozens of people walking along the plank walks that lined both sides of the streets. At intervals there were boards stretched all the way across the dirt streets to allow people a way to cross when the roads were full of mud. This seemed a totally unnecessary accommodation now, though, as it had been several weeks since the last good rain. As a result the passage of horses and wheeled vehicles stirred up the dust so that a brown-gray cloud seemed to hang in the air, no more than six feet above the ground.

"I'll ask that man over there where the federal court building is," Smoke said.

"No need to," Sally replied. "Look down there."

Sally pointed to a large and impressive brick and stone building that stood three stories high, with a tower in the center that stretched up one additional story. Stone steps climbed up to a porch that had an array of impressive-looking columns. A sign attached to the front of the structure said, UNITED STATES FEDERAL BUILDING.

"I would say that's the place we're looking for," Sally said.

"And I would say that you are right," Smoke replied.

Tying their horses to a hitching rail out front, the three went inside, examined the directory, then walked upstairs to the office of the federal judge.

Ezekiel B. Turner was the judge of the West Texas Federal Court, and he greeted them courteously after the judicial clerk announced their presence.

"Which of you gentlemen is Smoke Jensen?" Judge Turner asked.

"I am, Your Honor, though my real name is . . ."

"Kirby Jensen," Turner interrupted.

The expression on Smoke's face reflected his surprise at the judge knowing his given name.

"I beg your pardon?"

"That is your name, isn't it? Kirby Jensen?"

"Well, yes, that is true. But how in the world do you know that? To the best of my memory, we've never met."

"No, we haven't. But I know you. At least, I know of you. That is, if you are the same man who was appointed as a Deputy U.S. Marshal by Uriah B. Holloway."

"Yes, I am that man," Smoke replied. "Although, that was several years ago."

Turner smiled and nodded. "I thought so. Uriah and I are great friends from way back. He has spoken well of you."

"Marshal Holloway is a good man," Smoke said.

"That he is, Mr. Jensen, that he is. And this young lady?" Turner asked, smiling at Sally.

"This is my wife, Sally."

"Sally," Judge Turner said. "That is a beautiful name for a beautiful lady." He looked toward Pearlie.

"This is Pearlie," Smoke said.

"Pearlie?"

"That's what I'm called, Your Honor. My real name is Wes Fontaine."

"Now, Mr. and Mrs. Jensen, Pearlie, what can I do for you?"

"It's about Pearlie's sister. Pearlie is an employee of mine, and . . ." Smoke started.

"Smoke, Pearlie is much more than just an employee, and you know that," Sally interrupted.

"Yes, he is," Smoke said. "The truth is, Pearlie is more family than mere employee."

Pearlie smiled self-consciously at Smoke's beneficent description of their relationship.

"And you've always made me feel that way," Pearlie said. "But, Your Honor, my sister, Katie Abernathy, is why we're here."

"And Pearlie's nephew, Rusty Abernathy. Rusty was tried and convicted of murder."

Judge Turner held up his hand and shook his head. "I'm sure you realize that murder is a state offense."

"Your Honor, if I may," Sally said. "We are appealing to you on the basis of Judge Boykin's court violating Mr. Abernathy's rights under the Fourteenth Amendment, and that makes it federal. His trial was improper; therefore, his imprisonment was improper."

Judge Turner nodded. "That is an interesting tactic for appeal," he said. "How was the trial improper?"

"To begin with, Your Honor, Mr. Abernathy was given no choice in selecting his own lawyer. His defense was appointed by the court."

"Yes, well, when an indigent defendant is appointed a lawyer, he rarely has any say in it."

"That's just it, Your Honor. Mr. Abernathy isn't indigent. He could well afford his own lawyer but was denied that right. In addition there was no voir dire of a jury that was packed with Atwood men, and the court did not allow so much as one witness to testify in Mr. Abernathy's defense."

"Were there eyewitnesses who could have provided cogent testimony?" Judge Turner asked.

"Indeed there were, Your Honor, but as I said, they weren't allowed to testify."

"Is Mr. Abernathy in jail now?" he asked.

"No," Smoke replied. "Rusty escaped, and the marshal arrested Kate, his mother. Now they are saying that if Rusty doesn't return by a date certain, they are going to hang his mother in his place."

"What? Why, that is outrageous!" Judge Turner said.

"Yes, sir, that's what we thought, too," Smoke said. "We applied for bail through Judge Boykin, but he turned us down."

"Boykin," Judge Turner said, practically spitting the name. "If ever there was a man who dishonored the bench more than that miscreant, I have yet to hear of him. If you can get me some eyewitness accounts of the incident involving Mrs. Abernathy's son, I will, if those accounts justify it, overturn Judge Boykin and grant Mrs. Abernathy release on her own recognizance."

A broad smile played across Sally's lips. "We hoped you might say something like that," she said. Sally removed the paper she had recorded from the envelope, then handed it to Judge Turner. "Here is an affidavit, signed by every eyewitness to the event, and notarized."

Judge Turner read the document, reacting audibly to the part where it explained that no eyewitnesses were allowed to testify.

"You can forget about bail," Judge Turner said.

"What?" Smoke asked, surprised by the judge's announcement.

"There is no need for bail, neither for Mrs. Abernathy nor for her son. I am ordering the immediate release of Mrs. Abernathy, and I am officially vacating the conviction of

Rusty Abernathy. I have never seen such a travesty of justice as this in all my days on the bench."

Smoke smiled and reached out to shake Judge Turner's hand.

"Your Honor, I don't know how to thank you."

"No, Mr. Jensen, it is I who should thank you and Mrs. Jensen for bringing this to my attention. Oh, by the way, you might have a little trouble with Boykin and the marshal there, so the two of you hold up your right hand." He was referring to Smoke and Pearlie.

Smoke smiled. "I was going to ask you if you would be willing to appoint us as officers of the court."

"I'm more than willing. I'm proud to do it," Judge Turner replied.

Smoke and Pearlie raised their right hands as Judge Turner swore them in as United States Marshals.

When Smoke and Pearlie stepped into the marshal's office later that same day back in Etholen, Marshal Witherspoon was the only one present.

"Look here," Witherspoon said, pointing at Pearlie. "I ought to lock you up for what you done last time you was here. You assaulted an officer of the law, what with you stickin' your pistol in my mouth like you done."

"I didn't do that because you were an officer of the law," Pearlie said. "I did that because you are a low-life son of a bitch and I didn't like the way you referred to my sister."

"Yeah, well, maybe I was a little out of line, callin' her a whore 'n all. So, I'm goin' to let it pass this time," Witherspoon said, speaking as if he had any control over the matter. "But you better not do anythin' like that again. I reckon you're wantin' to go back there 'n see her, so, if you 'n Jensen will just go over there 'n shuck out of them pistol belts, you can go on back."

"We'll keep our guns, because we don't plan to go back and see her," Pearlie said.

"What do you mean? You aren't here to see your sister?"

"Oh, we're here to see her all right," Smoke said. "But we won't be going back there to see her. You are going to bring her up here, to us."

"Now, why would I want to do a damn-fool thing like that?"

"You should do it because we have an order from the court that says my sister is free," Pearlie said. "So we expect you to let her go."

"The judge is setting her free, is he?" Witherspoon smiled. "Good, then she's agreed to sell the saloon to Mr. Atwood. That probably means the judge will more'n likely drop charges against the boy, too. Hell, if Kate hadda agreed to sell the saloon to Mr. Atwood in the first place, none of this would've happened."

"What makes you think she has agreed to sell the saloon to Atwood?" Smoke asked.

"You said the judge said to let her out, didn't you?"

"Yes."

"Then that means she's willin' to sell the saloon to Mr. Atwood. Atwood told me hisself that that's all it would take for him to agree to allow Judge Boykin to let Kate out of jail."

"Are you telling me, Marshal, that Judge Boykin, an officer of the court, takes his orders from Silas Atwood?" Smoke asked.

"Hell, we pretty much all do," Witherspoon admitted. "Without Mr. Atwood, there most likely wouldn't be none of us have our jobs, the judge included."

"It really comes as no surprise to us that you and Boykin are in Atwood's pocket," Smoke said. "I just wanted to hear you say it aloud. But Boykin didn't set Mrs. Abernathy free."

"Wait a minute. You mean she ain't been set free? Well,

what did you tell me that for? Did you think I wouldn't check with the judge?"

"Oh, my sister has been set free, all right," Pearlie said. "But this court order doesn't come from Boykin, it comes from Judge Ezekiel B. Turner, in El Paso."

"El Paso? What does a judge in El Paso have to do with Etholen? He won't have any jurisdiction here. You'll need to get an order from Judge Boykin."

Smoke shook his head. "You don't understand. Turner is a federal judge. That means he has authority over Boykin, and every other judge in West Texas."

"Yeah? Well, I don't know about that," Witherspoon said. "I think maybe I should wait and see what Atwood thinks. I don't think I have the authority to let her go on my own."

"On the contrary, you have no authority to keep her on your own. I, on the other hand, do have the authority to see her set free," Smoke said. "And I intend to see to it that you do that, right now."

"You have the authority?" Witherspoon asked. "What authority do you have?"

"This," Smoke said, showing Marshal Witherspoon the paper. "And this," he added, pulling his pistol.

Smoke reached out to take the marshal's gun from his holster. "Get the keys, Pearlie. The marshal, here, is about to become a guest in his own jail."

"What are you doing? You can't do this!"

"Yeah, I can," Smoke said with an easy grin.

With the keys in Pearlie's hand, and a pistol in Smoke's hand, the three men went into the back of the jail. When they got to the back, they saw Kate standing in her cell with her hands grasping the bars.

"Pearlie, I thought I heard your voice out there." She saw that the man with her brother was holding a pistol on the marshal, and she gasped in fear. "What's going on?" she asked.

"We're getting you out of here, Katie."

"No!" Kate said, shaking her head. "I don't want you to break me out of jail! Wes, I mean Pearlie, I don't want you getting in trouble because of me!"

"Relax, we aren't in any trouble," Pearlie said. "We've got a court order from a federal judge, ordering your release. The only reason we've come back like this is because the marshal, here, didn't want to honor the court order. So, we just took it on our own to enforce the order."

"But, even with that letter, you don't have the authority on your own, do you?"

"I'll have you know, Katie, that Smoke and I were both appointed as officers of the federal court. That gives us all the authority we need."

While Smoke and Pearlie were freeing Kate, Deputy Calhoun, unaware of what was playing out back at the city jail, was in the back room of the courthouse, surrounded by cardboard boxes filled with yellowed and sometimes crumbling paper.

PROCLAMATION
of the
GOVERNOR OF MISSOURI

WANTED
for ROBBERY *and* MURDER

THE JAMES GANG :
JESSE JAMES, FRANK JAMES, COLE YOUNGER,
JIM YOUNGER, *and* BOB YOUNGER

REWARD OF $5,000
$1,000 ea.

Calhoun found dozens of other posters that he knew were outdated because the principals had already been captured or killed. He was about ready to give up when he found one that did catch his interest. This poster was brown with age, and the edges were curling up. He was sure it had probably been withdrawn or it wouldn't have been in this box with all the other outdated posters. Besides, it was a poster from Colorado, so he wasn't sure it would be applicable in Texas anyway. But he would let Marshal Witherspoon decide.

CHAPTER 13

"Miss Kate! You're out!" Peterson exclaimed in excitement when Kate, Pearlie, and Smoke stepped into the Pretty Girl and Happy Cowboy Saloon a few minutes later.

"Oh, Miss Kate! How good it is to see you!" Dolly shouted happily, running to her to give her an embrace. The other four girls did the same thing.

"Pearlie told me what all of you did for me," Kate said. "Sally, I thank you so much for writing up the paper telling what happened, and Mr. Peterson, Dolly, and all of you, I thank you for putting your names to it."

"It's only right," Dolly said. "Marshal Witherspoon had no business putting you in jail in the first place."

"Belly up to the bar, boys, and name your poison," Kate said. "Mr. Peterson, if you would, please, set everyone up with a drink of their choice, on the house."

"Thank you!" one of the patrons boomed in response, and all seventeen men present hurried to the bar to claim their drink.

"I'll bet Marshal Witherspoon is fit to be tied," Dolly said.

Kate laughed. "Funny you should mention that. Fit to be tied, I mean."

"Oh, oh," Sally said. "Smoke, what did you do? You didn't tie the marshal up, did you?"

"Why, no, there was no need to tie him up," Smoke said.

"I wouldn't put it past you."

"I mean, as long as we could put him in a jail cell, why bother to tie him up?"

"Smoke, you didn't!" Sally said, but she laughed as she made the comment.

"Did you say that Judge Turner overturned Rusty's conviction?" Kate asked.

"He sure did," Sally replied with a broad smile.

"Is there any way we can get word to him about that? I would sure like to have him come back home."

"I tell you what, Sis. I'll go get him and bring him back home," Pearlie said.

"Would you? Oh, that would be wonderful!"

"I'll go with you," Cal said.

"I suppose you folks will be going back home now that this is all straightened out," Kate said, though the tone of her voice indicated that this was not something she was particularly looking forward to.

"We have no intention of going back," Smoke said.

"Oh?"

"We don't have everything straightened out," Smoke said. "As I understand it, Atwood still wants to get control of your place, doesn't he?"

"I'm sure he does."

"Then, until he changes his mind, everything isn't straightened out. And we won't leave here until Atwood changes his tune."

Kate shook her head. "Oh, I don't think Silas Atwood is going to change anything very soon."

Smoke smiled. "Well then, we'll just have to change his mind for him, won't we?"

* * *

"I got that information on Smoke Jensen you was lookin' for," Deputy Calhoun said when he stepped into the marshal's office. He glanced toward the other side of the room and saw that the marshal wasn't sitting behind his desk. "Marshal? Marshal Witherspoon, are you in here?"

"Calhoun! I'm back here!" Witherspoon called.

"All right, I'll just leave this on your desk."

"Get back here!" Witherspoon shouted.

"What's up, Marshal? You havin' trouble with Kate?" Calhoun asked, and, putting the flyer he had located on the marshal's desk, he walked back to the cell area. "I'll be right there."

When Calhoun got to the cell area, he expected to see Marshal Witherspoon standing just outside of the prisoner's cell. To his total shock, he saw him standing inside the cell.

"Lord, have mercy, Marshal! What are you doin' in that jail cell?"

"Get me the hell out of here!" Witherspoon demanded angrily.

"How did you get in there?"

"Never mind all that. Just get me out, now!"

Calhoun hurried out to the front of the office, got the keys, then came back to let Witherspoon out.

"Where the hell have you been?" Witherspoon demanded to know. "I've been locked up back here for at least two hours!"

"I was doin' what you told me to do, Marshal," Calhoun replied. "I was seein' what I could come up with on Smoke Jensen."

"And did you?" Witherspoon asked as they returned to the office.

"Well, I'm not sure. I found somethin', but I'm not sure it'll be of any use to us."

"You let me decide on whether or not it'll be any use to us. What did you find?"

"I got a wanted poster on him for murder. But it's from Colorado, it ain't from Texas."

Despite the ordeal of having just been locked up in his own jail, a huge smile spread across Marshal Witherspoon's face. "The hell you say."

"Onliest thing is, that poster has to be over twenty years old."

"That doesn't matter," Witherspoon said. "I'm no lawyer, but even I know that there's no statute of limitations on murder." Witherspoon looked at the wanted poster. "And, as you can see here," he said, thumping his fingers on the paper, "he's wanted for murder. And for ten thousand dollars. Oh, yeah, Mr. Atwood is going to be really happy about this."

WANTED
DEAD *or* ALIVE
THE OUTLAW AND MURDERER

SMOKE JENSEN

$10,000 REWARD
Contact the Sheriff—Bury, Idaho Terr.

"You mean he *was* wanted for murder," Calhoun said. "Since this is the onliest one on him I found, why, like as not, it's done been called back."

"Maybe it was called back from Colorado," Witherspoon said with an evil smile. "But it wasn't called back from Texas."

"How do you know it wasn't called back from Texas?"

"You found it, didn't you? If it had been called back, most likely it would've been destroyed, not just put away."

"So, what do we do with it now?"

"I'll see Judge Boykin 'n have him issue a new one," Witherspoon said.

"Even if it's been withdrawn?"

"That's for the judge to decide, not you," Witherspoon said.

"I don't know if I have the authority to reissue this," Judge Boykin said after Witherspoon showed him the reward poster on Smoke Jensen. "This was issued by some sheriff up in Idaho, and it is offering a ten-thousand-dollar reward. Suppose someone did kill him, how would we come up with ten thousand dollars?"

"Hell, Judge, we won't actually be reissuing this poster," Witherspoon said. "We'll just be reprinting it for that marshal up in Idaho. If somebody kills Jensen and wants the reward, they'll have to contact that sheriff."

"But this poster is over twenty years old. There's very little chance that the man who originally posted this reward would still be the marshal, and whoever is there now probably knows nothing at all about this. I doubt seriously that the reward would even be paid."

Witherspoon chuckled. "Well now, that ain't really goin' to be our problem, is it? Once Jensen is dead, he's dead, 'n whether the sheriff up in Bury, Idaho, whoever he is, pays this reward or not, it don't really matter none to us."

"But if I am purposely issuing a wanted poster on a man who isn't wanted, I could get into a lot of trouble," Boykin complained.

"Are you a' tellin' me that you ain't goin' to reissue the poster?"

"I'm just saying it could be risky."

"Tell me this, Judge, have you ever received any information saying that Smoke Jensen ain't wanted no more?"

"Well, no, but then, I wasn't the judge back when this dodger was first issued."

"Then you have no information telling you that it has been withdrawn. As far as you know, you're just doing the state of Colorado a favor by authorizing the reprint of this.

"And, I might add, Atwood wants this done."

Judge Boykin smiled. "Yes," he said. "Yes, you're right, I would just be doing a community service by reissuing this document, wouldn't I?"

"You write out somethin' sayin' you approve of this, 'n I'll go over to the newspaper office 'n have 'em print up some reward dodgers for us," Witherspoon said.

"I wouldn't go to the newspaper office if I were you," Boykin said.

"Why not? I need to get these things printed."

"You've read some of Blanton's editorials, haven't you? I can't say that any of them have been particularly supportive. You'd better find someplace else to have it printed."

"Yeah, you're right," Witherspoon said.

"How many did you have printed?" Atwood asked.

"So far there's just this one. I told him I'd need to see what you thought about it before I'd have him print any more."

Atwood nodded. "Yes, it looks good, but we don't need any more. This one will be enough."

"One?" Witherspoon questioned, surprised by Atwood's reply. "What do you mean we only need one? How are we going to get them out there for people to see them if we only print one?"

"No need for a lot of people to see it," Atwood said. "The only one who needs to see it is the one who is going to try and collect the reward."

"Uh, Mr. Atwood, you do know, don't you, that there

might not be any reward at all? This was first printed a long time ago, and besides that, it was done up in Colorado."

"Paying the reward is not our problem," Atwood said. "According to this, it is the sheriff up in Idaho who will be paying the ten thousand."

"I suppose so. But I don't think Jensen is going to be all that easy to kill. It's not just that he killed Pardeen, from what I've been able to find out about him, he's better with a gun than just about anybody."

"Just about doesn't mean everyone. I may know of just the man who can handle him."

"Who would that be?" Witherspoon asked. "I know you've got some good men ridin' for you, but I'll be honest with you, Mr. Atwood, I don't think you've got anyone who's up to handlin' Smoke Jensen."

"Do you think someone like Lucien Critchlow would be good enough to take the measure of Mr. Jensen?"

"Someone like Critchlow? I don't know. He might be. That is, if he really is as good as Critchlow."

Atwood smiled. "Oh, I expect Critchlow is as good as Critchlow."

"You've got Critchlow?"

"Not yet, but I'll get him."

Witherspoon smiled and nodded. "Yeah, you get Critchlow, and our problem will be taken care of. Oh, wait, that might not be such a good idea."

"Why not?"

"Critchlow is for sure going to want the ten-thousand-dollar reward, and like I told you before, there might not even be a reward out for Jensen now. It's more than likely that this here reward was took down years ago. Otherwise, there would be fresh paper out on 'im, and I can tell you for a fact, there ain't none. And Critchlow ain't exactly the kind of a man I'd want to have thinkin' we cheated him."

"You let me worry about that."

* * *

"Why is it you're willin' to hire someone else to take care of Jensen?" Bo Willis asked. "Ain't that why you've got folks like me 'n Clark 'n Booker 'n the others? We ain't exactly your ordinary cowhands, you know."

"You had your opportunity to deal with him, and it didn't turn out all that well, did it?"

"Yeah, well, it wasn't just him, it was three of 'em, if you recall. 'N one of 'em sneaked up behind us."

"I do recall," Atwood said. "Look, Willis, don't misunderstand the situation here. You, Clark, and Booker are too valuable to me and I can't afford to lose you right now. If Critchlow succeeds, and Jensen is killed, I will be able to continue with the long-range plans I have. But if Critchlow is killed, it will merely be a temporary setback. I can replace him easily. You, not so easily."

"Oh," Willis said, mollified by Atwood's explanation. "Oh, well, yeah, if you put it that way, I see what you mean."

"Now, do be a good man and go to Carrizo Springs for me. I'm told that is where you will be able to find Critchlow."

CHAPTER 14

Bo Willis had never actually seen Lucien Critchlow, but he did have a good description of him, and when he stepped into the Bottom Dollar Saloon in Carrizo Springs, Texas, he saw someone standing, alone, at the far end of the bar. The man standing there had a narrow face with hollow cheeks and very thin lips. His eyes were dark, and deep—set beneath sparse eyebrows.

"What'll it be?" the bartender asked, stepping up to Willis.

"I'll take a whiskey."

The bartender poured a shot from an unmarked bottle.

"That man standing at the other end of the bar," Willis said quietly, as he paid for the drink. "Would that be Lucien Critchlow?"

"It might be. Who are you?"

"The name is Willis. I work for Mr. Atwood over in El Paso County, 'n he wants to make Critchlow an offer."

"What kind of offer?" the bartender asked.

Willis glared at him. "The offer is for Critchlow," he said.

"Yeah? Well, I wouldn't make 'im mad, if I was you," the bartender said as he walked away.

Willis tossed down his whiskey and looked over toward

Critchlow. Nobody knew for sure how many men Lucien Critchlow had actually killed. Seventeen, some said. Twenty-three, others insisted. Critchlow knew, but he never spoke about it. He didn't have to; his reputation spoke for itself.

Willis set the glass down on the bar, wiped his lips with the back of his hand, then screwed up his courage to approach the gunfighter.

"Mr. Critchlow?"

"Yeah?" Critchlow replied without turning around.

"I work for a man named Silas Atwood. He wants to make you an offer."

"An offer?"

"He wants to hire you for a job."

"I don't come cheap."

"Mr. Atwood isn't a cheap man."

"What is this job I'm supposed to do?"

"Have you ever heard of a man named Smoke Jensen?"

"Smoke Jensen? Yeah, I've heard of him. He come down here not too long ago and got into a little brawl with that Mexican feller that was raisin' so much Cain here about. Keno, I think his name was."

"Is that all you know about 'im?"

"Folks say that he's good with a gun," Critchlow said.

"Yeah, that's what I heard, too."

"What about Jensen? Why are you askin' me about 'im?"

"I'd rather let Mr. Atwood tell you about 'im," Willis said. "I can tell you this, though. He told me to tell you that if you can do the job, it'll be worth a lot of money to you."

Critchlow said nothing, but turned back to the bar and stared down into his whiskey glass. Willis, not quite sure what he should do now, stood there for a moment, then turned to walk away.

"Where are you goin'?" Critchlow asked with a low growl.

"Well, I, uh, am goin' to go back 'n tell Mr. Atwood you ain't interested."

"Did I tell you I wasn't interested?"

"You didn't say nothin' at all."

"Then don't be tellin' 'im nothin' if you don't know what you're talkin' about."

"You mean, you will come see Mr. Atwood?"

"Yeah, you can tell 'im I'll be there."

"When?"

"When I get there," Critchlow replied.

A couple of Atwood's Mexican employees were replacing shingles on the barn the next day when they saw someone ride in and dismount in front of the big house.

"*Pistolero*," one of them said.

"*Si, hombre asesina*," the other replied.

The two men spoke so quietly that it was impossible for Critchlow to have overheard them, but as he looped his horse's reins around the hitching post, he looked up toward them.

"*Madre de Dios*," one of them said prayerfully.

"It is all right, Ramon. He goes to see Señor Atwood."

Critchlow was shown into the library where, without being asked, he sat in what appeared to be the most comfortable leather chair to wait for Atwood.

When Atwood came into the room a few minutes later, it was obvious by the expression on his face that Atwood had chosen his chair. Critchlow made no effort to relinquish the chair.

"Mr. Critchlow, thank you for coming," Atwood said, finding another, less comfortable chair.

"Yeah, well, this ain't exactly what you might call a social visit," Critchlow said. "I was told that you might have a job for me."

"I do," Atwood said. "That is, if you are willing to take it."

"So, you want me to kill Smoke Jensen, do you?"

Atwood coughed. "You, uh, do get to the bottom of things very quickly, don't you?"

"You said you have a job for me. I don't punch cattle, and I'm no handyman. You know who I am, and what I do, so there's only one reason you would want to hire me. Your man asked me about Smoke Jensen, so I figure he's the one you want me to kill."

"Yes, you're right."

"Why do you want him killed?"

"I have personal and business reasons for wanting Smoke Jensen out of the way."

"Reason enough to pay for murder?"

"It won't exactly be murder."

"How will it not be murder?"

Atwood showed Critchlow the recently printed poster stating that Smoke Jensen was wanted, dead or alive, and that a reward of ten thousand dollars was being offered.

Critchlow studied the poster for a long moment. "Ten-thousand-dollar reward?"

"Yes."

"That's a lot of money."

"Yes, it is. Do you know this man, Jensen?" Atwood asked.

"Yeah, I know who he is," Critchlow replied. "I didn't know there was any paper out on 'im, though."

"This is new," Atwood said. "If you know him, then you also know that he is a man who, shall we say, enjoys somewhat of a reputation as one who is quite skilled with a gun."

"Yeah, so I've heard," Critchlow replied.

"Will you take the job?"

"What do you mean, will I take the job?" Critchlow held up the poster. "From the way I'm seein' it, this ain't exactly a job. There's a reward out for him, so what you're sayin' is that you want me to compete with all the others who are going after him."

"No," Atwood replied. "This poster hasn't been issued yet. You are the first one to see it, so you won't be competing with anyone."

"Once I kill 'im, who'll be payin' the reward?"

"It's like the poster says. The reward will be paid by the marshal up in Bury, Idaho. I'll see to it that the body is properly identified and reported, though. I'll have the local marshal and the judge verify it. You won't have any problem proving that you killed him. And of course, because Jensen is wanted, dead or alive, there won't be any unpleasant charges brought against the man who dispatches him."

"Who does what?"

"Who kills him."

"And you say that you've got personal reasons for wantin' 'im dead?"

"Yes."

"One thousand dollars."

"Ten thousand dollars."

"No, the reward is for ten thousand dollars, and in order to collect that, I'll have to contact some marshal up in Idaho. That means it could be a real long time before I get anything, if I ever get it at all," Critchlow said. "So when I say I want a thousand dollars, what I mean is, I want that thousand dollars from you, in addition to the reward. And I want it as soon as the job is done so I'll have some money while I'm waitin' for the ten thousand dollars to be paid."

"A thousand dollars? That's . . . uh . . . a lot of money."

"Yeah, well, if you want me to do the job, then that's what it's goin' to cost."

Atwood stroked his chin for a long moment before he replied. "All right, I'll meet your price. Just get the job done. Do you think you can handle Jensen?"

"I can beat 'im."

"You're sure you can?"

"Yeah, I'm sure."

"The reason I ask is, if, for some reason, you can't beat him, it might well come back that I'm the one who hired you."

"What do you mean, you hired me? Ain't you just showed me that there's paper out on him?"

"Yes, but still, I'm taking somewhat of a chance here."

Critchlow chuckled. "*You're* takin' a chance? I'm the one that's goin' to go up against him."

"Yes, I suppose that is true, isn't it?"

"I want the money now."

"I'll pay you when the job is done."

"Then you can get someone else to do the job." Critchlow turned to leave.

"Wait!" Atwood called to him. "What if I gave you one hundred dollars now and the rest of the money after the job is done? I promise you, I won't cheat you."

Critchlow moved his thin lips into what might have been a smile, though with a face like his, it was hard to tell. And if it was a smile, it didn't reach his eyes.

"Tell me, Atwood, do you really think I might be worried that you would cheat me?"

"No, I . . . I guess not."

"It's not 'cause I think you might cheat me. I just want a little walkin'-around money up front is all."

"All right," Atwood agreed. "I'll give you a hundred dollars now. But this one hundred comes off the one thousand."

"No. This one hundred dollars is what you might call expense money," Critchlow said.

"All right, all right. Kill Jensen, and I'll give you the entire one thousand dollars."

Ramon and Carlos saw Critchlow again as the *pistolero* rode away.

"He goes to kill someone, I think," Carlos said.

"*Si*," Ramon said. "I think so, too." Ramon crossed himself.

Gomez, Texas

"Really?" Rusty said as a huge smile spread across his face. "I'm not wanted anymore?"

"Judge Turner has overturned your conviction and has freed Katie as well," Pearlie said. He smiled at his nephew. "We've come to take you home to your mama."

"Thank you, Uncle Pearlie! Thank you!"

"I don't know about you two, but I'm kinda hungry," Pearlie said. "What do you say we find us a restaurant?"

Five minutes later Pearlie, Rusty, and Cal were enjoying their lunch at a café on Center Street called Susie's.

"Is Atwood still trying to take over Mom's saloon?" Rusty asked.

"He may try, but he won't get it," Cal said. "We'll make certain of that."

"By the way," Pearlie said. "Some of the customers at the Pretty Girl are wondering when you'll be back. It seems that they miss your piano playing."

Rusty smiled. "I miss playing it, too."

"Yeah, well I'd like to hear you play, so you can . . . damn!" Cal said. He had just started to take a bite when he spilled food all down the front of his shirt.

"Savin' some of your lunch for later, are you?" Pearlie teased.

"You think we have time for me to get a new shirt before we go back?"

"I think we need to; I sure don't want to be seen with a slob like you," Pearlie said.

* * *

"Hey!" someone called to them when the three men stepped out into the street. "You're Rusty Abernathy, ain't you?"

Rusty didn't answer.

"Yeah, I know you are. I've seen you play in the saloon over in Etholen."

Rusty smiled at the man who had called out to him. "Yeah, I'm Rusty. I hope you enjoyed . . ." that was as far as he got before the man, unexpectedly, drew his pistol and pointed it at Rusty.

"That's what I thought," the man said. "You're worth five hunnert dollars," he said.

"No, he isn't," Pearlie said. "A federal judge has set aside his guilty verdict. That means that the reward has been pulled back. He's not a wanted man anymore."

"Who the hell says so?" the man holding the gun replied.

"I say so," Pearlie said. "I was in the judge's office when he did that."

"Well, I've got a document in my pocket that says he's worth five hunnert dollars, 'n I intend to collect on it."

"I told you, that reward poster is worthless."

"Who are you?"

"I'm Rusty's uncle."

"Yeah? Well that tells me you're lyin' to save him. Only it ain't goin' to work, 'cause I'm pointin' this gun directly at him."

Pearlie drew so fast that he was holding a gun in his hand before the man realized it.

"And I'm pointing this gun directly at you," Pearlie said.

"Are you crazy, mister? Can't you see I'm already pointin' my gun at Abernathy? I told you, he's worth five hunnert dollars to me."

"And I told you, the reward has been withdrawn." Pearlie

smiled. "And even if it hasn't been, how are you going to spend five hundred dollars if you're dead?"

"I, uh . . ."

"Get his gun, Cal."

Cal reached out for the gun, which the man surrendered without resistance. Cal took out the cylinder, then handed the pistol, without the cylinder, back to the would-be bounty hunter.

"My friend is going to buy a shirt," Pearlie said. "When we're gone, you can pick up your cylinder over there, in the mercantile store."

"I want a red one," Cal said easily, as they headed toward the store, leaving the frustrated bounty hunter standing in the street, holding a useless pistol.

Back in Etholen, Sally and Kate were having lunch together.

"It has been a long time since I last saw my brother, but I must say he has made some wonderful friends."

"Pearlie has been almost a part of our family since we first met him," Sally said. "And over the years we have had to depend upon him more times than I can possibly count. He and Cal have been such a blessing to us."

"Yes, well, I don't know what would have happened to Rusty and me if he, you, Smoke, and Cal hadn't come along when you did. In fact, I don't want to know what would have happened."

Sally reached out across the table to lay her hand on Kate's hand. You don't have to wonder about it, because nothing bad is going to happen. We're here now, and Smoke told me he has no intention of our going back home until he is sure that you will be safe and not bothered."

CHAPTER 15

With Sally and Kate having lunch at the Palace Café, and with Pearlie and Cal gone to fetch Rusty, Smoke found himself alone in the Pretty Girl and Happy Cowboy Saloon. He was well aware that Atwood might still try to cause some trouble for Kate, so he was sitting at a table that offered a commanding view of the entire room. He had just taken a swallow of his beer when he saw someone come in who piqued his interest. As soon as the man stepped through the batwing doors, he moved in such a way as to put the wall to his back while he studied the saloon.

This was exactly the way Smoke entered a saloon, and the way this man did it, easily and without calling attention to himself, suggested to Smoke that he was either a man on the run or someone who had made many enemies in his life. And it was Smoke's experience that anyone who had made a lot of enemies had probably killed a lot of men. Also, the way the man wore his gun, low on his right hip, and slightly kicked out, suggested that he was quite proficient in its use.

Smoke wondered why such a man would be in Etholen, but even as he wondered, he had a gut feeling that he wasn't here by chance. There had been nothing overt in the man's actions, but Smoke had long ago developed an intuition about such things. That intuition, almost as much as his prowess with a pistol, had kept him alive through the years.

The gunman, and that was how Smoke was thinking of him now, stepped up to the bar and ordered a drink. Although the man was standing with his back to Smoke, Smoke could see that he was using the mirror to make a very careful study of the room. Then, when the man found what he was looking for, his searching eyes stopped.

And they stopped on Smoke.

That action validated Smoke's notion that the man was here for him. This wouldn't be the first time that a gunfighter, trying to make a name for himself, had called him out. But, he was out of his normal territory, so he rather doubted this was such a person. He believed that this could well be someone who had been sent by Atwood.

A couple of times Smoke looked directly at the gunman's reflection, wanting to look him in the eyes, but the man cut his gaze away both times.

Finally the gunman turned toward Smoke.

"Mister, why is it that you're a-starin' at me in the mirror?" he asked. He spoke the words loudly, and he put more reproach into the question than was required.

"Was I staring?" Smoke said. "I'm sorry, I don't mean to make you uncomfortable."

"Yeah? Well you are making me damn uncomfortable."

"I assure you, sir, any thought that I am staring at you is unfounded. I'll make certain not to do so in the future."

The gunman twisted his mouth into what might have been a smile. "Well now, Mr. Smoke Jensen, what makes you think you're even goin' to have a future?" he asked.

Here it was. This was no casual encounter. This man had called Smoke by name, and that could only mean that he was after him in particular.

"That's enough, mister!" Peterson said. "This man ain't

done nothin' to you, and he apologized even though he didn't do nothin'. Now back off."

The gunman held a hand out toward the bartender, though he didn't take his eyes off Smoke.

"This ain't none of your business, bartender. 'N if you don't keep your mouth shut, 'n stay out of this, I'll be takin' care of you, right after I take care of the famous . . . Smoke Jensen. That is your name, ain't it?"

"It is," Smoke replied.

"Tell me, would you be the same Smoke Jensen that a marshal from Idaho is offerin' a ten-thousand-dollar reward for?"

Smoke was rarely surprised by anything anymore, but this did surprise him.

"What?" he asked, practically shouting the response.

"You heard me. There's paper out on you from Idaho, ain't there? 'N it's for ten thousand dollars. I know this, 'cause I seen the dodger with m' own eyes."

"Mister, now, how about telling me your name?" Smoke asked.

"The name is Critchlow. Lucien Critchlow."

"Critchlow!" someone said, and though it was a whisper, it was loud enough that everyone in the saloon heard it.

The name was repeated a few more times, and in as much awe as was used by the first to speak it.

The gunman smiled. "I see several here have heard of me. But then most people have. Of course, some of 'em hear of me a little too late, if you get my meanin'."

Smoke, who was still sitting at the table, made no reply.

"Critchlow, I've heard of you," Peterson said. "But I've heard of Smoke Jensen, too, and if you're thinkin' about takin' him on, you might want to reconsider. I believe you're about to take a bigger bite than you can chew."

"Is that a fact? This man, Smoke Jensen, he's supposed

to be somebody, is he? I mean, other than a murderer 'n an outlaw that the marshal up in Bury, Idaho, is willin' to pay ten thousand dollars for."

"Critchlow, I don't know where you saw that, but that poster was issued more than twenty years ago," Smoke said. "And it was pulled soon after it was issued. There is no reward out for me, not here in Texas, not up in Colorado, not anywhere in the entire nation. So if you're prodding me so you can collect a reward, you're going to be disappointed, because nobody is going to pay you any money for my hide."

"Yeah? Well, now I know you're lyin', just tryin' to weasel your way out. I've seen the poster, mister, 'n the one I seen ain't twenty years old. Hell, it ain't hardly a week old, 'cause it was bright 'n shiny, brand new, which means that more'n likely it just come off the printin' press. Anyhow, why don't we let the marshal up in Idaho decide whether it's still any good or not?"

"I'm afraid Sheriff Reece isn't going to be able to tell you anything about this poster."

"Sheriff Reece? That's the lawman up in Bury, Idaho, that's wantin' you, is it?"

"He was the marshal when the poster was put out over twenty years ago. But he isn't there anymore."

"Yeah? Well he could be. I've heard of sheriffs bein' sheriffs for more'n twenty years."

"Not this one. He's dead."

"How do you know he's dead?" Critchlow challenged.

"I know he's dead, because I killed him."

At Smoke's words, spoken without inflection, there was another audible gasp of surprise from those present in the saloon.

"You'll never get your money, Critchlow."

Critchlow's mocking smile grew even wider. "So you're

sayin' I ain't goin' to get the money 'cause you killed a marshal? Well now, it just so happens that the lawman in Idaho ain't the only one wantin' to see you dead. Turns out there's another fella willin' to pay for it."

The bartender, measuring the conversation, knew that it had reached the pivotal stage and moved down to the far end of the bar.

Now it was Smoke's time to smile, and unlike Critchlow's forced smile, Smoke's smile was easy and confident.

"No. I'm saying you'll never get your money because if you actually try and go through with this, I'm going to kill you," Smoke said easily.

Critchlow was used to invoking fear in the men he faced. Smoke's calm, and almost matter-of-fact response unnerved him, and without saying another word, and without warning, the gunman's hand dipped with lightning speed toward his pistol.

Because Smoke was still sitting at the table, he was at a disadvantage, and Critchlow actually managed to draw his gun and get one shot off. The bullet punched a hole in the table just in front of Smoke. But Smoke had his gun out just as fast, firing at almost the same time. And unlike Critchlow, Smoke didn't miss.

Critchlow dropped his gun and grabbed his chest, then turned his hand out and looked down in surprise and disbelief as his palm began filling with his own blood.

"You . . . you was sittin' down! How the hell did you . . . ?" he started to say, but he was unable to finish his sentence. Instead, his eyes rolled back in his head and he fell back, then lay motionless on the floor with open, but sightless eyes staring toward the ceiling.

Gunsmoke from the two charges merged to form a large, acrid-bitter cloud, which drifted slowly toward the door. Beams of sunlight streaming in through the door and windows became visible as they stabbed through the cloud.

The other patrons in the saloon, shocked to have seen Critchlow beaten in a gunfight, and not only beaten, but by a man who was sitting down, moved with cautious awe toward the body that lay unmoving on the saloon floor.

"Did you see that?" someone asked.

"Hell, Cletus, we're in here, too," someone answered. "Yeah, we seen it. We all seen it."

"I seen it," another said. "But I ain't never seen nothin' like it."

"I thought Critchlow was fast."

"He was fast."

"Yeah? Well he warn't fast enough, was he?"

There were rapid and heavy footfalls on the wooden sidewalk outside as more people began coming in through the swinging doors. Marshal Witherspoon was one of the first ones to come in.

"What the hell happened here?" Witherspoon asked. Seeing that the dead man was Lucien Critchlow, Marshal Witherspoon nodded grimly. "I'll be damn. Someone got Critchlow."

"Yeah," Peterson said. He pointed to Critchlow's body. "And if there was ever anybody who needed killin' more than Lucien Critchlow, I don't know who it would be."

"Who done it?" Witherspoon asked.

"That would be me," Smoke said.

The marshal looked over at Smoke, who had placed his gun on the table, though his hands, also on the table, were clasped together.

"What'd you kill 'im for?" the marshal asked.

"I didn't have much choice, he drew on me." Smoke pointed to the bullet hole in the table. "Here is where his bullet went."

"You were sitting at the table?"

"Yes."

"Damndest thing I ever saw, Marshal. Critchlow drew first, and Smoke Jensen had to draw while he was sittin' down, 'n still he beat 'im," Cletus said.

"I never thought nobody would ever be able to beat Lucien Critchlow, neither," Doodle said.

"You ain't plannin' on arrestin' him, are you, Marshal?" Cletus asked. "Because I'll tell you right now, that ever'one in here will say what really happened. 'N we ain't goin' to let you 'n Boykin keep us from testifyin' this time."

"No, I ain't goin' to arrest him," Witherspoon said. He stared pointedly at Smoke. "This is the second man you've kilt since you come into my town. Killin' seems to be followin' you around, don't it?"

Smoke nodded. "Sometimes it does," he agreed.

Witherspoon looked back at Critchlow. "I'll get Welch down here to take care of the body," he added.

Cletus chuckled. "You don't have to be in too big a hurry, do you, Marshal? I expect there'll be quite a few folks who are goin' to want to come in here 'n see the body. Especially seein' as who it is."

"Yeah," Doodle said. "Hell, the Pretty Girl 'n Happy Cowboy will prob'ly wind up makin' twice as much money as they would have."

"Jensen, I'd advise you not to be leavin' town anytime soon," Witherspoon said.

"Oh, I'm not planning on going anywhere," Smoke replied. "Not until all this business with Atwood is cleaned up."

"What . . . what business is that?" Witherspoon asked.

Smoke chuckled. "You know what I'm talking about. Don't make yourself look any dumber than you have to, Marshal."

"Look here! You can't talk to me like that."

"Hell, Witherspoon, it looks to me like he just did talk to you like that," Doodle said to the laughter of the others in the saloon.

Clenching his fists in frustration, and with his cheeks flaming in embarrassment, Witherspoon spun on his heels and stormed out of the saloon.

CHAPTER 16

Shortly after Witherspoon left the saloon, Deputy Calhoun came in. His reaction, when he saw Critchlow's body lying on the floor, was ample indication that he knew nothing about what had just happened.

"Good Lord a'mighty! Is that Lucien Critchlow?" he asked.

"It sure as hell is," Cletus replied.

"What happened?"

"We've just been through all that with the marshal," Peterson said. "Smoke Jensen killed him."

"But it was a fair fight," Doodle said, and his declaration was validated by several other comments.

"How come Critchlow took Jensen on like that? I mean, what started the fight?"

"There warn't no fight," one of the other saloon patrons said. He reached over to the bar and picked up a flyer, then showed it to Calhoun. "Critchlow come in here carryin' this reward poster sayin' that they was a ten-thousand-dollar reward out for Jensen, dead or alive."

"Can I see that?" Calhoun asked in a small voice.

"Yeah, sure," the patron said, handing the reward poster over to the deputy. "It come from Idaho, so I don't know what it's doin' down here in Texas. Jensen said it warn't no good, but Critchlow didn't listen to 'im."

With the dodger in hand, Calhoun walked over to talk to Smoke, who was sitting back at his table.

"Critchlow tried to claim this reward?" Calhoun asked.

"Yes."

"I told Witherspoon that I didn't think this was any good."

"You saw it before?" Smoke asked.

"Yeah, I'm the one that found it. Well, not this one," Calhoun said, holding up the paper to look at it. "This looks like a new one, and I don't know where it come from. The one I found was so old it was near 'bout fallin' apart."

"Where did you find it? And why were you looking for it?" Smoke asked.

"I was lookin' for it, 'cause Witherspoon told me to look for it. 'N I found it in the courthouse records, but like I said, I told Witherspoon that, like as not, it was no good."

"You were right, it isn't any good."

"You're the one that got Kate let out of jail, too, aren't you?"

"I didn't do it by myself. My wife and Kate's brother were both with me."

"When I come back, I found Witherspoon in jail," Calhoun said. He laughed. "He was fit to be tied, too."

"Was he?"

"Yeah, he was. You know you're becomin' a real pain in the ass to him, don't you? Him and Atwood both."

"Am I?"

"Yeah," Calhoun said with a chuckle. "You are."

"You don't seem particularly upset by it."

"Yeah, well, I don't exactly agree with ever'thing Witherspoon does." Calhoun looked around at the others in the saloon, then spoke quietly. "Truth is, I don't agree with much of anything that he does. Like, I never thought we had no business puttin' Kate in jail in the first place, 'n if it had been up to me, I wouldn't of done it. It's Atwood that's causin' all this, but then, I figure you already know that. Atwood says jump, 'n the marshal 'n the judge, they kinda see which one of 'em can jump the highest. So if you put a burr under Atwood's saddle, it don't bother me all that much at all."

"Deputy Calhoun, from what several people have told me, you're a pretty good man. Why do you stay with Witherspoon?"

"The way I look at it, with the way Witherspoon is, I mean him 'n Judge Boykin bein' told what to do 'n all by Atwood, seems to me like there ought to be someone who has the good of the town in mind. 'Course, when it come to Rusty 'n his mama, I wasn't able to do nothin' about it, seein' as I was drunk when Rusty kilt Calley, and I don't remember anything about it. And when it come to puttin' Miss Kate in jail . . . I tried to talk 'em out of it, but they didn't listen to nothin' I had to say. That's why I'm glad you come to town when you did."

"It's good to hear that I've got a friend in the enemy's camp," Smoke said.

Calhoun laughed again. "A friend in the enemy's camp. That's a good one." He was still laughing as he left the saloon, meeting Welch, the undertaker, on his way out.

"Deputy, I'm told there's someone in need of my services in here," Welch said, glaring at Calhoun.

"Yeah, he's lyin' right over there."

"Why are you laughing, Deputy? I hardly think levity is appropriate around a dead body."

"Depends on who it is, Mr. Welch. For some people, you just want to celebrate when they're kilt. And Lucien Critchlow is just such a person."

"You mean the famous gunfighter? Oh, my. To think that

I'll be burying someone like Lucien Critchlow." Welch smiled in anticipation.

"You see what I mean, Undertaker? Sometimes you do want to smile."

"Hey, Marshal, I was just over in the saloon, and seen that Smoke Jensen killed Lucien Critchlow," Calhoun said when he stepped into the marshal's office a few minutes later.

"Yeah? Well, tell me somethin' I don't know."

"Here's somethin' you don't know. Or maybe you do know. Critchlow had a dead or alive wanted poster for Jensen."

"Did he now? Well, that's interesting."

"You want to know what's even more interesting? It was the same wanted poster that I found over at the courthouse, only, this here one wasn't all old and crumbly like the one I found. This here one looked like it was fresh off the press."

"You don't say."

"You know what I think?"

"What do you think?"

"I think maybe Judge Boykin took it on hisself to reprint that poster."

"Maybe the poster is still good," Witherspoon suggested.

"No, it ain't no good. If you ask me, the judge is just pissed off because Jensen went to the federal judge 'n got Miss Kate turned loose. 'N that's why he printed up a new poster."

"Could be," Witherspoon agreed.

"That wasn't right, Marshal. You know damn well that wasn't right. And now that I think about it, it was probably Atwood that put 'im up to it."

Witherspoon held his finger up. "I'll tell you this, Calhoun. You'd do well to remember who butters your biscuit."

"I'm not likely to forget that," Calhoun replied.

"See that you don't," Witherspoon said as he headed toward the door.

"Where are you goin'?"

"Out," the marshal snapped.

Even before Sally and Kate returned to the saloon, they had heard the news of the shoot-out. By the time they got back, though, the body had been moved and the small amount of blood had been cleaned up. There was nothing to remind anyone of the shooting other than the excited babble of conversation.

"You should've seen it, Miss Kate," Cletus said. "It was the damndest thing I ever saw. Critchlow drew first, and Jensen had to draw while he was sittin' down, 'n still he beat 'im."

"I never thought anyone would be able to beat Critchlow," yet another said.

"What did the marshal say?" Kate asked.

"We were all willin' to give a statement 'bout what happened here, I mean as to who drew first 'n all that, but the marshal didn't want it," Peterson said.

"Oh, dear. I hope he isn't planning on another trial like the one he gave Rusty."

"No, ma'am, we've already told 'im that we don't have any intention of lettin' 'im do that," yet another customer said. "He didn't like it much, but he seemed to take it without too much guff."

"You want to know what I think, Mr. Jensen? I think that even Witherspoon figures that you did us a favor, killin' Critchlow like you did," Peterson said. "He was a bad sort, but then I reckon you know about 'im."

"Truth to tell, Mr. Peterson, I had never even heard of Critchlow until right now."

"Really? You never heard of him, huh? It's too bad Critchlow didn't live long enough to hear you say that. He was about the most arrogant son of a bitch I've ever known," Peterson said. "I beg your pardon, ladies."

"Oh, heavens, there's no need to apologize, Mr. Peterson," Sally said. "As it so happens, that particular sobriquet is appropriate when applied to some people."

"Yes, ma'am, I suppose so," Peterson replied, not entirely certain what Sally said, though satisfied that she held no fault with him.

"Heavens! I feel guilty that someone tried to kill you. I know it is because of me," Kate said.

"If it hadn't been because of you, it would have been for some other reason," Sally said. "You have no idea how often someone tries to kill Smoke."

"Don't you worry about him?"

"Kate, if I worried about every two-bit gunman who had it in his mind to make a name for himself by killing Smoke, I would never draw an easy breath," Sally replied. "I have boundless confidence in his ability to take care of himself." She paused for a minute before she added, "and me."

"I'm glad to hear you say that," Smoke said. "Knowing that I don't have to be concerned about you worrying about me gives me an edge."

Sally smiled and put her hand on Smoke's shoulder. "That's good to know, because even though I don't worry about you, I do like for you to have every edge possible."

"Howdy, ever'body!" someone yelled from the front door.

"Rusty!" Kate shouted happily, as Rusty, Pearlie, and Cal came into the saloon then.

"Hi, Mom," Rusty replied with a broad smile.

Kate ran toward Rusty with her arms spread wide, embracing him firmly. "Oh, I'm so happy to have you back!"

The other patrons in the saloon joined in the welcome

back, including all the "Pretty Girls." Dolly was the only one of the Pretty Girls to add her embrace to Kate's, and she seemed to do so with particular vivacity.

As Smoke and Sally were witnessing the happy reunion, Smoke glanced over at Cal and smiled at the bright red shirt he was wearing.

"Whoa, that's some shirt you're wearing," Smoke said.

"You like it? I just bought it."

"You couldn't find one in red?"

"What are you talking about? This is . . ." Cal started to say, but he paused in midsentence, then grinned. "You're teasin' me, aren't you?"

"Maybe just a little," Smoke admitted, returning Cal's smile.

"Oh, is it safe for you to be here?" Kate asked.

"Uncle Pearlie says I'm not wanted anymore," Rusty said.

"Well, yes, but . . . who knows what Mr. Atwood might try next?"

"Katie, you and the boy can't be spending the rest of your life worrying about Atwood," Pearlie said. "For now the two of you just enjoy the fact that the law isn't after you anymore. You let us take care of Atwood."

"Take care of him? What do you mean, take care of him?"

"Take care of him," Pearlie said simply.

"Hey, Rusty, why don't you play the piano for us?" Peterson asked.

"Ha! So you have missed me, haven't you?" Rusty replied.

Peterson shook his head. "No, I can't say as we've missed you. But we have missed listenin' to someone play the piano," he added with a laugh.

"Play 'Old Dan Tucker,'" Cletus said.

Rusty held up his hand. "I will," he promised. "But first, I'm going to play whatever Mom wants me to play."

Kate smiled through her tears. "You know what I want you to play," she said.

Rusty nodded and, crossing his arm across his stomach, made a production of bowing to the audience there gathered. Then, walking over to the piano, he made a motion as if sweeping his tails back, took his seat on the piano bench, and stared at the keyboard for a moment.

"Oh, my," Sally said. "Is Rusty a classically trained pianist?"

"Yes," Kate answered proudly.

"How wonderful."

The saloon, which was normally filled with the cacophony of loud conversation, booming laughter, and high-pitched squeals, now waited in absolute silence. One of the patrons moved his chair just a fraction to better his position, and half a dozen cast a censoring gaze at him for the resultant squeak.

Then, with a flourish, Rusty began playing Tchaikovsky's Concerto Number Two. The music, coming from this piano, as opposed to the upright pianos that were so common in most of the saloons, was so rich and deep that it was almost as great as the difference between the voice of a solitary singer and a full chorus.

Smoke looked over at Sally and could see by the gleam in her eyes, and the expression on her face, how much she was enjoying this. Although Sally had never complained about it, he knew that one of the things she missed by having lived so much of her life out West was the opportunity for the cultural events living back East had afforded her. Because of that, he had spent much of their married time together taking her to concerts and plays presented by traveling troupes.

Rusty played only the second movement of the concerto. It was the most melodious of the three movements, and was only a little over eight minutes long. The entire concerto would have been well over half an hour long, and though Sally would have appreciated listening to the whole piece, she knew the people here would not be able to sit still for the whole thing.

It was, however, obvious that they enjoyed what they did hear, because the applause was loud and enthusiastic at the conclusion of the number. He stood and, with a broad smile on his face, bowed again at the audience.

"This was wonderful," Sally said.

Kate wiped her eyes. "Oh, how I would love to hear him play a real concert, in a real symphony hall," she said. "Maybe Atwood is right. Maybe I should sell out to him. I feel I have done Rusty such an injustice by making him stay here."

"Rusty is a grown man," Sally said. "If he is here with you, it is because he wants to be here with you."

CHAPTER 17

As the patrons of the Pretty Girl and Happy Cowboy Saloon were enjoying the impromptu concert, Allen Blanton, editor of the *Etholen Standard*, finished setting the type on the article, then leaned back to read it. When he first came into the newspaper business, it took him a while to read type because of it being set in reverse. But now he could read backward as easily as forward, and he smiled as he read what he intended to be the lead story to run in this evening's newspaper.

> Today, Lucien Critchlow, a man known for his skill with a pistol and his willingness, one might even say his eagerness, to employ that skill, met the fate that so often befalls someone of his ilk. He had the misfortune to engage in a gunfight with someone who was able to employ his pistol with even more effectiveness.
>
> The result was that Critchlow was killed by Smoke Jensen, who is a visitor to our town. Critchlow had opened the contest by presenting a Dead or Alive wanted poster that had been issued by a marshal in Bury, Idaho. Before undertaking to print this story, this

newspaper contacted, by wire, the current marshal of Bury, Idaho, and was told by the marshal that Kirby Jensen is not wanted in Idaho now, nor as far as that marshal is concerned, is he wanted anywhere else.

Witnesses to the gunfight have all stated that before the gunplay ensued, Mr. Jensen attempted to inform Critchlow that the reward poster was invalid, as he was not wanted. All the witnesses to the encounter are uniform in their declaration that Critchlow, unwilling to listen to Mr. Jensen's declaration, precipitated the gun battle that followed, and that Mr. Jensen was entirely justified in defending himself.

I hasten to put this story in the paper so that all might know the actual facts of the event. In this way it is to be hoped that the truth, published so that it is universally known, will prevent a repeat of the travesty of justice that condemned young Rusty Abernathy, and subsequently his mother, to death in a trial that defied all standards of legitimacy and fair dealing.

This editor has stated before, and by these published words I say again, that until our town has a new marshal and a new judge, independent of the improper influence of Silas Atwood, we will continue to be void of all semblance of justice.

Witherspoon had been absent from the marshal's office for the better part of the day, and Calhoun was alone when Elmer Welch, the undertaker, came into the marshal's office.

"Is the marshal here?" Welch asked.

"No," Calhoun answered. "But I reckon you have come

here to see how much money the county is goin' to pay you to bury Critchlow."

"No. It isn't going to cost the county so much as one penny to bury him."

"Oh? Why not?"

"It turns out that Critchlow had enough money in his pocket to pay for his own burial," Welch said.

"He did, did he? Well, that was very nice of him to be so accommodating, don't you think?" Calhoun replied with a chuckle.

Welch smiled. "Yes, it was. And here's the thing, Deputy. Not only is Critchlow paying for his own burial, he's goin' to wind up makin' me a lot more money 'n just what I'd get for buryin' 'im."

"Oh? And just how, pray tell, is he going to do that?"

"Well, sir, it was Phil Dysart who come up with the idea," Welch said.

"Dysart? The photographer?"

"Yep. What he's plannin' to do is, he's goin' to charge people two dollars to get their picture taken while they're standing alongside Critchlow's body. And for an extra fifty cents, he'll give 'em a gun to hold, so that it'll look like they were the one that shot 'im."

"By now everyone in town knows that it was Smoke Jensen that shot 'im."

"It was, but forty or fifty years from now, who's goin' to remember that? And a feller could show his grandkids a picture of him standing next to Lucien Critchlow, holding a pistol, and they're goin' to think it was their grandpa who did it."

Calhoun laughed. "Yeah," he said. "Hey, I wonder if Dysart would take my picture like that? I've got my own pistol, though, I don't plan on givin' him a half dollar to hold his gun."

"Yeah, I'm sure he would."

"I can see how that'll make money for Dysart, but what are you gettin' out of it?"

"I get one dollar for every picture that is taken."

"You said there was some money in Critchlow's pocket?"

"Yes, after subtracting the cost of the burial expenses there was seventy-three dollars and fifty-seven cents left over and to tell the truth, I don't have any idea as to what to do with it. As far as I know, he doesn't have any kin anywhere close by."

"Leave it with the county and I'll write you a receipt for it. If there's no claim against it, we'll put it in a special fund to pay for any other indigent burials."

Welch grinned. "Yeah, I thought you might want to do something like that."

"Leavin' that money so other folks can get a decent burial is probably the only decent thing Critchlow ever did in his whole life," Calhoun said.

"I don't doubt that," Welch said. "Well, I'd better get back to the parlor. I expect business is going fairly well, right now."

"What's this money for?" Marshal Witherspoon asked when he stepped back into the office a little later and saw the bills lying on his desk.

"Welch brought it here," Calhoun replied. "He said that he found it in Critchlow's pocket, and he figured he ought to turn it back in to the county."

"Ha, imagine 'im doing that." Witherspoon gave Calhoun twenty dollars and stuck the rest into his pocket.

"What are you doin'?"

"What's it look like I'm doin'? I'm dividin' up this money between us."

"But don't you think that money should go to the county, to pay for buryin' someone that might need buryin'?"

"If that happens, the county will come up with the money. Of course, if you don't want that twenty dollars, I'll take it back."

"No, I didn't say I didn't want it. I was just wonderin' about it is all."

"Well, you can quit wondering."

"Marshal, do you think Critchlow just happened to find that poster somewhere, or do you think someone might of give it to him most especial so's that he would come after Jensen 'n try 'n kill 'im?"

Marshal Witherspoon stared at his deputy through eyes narrowed. "Now, why would you suggest something like that?"

"Never mind," Calhoun said with a dismissive wave of his hand. "There's more'n likely nothin' at all to it." He turned to leave.

"No, hold up a minute," Witherspoon called.

Calhoun stopped.

"You got somethin' stickin' in your craw, you might as well spit it out."

"Well, think about it, Marshal. Critchlow had all that money in his pocket, and for all that he was a famous gunman, me 'n you both know he was most like to be dead broke." Calhoun chuckled. "All right, so we finally catch him when he ain't broke, but he is dead."

"I think perhaps I should pay a visit to Mr. Atwood," Witherspoon said.

"So Critchlow got himself killed, did he?" Atwood asked, as he lit the ever-present cigar. "Well"—he drew several puffs before he continued—"I can't say that the world has lost much."

"Did you pay Critchlow to kill Jensen?"

"What makes you think that?"

"He had a wanted poster in his pocket," Witherspoon said. "There was only one copy printed, and I gave it to you, so this had to be the same reward poster."

"All right, so what if I did pay him to kill Jensen? You haven't been able to do anything to get him out of the way, have you?"

"I haven't had any legal reason to go after him."

"There is that reward poster."

"Mr. Atwood, you and I both know that reward is bogus."

"We don't know that for sure," Atwood replied. "I mean, we didn't find anything that said it had been withdrawn, did we?"

"No. But if you ask me, Critchlow got hisself kilt for a reward that wasn't goin' to be paid."

Atwood smiled. "Well now, there's an idea. Maybe the wanted poster you've got on Jensen is no good, but it was Jensen who killed Critchlow. It seems to me like you could use that to arrest him for murder."

Witherspoon shook his head. "It wouldn't hold up. Ever'one in the saloon says that it was Critchlow who drew first."

"What difference does that make? They said the same thing about Rusty Abernathy, but we tried him for murder and got a conviction."

"It's not the same thing. There ain't nobody outside of Etholen that's ever even heard of Rusty Abernathy. Hell, people all over the country have heard of Jensen. Not even Judge Boykin could make it stick. Besides which, Jensen's got some kind of connection with Judge Turner, and Turner can overrule anything Boykin might say."

"We need to find some way to get Jensen out of the picture," Atwood said. "He has become quite a complication."

"Short of shooting the son of a bitch in the back, I don't know how we're goin' to do that," Witherspoon said. "I know I don't want to face him, not even if I had two or three more men with me."

"Then I'll just have to find someone who will be willing to face him," Atwood said.

"What makes you think you can find such a man?" Witherspoon asked. "Critchlow faced him, and you see what happened. I'll tell you the truth, Mr. Atwood, I'm not all that sure such a man even exists."

"I may have someone in mind."

"That's what you thought about Critchlow, isn't it?"

"Yes, but you know what they say. If at first you don't succeed, try, and try again."

Witherspoon chuckled. "Yeah, well, as long as it ain't me who's doin' all the tryin'."

After Witherspoon left, Atwood returned to the library to revisit an article he had read in the paper. It was a story that was reprinted from the *Morning Star*, a newspaper from the nearby town of Eagle Springs.

Gunfight in the Four Ten Saloon

Last Friday night, Milt Pounders, who has been making a name for himself through his prowess with a weapon, came to our fair city of Eagle Springs. His reason for coming soon became obvious, because he instigated a gunfight with Cain Conroy. Whatever their reason was, it was not well thought out because, while good, young Pounders was not

good enough. All witnesses to the gunfight
agreed that Pounders drew first, but even with
that advantage, he could not prevail.

Cain Conroy drew his weapon with the
speed of a flash of lightning, and as quick as
one could think about it, Pounders was on
his back on the saloon floor, his sightless
eyes still expressing the shock of having been
beaten. There are those who have made a
study of such a thing, who insist that Conroy
is the fastest, and most deadly, gunman ever to
employ the pistol in its most baneful extreme.

Atwood smiled as he lay the paper aside. Critchlow had
failed him, but he had an idea that Conroy wouldn't. He
decided to send for him.

Eagle Springs, Texas

When Cain Conroy stepped into the Four Jacks Saloon,
he moved quickly away from the door, then backed up
against the wall, standing there for a long moment while he
surveyed the room.

"Pedro," the bartender said to the old man who was
sweeping the floor. "Mr. Conroy is here. Go into the back
room and get his special bottle."

"*Sí,*" Pedro said, and leaned the broom against the cold
stove. He started toward the back at a shuffle.

"Hurry, man, hurry! Conroy don't like to be kept waitin'."

Pedro's shuffle increased imperceptibly.

Conroy walked over and sat at an empty table. He didn't
have to say anything to anyone. He knew that his drink
would be delivered, and he knew it would be what he
wanted. A moment later the bartender approached with

the drink in hand, and he poured a shot, then waited for Conroy's nod of approval.

There was someone standing at the bar who saw how everyone was treating the man who had just come in.

"Who is that feller?" he asked the bartender.

"You're new here, ain't you? Yeah, I know you are, 'cause ever'one in town knows that that is Cain Conroy."

"So that's Cain Conroy? Well, I ain't never met 'im, but I have heard of 'im."

"I should think you've heard of him. Why he's kilt hisself more'n forty men."

"Forty, huh?"

"At least that many. And truth to tell, they don't nobody really know just how many he has kilt. He might'a kilt a lot more'n that."

The questioner nodded. "Thanks," he said, turning away from the bar and taking a step toward the table where Conroy was sitting.

"Here, mister! Are you crazy? You don't want to go botherin' him now!"

The curious one didn't respond. Instead, he stepped boldly up to Conroy's table.

"Mr. Conroy?"

"Yeah, I'm Conroy."

"I've got a message for you."

"What kind of message?"

"I don't know, I didn't read it. I was just told to hand this envelope to you." He held the envelope out.

Conroy snatched the envelope from the man's hand, then opened it. A fifty-dollar bill fluttered out.

"What's this for?" he asked.

The man who had delivered the note, obviously a cowboy, shrugged. "I don't know. Like I said, all I was told to do was deliver this envelope to you, then wait 'n see what you said."

Conroy grunted, then read the note that accompanied the fifty-dollar bill.

Conroy, this fifty dollars is just to get your attention.
I wish to make a proposal and if you accept it,
there is much more money for you.
If you are interested, Bo Willis, the man who
delivered this to you, will lead you back to see me.
If you are not interested, tell him so, and you may
keep this money as compensation for the intrusion
into your time.

Conroy folded over the fifty dollars, then looked up at the cowboy. "Your name Bo Willis?"

"Yes."

"It says here that you're supposed to take me to see the man who wrote this note."

"Yeah, that would be Mr. Atwood," Willis said.

"Where is he?"

"He's got a ranch near Etholen."

Conroy tossed his drink down, then stood up.

"Take me to him."

CHAPTER 18

"A thousand dollars?" Conroy said. "Am I hearing you right? You're offerin' to give me a thousand dollars to kill Smoke Jensen?"

"After you kill him," Atwood said. "There's also a ten-thousand-dollar reward for him. You can keep that money as well."

"No, there ain't," Conroy said. "There was paper on 'im oncet, but that was pulled a long time ago."

"How do you know?" Atwood asked, surprised that Conroy would know that.

"I know, 'cause I've done me some bounty huntin' from time to time, 'n I know there ain't nothin' out on him."

"Hmm, I heard that there was, but you may be right," Atwood said, making no mention of the bogus flyer he had printed. "But the thousand dollars is good, and it's coming from me."

"Fifteen hundred," Conroy said.

"Fifteen hundred? That's asking a lot, isn't it?"

"I know that Critchlow couldn't take him."

Atwood gasped in surprise. "You heard about that, did you?"

"Yeah. When you are in the business I am, you follow other

folks who are in the same business. You hired Critchlow, did you?"

"Yes, but as you have pointed out, he was insufficient to the task."

"He was what?"

"He didn't get the job done."

"Yeah, well, the truth is, I figured the day would come when me 'n Critchlow would go up ag'in each other. Only Jensen beat me to it. I figure that ups the risk enough so that askin' for fifteen hunnert dollars ain't too much. Besides which, you must really want Jensen dead, or you wouldn'ta hired Critchlow in the first place. And if you want Jensen killed, it's going to cost you fifteen hunnert dollars, or you'll have to find someone else. Wait a minute, there ain't nobody else, is there?"

"All right, yes, I do want him killed," Atwood said. "And I'll meet your demand. But I would suggest that after you do the job, and I pay you, that you leave the area. With that much money you could go to some place like New Orleans, or Saint Louis, or even Chicago."

"Why would I want to do that? If I kill Smoke Jensen, I'll be about the most famous man in the whole West."

"Is that really what you want? You would be a marked man. Can you imagine how many people would want to kill the man who killed Smoke Jensen? You'll have them coming from everywhere, some who will want to avenge Jensen, and some who will just want the fame it will bring them."

"Yeah, well, I guess there is that to think about."

"I'm glad you understand. And of course, it will also be to my advantage for you to be gone, because that way, there will be less of a likelihood that I would be connected with it."

"When do I get the money?"

"I told you, you'll get it after you do the job. I didn't give Critchlow what I had agreed to pay him before the job, and it's a good thing I didn't. If I had, I would have been out the money. I didn't get where I am today by paying for failure."

"You just have the money ready when I come back," Conroy said.

"It'll be here for you."

"If it ain't, there'll be another killin' that I won't be paid for. But I'll be doin' that killin' for me . . . if you know what I mean."

"I fully understand what you mean, Mr. Conroy. You just do your job, and the money will be here for you."

Atwood walked out onto the front porch and watched Conroy until he rode away. Then Atwood sent for Al Booker, one of his men. But, like Willis, Booker couldn't exactly be called a cowboy. He was one of the nearly dozen or so men that Atwood referred to as his special cadre.

As soon as Booker arrived, Atwood gave him fifty dollars. "I want you to do a little job for me," he said.

Booker looked at the money. "It must be more than a little job if you're willing to pay fifty dollars for it."

"There's not that much to it. I want you to go into town and keep an eye on a man named Cain Conroy."

"Conroy?" Booker replied nervously. "That's the feller you sent Willis after, ain't it?"

"Yes, it is."

"Willis tells me that Conroy has kilt more'n fifty men."

"I really don't care how many he has killed," Atwood said. "I'm only interested in who he is going to kill."

"Yeah, well, what do you mean by 'keep an eye on 'im'? On account of I don't plan on me bein' the next man that he kills."

"Good, then that means you'll be very careful around him, doesn't it?"

"When you say around him, what exactly do you mean? I mean, how close do I have to get to him?"

"It would be better for you, and for me, if he doesn't even

know you are around. If you can, keep an eye on him from some distance."

Booker smiled. "I don't mind keepin' my distance from him. But what is it, exactly, that you want me to do?"

"I've hired him to do a job for me, and I want you to tell me whether or not he does it."

"What is the job?"

"You don't need to know that."

"Mr. Atwood, I don't understand. If I don't know what his job is supposed to be, how will I know whether or not he has done it?"

"If he does his job, you'll know what it is. Everyone in town will know. And if nothing at all happens, oh, say within the next day or two, then you come back and tell me that nothing has happened. That's all you need to do."

"All right," Booker said. "That sounds like an easy enough job."

Etholen

Smoke, Pearlie, and Cal were in the Pretty Girl and Happy Cowboy Saloon when Sally and Kate returned from an impromptu shopping trip. Sally was carrying a package.

"Did you find something you liked?" Smoke asked.

"That isn't the question you ask," Kate said. "The question is, will *you* like it? Surely you know by now that women buy clothes, not to please themselves but to please the men in their lives. Is that not true, Sally?"

Sally laughed. "Now, Kate, don't you go giving away all our secrets."

"I know I will like it," Smoke said. "Anything Sally chooses, I will like."

"Ha, way to go, Smoke. That was exactly the correct answer," Pearlie said.

"Smoke, I didn't have lunch," Sally said. "Why don't you take me out?"

"We could get something here if you're hungry," Smoke said.

"I believe you said you were going to take me out."

"I did say that, didn't I?" Smoke replied.

"Katie and I ate at the Palace Café the other day, and it was a most pleasant experience."

"Oh, yeah," Pearlie said. "The food is real good there, I'll vouch for it."

Smoke laughed. "Your endorsement would carry some weight with me, Pearlie, if I didn't know that you had never found any place to eat that you didn't think was really good."

"Well, you tell 'em, Katie. I mean, you live here. I'm sure you know the place," Pearlie said.

"Yes, I've eaten there many times, and the food is quite good," Kate said, her words validating Pearlie's stamp of approval.

"All right, you've sold me on it. Let's go," Smoke said.

"Good, I'm starving," Cal said.

Until that moment there had been no mention that Cal was to be a part of the visit to the café, but after his comment, there was no way he would be excluded.

Pearlie cleared his throat. "Cal, if you're that hungry, we could just eat here," Pearlie suggested. The suggestion was pointed enough that Cal understood.

"Oh, uh, yeah, that's right. We could eat here, couldn't we?" Cal replied. "Maybe you two had better go on without me."

"The lack of your company leaves me bereft," Sally said.

"It leaves you what?"

Sally chuckled. "Never mind. Enjoy your lunch with Pearlie."

"Yes, ma'am, I expect I will."

"Smoke, can we stop by the hotel room so I can change clothes?" Sally asked as they left the saloon. "I'd like to wear my new dress."

"Sure," Smoke agreed.

Half an hour later, with Sally now wearing her new dress, she and Smoke approached the Palace Café, which was just down Waling Street a short distance from the saloon. They were assailed by delicious-smelling aromas as they approached.

"Well, if it tastes as good as it smells, I'd say the food is going to be very good," Smoke said.

There was a counter to the left as they entered, then eight smaller tables spread out through the dining room, and one long, banquet table at the back of the room.

The woman behind the counter was a very attractive redhead, who looked to be in her late thirties.

"Hello, Sue Ellen," Sally said.

"Hello, Sally," the woman replied. "It was so good to see you and Kate in here the other day. I'm glad she has been set free."

"I think everyone is."

"Well, almost everyone, if you know what I mean," Sue Ellen replied.

"Any table?" Smoke asked Sue Ellen.

"Yes, sir, you all just find an open table and seat yourselves," the woman said. "I'll be right with you. I hope you enjoy the food."

"Believe me, he will enjoy it, I guarantee," Sally said.

The Bull and Heifer Saloon was a block and a half away from the Pretty Girl and Happy Cowboy Saloon, on the corner of Cavender and Martin Streets. Bull Blackwell, owner of the Bull and Heifer, wasn't exactly in direct competition with Kate Abernathy, because there was a vast difference in their establishments.

The Pretty Girl and Happy Cowboy Saloon featured blended whiskeys and fine wines, and was a genteel enough place that women could visit without danger to their reputation. The Bull and Heifer, on the other hand, used only the cheapest whiskey and beer . . . and no wines at all. The Bull and Heifer did serve a purpose though . . . it served a clientele who either couldn't afford the Pretty Girl and Happy Cowboy, or preferred a somewhat more coarse atmosphere when they were drinking.

The Bull and Heifer also offered something else that the Pretty Girl and Happy Cowboy Saloon did not. For a price, the girls at the Bull and Heifer would take a customer upstairs to their room, whereas the girls at the Pretty Girl and Happy Cowboy Saloon offered nothing but drinks and friendly smiles.

Cain Conroy, after arriving in Etholen this morning, had just taken advantage of the services offered by Lucy, one of the accommodating young women of the Bull and Heifer. At the moment, Lucy was sitting up in bed, covered to the waist only by the bed sheet. She was topless and smoking a cigarette she had just rolled for herself. Conroy was sitting on the edge of the bed, pulling on his boots.

"You know, honey, if you would like to spend the night with me, tonight, I'll give you a special deal since we've already had one visit today," Lucy said. "That is, if you can do it twice in one day," she added with a suggestive smile.

"I more'n likely won't be here tonight," Conroy said. "I got me some business to take care of in this town, 'n once I do that, I'll be leavin'."

"Oh? What kind of business are you in, honey?"

Conroy chuckled. "You might say I'm in the arrangin' business, seein' as someone arranges for me to do somethin', 'n then I do it. This here job involves a fella by the name of Smoke Jensen. Do you know him?"

"Smoke Jensen? Yes, he's only just come to Etholen, but he's already made a name for himself. Why, he's killed two people, did you know that?"

"Two people? I heard that he kilt Lucien Critchlow. Who else has he kilt?"

"He killed Rufus Pardeen. Pardeen worked for Atwood."

"Do you know how I can find him?"

"He hangs out most of the time over at the Pretty Girl," Lucy said.

"Pretty girl?"

"It's the name of a saloon," Lucy said. "They call it the Pretty Girl and Happy Cowboy, but if you ask me, the girls that works there ain't no prettier than the ones that works here. And we're a lot more friendly, if you know what I mean," she added with a seductive smile.

Booker had seen Conroy go upstairs with Lucy, so he just stayed at the corner of the bar, nursing his beer and keeping his eyes on the stairs, waiting for the gunman to come back down. He wasn't up there for more than fifteen minutes, and Booker smiled. He knew Lucy, and he knew that she prided herself on how short she could make the visits with her clients. He watched as Conroy stepped up to the bar to order a drink.

"You got 'ny idea where I might find Smoke Jensen?" Booker heard Conroy say.

"I just seen him 'n his wife goin' into the Palace Café," one of the saloon patrons said.

"Where's that at?"

"It's just sort of catty-cornered across the street from the Model Barbershop."

"Can you see the Palace Café from the barbershop?"

"Well, yeah, I mean, it bein' just across the street 'n all."

"Thanks."

Conroy tossed the whiskey down, then left the saloon. He didn't notice Booker, who had been eyeing him from the other end of the bar. If he had noticed him, he wouldn't have paid any attention to him. He had never met Booker, and had no idea that Booker worked for the same man who had just hired him.

CHAPTER 19

"Haircut, sir?" the barber asked when Conroy stepped into his shop.

"Yeah. Which chair gives me the best view of the Palace Café?"

"You can see it well from here," the barber said, pointing to the chair. "Are you planning to eat there? It's a fine restaurant. But so is Dumplin's."

"Do you know Smoke Jensen?"

"Well, I can't say as I actually know him," the barber replied. "But I must say that since he has come to town, he has certainly made himself known." The sign behind the barber chair read EARL COOK, and after Conroy got into his chair, Cook put the cape around him.

"Would you know this Jensen feller if you seen 'im?" Conroy asked.

"Oh, yes."

"I'm told he's takin' his dinner in the Palace Café today."

"Indeed he is, sir. I saw him and his wife going into the place a few minutes ago. She's such a pretty thing. It almost makes you wonder how somebody like Smoke Jensen could get himself such a pretty wife."

"What do you mean, somebody like Smoke Jensen?"

"Well, maybe you don't know that much about him. But

since he came to town, he's already let people know he was here. First thing he did was he got Miss Kate out of jail."

Cook began cutting Conroy's hair.

"Who is Miss Kate?"

"Oh, she owns the Pretty Girl and Happy Cowboy Saloon. It's quite a fine establishment, I go in there myself, from time to time. Anyhow, there was some trouble there, her son killed one of Mr. Atwood's men, then he wound up being tried and sentenced to hang. But he escaped, and when he did, why Atwood got Miss Kate put in jail."

"Atwood did?"

"Yes, well, it was the judge who actually did it, but ever'body knows that Atwood controls the marshal and the judge in this town. Anyway, Smoke Jensen got Miss Kate out of jail, then he shot and killed Lucien Critchlow. I reckon you've heard of Critchlow, haven't you?"

"Yeah, I've heard of 'im."

"They say that Critchlow is the fastest gun in Texas; only, he wasn't fast enough. I can see now why they've written so many dime novels about Smoke Jensen. I bought one."

Cook put down the scissors and picked up a book. "I don't know how true this story is, but it's mighty exciting reading, I can tell you that, for sure," he said, showing the book to Conroy.

Smoke Jensen, King of the Western Range

"If you've never read anything about him, you should," Cook said.

"They ain't come back out yet, have they?"

"I don't think so. At least, I haven't seen them come back out. Anyway, I don't think they have been in there long enough to have actually eaten a meal."

"I've got some business with him, but I don't want to disturb him while he's eatin'."

"Yes, I think you are right to let the man eat in peace.

You say you have business with him. Do you know Mr. Jensen?"

"No, I ain't never seen him before. If he comes out while I'm here in the chair, point him out to me, would you?"

"Why yes, I'd be glad to," Cook replied. Having put the book down, he was once more employing the scissors, and Conroy could hear them clicking beside his ear.

Conroy sat in the chair, then, under cover of the barber's cape, he pulled his pistol from his holster and held it in his lap.

"In the book I'm reading, it seems that Smoke Jensen is tracking down a young lady who was kidnapped by . . ."

"I don't like talkin' while I'm gettin' a haircut," Conroy said gruffly.

"Very good, sir. I shall be as silent as the sphinx."

Conroy had no idea what a sphinx was, or why it might be silent, but he was grateful that the barber had shut up.

"You sure he ain't come out yet?" Conroy asked after a few minutes.

"Oh, yes, sir, I'm quite sure."

Booker left the Bull and Heifer shortly after Conroy did, and now he was sitting on a bench in front of the Buckner-Ragsdale Emporium, keeping an eye on both the Model Barbershop and the Palace Café. While in the saloon, he had heard Conroy ask about Smoke Jensen, so he had a pretty good idea about what Conroy had in mind. If there was going to be a shoot-out between Conroy and Jensen, he would have a front-row seat.

Because Conroy had told the barber that he didn't want to talk, the only sound that could be heard in the barbershop at the moment was the click and snap of the scissors as Earl Cook worked. Then, Conroy broke the silence.

"You be sure and keep an eye open and let me know soon as you see Jensen."

"Yes, sir, I will," Cook said.

The sound of clicking scissors continued for another minute, then Cook stopped.

"Oh, there he is now, him and his wife," the barber said, interrupting Conroy's comment. "They're just now comin' out. She's such a pretty thing, don't you think?"

Even as the barber was talking, Conroy leaped up from the chair and rushed through the door.

"Sir, I'm not finished, you . . ." At that moment the barber saw Conroy raising his pistol to point at an unsuspecting Smoke who was looking toward Sally.

"Mr. Jensen! Look out!" the barber shouted at the top of his voice.

Smoke's reaction was instantaneous. With his left hand he pushed Sally down. He didn't have to push her all the way down; she was smart and reflexive, and she went all the way down and then rolled out of the way without any further effort.

Conroy fired, and Smoke felt the concussion of the bullet as it fried the air just past his ear and slammed into the door frame just behind him.

Conroy didn't even realize he had missed, because even as his bullet was burying itself in the door frame, Smoke had already drawn and fired, his bullet plunging into Conroy's heart. Conroy fell facedown in the middle of the street, the barber's cape spread out on the ground under him. His right arm was outstretched and his hand still wrapped around the gun.

The shooting, happening as it did right in the middle of town, began to draw a crowd as people came out of the Pretty Girl and Happy Cowboy Saloon, the Bull and Heifer Saloon, Palace Café, Dereck's Gun Shop, the Buckner-Ragsdale Emporium, as well as the feed and seed store.

Smoke leaned down to help Sally back to her feet.

"Are you all right?" he asked anxiously.

"Yes. I must say, though, that this was certainly not how I intended to break in the new dress I just bought."

"What happened here?" Marshal Witherspoon asked, hurrying up to Smoke.

"That fella over there took a shot at my wife," Smoke said.

"You say he shot at your wife?" Witherspoon asked.

"Well, it might have been at me, but Sally was standing right next to me, and I have to tell you that did get me some riled."

"What's that he's lying on?"

"It's a barber's cape, Marshal," Earl Cook said, arriving at that point. "He was getting a haircut, and he asked me to point Mr. Jensen out to him. Mr. Jensen, I'm so sorry. He said he had some business to do with you. I had no idea he intended to shoot you."

"No need for you to apologize," Smoke replied. "Your shout for sure saved one of our lives, either my wife or me."

"Jensen, this is the third man you have killed in my town in less than a week," Witherspoon said.

"This is the third man who has tried to kill me," Smoke replied.

"Do you know him?" Witherspoon asked.

"To be honest I didn't get that good of a look at him," Smoke said. "Let me see if I know him."

Smoke and the marshal walked across the thirty yards that separated them from the body, but, by now, they had to pick their way through the crowd that had gathered. Marshal Witherspoon turned him over so he could be seen.

"Do you know him?" the marshal asked.

Smoke shook his head. "I've never seen him before."

"His name is Cain Conroy," Booker said. By now several

of the citizens of the town had collected around the body, and Booker was one of them.

"You ever heard of 'im?" Witherspoon asked Smoke.

Smoke shook his head. "No, I'm afraid not. The name doesn't mean anything to me."

"Well, your name must've meant something to him," Witherspoon said. "That is, if you're tellin' the truth, 'n he shot at you first."

"Mr. Jensen is telling the truth," the barber said. He pointed to Conroy's body. "This gentleman was getting a haircut, and he asked me to point out Mr. Jensen when I saw him. When I saw Mr. and Mrs. Jensen come out of the café I mentioned it, and, without so much as a fare-thee-well, he leaped up from the chair with his gun in his hand. I had no idea that he had such a thing in mind."

"Booker, how come it is that you know him?" Marshal Witherspoon asked.

"I can't say as I actual know him," Booker replied. "It's more like I know of him. Anyhow, I seen 'im oncet when I was over in Eagle Springs, and then I seen 'im a while ago over in the Bull and Heifer."

"That's right," someone else said. "He was in the Bull and Heifer a few minutes ago, 'cause I seen 'im, too. 'Course, I didn't know who he was, then."

Atwood hadn't told Booker what he was supposed to be looking out for, but he did tell him that when it happened, he would know. Well, now he knew.

"So, Smoke Jensen shot Cain Conroy, did he?" Deputy Calhoun said with a little chuckle back at the marshal's office. "It looks to me like he's goin' to be a pretty hard man for Atwood to kill."

"What do you mean for Atwood to kill?" Witherspoon asked.

"Well come on, Marshal. Atwood is the one who wanted us to see if we could find a wanted poster on Jensen. We found one, I mean it was so old that I knowed soon as we found it that it warn't no good anymore. But we found it, 'n the next thing there was a new, fresh poster printed up, and since then there's been two gunmen who come after him, Critchlow and Conroy. You don't think they just took it on their own to try 'n kill Jensen, do you? Like I said before, Atwood had to be behind them. Leastwise, that's what I think."

"You know what I think?" Witherspoon replied.

"What?"

"I think there are some things you'd be better off just keeping your nose out of it."

"Well, yeah, I'll do that, Marshal. I was just talkin' is all."

"You talk too much. I've got something I have to check on. If Welch comes to ask you about Conroy's body, tell 'im he can have 'im, I don't need to do any investigatin'."

"All right," Calhoun said. "More'n likely there'll be money in Conroy's pockets, too, so I don't figure the county's goin' to have to pay for this one, neither."

Eagle Shire Ranch

"You came back pretty quickly," Atwood said when Booker returned to the Eagle Shire.

"Yes, sir, but there warn't no need to stay around no longer," Booker said.

"Good, good!" Atwood rubbed his hands together in satisfaction and smiled broadly. "That means Conroy did the job and will be back soon."

"No, sir, he won't be back soon. Fac' is, he won't be back at all," Booker said. "Conroy got hisself kilt."

"What?"

"Yes, sir. Turns out Conroy tried to kill Jensen; onliest thing is, Jensen wound up killin' Conroy."

"Damn!" Atwood said, striking his fist angrily into the palm of his hand. "Damn!"

"That was what you sent him to do, warn't it?" Booker asked. "You wanted him to kill Smoke Jensen?"

"Booker, do you like your job here?" Atwood asked in a sharp and challenging tone of voice.

"Well, yes, sir, I like my job here. I like it a lot."

"Then don't ask so damn many questions."

"No, sir, I won't ask no more," Booker replied.

While the two men were talking, Marshal Witherspoon rode up.

"Booker, find something to do," Atwood ordered. "The marshal and I need to talk."

"Yes, sir," Booker said.

Atwood waited until Witherspoon dismounted.

"Marshal," he said by way of greeting.

"I thought you might like to know that . . ."

"Jensen killed Conroy," Atwood said, interrupting him.

"Yeah."

"Maybe we're concentrating on the wrong person," Atwood suggested.

"What do you mean?"

"I've been doing some checking on my own," Atwood said. "It turns out there was also a reward offered for Kate's brother, Wes Fontaine. The reason he left Texas some time ago, it was because he had just killed a marshal. He's wanted for murder."

"It must have been a long time ago, 'cause I've been marshalin' for fifteen years, and I never even heard of him until he 'n the others come into town," Witherspoon said.

Atwood showed the wanted poster to Witherspoon and, like the original one for Smoke, this flyer was browned, with curling edges.

"That looks as old as the one for Jensen," Witherspoon said.

"It doesn't matter how long ago it was. It was for murder, and there's no statute of limitations to murder. Better yet, it's from Texas."

"That federal judge will just throw it out," Witherspoon said.

"No, he can't. Murder is a state crime, not a federal crime. He won't have any say-so on this one at all."

"He threw out the verdict on Kate and her boy, and those was both state crimes."

"That's because he found fault with the trial," Atwood said. "But we haven't had a trial for Wes Fontaine. In fact, there never has been a trial for him, because he disappeared and nobody knew what happened to him. We know where he is now. Get some new paper printed up for him, and I guarantee you that the federal judge will do nothing about it."

"Yeah, but if we try him, and . . ."

"Who said anything about bringing him to trial?" Atwood asked.

"All I asked you to do is get a wanted poster out on Fontaine. Only don't stop at just one this time. I want you to print up about a thousand copies and spread them around. Make certain they say dead or alive. That way anyone who wants to take on the job won't have to go up against him face to face. When it says dead or alive, you're just as dead if you're shot in the back as you are if you're shot in the front. And the reward is just as high."

"Who's goin' to pay the reward?"

"It's a Texas crime, so we'll get the state of Texas to pay it."

Witherspoon shook his head. "Mr. Atwood, look, I've gone along with you on just about ever'thing you've wanted."

"And you have been well compensated," Atwood replied.

"Yes, sir, I have, 'n I'm real grateful to you for that, too. But what you're sayin' now, put out a flyer that's near twenty years old, I don't know. What if that flyer was withdrawn, like the one on Smoke Jensen was? I mean for Jensen, that was a flyer up in Idaho, 'n it didn't much matter down here in Texas whether it was withdrawn or not. But this here was a Texas warrant, 'n if it's been withdrawn, the state ain't only not goin' to pay the reward, but they could maybe charge whoever kills Fontaine with murder."

"You aren't planning on trying to collect the reward on him, are you?" Atwood asked.

"Well, no sir, but I couldn't collect it anyway, bein' as I'm a marshal."

"Then what difference does it make to you whether whoever kills Fontaine is charged with murder or not? Now just get the new poster printed, and put it out like I told you to," Atwood ordered.

"All right," Witherspoon acquiesced. "If you say so."

"I do say so."

"But I can tell you right now, it ain't goin' to do you no good to print that thing. It ain't goin' to do you no good at all," Witherspoon said.

"Just do it, Witherspoon," Atwood said.

"Yes, sir, if you say so. Only, I don't think it's going to do no good."

After Witherspoon left, Atwood poured himself a drink and called for his butler.

"Sí, señor?"

"Sanchez, fetch Mr. Willis for me."

Sanchez nodded, then left on his task. A few minutes later Sanchez showed Willis into the parlor.

"You sent for me, Mr. Atwood?" Bo Willis asked.

"Yes, I've decided to make you the new marshal," Atwood said.

"You mean Witherspoon ain't plannin' on runnin' in the next election?" Willis replied.

"There ain't goin' to be another election. I'll have Judge Boykin appoint you."

"What about Witherspoon? You mean he's going to resign?"

"I'm afraid Marshal Witherspoon has become somewhat troublesome and argumentative," Atwood said. "Such a person can be deleterious to my long-range plans. His usefulness has expired and I need a new marshal, someone I can depend on. I can depend on you, can't I, *Marshal* Willis?"

A broad smile spread across Willis's face. "Yes, sir!" he said exuberantly. "You can depend on me, for sure."

CHAPTER 20

"This ain't goin' to do no good," Calhoun said when Witherspoon ordered him to print up new posters for Pearlie. "This won't be no different from the posters that we printed for Smoke Jensen."

"It ain't the same thing," Witherspoon said. "Jensen wasn't wanted in Texas, Fontaine is."

"This was near twenty years ago," Calhoun said. "You know it ain't good now. Like as not, there don't nobody even remember it."

"It's murder," Witherspoon said. "It don't matter whether anyone remembers it or not. Now, get them posters printed up like I told you to."

"If you're goin' to arrest him, why do you need the posters printed?" Calhoun asked. "Why not just arrest him?"

"Who said anything about arresting him?" Witherspoon asked with an evil smile.

"This is Atwood's doin', ain't it? He don't want Pearlie arrested, he wants him kilt."

"What if it is?"

"It ain't right," the deputy replied.

"You want to turn your back on the money Atwood is givin' us 'n just live on the salary the city pays?"

"I'll get the posters printed," Calhoun said.

"Yeah, I thought you might see it my way."

* * *

It was dark by the time Calhoun returned to Etholen with the printed flyers. There was a huge difference between the daytime Etholen and the town at night. In the daytime the population was given to the normal pursuits of a small community, freight wagons rolling in out of town, the arrival and departure of trains on the Southern Pacific Railroad, and merchants and shoppers in the stores.

At night, though, the population of the town increased precipitously, and its character changed, tone and tint. The cowboys who came into town did so in quest of fun and relaxation from a long day of work on the ranch, and most found that fun in the town's two saloons. Liquor flowed, laughter, shrieks, loud voices, and occasionally gunshots sounded in the night. In some unfathomable way, the citizens of the town learned how to discern the difference between gunshots that were fired in celebration and those fired in anger.

Calhoun rode down the dark street, sometimes passing through the golden bubbles of light that came from the streetlamps or was projected into the street from lighted windows. He stopped in front of the marshal's office, then went inside.

"Here they are," he said, dropping the bundle onto Witherspoon's desk.

"I'll get 'em put out tomorrow," Witherspoon said.

"This ain't right. I mean especially if you ain't even plannin' on arrestin' him."

"Make your rounds and quit your bitchin'," Witherspoon said.

When Deputy Calhoun came into the Pretty Girl and Happy Cowboy Saloon a few minutes later, he was holding one of the reward flyers in his hand.

"Hello, Deputy," Peterson said. "Making your rounds?"

"Yeah," Calhoun said. "Listen, is Kate's brother in here?"

"You mean Pearlie? Yes, he and the others are all sitting around the table back by the piano. See them?"

"Yeah, thanks," Calhoun said as he started toward the table the bartender had pointed out.

"Hello, Deputy," Pearlie said when Calhoun approached. "Something we can do for you?"

"Mr. Fontaine, I've got something I think you should see."

"What is it?" Pearlie asked.

Without answering him directly, Calhoun handed Pearlie the paper he was holding.

WANTED
DEAD *or* ALIVE
For MURDERING *a* SHERIFF :

WES WESLEY FONTAINE
Alias: "PEARLIE"

$2,500 REWARD
Contact: MARSHAL WITHERSPOON, *Etholen, Texas*

"Damn," Pearlie said after he examined it.

"There's been about a thousand of these things printed up 'n Witherspoon plans to have 'em all posted tomorrow," Calhoun said. "I thought maybe you ought to know about 'em."

"Smoke, take a look at this. They've got paper on me, too. Where the hell did they come up with these things?"

"Where did they come up with it, Deputy?" Smoke asked after he looked at the document. "This one, like the wanted poster Critchlow had on me, has been freshly printed."

"Yeah, look, it even calls me Pearlie. I mean when this happened, nobody called me Pearlie."

"I got it printed over in Sierra Blanca," Calhoun replied.

"Witherspoon sent me over there, 'cause he knew that Blanton wouldn't print it here."

"You got it printed?"

"Yeah, Witherspoon ordered me to do it. And Atwood ordered him," he added.

"You're not looking to arrest me, are you, Calhoun?"

"No!" Calhoun said quickly. "No, I'm not. Truth to tell, I don't think Atwood wants you arrested, either, which means the marshal doesn't want you arrested."

"Then I don't understand," Kate said. "If they don't want him arrested, why did they have these old posters reprinted?"

"They don't want him arrested, 'cause they want some bounty hunter to kill 'im," Cal said.

"Oh, Pearlie!" Kate said.

"Cal, must you be so blunt?" Sally scolded.

"Sorry, Miz Sally, but you know it's true," Cal replied.

"And he's right, ma'am. I'm pretty sure that's exactly why Atwood had them printed. I'm sorry to be the one to show you this," Calhoun said.

"No, you did right to show it to him," Smoke said. "Better to be approached with a reward poster than a bounty hunter's gun."

"Tell me, Calhoun, why did you show me this?" Pearlie asked. "Did Witherspoon ask you to?"

"Ha, Witherspoon would just as well want you to not know nothin' about it till some gunny took a shot at you," Calhoun said.

"Well, I appreciate the warning."

With a departing nod, Calhoun left the saloon.

"You shouldn't have come back to Texas. This is all my fault," Kate said.

"No, Mom, it's my fault," Rusty said. "I'm the one started all this when I shot Calley."

"Don't be ridiculous. If you hadn't shot him, he would have shot you."

"If it is anybody's fault, it is mine," Pearlie said. "I'm the one that killed Miller, and Marshal Gibson. And I'm the one that ran away after my name wound up on a wanted poster. I've put this off long enough. I think it's time I faced up to it."

"Maybe so, but not with Judge Boykin," Rusty said. "Boykin is an evil man who will do anything Atwood tells him to do."

"Rusty is right," Kate said. "You won't get a fair trial with Boykin."

"We could go see Judge Turner again," Sally suggested.

"That won't do any good, Miz Sally," Pearlie said with a shake of his head. "This happened in Texas, and unlike the dodger Critchlow had on Smoke, this one didn't cross state lines. Also I'm sure it has never been pulled back."

"Judge Turner can order a change of venue," Sally said.

"What's that?" Cal asked.

"It means he can order that the trial can be held somewhere other than in Judge Boykin's court."

"Well then," Rusty said with a wide smile. "That's something else. If you have a chance to have a fair trial, without Boykin having anything to do with it, then maybe everything will be all right."

Bo Willis, Al Booker, Emile Clark, and Johnny Sanders were in the Bull and Heifer Saloon when Willis saw Calhoun step in through the batwing doors.

"Well now," Willis said. "We ain't goin' to have to look for Calhoun, there he is."

"Hello, Deputy. How are you doin' tonight?" Bull Blackwell asked, greeting Calhoun when he stepped up to the bar.

"Hello, Bull."

"Good to see that you are visitin' my place tonight. I

thought the Pretty Girl and Happy Cowboy was more your style."

"That ain't true. I come in here as much as I go in there."

"Hello, Calhoun," someone said, approaching the bar then.

Turning toward the voice, Calhoun saw one of Atwood's men. And "men" was the way he thought of it, because Willis wasn't one of Atwood's cowboys. He was one of the people Atwood called his special cadre, one of his gunhands.

"Hello, Willis."

"Why don't I buy you a drink, Deputy?" Willis asked.

"I don't know if I should. I'm on duty." Calhoun paused for a moment. "On second thought, maybe I'm not on duty."

"What do you mean?" Bull Blackwell asked.

Calhoun reached up to the star pinned to his shirt, took it off, then lay it on the bar. "I'm not on duty, 'cause I ain't the deputy anymore, seein' as I just quit. You know what I plan to do? I aim to get good 'n drunk, one last time. Then I'm goin' to quit drinkin' for real. I mean, if I ain't workin' for Witherspoon no more, I don't see as I'll have any need to be gettin' drunk anymore."

Willis laughed. "There you go. Blackwell, give me 'n the deputy . . ."

"I told you, I ain't the deputy no more," Calhoun said.

"That is, give me 'n my friend a bottle. Come on, Calhoun, let's me 'n you get us a table 'n get drunk together."

Willis took Calhoun back to the table where, earlier, he had been sitting with Booker, Clark, and Sanders. The table was empty now.

Booker left the saloon and went straight to the office of the city marshal. "Marshal?" Booker said.

Witherspoon was sitting at his desk in the marshal's office, playing a game of solitaire.

"Yeah? What's Atwood want now?" he asked without looking up.

"No, this ain't got nothin' to do with Atwood. Did you 'n Calhoun have a fallin' out over somethin'?"

"A fallin' out? No, what do you mean, a fallin' out? What are you talkin' about?"

"I don't know if he's mad at you over somethin', or if he's just suddenly got ambition. But he's over at the Bull and Heifer now, tellin' Willis that he's plannin' on killin' you the next time he sees you, then he's goin' to pin on your badge."

"The hell you say? Calhoun said somethin' like that? That don't sound like him. Unless he's drunk again."

"Well, he is drinkin', but he ain't drunk yet, so it ain't the whiskey that's talkin'. But as for what he's sayin', I'm tellin' you the straight of it, 'cause I was right there listenin' to 'im. He said next time he seen you, he wasn't goin' to give you no warnin' at all. What he was goin' to do was shoot you down like a dog. Them's his exact words. 'I'm goin' to shoot him down like a dog,' he says. Then, he says, he'll be the new marshal."

"We'll just see about that," Witherspoon said. "Where'd you say the son of a bitch was?"

"He's over at the Bull and Heifer. But I wouldn't go in there if I was you. I'm tellin' you, Marshal, he aims to shoot you on sight!"

"Hello, Clark," Willis said when Clark came over to the table. "Why don't you join me 'n my friend for a drink?"

"There ain't no time for that," Clark said. "I come here to tell Calhoun, he'd better get out of town."

"Get out of town? What for?" Calhoun replied.

"I don't know what it is that you done to get Witherspoon

all mad at you 'n ever'thing, but he's tellin' ever'one that he's comin' over here to kill you."

"Now that don't make no sense at all. Why would he want to kill me?"

"I don't know, but if I was you, I'd get out now, before he comes over here."

"I'm not goin' anywhere. Besides which, I'm not the deputy anymore, so nothin' I do has anything to do with him."

Clark looked around to the others in the saloon. "Listen to me, all of you," he said. "I just told the deputy here that the marshal is gunnin' for him. I want it well known that I give him the warnin', and as to what he does about it, well, I reckon that's his business."

"And I want ever'one to know that I ain't the deputy no more, which means the marshal ain't got no truck with me no more," Calhoun said. He raised the glass of whiskey to his lips to show that he wasn't concerned. He had just begun to take a sip when Witherspoon burst through the batwing doors, and burst through was the most accurate way of describing it.

"Where is that scum-sucking son of a bitchin' deputy of mine?" Witherspoon shouted. He already had his gun in his hand.

Calhoun put the glass down quickly. "Marshal, I . . ."

"Here I am, Calhoun! You want to shoot me?"

Even as Witherspoon shouted his challenge, he pulled the trigger. Immediately after, both Clark and Willis shot back at him. Within a matter of a moment, both the marshal and Calhoun lay unmoving on the floor of the Bull and Heifer Saloon.

"Son of a bitch! Did you all see that?" one of the saloon patrons asked.

"What was that all about?" another asked.

Clark and Willis still had the smoking guns in their hands.

Willis put his gun away and checked Calhoun. "Calhoun's dead. What about the marshal?"

"He's deader 'n a doornail," Booker said, having come into the saloon immediately after the shooting.

"What was that all about?" Bull asked.

"I don't know," Willis replied. "You seen it same as we did. Witherspoon come in here just blazin' away. Hell, we didn't have no choice but to kill 'im. There was no tellin' how many people he would shoot afore he was all done."

CHAPTER 21

The next morning, in a brief ceremony held in front of "Old Thunder," the cannon that the "officers and men" of Fort Quitman had donated to the town, Judge Boykin swore in Bo Willis as the new City Marshal of Etholen. Willis's first act was to appoint Clark as his deputy.

Almost immediately thereafter, Willis and Clark began strutting around town, showing their badges and exercising their new authority. Allen Blanton, editor of the *Etholen Standard*, called upon Mayor Cravens.

"That was sort of quick, wasn't it, Joe? I mean appointing a new marshal and deputy without even calling a meeting of the city council?" Blanton asked.

"We did have a city council meeting."

"And the city council wanted Willis and Clark? Hell, Joe, those two are Atwood's men, part of his special cadre. They don't even live in town."

"I know that, Allen, and believe me, if it had been up to me, they would not be wearing badges today. But there is nothing I can do about it. The city council appointed them, and you know as well as I do that all five of them are in Atwood's pocket. The vote on the council was five to zero."

"That's not right," Blanton said. "There's nothing right about that."

"Let's face it, Allen. Whether we like it or not, Atwood controls this town. And with the city council in his back pocket, I am as useless as tits on a boar hog."

"Maybe all it takes is a little reminder to the citizens of the town that, as Americans, we can control our own destiny," Blanton suggested.

"What do you have in mind?"

"You'll see."

Blanton didn't waste any time printing a scathing editorial in the *Etholen Standard*.

Marshal and Deputy Killed
In Shoot-Out!

Yesterday in an act, the motive of which we shall probably never know, Marshal Seth Witherspoon stepped into the Bull and Heifer Saloon shouting vituperative challenges at Tim Calhoun. Even as he mouthed the scurrilous words, he was engaging his pistol with devastating effect. Deputy Calhoun dropped to the floor with a bullet in his heart.

Bo Willis and Emile Clark, both of whom were standing near the deputy, fired at the marshal, killing him instantly. Although there was no witness testimony, nor evidence to indicate that Witherspoon represented a threat, their claim of self-defense was immediately accepted by Judge Boykin, and no charge of homicide has been filed.

With the death of both Marshal Witherspoon and Deputy Calhoun, our fair community was left without the services of either, though a case could well be made that neither the marshal nor his deputy represented the people's interest in the first place. The absence of law enforcement did not last very long, however, for in a move that can only be described as bizarre, the city council, by unanimous vote, appointed Willis as our new marshal and Clark as our new deputy. The very men who had, by their action, rendered the vacancy available were selected to fill it. The city council wasted no time in making the appointments, no doubt directed to do so by Silas Atwood.

While this newspaper agrees that it is good to fill such a vacancy as quickly as possible, we do not agree that the wisest choice was made. Atwood's influence over Marshal Witherspoon had already been a point of concern by the good citizens of our town. Now that influence shall be even greater, for this paper believes that Willis and Clark have been appointed as the newest officers of the law in order to give Atwood even more control.

I would be remiss in my duty if I did not urge my fellow citizens to rise up against this usurpation and demand an immediate popular election to either sustain, or override, the action of the city council. We cannot allow Atwood to continue to exercise his tyrannical reign over our fair community.

"Just who the hell does Blanton think he is, anyway?" Atwood shouted angrily, throwing the newspaper down.

"I couldn't understand about half of them words, but I

was pretty sure they wasn't good ones. That's why I brung the paper to you soon as it come out," Willis said.

"I think, perhaps, Mr. Blanton needs to be taught a lesson," Atwood said.

"You want me 'n Clark to rough 'im up a bit?"

"No, I'll have Sanders and Booker pay his office a visit. You're the marshal. It'll be your job to investigate, to find out who did it."

"Well hell, Boss, if Sanders and Booker does it, there won't be no need to investigate. We'll know who done it," Willis said.

"You won't know that they did it."

"Sure I will, you just told me you was goin' to have them do it."

"Willis, I didn't make a mistake in making you the marshal, did I? Please tell me you aren't that dumb."

"What do you mean? I mean, if Sanders and . . ." Willis stopped in midsentence, and a smile spread across his face. "Oh!" he said. "Oh! Yeah, I get it! I ain't *supposed* to know who done it. That way I'll be tryin' to figure it out."

"Aren't you the brilliant one, though," Atwood said.

"Yeah, I am pretty smart at that," Willis replied, not catching the sarcasm in Atwood's remark.

Allen Blanton was still at breakfast the next morning when there was a loud knock on the door. When he opened the door he saw Oscar Davis, his all-around handyman.

"Hello, OD. Lose your key?"

"No, sir," OD replied. "And truth is, even if I had, it wouldn't have mattered this morning. There was no key needed."

"Damn! Did I leave the door unlocked last night?"

"No, sir. That is, not that I know of," OD said. "Anyway

you don't need a key to open the front door this morning because there is no front door. That's why I'm over here."

"What?"

"I think perhaps you should come take a look," OD suggested.

Five minutes later Blanton was standing in the front room of the *Etholen Standard*, looking at the disarray. In addition to the fact that the door was lying on the floor, all the glass of the front window had been broken, the composing tables turned over, the type trays emptied, and type scattered everywhere.

"Who would do something like this?" Blanton lamented.

"Do you really need to ask that question, Mr. Blanton? Don't you know who it was?" Smoke asked. Smoke was but one of several of the town's people who had gathered at the newspaper office, not only from curiosity, but, for many, a genuine desire to help put things back in order.

Blanton shook his head. "No, I don't know."

"Think about it, Mr. Blanton. Who has been the most frequent subject of your recent editorials?"

"Surely you don't think Atwood would do something like this, do you? I'll admit, he is a bit overly ambitious, but he is a wealthy and influential man. I just can't see someone of his social and economic status stooping to do something like this."

"I have been around a lot of wealthy men," Smoke said. "Believe me, a sizable bank account has very little bearing on their behavior."

"Yes," Blanton said with a troubled nod of his head. "You are right, of course."

"What happened here?" a loud voice called, and looking toward the front door, Smoke and Blanton saw the newly appointed Marshal Willis standing there.

"It's fairly obvious what happened here, isn't it?"

Smoke replied. "Some of your friends took issue with Mr. Blanton's editorial."

"What do you mean, some of my friends? Are you telling me you think I know something about this? That's a damn lie, and you know it."

"You may well be right," Smoke replied. "Now that I think about it, it is foolish of me to believe that you actually have any friends."

Many of those who had been drawn to the scene laughed at Smoke's reply.

Blanton chuckled as well. "Thanks," he said. "I needed a laugh, especially now."

"What do you mean I ain't got no friends? I got friends," Willis asked, not catching the sarcasm. "I got lots of friends."

"I'm sure you do," Smoke replied.

Blanton got down on all fours and began gathering the type that had been scattered all over the floor.

"We'll help you, Mr. Blanton," someone else said.

"Each of you just choose one letter to pick up at a time," Blanton suggested. "It will be easier to separate them that way."

"I've got the z's," someone said.

"Ha! Leave it to Doodle to do the least work," another said. "I'll do the x's."

"Wait a minute, wait a minute!" Willis called. "You folks ain't got no right to start pickin' up the type, or to do anythin' like that till I tell you."

"What do you mean till you tell us, Willis?" one of those in the crowd asked.

"This here is a crime scene, as I'm sure all of you know. 'N bein' as it is a crime scene, it needs to be left just the way we found it, till I'm through investigating."

"Willis, either help us get this place cleaned up, or get out of the way," Smoke said with an angry growl.

"Well, I was just . . . I mean . . ." Willis started to respond, but he realized that he wasn't going to be able to stop the cleanup of the newspaper office because by now at least ten of the citizens of the town were involved in putting it back together again.

Willis remained for no more than a moment longer, then he turned and left the office as even more townspeople joined the first group, picking up type and setting the press and furniture to rights. At least two people were reattaching the door, while a couple more were cleaning out the rest of the broken window so a new plate of glass could be put in place.

Smoke, Sally, and Pearlie had planned to go to El Paso to visit Judge Turner this morning, but they put the trip off, staying to help the rest of the town put the newspaper office together again.

"This is great," Blanton said as the newspaper office continued to be put back to normal. "I never would have expected anything like this."

"Mr. Blanton, you know what this tells me?" Kate, who had also joined the helpers, asked.

"What's that?"

"It tells me that you have a lot of friends, and that, despite everything, Etholen is a very nice town."

"Yes, it is, or at least it could be, if we could ever get out from under Atwood's thumb," Blanton replied.

"We will," Kate said. "I have no doubt about that."

It was late afternoon before the newspaper office was completely reassembled, with the type and composing tables back in place, along with a new door and new glass in the front window. Afterward, everyone who had showed up to help put the newspaper office together again gathered at the Palace Café for dinner. Sue Ellen Johnson, proprietor of the café, pushed several tables together so there was one long table to accommodate everyone.

"Who could have done such a thing as try and destroy the newspaper?" someone asked. "And what could possibly be their reason?"

"That shouldn't be all that hard to figure out," Cletus said. "I mean, all you have to do is read yesterday's issue, when he talked about Atwood. There's no doubt in my mind but that Atwood done it. Or leastwise he had some of his men do it."

"But Willis was one of Atwood's men before he become marshal, wasn't he? And now he's investigating it. If it was one of Atwood's men that did it, don't you think Willis would know that?" one of the men around the table asked.

The others looked at him.

"Oh," he said. "Yeah, he probably already knows, don't he?"

"If he didn't do it himself," another offered.

Blanton struck his fork against the glass and, getting everyone's attention, stood to speak.

"My friends," he said. "And you are, all of you, indeed my friends. I will be honest with you. When Rusty Abernathy was convicted in the sham of a trial, and then Kate arrested and put in jail to take Rusty's place when he escaped, I had just about given up all hope for this town. Indeed, I had started looking into other towns where I could take my printing press and start my newspaper all over again.

"But now there are things that are giving me hope that our town will be able, not only to survive, but to escape from these oppressive shackles placed upon us by Silas Atwood and his gunhands. And the people we can most thank for that are here with us tonight. I'm talking about Smoke Jensen and his wife Sally, Pearlie Fontaine, and Cal Wood."

"Hear! Hear!" Joe Cravens said, lifting his glass toward Smoke, Sally, Pearlie, and Cal, and the others joined the mayor in lifting their own glasses in salute.

Eagle Shire Ranch

"Are you telling me that the people of the town actually turned out to help Blanton get his newspaper office put back in shape?" Atwood asked, the tone of his voice showing his anger.

"Yes, sir, that's exactly what happened, all right," Willis said. "Why there musta been fifteen or twenty people there helpin', fixin' the door, puttin' in a new window, pickin' up all the type and such."

"I think the townspeople are feeling pretty emboldened right now, because Smoke Jensen and Kate's brother, what is it they're callin' 'im?"

"Pearlie," Willis said.

"Yes, Pearlie. Witherspoon didn't get any of the reward posters out for him, did he?" Atwood asked.

"No, sir, he never got the chance."

"As soon as we get them distributed, I have a feeling that Kate's brother will concern us no further."

Blanton had more to say in the next edition of the *Etholen Standard*.

ATTACK ON FREEDOM OF THE PRESS

As many of you know, the *Standard* offices were attacked last night. The vandals broke out the front window and knocked the front door off its hinges. Once they had gained access to the building, they scattered the type around and overturned the press. This scurrilous action was not only an attack on the newspaper, it was an assault on the free press, which means that every citizen of Etholen was as much a victim as was the *Standard*.

But this heinous attack aroused a wave of righteous discontent among the population. For, dear readers, dozens of right-minded citizens of our city came to my aid, and in so doing, expressed their belief in, and their willingness to defend, freedom of the press.

Now, and for some time, our fair city has been subjected to the heavy-handed activity of one Silas Atwood. Atwood, as our readers know, is a very rich man . . . one of the most affluent in West Texas, if, indeed, not in the entire state. This has given him a sense of entitlement, and no despotic ruler in the history of the European feudal system has ever been more tyrannical in the ruthless application of wealth and power than the owner of Eagle Shire Ranch, who used his position to force out all the other area ranchers, and now, through his control of our city council, judge, and city marshal's office, is, by fear and intimidation, doing all that he can to establish his own fiefdom in El Paso County.

We cannot let this happen, and it is my belief, as evidenced by the courageous reaction of our town when this newspaper was attacked, that the time will come when our citizens will arise and throw this despot out.

CHAPTER 22

El Paso

On the very morning that Allen Blanton's defiant article appeared in the *Etholen Standard,* Smoke, Sally, and Pearlie went to the courthouse in El Paso to pay another visit to Judge Turner.

"Is the information on this poster true?" Judge Turner asked.

"If you are asking is it true that I killed Marshal Gibson, then the answer is yes, that is true," Pearlie said. "But it isn't true that I murdered him. I killed him in self-defense."

"Where did this happen?" Judge Turner asked.

"Bexar County," Pearlie replied.

"Bexar, not El Paso?"

"No, sir. It was Bexar."

"But the information says contact Marshal Witherspoon in Etholen. By the way, I understand that he was recently killed."

"Yes, sir, he was."

"He was killed by the man who is now the marshal," Smoke added.

"When did this happen?" Judge Turner asked. He held up the poster. "It must be very recent, judging by this poster."

"It happened a long time ago, Your Honor," Pearlie replied. "When I was fifteen."

"But these reward posters are new."

"Yes sir, they are," Smoke said.

"Still, there is no statute of limitations on murder," Judge Turner said.

"It wasn't murder, Your Honor. It was self-defense," Pearlie insisted.

"That may be, but there is going to have to be a resolution to the charge."

"Yes, that's why we came to you," Smoke said.

"What, exactly, are you asking me to do?" Judge Turner asked.

"I want to go to trial, Your Honor, and get this behind me. But I don't want to be tried by Judge Boykin," Pearlie said.

"We're asking for a change of venue," Sally said. "We know that you can't arbitrarily dismiss all charges, but, as a federal judge, you can at least position us in such a way as to guarantee a fair trial."

"Yes, I can at least do that," Judge Turner replied. "Tell me the story of what happened. Don't leave anything out," the judge added.

As he had when he related the story back at Sugarloaf, before they left to come to Texas, Pearlie laid out all the facts of that afternoon when he had gone into town with his friends with no more intention than to enjoy a cool lemonade.

When Pearlie was finished with his story, Judge Turner smiled, then held up his finger. "Come with me," he said mysteriously.

The four followed Judge Turner downstairs, then to an office in the back of the building. The sign on the door leading into that office read FIELDING POTASHNICK, JUDGE OF CIRCUIT COURT.

"Zeke," Judge Potashnick said when Turner took them into his office. "What can I do for you?"

"Fielding, I want you to conduct a trial for this young man," Judge Turner said.

"What kind of trial? And when?"

"A murder trial, and right now."

"Whoa, hold on there, Zeke. What do you mean, right now?"

"I am acting as his attorney," Judge Turner said. "And we waive trial by jury . . . we will accede to your finding."

"We'll need a prosecutor."

"Is David Crader in his office?"

"Yes," Potashnick said. "Wilma, step down to Mr. Crader's office, and tell him to meet us in the courtroom."

"Yes, sir," his clerk answered.

"I found an article about the incident in the newspaper morgue," Crader said two hours later, when he returned to the courtroom after learning what it was about. "I'm prepared to make my case."

Potashnick turned toward Judge Turner. "Your Honor, are you . . . ?"

"Your Honor . . . we can't be Your Honoring each other all day," Turner replied. "As you are conducting this trial, I will refer to you as Your Honor. But as I will be acting as Mr. Fontaine's defense attorney, suppose you just refer to me as Counselor?"

Potashnick chuckled. "All right, Counselor it is. Counselor, are you ready to present your case?"

"I am."

"Mr. Prosecutor, you may begin."

"Your Honor, according to the information I have before me, Wes Fontaine, then a boy of fifteen, shot and killed two men within a period of one hour. And one of the men he shot was the marshal, who was attempting to arrest him for murdering the first gentleman."

"Have you any witnesses to call?" Judge Potashnick asked.

"No, Your Honor, I do not. As it happened nearly twenty years ago, and given the constraint of time since being assigned this case, I have been unable to find any witnesses, other than the printed witness of the newspaper article I have used as my source."

"Objection," Turner said. "A newspaper article is, by definition, hearsay evidence."

"But, Your Honor," Crader replied. "Hearsay or not, it is the only evidence Prosecution has. And, I hasten to point out that it is a contemporary account."

"Objection overruled. The newspaper account will be considered as evidence. Have you anything else?"

"No, Your Honor."

"Do you rest your case?"

"I do."

"Defense counsel?"

"Your Honor, Defense has a witness to the event, a very good witness as he was also one of the principals to the case. I call the defendant, Mr. Wes Wesley Fontaine."

Pearlie was sworn, then he took his seat in the witness chair.

"You go by Pearlie, I believe? Do you mind if I address you as Pearlie?"

"No, sir, I don't mind at all."

"A moment ago, the prosecutor said that you killed the marshal when he tried to arrest you for murder. Is that true?"

"No, sir, that isn't true."

"What is untrue?"

"He wasn't trying to arrest me," Pearlie said. "Emmett Miller was the first man I killed. He drew on me, and everyone in the saloon saw it. When Marshal Gibson arrived very shortly thereafter, everyone in the saloon who had seen it told him that Miller drew first, and I had no choice but to defend myself."

"And did the marshal believe you?"

"Yes, sir, he did."

"But he attempted to arrest you, anyway?"

"No, sir, he did not."

"Then I don't understand. If he wasn't trying to arrest you, how is it that you wound up shooting him?"

Pearlie told how the marshal had ordered him out of the county, and when he said he didn't want to leave, that he had a good job and friends, the marshal said that he would either leave or get killed.

"When I said I wasn't going to go, he went for his gun."

"And you beat him?"

"Yes, sir."

"What happened then?"

"Everyone in the saloon told me that I'd better leave because I had shot a lawman, and it wouldn't matter if I was right or wrong. Shooting a lawman meant I would probably be hanged for it. So they all took up a collection for enough money for me to leave Texas. As I look back on it now, I think I should have stayed there and gone to trial. But I was a fifteen-year-old kid, I was scared, and I listened to everyone when they told me I should run."

Turner returned to the defense table and picked up a piece of paper. "Your Honor, I enter this as a defense exhibit. It is a wanted for murder poster issued on Wes, Pearlie, Fontaine, offering a reward of twenty-five hundred dollars, dead or alive."

"Let me get this straight, Counselor," Judge Potashnick said. "This is a wanted for murder poster, issued against your client, and you are putting this up as evidence for the defense?"

"I am, Your Honor. Its relevance shall come clear, shortly."

"Very well, let the clerk note that this is accepted as evidence for the defense."

"Is this an original poster, Mr. Fontaine?" Turner asked.

"No, sir. As you can see, it's clear that this poster isn't twenty years old."

"Yes, I can see that. I'm also interested in the way your name is listed here. Pearlie. When the incident in question happened, were you known as Pearlie?"

"No, sir," Pearlie replied.

"How did you come by the name Pearlie?"

"I figured I needed to change my name, in order to keep anyone from tracking me down."

"Where do you think this reward poster came from?"

"Objection, Your Honor, leading the witness," Crader said.

"Sustained."

"Let me restate the question. Do you know where this document came from?"

"I'm sure that Silas Atwood had it printed."

"Objection, Your Honor. That's not a definitive response."

"Objection sustained."

"I have no further questions, Your Honor," Turner said.

"Cross, Mr. Prosecutor?" Potashnick asked.

Crader started to approach the jury box, then, realizing that there was no jury, smiled sheepishly and came back to the witness stand.

"Mr. Fontaine, how old were you when this happened?"

"I was fifteen."

"You were fifteen, but you expect this court to believe that you, a fifteen-year-old boy, could draw faster and shoot straighter than an experienced marshal?"

"Yes, sir."

"Why is that? How were you able to draw faster and shoot straighter than an experienced law officer?"

"I had been practicing."

"So, you practiced drawing and shooting?"

"Yes, sir."

"Why?"

"I thought I might need the skill in order to defend myself."

"Isn't it also possible that you had this great skill, and you wished to show it off, and were willing to do so at the slightest provocation?"

"No, sir."

"But that is what happened, isn't it? In both cases, when you shot and killed Miller, and when you shot and killed the marshal, you could have avoided killing them?"

"Both Miller and Marshal Gibson drew first."

"After you provoked them into it."

"No, sir, I don't see it that way at all."

"You say your friends all took up a collection for you?"

"Yes, sir."

"And you left Texas?"

"Yes, sir."

Crader stroked his chin for a moment as he stared at Pearlie. "Mr. Fontaine, if what you are telling us is the truth, have you ever considered the irony of it?"

"The irony, sir?"

"Yes," Crader said. "According to you, the entire incident happened because you refused to leave Texas when the marshal ordered you to do so."

"Yes, sir, that's right."

"But you wound up leaving, anyway."

"Yes, sir."

"Wouldn't it have been better, under the circumstances, to have left when he told you to? As it turned out, you left anyway, and the marshal wound up getting killed."

"Yes, sir," Pearlie said contritely. "I've thought about that a thousand times over the last several years. And I wish to hell I had left when he first asked me."

"So you admit that you did provoke the marshal into shooting you."

"I . . ."

"No further questions, Your Honor."

"Redirect, Mr. Turner?" Judge Potashnick asked after Crader sat down.

Turner stood up but didn't leave the table.

"Mr. Fontaine, prior to the incident we are debating, how did you and Marshal Gibson get along?"

"We got along fine," Pearlie responded. "I guess," he added.

"You guess?"

"Yes, sir. Well, the truth is, I don't think the marshal even knew who I was. There was no need for him to. I mean, I had never done anything to cause him to know me. We never even spoke, at least, not before that night."

"Did you feel you had something to prove?"

"Something to prove?"

"Yes. When you went into town with your friends that night, did you have it in your mind that you were going to prove to the others that, even though you were only fifteen, you could take care of yourself?"

"No, sir. The only reason I went into town that night is because I wanted to have a lemonade, and I wanted to have it with my friends."

"No further questions."

"Closing statement?"

"None, Your Honor. Defense rests."

"Prosecutor?"

"Prosecution rests."

Potashnick looked out over the court and, for a long moment, drummed his fingers on the bench.

"Would the defendant please stand?"

Pearlie, and Judge Turner, acting as his defense counsel, stood.

"After careful consideration, I find the defendant not guilty, and hereby order the recall of any and all wanted posters that may be, or may come to be in existence, as it pertains to this particular incident.

"Court is adjourned."

With a big smile, Pearlie reached out to shake Judge Turner's hand. By the time he turned around, Sally had stepped up to the defense table, and she gave him a big hug.

"Oh, Miz Sally, do you know how long that's been hanging over me?" Pearlie asked. "I mean, I wasn't ever really worried about it, but still, it sometimes sort of nagged at me. And now, it's all over."

"It is indeed," Sally said.

CHAPTER 23

Etholen

"I got a telegram for you," Dennis Hodge said, stepping into the marshal's office.

"You have a telegram for me?" Willis asked.

"You're the city marshal, aren't you?" the Western Union operator said.

"Oh, yeah, I guess I am."

"Well, then this is for you. It came for you about five minutes ago."

"Do I have to pay for it?"

"No, it's already been paid for. Are you going to take it or not? I have to get back over to the office."

"Yeah, sure, I'll take it," Willis said, reaching for the sheet of paper. He waited until Hodge left before he read it.

WES WESLEY PEARLIE FONTAINE FOUND
NOT GUILTY OF ALL CHARGES. IMMEDIATE
RECALL OF ALL REWARD POSTERS
ORDERED BY JUDGE F. POTASHNICK.

"Damn," Willis said. "Atwood ain't goin' to like this."

"He ain't goin' to like what?" Clark asked.

"He ain't goin' to like it that we have to take up all them posters we put out on Fontaine."

"What do you mean?"

Willis showed Clark the telegram. "What the hell? Does this mean we have to go out 'n find all them posters we done put out?"

"That's what the telegram says."

"What if we can't find 'em all? What if some people have already took some of 'em, 'n is lookin' for Pearlie?"

Willis chuckled. "Well, now, it'd just be a real shame if someone was to kill 'im by mistake, wouldn't it?"

Booker laughed as well. "Yeah," he said. "A real shame."

"Look at this!" Cal said excitedly, holding out the telegram he had just received from Smoke. "Pearlie has been tried and found innocent already. Miz Kate, you don't have to worry about him ever again. Whatever happened all those years ago is behind him now."

"Oh!" Kate said. "Oh, I'm so happy!"

"I think the smartest thing I ever did was go to Colorado to find Uncle Wes," Rusty said.

"I agree," Kate said. "I just know, now, how foolish I was once I learned that my brother was still alive, and where he lived, that I didn't make any effort go see him long before now."

Reeves County, Texas

Dingus Lomax rode into Salcedo, stopped in front of the Longhorn Saloon, dismounted, and went inside. Stepping up to the bar, he slapped a silver coin down in front of him.

The sound of the coin made the saloonkeeper look around. The man waiting to be served looked like a piece of rawhide. He was smaller than average, with a craggy face and an oversized, hooked nose.

"What'll it be, Mr. Lomax?" the bartender asked, stepping up to him.

"Whiskey."

Lomax was a bounty hunter, who was well known for the dispassionate way he could kill. His very name instilled fear. He wasn't surprised that he was recognized by the bartender, but in his profession that was a mixed blessing. On the one hand, it often gave him an edge, by inducing fear in his quarry. On the other hand, it also forewarned them, so they could get away.

Lomax specialized in those fugitives who were wanted "dead or alive." So far he had hunted down and been paid reward money for seventeen such fugitives. Not one of the fugitives for whom the reward was paid had been brought in alive.

"Why should I bring 'em in alive?" Lomax replied when a marshal queried him about his method of operation. "They're easier to handle when they're dead, 'n besides which, I don't have to feed 'em."

When Lomax had ridden into the small town of Salcedo a few minutes earlier, news of his arrival spread quickly. Old men held up their grandsons to point him out as he rode by so that the young ones could remember this moment and, many years from now, tell their own grandchildren about it. Those grandchildren would ultimately tell their grandchildren that their grandfather had once seen Dingus Lomax, so that the legend of the man would span seven generations.

Lomax picked up his drink, then slowly surveyed the interior of the saloon. He was on the trail of Mort Bodine, and a chance remark he had overheard down in Wild Horse suggested that Bodine might have come to Salcedo.

The saloon was typical of the many he had seen over

the past several years. Wide, rough-hewn boards formed the plank floor, and against the wall behind the long, brown-stained bar was a shelf of whiskey bottles, their number doubled by the mirror they stood against. Half a dozen tables, occupied by a dozen or so men, filled the room, and tobacco smoke hovered in a noxious cloud just under the ceiling.

At the opposite end of the bar stood a man wearing a slouch hat and a trail-worn shirt. Lomax thought this might be Bodine, and because the man looked away from him the few times Lomax glanced that way, he was sure this was the man he was looking for.

Hanging low in a well-oiled holster on Bodine's right side was a Colt .44 with a wooden grip. The man was slender, with dark hair and dark eyes, and there was a gracefulness and economy of motion about the way he walked and moved.

The longer Lomax studied him, the more he was convinced this was his man. Bodine, if that really was his name, had not turned around since Lomax arrived.

"Hey, you," Lomax called.

The man did not turn.

"I'm talkin' to you, Bodine. Your name is Bodine, isn't it? Mort Bodine? That who you are?"

Lomax studied him from the back and saw a visible tightening of the man's shoulders. Then, with a sigh, he turned around. "Yeah," he said. "I'm Bodine. You're Lomax, ain't you?"

"That's me," Lomax said with a smile. "There are wanted dodgers out on you," he added.

"Yeah, I know. I'm a little surprised to see you here, though. I thought you shot most of the men in the back."

Lomax's smile grew bigger. "Try me," he said.

"Draw!" Bodine shouted, going for his own gun even before he issued the challenge.

Bodine was quick, quicker than anyone else this town had ever seen. But midway through his draw, Bodine realized he wasn't quick enough. The arrogant confidence in his eyes was replaced by fear, then the acceptance of the fact that he was about to be killed.

The two pistols discharged almost simultaneously, but Lomax had been able to bring his gun to bear and his bullet plunged into Bodine's chest. The bullet from Bodine's gun smashed the glass that held Lomax's drink, sending up a shower of whiskey and tiny shards of glass.

Looking down at himself, Bodine put his hand over his wound, then pulled it away and examined the blood that had pooled in his palm. When he looked back at Lomax, there was an almost whimsical smile on his face.

He coughed, then fell back against the bar, making an attempt to grab on to the bar to keep himself erect. The attempt was unsuccessful, and Bodine fell on his back, his right arm stretched out beside him, his pistol still connected to him, only because his forefinger was hung up in the trigger guard. The old slouch hat had rolled across the floor and now rested in a half-filled spittoon.

Lomax turned back to the bar where pieces of broken glass and a small puddle of whiskey marked the spot of his drink.

"Looks like I'm going to need a refill," he said.

One hour later Dingus Lomax dismounted, then stepped over to the side of the road to take a leak. He was riding one horse and leading another. Mort Bodine was belly-down across the saddle of the led horse. It wasn't uncomfortable for Bodine, because he was dead. Bodine was wanted in Presidio County. The county seat was Marfa, but that was farther away than Lomax wanted to go, so he was headed for Wild Horse, which was the closest town.

As Lomax buttoned up his trousers, he saw a poster pinned to a nearby tree, and he walked over to examine it.

"Twenty-five hunnert dollars, huh? Seems to me like you coulda at least put a drawin' o' this feller, Fontaine, so that folks that might be after 'im would know what this here Wes Pearlie Fontaine looks like."

Lomax planned to turn the body over to the marshal, or the sheriff, whoever the local law was in Wild Horse, then he figured on going on to Etholen to find out whatever he needed to know about Fontaine.

"Pearlie," he said. "I reckon that's the name you go by. Is that the name you want on your tombstone?"

Lomax giggled at his question, then he swung into the saddle.

"Hey, Bodine," he called back to the body behind him. "You ever been to Wild Horse before? It'd be kind of funny, don't you think, if you ain't never been there before? Funny, I mean, 'cause you're likely goin' to wind up gettin' buried there instead of Marfa, 'n that's where you'll be for all eternity.

"'Course, when you stop to think about it, I reckon you wasn't all that different from me. I mean, I was born just outside Dayton, Ohio, but I ain't been back in Ohio for more'n twenty years now, 'n I don't reckon I'll ever go back. I don't know where I'll wind up planted, but more'n likely it'll be someplace just like you, someplace I ain't never been to before."

Wild Horse

"Which one of you's the marshal?" Lomax asked when he stepped into the marshal's office where two men were engaged in conversation.

"I'm Marshal Wallace," the larger of the two men said, looking toward Lomax. "What do you want?"

"Marshal, my name is Lomax."

"Lomax?" the marshal asked, the expression on his face becoming more animated. "Would that be Dingus Lomax?"

"Yeah. Look, I got Mort Bodine outside, 'n ole' Mort has a fifteen-hunnert-dollar reward on 'im."

"And you're wantin' me to put him in my jail?"

Lomax laughed, a dry, high-pitched cackle. "You can put 'im in jail if you want to, onliest thing is, he's liable to start stinkin' in another day or two."

"What do you mean, he's liable to start stinkin'?"

"That's what happens to a dead body iffen you let it lie around long enough. When I told you I had Mort Bodine outside, I didn't tell you he was belly-down on his horse."

"I don't understand," the marshal said. "If he's already dead, what did you bring 'im to me for?"

"Damn, how long you been a marshal?" Lomax asked.

"What difference does it make how long I've been a marshal?" Wallace replied, clearly agitated by Lomax's question.

"The thing is, you can't have been one for too long, or you'd know what this is all about. You see, what you have to do is send a telegram back to the Pecos City marshal, 'n tell 'im that you are a lawman, and say that Bodine is dead, and I'm the one that kilt 'im."

"Lomax, I wouldn't know Mort Bodine from Mrs. Smith's housecat. How am I supposed to be able to say he's dead?"

"Maybe, for two hundred and fifty dollars, you might remember that you saw him somewhere before."

"But I ain't never . . ."

"Sure we did, Harold, me 'n you seen 'im back in Van Horn oncet, don't you remember?" his deputy asked.

"No, I don't recall that we . . ."

"You said to me, 'Carl, I do believe that feller over there is worth a hunnert 'n twenty-five dollars to each of us,'" Carl said very pointedly.

Wallace's frown deepened for just a moment, then he realized what his deputy was saying, and a broad smile spread across his face.

"Yes!" he said. "Yes, I do remember that now. Them was my exact words! Come on, Mr. Lomax, let's get a look at this dead prisoner of yours, so I can send word back to Pecos County that this Bodine feller has done been caught."

Lomax's smile was without mirth. "Well now," he said. "I'd say you two is pretty smart law officers. Yes, sir, real smart."

CHAPTER 24

Etholen

"I wonder if Katie's got any champagne in her place," Pearlie said as he, Smoke, and Sally rode back into town.

"Champagne?" Sally asked.

"Sure. Isn't that what you drink when you want to celebrate something? I'm that relieved that this has finally been cleared up after all these years that I plan to celebrate with champagne, and I want you all, and Cal, Katie, and Rusty to celebrate with me."

"That's a bit extravagant," Sally said. "But, under the circumstance, I think it may be appropriate."

They tied up in front of the Pretty Girl and Happy Cowboy Saloon, then, Pearlie let out a shout as soon as they stepped inside.

"Yahoo! Katie! Did you get my telegram?" Pearlie asked as he, Smoke, and Sally pushed through the batwing doors.

"Yes!" Katie said happily. "You're a free man!"

Kate, with her arms spread, and a wide smile on her face, hurried over to Pearlie to give him a hug.

"There's not one thing out of my past that's hanging over me now. Katie, I plan to buy a couple of bottles of champagne so we can celebrate."

"Mr. Peterson, how many bottles of champagne do we have?" Kate asked.

Peterson looked under the bar. "Six," he said.

"Open them up, Mr. Peterson. Open every bottle and serve it to anyone who wants it, until it's all gone."

"Champagne?" Cletus said. "Damn! I ain't never tasted any champagne in my whole life."

"Well, you're about to now," Rusty said with a happy laugh.

Over the next few minutes, corks popped loudly, glasses were filled with the bubbly beverage, and the patrons, Dolly, and the other Pretty Girls joined Pearlie in celebrating the outcome of Pearlie's trial.

"Oh! This tickles my nose!" Dolly said, giggling as she took the first drink.

"Sure, champagne always does that," Rusty said.

"Ha! You talk like you've drunk a lot of champagne," Cletus said.

"I've drunk it, before."

"Well, I've got two reasons to celebrate," Dolly said.

"What two reasons?" Rusty asked.

"One, because your uncle Pearlie got everything from his past taken care of, and one because it is my birthday."

"Today is your birthday?"

"Actually, tomorrow is my birthday," Dolly said.

"Well, happy birthday, tomorrow," Rusty said, lifting his glass. "How old will you be?"

"Rusty!" Sally scolded. "That's not something you ever ask a lady. Not even someone as young as Dolly."

Dolly laughed. "She's right, you know. But I'll tell you. I'll be nineteen tomorrow."

"Good, I'm a year older than you are," Rusty said.

"Why do you say good?"

"Because it's just good, that's all."

"Rusty?" Sally said. "I wonder if you would do me a huge favor and play Beethoven's Sonata Number Fourteen?"

"Oh, yes, please do!" Dolly said. "That's one of my favorites."

"Why, Dolly, I didn't know you liked classical music," Sally said.

"I didn't used to like it. Well, I can't say I didn't used to like it . . . it's just that I never actually heard any of it until I heard the kind of music Rusty plays. Now, I love classical music, and I could sit here and listen to it all day."

"Then, why don't you come over here and sit beside me?" Sally invited. "We can enjoy it together."

"Oh, yes," Dolly said. "That would be wonderful. Thank you!"

The celebration stilled, and the patrons of the saloon grew quiet, as Rusty approached the grand piano. Before he sat down, he addressed the saloon patrons.

"The piece I'm about to play, Beethoven's Sonata Number Fourteen, is sometimes known as Moonlight Sonata. Beethoven composed it and dedicated it to the Countess Giulietta Guicciardi, a pupil of Beethoven. He was in love with her, you see, and he proposed to her shortly after playing the piece in public for the first time. She loved him as well, but she was forbidden by her parents to marry him, so, sadly, the marriage never happened.

"Beethoven's Moonlight Sonata," Rusty concluded, then he held his hands over the keyboard for just a moment before he started to play.

The opening notes were haunting, the melody almost a whisper. The music filled the saloon and caressed the collective soul of the patrons. If there was anyone left in Etholen who was unaware of Rusty's talent, it took but a few bars of music to convince even the most skeptical that they weren't hearing a mere saloon piano player, they were listening to a concert pianist of great expertise. As Rusty's fingers caressed the piano keyboard, he created magic. It was as if, through his skill, he had actually been able to resurrect the great composer.

When Rusty finished, the applause was spontaneous, genuine, and sustained, from the Pretty Girls, who were also Dolly's friends, to the men who punched cows or drove freight wagons or worked for the railroad. Those who had never even heard of Beethoven were applauding as enthusiastically as Sally, Kate, and Dolly.

"Oh, Rusty, that was so pretty that it made me cry," Dolly said when Rusty came back over to her.

"Dolly is right," Sally said. "I've heard Ricardo Castro and J. E. Goodson in concert, and neither of them have anything on you."

Rusty beamed at the compliment. "I've heard both of them play as well," he said. "And while I can't agree that I play as well as they . . . I certainly do appreciate you saying so."

"Well, this has been a most enjoyable celebration," Sally said. "But, Smoke, if you don't mind, I'd like to clean up before dinner tonight, so I'm going back to the hotel."

"I've got a little trail dust I'd like to get off as well, so I'll join you," Smoke said.

When they returned to the hotel, they made arrangements to have a tub and hot water brought up to their room.

"You can go first," Smoke said, once the tub was filled with hot water.

"That's nice of you to let me have the clean water," Sally said.

Smoke chuckled. "Letting you have the clean water has nothing to do with it. I just want to see you naked."

"Smoke!" Sally said, dipping her hand down into the water and splashing some of it on him. "You're awful!" She laughed. "I have to admit, though, that I'm flattered you would still say something like that."

"Tell me, do you think Rusty has ever watched Dolly take a bath?" Smoke said.

"I don't know," Sally replied. She giggled. "But I'll bet he would like to."

"Ha! Now who is being awful?"

Blanton wasted no time declaring Pearlie's innocence in the *Etholen Standard*.

WESLEY FONTAINE FOUND INNOCENT

Why, readers may ask, does this paper print an article declaring the innocence of this man Wesley Fontaine? Recently questionable wanted posters have been freshly printed, and circulated, offering a reward of twenty-five hundred dollars, dead or alive, for Mr. Fontaine. I say questionable, because the event for which the reward was being offered happened many years ago in another county.

Upon learning of the existence of these posters, Mr. Fontaine presented himself before a valid court, requested, and was granted a trial. The result of that trial was absolution of any guilt implied by the reward circulars. As publisher of this newspaper, I feel it is my obligation to make certain that everyone knows the reward is no longer valid, and if you see one of these dodgers still posted, you should, as a matter of civic duty, destroy it, in order to prevent what could become a tragic mistake.

Mr. Fontaine, who is better known by the sobriquet "Pearlie" is the brother of Mrs. Kate Abernathy. Kate Abernathy is not only one of our town's most successful business leaders, she is also generous of spirit and resources. It was she, you might remember, who organized and was the major contributor to a special fund last year that made Christmas an enjoyable event for the less fortunate of our community.

Pearlie arrived in town along with Mr. and Mrs. Smoke Jensen in order to have overturned the unjust conviction of Rusty Abernathy and to free, from illegal incarceration, Pearlie's sister, the above mentioned Kate Abernathy.

Shortly after Smoke and Sally left, Willis came into the saloon, and he saw everyone laughing and toasting each other. Seeing the marshal, the mood changed quickly.

"Is there something we can help you with, Marshal?" Kate asked.

Willis pointed to the glasses several were holding. "What's that stuff you're all drinkin'?" he asked.

"It's champagne. We're celebrating my trial, Marshal," Pearlie said. "You may not have gotten the word yet, but I was tried and found innocent of all charges. So that reward poster that Witherspoon had put out is worthless."

"Yeah," Willis said. "I got a telegram tellin' me that." He looked over toward Kate.

"Have a glass with us, Marshal. Help us celebrate," Kate invited.

"A beer's fine," Willis replied with a growl.

As the others continued to celebrate, Willis stood alone at the bar, finished his beer, then left.

"You know what, Pearlie? I don't think the new marshal was all that interested in celebrating you being found innocent of all those old charges," Cal said.

"It didn't appear like he was, did it?" Pearlie replied with a chuckle.

"Hey, Cal," Rusty said a moment later when Dolly returned to work. "Dolly's birthday is tomorrow. Did you know that?"

"No, I didn't know."

"Yeah, she just told me. I'd like to buy her a birthday present. Would you come with me to help me pick something out for her?"

"Yeah, sure."

When Cal and Rusty left the saloon, they had to wait for a rider to pass before they could cross the street. The rider was Dingus Lomax who had just arrived in town twelve hundred and fifty dollars wealthier than he was when he woke up this morning. He hadn't actually been paid the reward yet, but he was told that the money would be waiting for him in the Bank of Wild Horse within three days. He decided that, while waiting on that money, he might as well investigate the twenty-five hundred dollars that was being offered for Fontaine, and for that, he had to come to Etholen.

If he could find Fontaine, that would make today the best payday he had ever had. And he decided that the best place to start would be with Marshal Witherspoon, since his name was on the dodger. Tying up in front of the city marshal's office, he stepped inside.

"You Marshal Witherspoon?" Lomax asked.

"Witherspoon is dead. I'm the marshal now," Willis said. "Who's askin'?"

"Lomax is the name." Lomax took the reward poster from his shirt pocket. "Tell me, Marshal, what do you know about this man, Fontaine? It says that Witherspoon is the one that's a' wantin' 'im. Bein' as you're the new marshal, are you a' wantin' 'im, too? Or has somebody done brung 'im in?"

"There ain't nobody brung 'im in yet, but . . ."

Willis was about to tell Lomax that the reward posters were being withdrawn, but he changed his mind. He knew that Atwood wanted Pearlie taken care of . . . so why not let Lomax do it?

Glancing down toward his desk, Willis saw the newspaper article proclaiming Pearlie's innocence, and he turned the paper over so that the story wasn't visible.

"But what?" Lomax asked.

"But there don't nobody need to bring 'im in 'cause he's here, in town, now," Willis said.

"He's here? You mean, you got 'im in jail?"

"No, he ain't in jail."

"Well, if he's in town, 'n he ain't in jail, how come it is that you ain't arrested him?"

"I was fixin' to go over 'n arrest 'im, but the onliest thing is, bein' as I'm the law, I can't collect on the reward. So I was thinkin' . . ."

"I know what you was thinkin'," Lomax said. "You was thinkin' that if you let me bring 'im in, that maybe I'd give you some of the reward money."

"Yeah, that's what I was thinkin' all right."

"Only thing is, if you know anything about me, you know I don't bring 'em in alive."

"Oh?"

"This here poster says dead or alive, don't it?"

"Yes."

"That means that when I bring 'em in, he'll be dead."

Willis nodded. "Yes, well, like you said, the reward is for dead or alive."

"Where is he?"

"If I tell you where to find 'im, I'll be expectin' some of the money."

"I'll give you two hunnert and fifty dollars."

"Uh-uh. Fontaine is worth twenty-five hunnert dollars. I want five hunnert."

Willis knew that there was no reward being offered, but he carried out the charade because he wanted Lomax to think that the poster was valid. That way Lomax would kill Fontaine. And because Atwood wanted Fontaine taken care of, Willis was reasonably sure that after he explained how it was all set up, the rancher would be generous to him, if not to Lomax.

"How 'bout if I give you three hunnert dollars?" Lomax asked. He smiled. "And all you have to do to earn that is sit here 'n wait for me to kill 'im for you."

"All right. He's in the Pretty Girl and Happy Cowboy Saloon," Willis said.

"What's he look like?"

"He's wearing a low-crown black hat with a silver band around it. 'N he's got on a yeller shirt."

CHAPTER 25

When he went into the Pretty Girl and Happy Cowboy Saloon a few minutes later, Lomax saw the man Willis had described. He was fairly tall, but then to Lomax, who was only five feet four inches, everyone was tall. The man Lomax saw was also wearing a yellow shirt, and though he wasn't the only one in the saloon with a yellow shirt, he was the only one with a yellow shirt and a black, low-crowned hat with a silver hatband.

"Yes, sir, what can I get for you?" the bartender asked, stepping down to greet Lomax as he stepped up to the bar.

"Whiskey," Lomax replied. He thought about asking the bartender if the man at the other end of the bar was Pearlie Fontaine, and he knew that someone with less experience would probably do just that. But he also knew if he did ask, it would draw attention to him, and, in his business, that wasn't something you wanted to do.

Because Lomax was nearly as good with a knife as he was with a pistol, that was sometimes his weapon of preference. It was more stealthy than a pistol, and as the reward poster specifically said, "dead or alive," there was no need to give his quarry any warning. Rewards were paid no matter how the subject was killed, and that same reward poster would insulate him against any murder charge, no matter how he killed him.

The knife was perfectly balanced for throwing, and, slowly and without being observed, Lomax pulled the blade from its sheath. He held the knife down by his side, waiting for the opportunity to present itself.

"You know what I think?" Pearlie was asking Peterson. "I think my nephew has his cap set for Dolly."

"You just now noticing that are you, Pearlie?" Cletus asked from the other end of the bar. "Why ole' Rusty's been sniffing around that little ole' girl ever since she come here. Ever'body knows that."

Pearlie turned toward Cletus, momentarily showing his back to Lomax.

"Well, you can't blame him, can you, Cletus? I mean she is a pretty little thing, and . . ." Pearlie raised his hand and when he did, he spilled some of his drink on his shirt. "Damn," he said about the spill. He took a step back from the bar to wipe it off, just as something flashed by in front of him. It was a knife! The blade buried itself about half an inch into the bar with a thocking sound, the handle vibrating back and forth. It missed him, only because of the fortuitous spill that had caused him to move.

Instantly, Pearlie drew his pistol and turned toward the direction from which the knife had come. He saw a man with a gun in his hand standing at the other end of the bar. However, when the man saw how quickly Pearlie had drawn, he held his hands up, letting the pistol dangle from its trigger guard.

"No, no," he said. "Don't shoot, mister. Don't shoot!"

"Why the hell not?" Pearlie growled. "If you would've had your way, that knife would be sticking out of me instead of the bar."

"No, it wouldn't. If I'da been throwin' it at you, I woulda hit you. I was just wanting to get your attention is all," the man said.

That was a lie; Lomax had every expectation of seeing the knife plunge into Pearlie's back, and it would have had not Pearlie moved at that precise moment.

"Well, you got it," Pearlie said. "Now, what do you want?"

"Is your name Wesley Fontaine? You go by Pearlie?"

"Yep. Who are you?"

"The name is Lomax. Dingus Lomax. And I just wanted to make sure you was who I thought you was, is all. We need to talk."

"What do you want to talk about?" Pearlie asked.

"Oh, first one thing, then the other," Lomax replied.

"Mister, you aren't making a lick of sense," Pearlie said. "But if we're goin' to talk, I'd feel better if you hand that gun over to me."

"I can't do that, 'less I put my hands down."

"You can lower them."

Lomax lowered his hands, smiled, then slowly turned the pistol around so that the butt was pointing toward Pearlie. Pearlie had started across the floor for the gun, but before he went half a step, Lomax executed as neat a border roll as Pearlie had ever seen. Pearlie wasn't often caught by surprise, but this time he was . . . not only by the fact that Lomax would try such a thing, but by the skill with which Lomax was able to do it.

Pearlie had relaxed his own position to the point where he had actually let the hammer down on his pistol and even lowered the gun. Now he had to raise the gun back into line while, at the same time, cocking it. And he was slowed by the fact that he first had to react to Lomax's unexpected action.

The quiet room was suddenly shattered with the roar of two pistols snapping firing caps and exploding powder almost simultaneously. The bar patrons, also caught by surprise, yelled and dived, or scrambled for cover. White gunsmoke billowed out in a cloud that filled the center of the room, momentarily obscuring everything.

As the smoke began to clear, Lomax stared through the white cloud, smiling broadly at Pearlie.

"I'll be damn," he said. "I'm goin' to wind up in the boot hill of someplace I ain't never even heard of before today."

The smile left his face, his eyes glazed over, and he pitched forward, his gun clattering to the floor.

Pearlie stood ready to fire a second shot if needed, but a second shot wasn't necessary. He looked down at Lomax for a moment, then holstered his pistol.

"Pearlie! Are you all right?" Kate asked. She had been back in her office when the shooting happened and, coming out quickly, was now standing next to her brother.

"You didn't know that fella, did you, Pearlie?" Peterson asked. The shooting had all happened so fast that neither Peterson nor anyone else in the saloon had had the opportunity to get out of the way.

"I never saw him before in my life," Pearlie said.

Cletus walked over to the body, squatted down beside it, then pulled a piece of paper from Lomax's pocket.

"Here's what this was all about, Pearlie," Cletus said. "Looks like this feller didn't get the word that you ain't wanted no more."

Pearlie looked at the reward dodger. "I can see right now that a court order calling them back isn't going to mean there's an end to it."

"You think she'll like this?" Rusty asked, holding up a cameo broach.

"Yes, I don't know why she wouldn't, it's really . . ." that was as far as Cal got in his response before they heard gunshots.

"That was from Mama's place!" Rusty said. He lay the broach back down and he and Cal ran across the street and into the Pretty Girl and Happy Cowboy Saloon.

As soon as they stepped inside they saw a body lying on the floor, with a few people staring down at it. Dolly and the other girls were standing down at the far end of the bar, looking on with horror-struck faces. Kate was next to Pearlie, with her hands on his arm, and the expression on both her face and Pearlie's left no doubt as to who did it.

"You did this, Pearlie?" Cal asked.

Pearlie sighed. "Bounty hunter," he said.

"Then you didn't have any choice. It's probably going to be a while, and I blame Atwood for putting out the posters in the first place."

"Atwood?" one of the bar patrons said. "The name on here is Witherspoon."

"Tell me, Doodle. Who controlled Witherspoon?" Cletus asked.

"Oh, yeah," Doodle said. "You're right."

When Willis stepped into the saloon a moment later, he fully expected to see Pearlie lying dead on the floor. Instead, the body he saw was the small, wiry man who had been in his office a few minutes earlier. He gasped in surprise and disappointment.

"What's goin' on in here?" Willis asked. "What's all the shootin' about?"

"This here feller just come after Pearlie," Cletus said, pointing to Lomax's body.

"You kilt 'im?" Willis asked.

"Yes," Pearlie replied without elaboration.

"You can't seem to stay out of trouble, can you, boy?

I mean you just got yourself cleared of one killin', 'n here you've done kilt yourself another 'n."

"I didn't have any choice," Pearlie said.

"Seems to me like ever since you and Jensen, and—" Willis paused, then glanced toward Cal—"this feller here, come into town, folks has been dyin' left 'n right all around you. And you always say you didn't have no choice."

"Willis, there were twelve people in here when this happened, and every one of us will swear that the man lying dead on the floor is the one who started this," Peterson said.

"You're askin' me to believe that Lomax come in here, 'n for no reason at all, just started shootin'?"

"How did you know his name?" Pearlie asked.

"What?"

"How did you know his name was Lomax?"

"Well, I, uh, just knew, that's all. He was a bounty hunter. Lot's of people know'd him."

"How did he know me?" Pearlie asked.

"What do you mean, how did he know you? Your name is on a thousand or so reward posters."

"Those posters have all been recalled."

"I just got the word to recall 'em today, there ain't no way in hell they could all be called in this quick." Willis smiled. "The thing is, boy, you're famous."

"My name, yes. But my picture isn't on any of the posters, so how did he recognize me? Mr. Peterson, did he ask you who I was?"

The bartender shook his head. "No, all he asked for was a whiskey."

"Willis told 'im who you was," one of the saloon patrons said. "Just afore I come in here, I seen that feller there," he pointed toward Lomax's body, "leavin' the marshal's office."

"Is that right?" Pearlie asked. "Did Lomax come to see you? Did you tell him what I looked like and where to find me?"

Willis's eyes darted nervously back and forth between Pearlie and the man who had reported seeing Lomax leaving the marshal's office.

"No, I didn't tell him no such thing. I mean, yeah, he come over to see me 'n showed me that dodger 'n all, but I tole' 'im it warn't no good no more, that they'd all been called back." He smiled. "I even showed him the story that Blanton wrote 'n put in his newspaper today. I don't have no idee why he'd a' come over here after you, seein' as I told him you wasn't wanted no more."

"Get this body out of my saloon," Kate said.

"What do you mean, get this body out of your saloon?" Willis replied.

"You are the city law now," Kate said. "When something like this happens, it is your responsibility to take care of it."

"You two," Willis said, pointing to two of the patrons in the saloon. "Get his carcass down to the undertaker."

"Why should we do that?" one of the men asked.

Willis drew his gun. "Because if you don't, I'll have to find somebody to get three bodies moved."

With grumbling compliance, the two men picked up Lomax's body and Willis followed them out.

"Maybe I had better go tell Smoke what happened," Pearlie suggested a moment later.

"No need to. I'll go tell 'im," Cal promised.

"Cal, before you go," Rusty called to him. "That thing I showed you a while ago?"

"What thing?"

"You know. That thing," Rusty said, making a head motion toward the street.

Cal realized then that he was talking about the cameo broach.

"Oh, yeah, that thing," he said.

"You think she'll lik . . . uh . . . that is, do you think it'll be all right?"

"I think it'll be just fine," Cal replied with a smile.

"Then I'm goin' to go get it!" Rusty said with an even broader smile.

"Smoke? Smoke?" The call was accompanied by a relatively loud knock on the door.

"That's Cal," Sally said. Fresh from their baths, Smoke and Cal were dressed now and about to go out for dinner.

Smoke chuckled. "You can always count on him to show up in time to eat." Smoke opened the door, but his smile disappeared when he saw the expression on Cal's face.

"Cal, what is it?"

"Some bounty hunter just tried to bring Pearlie in," Cal said.

"Oh, Cal!" Sally responded in alarm. "Is he . . . ?"

"Pearlie's fine," Cal said. "But the man that threw down on him isn't so fine. Pearlie killed him."

CHAPTER 26

In order to celebrate Pearlie's acquittal, Smoke invited Pearlie, Katie, Rusty, and Cal to have dinner that evening with Sally and him.

"Uh, Mr. Jensen, would you mind if Dolly came as well?" Rusty asked. "I'll pay for it. It's just that tomorrow is her birthday."

"Of course she can come as well," Smoke said. "And no, you will not pay for it."

They took their dinner at the Palace Café that evening, Sue Ellen Johnson putting them at a table that was long enough to accommodate all eleven of them, the extra numbers made up by the four other Pretty Girls from Kate's saloon.

The meal was enjoyable, and would have passed without incident, had it not been for three extraordinarily rude customers who were sitting at one of the other tables in the dining room.

"Hey, Clinton," one of the men said, speaking loudly enough to be heard at every table. "There ain't goin' to be no need for us to be a-goin' over to the Bull 'n Heifer tonight. Why put up with their whores, when all the whores from the Pretty Girl has come over here to us."

Clinton laughed. "Tell me, Reed, which one o' them whores do you like best?"

"I think I like that redheaded one down at the end of the table," Reed said. "What about you?"

"Me? I like that little black-eyed girl that's sittin' in front of the cake. Her name is Dolly, 'n I've had a few drinks with her, but she ain't never let nobody do nothin' but talk to her. What about you, Warren? Which one do you like?"

"Hell," Warren replied in a low, rumbling voice that rolled out across the entire dining room. "A whore is a whore, 'n I like 'em all."

"Who are those idiots, Katie?" Pearlie asked.

"I don't know their first names. The one with the beard is Clinton, the one with just the mustache is Reed, and the clean-shaven one is Warren. They work for Atwood."

"Yeah, they would," Pearlie said.

"Hey! If we buy you whores some coffee, will you come over here and drink with us?" Clinton called out.

Sally turned toward Clinton. "May I make an inquiry of you, sir?" she asked.

Clinton was surprised that the woman had spoken to him, even if he didn't know what she had asked.

"What?" he replied. "What is it you are wanting to do?"

"Please forgive me for not wording my question to your level of understanding. What I said was, may I ask you a question?"

"Oh. Yeah, sure, go ahead."

"I would be interested as to which characteristic Atwood most values in his employees. Would it be depravity or retardation?"

Clinton blinked his eyes several times. He had absolutely no idea what Sally had just asked him, but he did have an idea that she had just insulted him. When the others at the birthday table laughed, he knew he had been insulted and he stood up so quickly that the chair turned over and he started to reach for his gun. He stopped in mid-draw when he saw that Sally was pointing a pistol at him.

"You don't really want to carry this any further, do you, Mr. Clinton?" she asked.

Clinton stared at her for a moment longer, then reaching down he righted his chair and, once more, took his seat. Nothing else was heard from them until, about half an hour later, when the three men then left.

With the situation calm again, the celebration continued. That was when Rusty took the broach from his pocket and gave it to Dolly.

"Oh!" Dolly said. "Oh, this is the most beautiful thing I have ever seen. I'll be so proud to wear it!"

"Nobody will see it," Rusty said.

"What do you mean, nobody will see it? Why won't they see it?"

"Because, if you are wearing it, they'll have something even prettier to look at," Rusty said.

Dolly laughed self-consciously. "Rusty, you do say the sweetest things," she said.

When Willis rode out to Eagle Shire the next day to report what happened, Atwood invited him into the library.

"Who is the man you said Pearlie killed?"

"His name was Lomax," Willis said. "Dingus Lomax. He was a bounty hunter, and he come into town yesterday carryin' one o' them reward posters."

"So, you are tellin' me that all the reward posters on Pearlie haven't been pulled back, are you?"

"We've pulled back the ones that's still in town, but there is just too damn many of them still out that we ain't got back, 'n more'n likely a lot of 'em has done been took by bounty hunters like the one Lomax brung with him when he come into town."

"Did you happen to see Lomax before this happened?"

"Yes, sir, he come by the marshal's office to see what kind of information he could get from me about Pearlie."

"You mean to tell me, Marshal Willis, that a bounty hunter came to see you with one of those reward posters, and you didn't tell him that the posters had all been rescinded?"

"Uh . . . well . . . I thought . . ."

Suddenly, and unexpectedly, Atwood laughed out loud.

"You mean you ain't mad?"

"No, I'm not mad. You did just the right thing," he said. "Like you said, we can't call in all the posters, and if another bounty hunter wants to try Pearlie, or Smoke Jensen, well, who are we to stop him?"

"Yes, sir, that's just what I was thinkin'," Willis said with a relieved grin.

"I knew that Jensen was fast with a gun," Atwood said. "Now it would appear that Kate's brother, Pearlie, is also quite skilled with a pistol. So, even though there may be a lot of posters still out there, we can't depend upon them to get the job done, because if they attempt to face Pearlie or Jensen the result of such an encounter can be predicted."

"So, what do we do next?" Willis asked.

"Step out to the bunkhouse and have Clinton, Reed, and Warren come see me. I'll give them the task of taking care of Smoke Jensen."

"Why are you sending them, Mr. Atwood?" Willis asked, obviously disturbed that Atwood was giving the task to someone else. "What can they do that me 'n Clark can't do?"

"They can get killed," Atwood replied simply. "And right now it's to my advantage to keep you and Clark alive."

Willis frowned for a moment until he realized what Atwood was saying. Then he smiled broadly.

"Yeah," he said. "Yeah, I can see that. I'm all for stayin' alive."

"I thought you might understand," Atwood replied with a condescending smile.

"You wanted to see us, boss?" Warren asked.

"Yes. I understand you three men had an encounter with Smoke Jensen last night."

"Who told you that?" Clinton asked.

"I have ways of keeping track of things that I need to know."

"Yeah, we did. Well, it was more Jensen's wife than it was him."

"Yes, so I heard. She beat you to the draw."

Clinton held up his hand and shook his head. "Now she didn't do no such thing. She already had her gun drawed when she started mouthing off at me."

"Would you be interested in a little revenge?"

"Yeah," Clinton said. "Yeah we would. Or at least, I would."

"Warren? Reed?"

"She didn't pull 'er gun on me or Reed," Warren said.

"So, you have no interest in revenge?"

"Not particular," Reed replied.

"But, if it paid very well for you to help Clinton get his revenge, you might be more interested?"

Warren and Reed glanced toward each other, then smiled.

"Yeah," Warren said. "I think we might be."

"I told you men when I hired you that from time to time I would ask you to take care of a specific job for me. This is such a time. You would be killing two birds with one stone, so to speak. You would be taking care of a job for me, and you would be helping Clinton get his revenge."

"You said something about payin' really well?" Reed said.

"I did indeed, and I will make good on that promise as soon as you handle the job I'm going to give you."

"What do you have in mind?" Warren asked.

"I want you three men to kill Smoke Jensen."

"Smoke Jensen?" Reed asked, the tone of voice in his response showing his nervousness over the prospect.

"Yes, the way I have it planned, you will be killing Jensen and his wife. It should be an easy enough job for you."

"Mr. Atwood, I don't know what you know about this feller Jensen, but I've heard a lot about him," Warren said. "And believe me, from all that I've heard, he ain't all that easy to kill."

"His wife ain't goin' to be all that easy, neither," Reed added, "most especial when you think back on how fast she got that gun out."

Atwood smiled. "Yes, well, what if I told you that you wouldn't have to go up against either one of them? If you take this job, it will be as simple as shooting someone while they are lying in bed, in the middle of the night, sound asleep? Do you think you could handle the job then?"

"Asleep? Where are we going to find them asleep?"

"In their hotel room, tonight," Atwood said.

"How are we supposed to get to them if they're in a hotel room?" Warren asked.

"I will make all the arrangements you need. And I will pay each of you two hundred dollars apiece to do the job."

"Two hunnert dollars, 'n all we have to do is kill him while he's asleep?" Clinton asked.

"Not just him. You are going to have to kill both of them. Do you think you can handle that?"

"What about the law?" Reed asked.

"What law would that be?" Atwood replied. "I control

the city council, the marshal, and the judge. You don't have to worry about the law."

"Yeah, that's right, you do, don't you?" Reed said with a big smile.

"Mr. Atwood, I can tell you right now, you ain't goin' to have to worry none about Smoke Jensen no more after tonight," Warren said.

Atwood gave the men twenty dollars apiece. "Here's a little spending money for you while you're waiting."

CHAPTER 27

"I think Dolly really appreciated her birthday gift from Rusty," Sally said.

"Yes, I think so, too," Smoke said. "I mean, the way she took on about it. Especially when I don't think it was really all that expensive."

"Expensive? What does that have to do with it?" Sally asked.

"Well, I was just talking about how much she seemed to appreciate it, way beyond what it was actually worth."

"Oh, Smoke, for heaven's sake, just how obtuse are you, anyway?" Sally asked.

"Obtuse? What are you talking about, obtuse?"

"It isn't how expensive it is . . . it's that Rusty gave it to her."

"Oh," Smoke replied, then it dawned on him what Sally was actually saying, and he smiled. "Oh," he repeated, mouthing the word this time in a way that showed he really did understand it.

"I'm glad I don't have to explain in minute detail. It renews my faith in you," Sally said.

"I like it that Pearlie has been able to reestablish a relationship with his sister," Smoke said.

"Not only his sister but finding a nephew that he never knew he had," Sally said.

The conversation was taking place in their hotel room. It was too early for bed, so Smoke and Sally were sitting in the two chairs furnished by the room, with a table lantern lighting the distance between them.

"Do Kate and Rusty remind you of Janey and Rebecca?" Sally asked.

Janey was Smoke's sister, and Rebecca was the niece he never knew he had until he discovered her one Christmas.*

"Well, Pearlie finding Rusty does remind me of my finding Rebecca, I suppose," Smoke said. "But if you remember, Janey and I had managed to make contact from time to time before she died, and the contacts weren't always that pleasant."

"I liked Janey," Sally said. "I think that if the situation had been different, the two of you would have gotten along well."†

"Maybe," Smoke admitted.

"Smoke, do you think Atwood is ever going to leave Kate alone?"

"If you mean do I think he will have a change of mind, no, he won't. But it isn't just Kate. He dominates the entire town."

"What do you think is going to happen?"

"I think Atwood is going to push this town too far," Smoke said. "And when he does, the town is going to fight back."

"Will the town win?"

"Yes," Smoke answered.

A soft breeze came up, lifting the muslin curtains away from the open window.

*A Lone Star Christmas.
†Sally met Janey in Smoke Jensen, The Beginning.

"Uhmm, the breeze feels good," Sally said.

"Yes, I'll sleep well tonight," Smoke said.

Sally chuckled. "What do you mean, you'll sleep well *tonight*? Smoke Jensen, you sleep well every night. Why, you can sleep outside in the rain. I know that, because I have seen you do it."

"Maybe, but some nights are better than others. Put out the lantern and let's go to bed."

Cal also had a room in the hotel, but Pearlie did not. Kate had an apartment at the back of the Pretty Girl and Happy Cowboy Saloon, and she invited Pearlie to stay in the spare bedroom. On the one hand, Pearlie felt, somewhat, as if he had abandoned Smoke, Sally, and Cal. But on the other hand, he felt good at being able to reestablish a connection with his long estranged sister.

Smoke and Sally might have turned in for the night, but Cal was still at the saloon visiting with Pearlie, Rusty, Dolly, Linda Sue, and Peggy Ann. Linda Sue and Peggy Ann, like Dolly, were part of the Pretty Girls that gave the saloon its name. At the moment, all six were sharing a single table.

"Seems like Smoke and Sally are turnin' in earlier 'n earlier now," Cal said. "They must be getting old."

"Ha!" Pearlie said. "I'd like to see you say that to Miz Sally's face."

"Well, I don't mean old, old," Cal said. "I just mean older than me."

"Honey, seems to me like almost ever'one is older than you," Peggy Ann said.

"Darlin', don't let these boyish good looks fool you," Cal said. "I've been rode hard and put away wet more than a few times."

Peggy Ann laughed. "I'm just foolin' you, honey. I'm

sure you've had more than your share of experiences. But, you do have boyish good looks, and that I appreciate." Her words were teasing as she traced her fingers along his cheek.

"Well I'll be damn, Cal, who would have thought it? Peggy Ann just made you blush," Pearlie said with a little laugh.

"No, she didn't."

"Yeah, she did," Rusty said.

"Now quit it! I'm not blushing!" Cal insisted.

"Ya'll quit picking on him now," Peggy Ann said.

"Ahh, I'm not picking on him," Pearlie said. "Cal was just being modest when he said he had been ridden hard and put away wet. He could say more than that. Besides, he's my closest friend and he's saved my bacon more than once."

"I thought Mr. Jensen was your closest friend," Rusty said.

"I suppose that, by definition, you can have only one 'closest' friend," Pearlie said. "But in this case, the dictionary be damned, I have two closest friends."

"Me, too," Cal said.

"How long have you two been cowboyin' for Mr. Jensen?" Linda Sue asked.

"We don't cowboy for him," Pearlie said.

"What? But I thought you did."

"We are full-time riders for the brand," Pearlie explained.

"Isn't that the same thing as cowboying for him?"

Cal shook his head. "Most cowboys are temporary hands. Pearlie and I are not only full-time . . . you might say that we are partners with him."

"Partners? You mean, you and Pearlie own part of the ranch?"

Pearlie laughed. "No, we can't say that. But Cal and I have about a thousand head of livestock that we run on the ranch, along with Smoke's cattle. And he and I also have land claims that run adjacent to the Sugarloaf, and since they are without fences, you can't really tell where Smoke's property ends and ours begins."

The six visited for a while longer, then the three girls, declaring that they had to "earn their pay," excused themselves and began moving through the saloon, visiting, smiling, talking, and laughing with the other patrons.

"I know you two think it's prob'ly wrong for me to like a girl like Dolly," Rusty said. "But no matter what it looks like, she's not a whore. All she does is be nice to people."

"Rusty, there is no need for you to apologize for anything. I once had a, uh, friend like Dolly. Her real name was Julia McKnight, but her working name was Elegant Sue."

"Her working name? You mean she was like Dolly?"

"Yeah, only more so," Cal said.

"By more so you mean . . . ?"

"She really was a whore when I first met her."

"When you found that out, is that when you . . . what I mean, you said you once had a friend like Dolly. I take that to mean that you don't have her anymore."

"No, I don't."

"What happened?"

Cal was silent for a long moment before he answered. "She was killed," he said, the words barely audible.

"She was a sweet girl, Cal," Pearlie said, reaching over to put his hand on his friend's shoulder.

"Oh! Cal, I'm sorry! I didn't mean . . ."

"No apology needed," Cal replied. Then he let a smile replace the melancholy expression on his face. "Well, gents, I think I'll get on back to the hotel," he said. "I'll see you both tomorrow."

* * *

When Warren, Clinton, and Reed rode into Etholen that night, they stopped at the Bull and Heifer Saloon. They were met by one of the girls as soon as they stepped inside. The girl, who was known at Cactus Jenny, may have been attractive at one time, but the dissipation of her profession had hardened her features.

"Well, how are you boys tonight?" she said, flashing a smile. The smile disclosed a two-tooth gap, the result of a drunken cowboy. "Which one of you are going to buy me a drink?"

"Why do I have to buy you a drink?" Warren asked. "Seein' as how last time I was here you told me how much you love me."

"Honey, I love all the boys," Cactus Jenny said. "That is, I love 'em as long as they've got the money."

"Tonight, I got the money," Warren said.

Cactus Jenny smiled again.

"Don't smile so much," Warren said. "You can see where you ain't got teeth, 'n that ain't purty."

The smile left her face, replaced with a hurt look. "You say you've got money?"

"Yeah."

"Well then, let's just go upstairs." Cactus Jenny's invitation was even more business-like than usual.

Clinton and Reed watched Warren and the girl go up the stairs, then they turned toward the bartender and ordered a couple of beers.

"How long you reckon he'll be up there?" Clinton asked.

"About two or three minutes," Reed replied, and they both laughed.

"Atwood said he'd give us two hunnert dollars apiece," Clinton said. "You ever had two hunnert dollars before?"

"Not all at one time," Reed admitted.

"I ain't never had that much money, neither. What are you goin' to do with your money?"

"First we got to earn it."

"Hell, how hard can that be? I mean he'll be asleep, so it ain't like we're goin' to be a' callin' 'im out, or anything," Clinton said. "Besides which, if that bitch is lyin' there alongside 'im, I'm goin' to take particular pleasure in shootin' her."

"Shhh!" Reed said. "You want the whole world to know our business? Anyhow, from all I've heard about Smoke Jensen, this ain't the kind of job we want to mess up on. I know that I sure as hell don't want him comin' after me."

"How many men do you reckon Smoke Jensen has kilt?"

"I don't know. Twenty, thirty . . . maybe a lot more'n that," Reed replied.

"If he really has kilt that many, how come he ain't never been put in prison?"

"On account of folks say that ever'one he's kilt was tryin' to kill him."

"Like us, you mean?" Clinton asked.

"Yeah, like us. Well, no, not really like us. They say that he's some kind of a hero, on account of the way he is. They've actual writ books about him, did you know that?"

"No they ain't, you're just spoofin' me. They ain't writ no books about him."

"Yes, they have. I've seen them."

"Wow! You think we'll be famous after we kill 'im?"

"We plan on killin' the son of a bitch while he's a' sleepin', don't we? How's that goin' to make us famous? Besides which, when you kill someone like that, you don't particular want no one to know that you was the one to do it," Clinton said.

"Yeah, I reckon that's right. And I don't care how good he is with a gun, there ain't nobody that can shoot in their sleep."

"Shh," Clinton said. "Bartender's comin' back this way again."

"You gents 'bout ready for a refill?" the bartender asked.

"We'll tell you when we're ready," Clinton said. "Don't be botherin' us none."

"I'm just trying to be helpful."

"Yeah, well, don't be."

Chagrined, the bartender walked away.

"How much longer you think Warren's goin' to be?" Reed asked.

"I don't know he . . . wait, here he comes now," Clinton answered.

Warren joined the other two at the bar.

"Damn, Muley, you smell like a whore," Reed said.

"Yeah, well I just been with a whore, so what the hell am I s'posed to smell like, roses? Anyhow, that's better 'n smellin' like horse shit, which is what you two smell like," Warren replied with a broad smile.

"How was she?" Clinton asked.

"How was she? Hell, why don't you find out for yourself? It don't cost but two dollars."

"No, thanks. I'll wait till we do this job 'n get the money Atwood's promised us, then I'm goin' to go down to the Pretty Girl 'n get me one of the women that works down there," Clinton said.

"Them women don't do nothin' but sit with you while you drink," Reed reminded them. "They ain't actual whores, 'n they won't none of 'em let you take 'em to bed. Don't you 'member, they was all in the Palace Café?"

"Yeah, I remember, and I also remember how snooty all of 'em was actin'. But I reckon if I offered one of 'em enough money, she'd go to bed with me, all right."

"Ha! As ugly as you are, it'll take a lot of money," Reed teased.

CHAPTER 28

The three men moved from the bar to one of the tables where, for the next hour or so they "spent" the money they were going to get from Atwood.

"I'm goin' to New York," Reed said.

"What are you goin' there for?" Warren asked.

"You ever been around any of them Eastern dudes?" Reed replied. "Hell, you can push 'em around like babies. I figure if I go to New York 'n I've got a little money, it won't be no time a-tall till I got me a gang put together, 'n I can take anythin' I want."

"It'll take a lot more money than a couple hundred dollars if you're plannin' on goin' to New York."

"Well, who knows, I might just pick me up a little more money on the way," Reed said.

"I'm goin' to China," Clinton said. "I used to live in San Francisco, 'n near 'bout all them Chinese women is purty. Just think how many Chinese women there is in China."

"What time is it?" Warren asked.

Clinton pointed to the clock on the wall behind the bar. "Accordin' to that, it's near onto midnight," he said.

"You think the son of a bitch is asleep yet?" Reed asked.

"I reckon he is," Warren replied. He loosed the pistol in his holster. "What do you say we go get this job done?"

Draining what remained of their beers, the three men left the saloon.

"First thing let's do, let's get our horses took care of," Warren said.

"Hell, can't we just tie 'em off in front of the hotel?" Reed asked. "That way they'll be there when we come out."

"I think we'd be better off leavin' 'em tied off over on Center Street. That'll keep 'em out of sight, 'n we can slip through between the buildings of the hardware store and the feed store. There ain't no light in between the stores, so we can get away real quick."

"What are we gettin' away from?" Reed wanted to know. "Jensen will be dead, 'n the law is on our side."

"I think it would just be better this way," Warren said.

"I agree with Muley," Clinton said.

For now, the three horses were tied in front of the Bull and Heifer Saloon. After they were mounted, Warren, Clinton, and Reed rode as if they were leaving, then once out of town, they doubled back on Center Street, which was one block over. They tied their horses off on a hitching rack that was in front of the apothecary, then came back to Waling Street by passing between the hardware and feed store. As Warren had said, it was very dark between the stores.

"Damn, I can't see nothin' in here," Reed said.

"That's good; it means nobody can't see us, neither," Warren replied.

When they reached the Milner Hotel, they stopped.

"See anyone watchin' us?" Warren asked.

"No, the onliest people that's still up is all in one of the saloons," Clinton said.

As if validating Clinton's comment, a woman's high-pitched squeal, followed by laughter, came from the Pretty Girl and Happy Cowboy.

"All right, let's go in," Warren said.

Low-burning lanterns sat on a table, illuminating the

middle of the lobby but leaving the outer edges shrouded in shadow. The lobby was deserted, and the scattering of chairs and sofas that in the daytime were often occupied by guests were now empty.

Walking quietly across the carpet, the three men approached the front desk. The night clerk was sitting in a chair behind the desk. He had his chair tilted back on its rear two legs, leaning against the wall. His chest was rising and falling in rhythm with the snoring, which came in snorts, wheezes, and fluttering lips.

"What room are they in?" Reed asked in a low whisper.

"Atwood said they were in room two ten. That's up on the second floor, nearest the street," Warren replied. "Let's get on up the stairs, but be quiet about it." He pulled his pistol.

With guns drawn, the three men stepped softly back across the carpeted lobby and through the shadows until they reached the foot of the stairs. They were surprised when they reached the second floor, because in contrast to the lobby and stairwell, the hallway was incredibly bright. That was because there were four sconce-mounted kerosene lanterns on both walls, flanking the hallway.

"Let's get these damned lights out!" Warren ordered in a whisper, and Clinton went down one side of the hall and Reed the other side, snuffing out the lanterns one at a time. The hallway grew progressively dimmer as each of the kerosene lanterns was extinguished.

Sally had no idea what woke her up. One minute she was sleeping soundly, and the next minute she was wide awake, and alert. She had the strangest foreboding of danger, a sense that someone was close by, though there was nothing immediate to suggest that. Nevertheless, as she lay in bed she continued to experience a sense of unease. She looked toward the door, where she saw a narrow bar of light that slipped in under the crack. Had it actually dimmed slightly, or was this her imagination?

As she continued to stare at the light bar under the door, she realized that it wasn't merely an illusion, the light was progressively fading.

"Smoke!" she whispered. "Smoke, something is wrong!"

Smoke was awake instantly. "What is it?" he asked.

"I'm not sure."

Smoke needed no further explanation. Sally's intuition was enough.

"Out of bed!" he ordered quietly, and Sally reacted quickly. When Sally saw Smoke putting a pillow under the bed sheet, she did the same thing. She grabbed a housecoat, and when Smoke pulled his pistol from the holster that hung from the head of the bed, she drew her own gun.

Smoke moved quietly to the already open window, then raised it high enough so he and Sally could step through it. Their room opened onto the front of the hotel, and just below the window was the roof that covered the entry porch below.

"Out here," Smoke said, and after helping Sally through the window, he followed her out onto the roof.

"We should have slept out here," Sally said quietly and with an easy smile. "It's a lot cooler."

"Come on!" Warren said in a loud hiss. "That's his door down there!"

The three men moved silently through the now dark corridor toward the front end of the hallway.

"Are you sure his wife is goin' to be with 'im?" Clinton asked.

"Yeah, that's what Atwood said."

"Good. When the shootin' starts, she's mine. I'll show that bitch to pull a gun on me."

The conversation had been carried on in a very low voice as the three men made their way toward the room that had been identified as the room occupied by their targets. Now they were standing in front of a door to which had been attached, in white-painted tin numbers, 210.

"Shall we break it in?" Reed asked.

"No need for that," Warren said.

"How we goin' to get in?"

"Atwood not only give us the room number, he also give us the key," Warren said, holding it up for the others to see.

"How the hell did he get the key?" Reed asked.

"We're talking about Atwood, remember? He can get anything he wants."

Warren slipped the key into the keyhole, then turned it. It moved the tumblers, but as they were tripped they made a clicking sound that seemed considerably louder than any of them had expected. Startled, the three men stepped to either side of the door, staying there for a long moment to see if there was any reaction.

There was none.

"He must not have heard nothin'," Warren said, and reaching out to the cut-glass knob he turned it and, slowly, swung the door open. To his relief, it opened quietly.

"You two go in first," Warren ordered, making a motion with his hand. It didn't actually occur to the other two that by so doing, Warren was putting them in harm's way before he submitted himself to any possible reaction from someone who might be waiting just inside the room.

The room was slightly brighter than the hallway because of the pale moonlight that fell in through the open window. That allowed them to see the two mounds under the bedclothes, as well as a hat that was hanging from the brass bedpost:

"There's his hat," Warren whispered. "That means he's here."

"Of course he's here, I can see 'im in the bed," Clinton replied, pointing to the two covered mounds.

On a chair, near the bed, there was a dress.

"Look at that!" Reed said excitedly, pointing to the dress. "Damn, I'll bet she's nekkid!"

"Quiet, you fool! You want to wake them?" Warren said. He aimed at the bed.

"Now!" he shouted as he pulled the trigger. The other two began firing as well, and for a moment, all three guns were firing, lighting up the darkness with white flashes and filling the room with thunder.

In his room at the far end of the hall, Cal suddenly sat up in his bed. Those gunshots were coming from this very floor, and they were coming from the other end of the hall. Could they be coming from Smoke and Sally's room?

Cal reached for his pistol.

After firing three shots apiece, Warren called out to the other two men. "Stop your shootin'!" he shouted. "We've made enough noise to wake the dead, 'n the whole town is goin' to be comin' up here in a minute. We got to get out of here," he said. "Clinton, you check on 'em, 'n make sure that both of 'em is dead."

Clinton walked over to the bed and felt around, then gasped in surprise.

"Son of a bitch!" he shouted. "Muley, there ain't nobody here!"

"What? What do you mean there ain't nobody there? If they ain't there in the bed, then where in the hell are they?"

"We thought we'd sleep out here tonight. I mean, it is a

lot cooler," Smoke said. He was standing on the porch roof just outside his window, his large frame back-lit by the ambient light of the streetlamps.

"Son of a bitch! He ain't dead!" Reed shouted.

"Shoot 'im, shoot 'im!" Warren yelled.

With shouts of frustrated rage and fear, all three would-be assassins turned their guns toward the window and began firing. Bullets crashed through the window, sending large shards of glass out onto the porch roof. They found no target though, because Smoke had jumped to one side of the window as soon as he spoke, and by so doing was able to avoid the initial fusillade. The outside walls of the hotel building were of brick construction, so shooting into the wall beside the window would have been an exercise in futility.

After the first volley, Smoke leaned around and fired through the window. One of the would-be assassins went down as he stumbled backward into the hallway.

"Clinton! He shot Warren!" someone said.

"Come on, Reed! Let's get the hell out of here!" a second voice replied.

Cal had taken time to slip on his trousers before leaving his room and was moving up the hallway as quickly as he could. Although the hall lanterns had been extinguished, several of the doors had been opened, and the occupants were standing in the open door of their rooms. Some of them were holding lit lanterns, which cast enough light out into the hall for Cal to see his way.

"What is it?" one of the men asked.

"What's going on?" another questioned.

Cal saw two shadowy forms darting down the stairs, and he gave a passing thought to going after them, but frightened for Smoke and Sally, decided to check on their condition first.

When the remaining two men left the room, Smoke started to climb back through the window.

"Smoke, wait!" Sally called out to him. "You know they'll be coming out through the front door of the hotel."

"Yeah!" Smoke said with a chuckle. "Yeah, you're right."

"Smoke!" Cal shouted.

"We're out here, on the roof, Cal!" Smoke replied.

Cal hurried through the room to the window.

"Cal, watch your feet," Sally cautioned. "There's glass everywhere."

Carefully, because he was barefooted, Cal picked his way through the broken glass, then stepped out onto the edge of the porch. He no sooner got there, when two men ran out into the street.

"Hold it right there!" Smoke called down to them.

One of the men turned and fired, the bullet whizzing by Smoke's ear, much closer than he would have liked.

Smoke, Sally, and Cal returned fire, all three of them shooting at the same time, and the shooter went down.

The remaining gunman darted across the street and disappeared into the darkness between two buildings on the other side.

Smoke stepped to the edge of the porch, preparatory to jumping down into the street.

"Smoke, wait! You're wearing your underwear!" Sally said.

"Yeah," Smoke replied with a chuckle. "I suppose I am at that."

By now others in the town had begun to react to the shooting. Several men came out of the two saloons, and a few even came out from the houses that fronted Waling Street.

In addition to the few hotel guests Cal had seen during his traverse of the hall, others had been awakened as well, and now several of them were gathered in the hallway, asking questions.

"What was all the shootin'?"

"What happened to the hallway lights?"

"Good Lord! There's a body lyin' right here on the floor!"

Smoke knew that someone from the law would be here shortly, so he pulled on his trousers and boots, then put on a shirt. Sally took the dress from the chair and slipped it on as well so that, dressed, Smoke and Sally joined as many as a dozen of the hotel patrons out in the hall, where the lanterns closest to Smoke's room had now been relit. Cal, who had been wearing only trousers, borrowed one of Smoke's shirts before he, also, stepped out into the hall.

"Well now," Cal said. "Look here. This is one of the men who was giving us trouble last night."

"Smoke, you don't think they came here because I . . ." she was about to say because she drew on them, but Smoke held up his hand to stop her.

"No," he said. "I don't think that had anything to do with it at all."

CHAPTER 29

"What happened here?" the hotel clerk asked. "What was all the . . . oh, my goodness! Is that man dead?"

"Deader 'n a doornail he is, 'cause I just checked," one of the hotel guests replied to the question.

"Who is it? Does anyone know?"

"His name is Warren," Smoke replied.

"Make way! Make way! You folks get out of the way!" an authoritative voice was shouting as he came up the stairs. Deputy Clark pushed his way through the others until he reached the body.

"I'll be damn! This is Muley Warren," he said. "And the one lyin' dead down there in the street is Danny Reed."

"You know both of them, do you, Deputy?" the hotel clerk asked.

"Yes, I know 'em. They both ride for . . . that is, they rode for Mr. Atwood, out at the Eagle Shire Ranch. They don't ride none for 'em now, seein' as they're both dead."

"If they both rode for Atwood, what do you suppose they were doing here, in the hotel?" Smoke asked.

"I don't know what they was doin' here. Who kilt 'im, anyway?"

"I did."

"Damn, Jensen, that makes the fourth man you've kilt

since you've been here. Pardeen, Critchlow, and Conroy. And one of them fellas that come with you, the one called Pearlie? Why, he kilt one, too."

"Actually, I've killed five," Smoke said dispassionately. "Don't forget the one that's lying out in the street. I killed Reed as well."

"Wait a minute, Smoke," Sally said. "If there are two bullets in him, one of them is mine."

"I was shooting, too, don't forget," Cal added.

Smoke chuckled. "I guess that's right."

"So you might say all three of us killed him," Sally said.

"What did you kill 'em for?" Clark asked.

"Come in here, and I'll show you," Smoke invited.

Clark followed Smoke, Sally, and Cal into the room, where Smoke showed the deputy the bullet holes in his bed.

"We killed them because they came into our room and tried to kill us," Smoke said. "We're sort of funny that way."

"Wait a minute, if they come in here 'n put these bullet holes in your bed, how come you two wasn't kilt?"

"Yes, that has to be disappointing to Atwood, doesn't it?" Smoke asked.

"What do you mean, disappointin' to Mr. Atwood?"

"You did say that these two men worked for Atwood, didn't you?"

"Yes, but . . ."

"I believe Atwood sent them here to kill me. And not just me, but my wife as well."

"Or maybe you was just finishin' the job you started last night," a new voice said. This was Marshal Willis, who had just arrived.

"What are you talking about?" Smoke asked.

"I was told you got into it with these three men last night."

"These *three* men?" Smoke asked.

"Yes. Wasn't all three of 'em at the Palace Café last

night?" Willis pointed to Sally. "And didn't you pull a gun on 'em for no reason at all?"

"What three men would that be, Marshal?" Smoke asked. "There are only two men that I can see. Warren, here, and Reed, who is laying out in the street."

"Well, yes, but . . ." Willis stammered.

"You think there were three men who came to kill us?"

"Well maybe it was just these two," Willis said. "Thing is, they was three of 'em last night and I just sorta thought that . . . uh, maybe all three of 'em come in town together."

"To kill my wife and me," Smoke said.

"Uh, listen, you ain't goin' to leave town, are you?" Willis asked. "I'm goin' to need to investigate this."

"You don't have to worry about me leaving town, Marshal. I'm not going anywhere until this business with Atwood is settled."

"Settled? What do you mean, settled?"

"Settled," Smoke said, repeating the word without further amplification.

From the *Etholen Standard:*

ATTEMPTED MURDER THWARTED

Last night, as Mr. and Mrs. Smoke Jensen lay peacefully sleeping in their bed at the Milner Hotel, three brigands gained access to their room in the middle of the night. Once in the room the three men began shooting into the bed where they believed Mr. and Mrs. Jensen to be. Their nefarious scheme was foiled, however, because the Jensens, sensing not only their presence but their evil intent, managed to step out onto the porch roof, their room being at the front of the hotel, thus allowing their egress.

In the exchange of gunfire that transpired, two of the three attackers were killed, their names being Muley Warren and Danny Reed. The identity of the third man is unknown.

Reed and Warren were both in the employ of Silas Atwood, as was Jeb Calley, who readers will remember attempted to kill Rusty Abernathy. Marshal Bo Willis and Deputy Clark were also once employees of Silas Atwood, and one can't help but think that, though they are supposed to be servants of the public, they are still at the beck and call of their former employer. No villain in literature has visited as much evil upon others as Silas Atwood has upon our fair community.

"My name is in the newspaper this morning," Smoke said as he and Sally ate their breakfast. "I'm famous."

"Oh, for heaven's sake, Smoke, you have more than a dozen books written about you. You are already famous, so you don't need a story in a newspaper to make you famous."

"But you're famous, too, now," Smoke said. "Your name is in here as well."

"Let me see it," Sally said, reaching for the paper.

Smoke pulled the paper back from her. "Ha! Good to see that you have a little vanity."

"Give me the paper," Sally said again, grabbing it from him.

"'The two were having breakfast at the Palace Café. They had invited Cal, but he decided to have breakfast with Pearlie and Rusty.'

"Wow, he really is letting Atwood have it, isn't he?" Sally said when she finished the article.

"He hasn't printed anything about him that isn't true," Smoke replied. "This town is suffering under him."

"I just hope he doesn't wind up with his newspaper office damaged again. This time could be worse than the other time," Sally said.

"I've got a feeling that Mr. Blanton is not the kind of man who would let a little intimidation cause him to back away from printing the truth."

Of the three men who had gone into town to kill Smoke Jensen, only Tony Clinton returned to the Eagle Shire Ranch, and now, as Smoke and Sally were having their breakfast, Clinton was standing in the parlor of Atwood's house, nervously rolling his hat in his hands as he reported their failure to his boss.

"Let me understand this," Atwood said. "There were three of you. You attacked Smoke Jensen in the middle of the night, and you not only didn't kill him, but he, while asleep in his bed, managed to kill Warren and Reed?"

"That's just it, Mr. Atwood, he warn't in his bed. Him 'n his woman was outside, standin' on the roof of the porch, 'n when we went into his room, why they commenced a' shootin'.'"

"Still, there were three of you, which made the odds three to one."

"No, sir. They was three of 'em, too."

"Three?"

"Well, not at first. They was only Jensen 'n his wife at first, 'n both of them was shootin'. But by the time me 'n Reed got outside, they was three of 'em, 'cause another man had come out on the porch, 'n he was shootin', too. Me 'n Reed was outnumbered then, 'n when they kilt Reed, well, sir, I was bad outnumbered. Seemed to me like the best thing for me to do was get away, so's I could come back here 'n tell you what happened."

"If this happened last night, why are you just now telling me?"

Clinton didn't tell him when he first returned, because he was afraid to tell him.

"Well, I, uh, didn't want to wake you up, it bein' in the middle of the night 'n all."

"Well, I didn't need you to tell me what happened, anyway," Atwood said. "Something like this, everybody in town will soon know, and it would get back to me."

"Does this mean I ain't goin' to get none of that money you was talkin' about?"

"Did you kill him, Clinton?" Atwood asked challengingly.

"Why no, sir, we didn't kill him. It's like I told you, he wound up killin' Warren and Reed instead."

"Then what makes you think I would give you anything? I've a good notion to take back the twenty dollars I did give you. The only way you can get the money I promised is by doing the job I asked. Would you like to go into town and try again?"

"No, sir, I wouldn't like that a-tall," Clinton said.

"I didn't think you would. But it makes me wonder, just what in the hell is it going to take to kill Smoke Jensen?" Atwood asked.

Slim wasn't proud to be riding for the Eagle Shire, and he knew that some of the other cowboys weren't, either. Most of them, that is, the real cowboys, had ridden for legitimate spreads before. It may have been that, from time to time they might have put a running brand on a few new calves that didn't exactly belong to the spread, or thrown an occasional long rope . . . but none of them had ever before worked for a man who was as ruthless as Silas Atwood. But they felt they had no choice. Atwood was so successful in his ruthlessness . . . that there was no place else for them to work, unless they left West Texas entirely.

Slim had seen Warren, Clinton, and Reed leave last night, but this morning only Clinton seemed to be around. He wondered what happened to the other two men, but there was no way he was going to ask Clinton. Slim tended to avoid the men who lived in the special bunkhouse as much as he could. He wasn't sure what they did, and not long after he came to work at Eagle Shire, he asked some of the older hands about the mysterious group of men who occupied the other bunkhouse. It appeared to him that they did nothing for their pay, but he was told that it would be better if he didn't ask questions.

He was working on the windmill when he saw Bo Willis come riding up. Until very recently, Willis had been one of the men who lived in the special bunkhouse, but now he was the new marshal in town. Slim couldn't help but wonder how Willis had ever gotten the job. Slim's idea of a lawman was someone who looked out for the people, and from what he knew of Willis, the new man didn't give a damn about the people.

"Did Clinton come back here, or did he run off?" Willis asked.

"He came back," Atwood said.

"I wasn't sure he would, after what happened last night. I reckon he told you."

"Yes."

"Jensen kilt Warren and Reed."

Atwood had answered in the affirmative, but Willis didn't want to be denied the pleasure of telling him specifically.

"Yes, sir, he kilt Warren just outside his hotel room, 'n he shot Reed after Reed run out of the hotel 'n was already down on the street. Shot 'im from his hotel room, he did."

"Clinton said there were three of them shooting at him and Reed."

"Yeah, they was. Jensen, his wife, 'n one of them two fellers that come to town with 'em."

"His wife was one of the shooters?"

Willis nodded. "I expect she's right good with a gun. From what I heard, when Clinton 'n the others started raggin' on them whores from the Pretty Girl Saloon, why, Jensen's wife draw'd her gun quicker 'n Clinton did."

"So, what you are saying is it isn't just Jensen and Pearlie we have to worry about. It's four of 'em."

"Yeah. Well, I don't know how good the youngest one is, the one they call Cal. But turns out he was one of the ones shootin' last night."

"I expect he is about as good as the others."

"Yes, sir, I expect so, too."

"You know what I think?" Atwood asked. "I think you need some more deputies."

"What do you mean, I need more? Witherspoon never had but one deputy."

"Yes, but Witherspoon didn't have three, and maybe four gunmen to deal with. And Witherspoon wasn't collecting the special taxes."

"What special taxes?"

"The special taxes we'll need so I can pay you and your new deputies more money."

Willis smiled. "I like the idea of more money," he said. "But I don't understand what kind of special taxes you're talkin' about."

"We'll call it the Law Enforcement Capitalization tax. I'll have the city council put on the new tax for the protection of the citizens of Etholen. It will apply to all the citizens in the town in order to pay all the extra deputies you're going to put on," Atwood said. He smiled. "And you'll need the extra deputies to collect the taxes."

"Do you think the city council will go along with this new tax?"

"Of course they will, when they learn that the new taxes will allow the council members to be compensated for their service to the community."

Willis laughed. "Yeah," he said. "Yeah, I can see where they might go along with that."

"When you go back into town, I want you to take Booker, Sanders, Creech, and Walker with you. That will give you five full-time deputies, and if it actually comes to a show-down, I'll provide you with some additional support."

"I'm pretty sure the six us will be able to handle just about anything that pops up," Willis said confidently.

CHAPTER 30

"All right, Willis, you called for a meeting of the city council," Mayor Joe Cravens said, when Willis, Mayor Cravens, and the five members of the city council were gathered in the city hall. "What do you want?"

"One of the first things I realized, after becoming marshal, was the need for deputies," Willis said.

"What do you mean, a need for deputies? You've got Clark," Mayor Cravens said.

Willis shook his head. "Just havin' Clark ain't enough. Maybe you ain't noticed it, but what with all the killin' that's been happenin' lately, why we practically got us a war goin' on here in town. It started with Rusty Abernathy killin' Jeb Calley. Then, his mama helped him escape. Then, the next thing you know Smoke Jensen come into town with Kate Abernathy's brother, 'n since they come to town, why they's been a lot more that was kilt, even Deputy Calhoun and Marshal Witherspoon."

"What the hell, Willis? You are the one who killed Witherspoon," Cravens said.

"Yes, 'n that's what I'm talkin' about. You might 'member that I kilt Witherspoon right after he kilt Calhoun, 'n with him still shootin' 'n all, why who knows who else he woulda kilt? 'N don't forget, Kate's brother was already wanted afore he even got here."

"It is my understanding that he was tried and found not guilty," Cravens said. "That means he is no longer wanted."

"Yeah, well, whether he's wanted or not, that didn't stop the killin', did it?" Willis said. "Two of 'em was kilt just last night. Smoke Jensen, his wife, and one o' them two fellers who come to town with 'im, shot 'n kilt Muley Warren 'n Danny Reed."

"After they broke into Mr. and Mrs. Jensen's room and tried to kill them," Cravens said.

"Could be. But even that proves my point," Willis said. "It's just that much more shootin'. Which is why we need to raise taxes so's I can put on more deputies."

"Raise taxes? Why, don't be silly, Willis. You know the town would never put up with having their taxes raised," Cravens said.

"It don't matter whether the town is willing to put up with it or not," Willis said. "The town don't have nothin' to say about it. All it needs is a vote by the city council to pass it."

Mayor Cravens sighed, then looked at Jay Kinder, who was Speaker of the City Council.

"I've got an idea that you are going to pass it," he said.

Kinder smiled. "And there's nothing you can do about it."

The first place to feel the manifestation of the new taxes was the railroad depot. Booker and Creech, two of the new deputies, set up a table in the waiting room of the depot, charged with the task of collecting a "visitor's tax" from all the arrivals.

"Visitor's tax? Why, I've never heard of such a thing," an arriving salesman said. "I travel to towns all over West

Texas, and nobody has ever asked me to pay a visitor's tax before."

"Well, it's the law here in Etholen," Booker said. "And you'll either pay it or get on the train and go on to the next stop."

"How much is it?" the drummer asked.

"The town charges visitors a tax of a dollar a day as long as you are in town."

"All right," the salesman said. "I've got too many good customers in town not to call on them. I'll pay it. I don't like it, but I'll pay it."

"You!" Creech called to a passenger who walked on by the table without stopping. "Get over here! We haven't collected the visitor's tax from you yet."

"What do you mean, visitor's tax? My name is Ron Gelbman, and I live here. I own Gelbman's Department Store and I have lived here for as long as the town has been here. I'm just coming back home from a business trip."

"Then you're lucky," Creech said. "You only have to pay the tax for one day. Iffen you was just visitin', you'd have to pay a tax for ever'day you're in town."

"This is outrageous," Gelbman said as he paid the dollar fee.

Very quickly, the rest of the town learned that the taxes weren't limited to the visitors. The new taxes had an impact on everyone, sales taxes upon purchases, operating taxes on businesses, service taxes on people who provided services, from doctors to blacksmiths, and from lawyers to whores.

That same morning, one of the deputies came into the Pretty Girl and Happy Cowboy Saloon. Seeing Cal sitting at a table with Rusty, the deputy walked back to them.

"You ain't a resident of this town, are you?" the deputy asked.

"No, I'm not, but I'm sure you already know that," Cal replied.

"What are you doin' here, in Etholen?"

"I thought everybody knew by now, Mr. Booker. This is a friend of my uncle, and they are visiting my mother and me," Rusty said.

"That would be Deputy Booker. So, what you're sayin' is, he is a visitor."

"Yes, I just told you, he is visiting my mother and me. But why is this any concern of yours?" Rusty asked.

Booker pointed a finger at him. "Now, don't you go gettin' smart with me, boy. I'll throw you back in jail for mouthin' off at a deputy."

"Are you aware of the First Amendment, Deputy?" Cal asked.

"The first what?"

"The First Amendment to the Constitution. It guarantees all Americans the right of free speech. That means that Rusty can say anything he wants to you, short of a physical threat, and you have no authority to put him in jail."

"Yeah, well, he ain't the one I'm concerned about anyhow. You're the one I'm concerned about. On account of because I don't believe you have paid your visitor's tax."

"My what?"

"Your visitor's tax," Booker repeated.

"What visitor's tax?" Rusty said. "I've never heard anything about a visitor's tax."

"That's 'cause it's a brand-new tax that the city council just put on today. We're collectin' from ever' man that visits the town. It's called the Law Enforcement Capitalization tax."

"How much is this visitor's tax?" Cal asked.

"It's a dollar a day, for ever' day you're here," Booker said. "Now, hand it over."

"You know what? I don't think there is any such thing as a visitor's tax."

Booker pulled his gun and, cocking it, pointed it at Cal. "You'll pay the dollar now, or I'll shoot you dead and take it from you."

"You'd shoot a man for a dollar?" Cal asked.

"It ain't just the dollar. It's the law," the deputy replied.

"Why do you suppose it is that I have the feeling you haven't always been such a stickler for the law?" Cal asked.

"It don't matter none whether I have or I haven't. Right now I'm a deputy city marshal, 'n I'm askin' you, polite like, to pay the taxes you owe."

"Polite like? Asking somebody at the point of a gun doesn't seem all that polite to me," Cal said. "But here's my dollar."

Booker took the dollar.

"Do I get a receipt?"

"What do you need a receipt for?"

"Suppose one of the other deputies approaches me and asks for a dollar? If I just told them I had already paid it, they might not believe me. So, I'd like a receipt."

"Yeah, all right, I'll write you out a receipt."

"Where are them other two?" Booker asked as he handed the receipt to Cal.

"What other two?"

"You know what two. The ones that come with you, Jensen and Kate's brother."

"They aren't in town right now."

"Where did they go?"

"It's such a nice day, I think they just decided to take a ride through the country."

"When they come back, you tell 'em they owe me a dollar apiece."

"They owe you a dollar?" Cal asked. "And here I thought the tax was going to the town."

"You just tell 'em," Booker said gruffly as he left.

"Who are you?" the rancher asked suspiciously, as he stood on the front porch of his small house, holding a shotgun. Smoke could see the anxious face of a woman, and a child, through the front window.

"Mr. Barnes, my name is Smoke Jensen. This is Pearlie Fontaine. Joe Cravens suggested that we come talk to you."

"Talk to me about what?"

"So far you've managed to resist having your ranch taken over by Silas Atwood."

"If you're here to make me another one of those offers to buy my ranch, you can just forget about it," Barnes said resolutely. "It ain't for sale!"

"You don't understand, Mr. Barnes. We aren't here to take your ranch. We're here to help you keep it."

In the office of the *Standard,* Allen Blanton learned quickly that his business was no different from all the other businesses in town when he was assessed five dollars for every issue he published. Unlike the other businesses in town, though, Blanton published a newspaper, which gave him a voice, and he was using it.

After he finished setting the type, he leaned back to read it. Because he could read backward as easily as he could forward, he smiled as he read the opening paragraph of his editorial, to which he had added a title reminiscent of an earlier time in the nation's history.

TAXATION WITHOUT
REPRESENTATION

Our forefathers fought a war of revolution against the British because they insisted upon taxing the colonies without giving the colonies any say in their own fate.

Unfortunately the people of Etholen are now facing the same thing because Atwood's bought and paid-for city council, in a closed hearing, which by its very nature prevented the attendance of our citizens, enacted a series of draconian taxes. That is, by any definition, taxation without representation.

These taxes, once they are fully implemented, cannot help but have a most deleterious effect on the economy of our fair community.

Blanton stroked his chin. Was "draconian" the correct word? Yes, he was sure of it. But would all his readers understand it?

He reached for the word to remove it, then had second thoughts. He smiled. Let them learn a new word.

Suddenly there was the crashing sound of glass being broken in his front window, and looking around in fright, he saw a brick lying on the floor. There was a note tied to the brick, but before he picked it up, he stuck his head out the front door and looked around in an attempt to see who had done this.

He saw nobody.

Stepping back inside, he removed the note.

We are watching you.

* * *

"This is all it says?" Willis asked after reading the note that Blanton had brought to him. "Just, 'we are watching you'?"

"Yes."

"Nobody said anything to you?"

"No. I didn't even see anyone," Blanton said. "I was about ready to start my print run when the brick crashed through the window."

"If you didn't speak to anyone, or even see anyone, how do you expect me to help you?"

"I don't know, but you're the marshal. Who should I ask to look into it for me? The doctor?"

Failing to catch the sarcasm, Willis handed the note back to the editor of the *Standard*.

"There's nothing I can do. I don't even know why you came to me."

"Neither do I," Blanton said, and again Willis missed the sarcasm.

CHAPTER 31

It was just before noon, and business was slow in the Pretty Girl and Happy Cowboy Saloon, with only one man standing at the bar and nursing a beer. Peterson was behind the bar, polishing glasses, not because they needed it, but because he was wont to stand there and do nothing. None of the girls were working yet, and the only other people in the saloon at the moment were Cal, Rusty, and Kate, who were sharing a table.

"It was bad enough when Atwood had Witherspoon and Calhoun to run roughshod over us, but now he's got an entire army to do his bidding for him."

"Well, to be fair, Mom, Deputy Calhoun wasn't all that bad."

"I know but he had his hands tied so that, even when he wasn't drunk, which was most of the time, there wasn't much he could do for us."

"These taxes may turn out to be a good thing, though," Cal said.

"What?" Kate asked, surprised by the remark. "What do you mean? How could anything good come from these taxes?"

"It might be just the thing needed for the town to fight back," Cal said.

Kate nodded. "Yes," she said. "You might be right."

"Say, Rusty, what do you say we go down to the Palace Café and have a good lunch?" Cal suggested. He glanced across the table at Kate. "Of course, that invitation includes you as well, Miz Kate."

Kate smiled. "No, I'd just be a fifth wheel, I'm afraid. You two go on, have a good meal, and enjoy yourselves. And tell Sue Ellen I send my regards, will you?"

"Yes, ma'am," Rusty said.

"There are four ranchers who haven't given in to Atwood," Rusty said. "Jim Barnes, Burt Rowe, Bill Lewis, and Tom Allen. I don't know how much longer they're going to be able to hold him off, though."

"Smoke and Pearlie are out talking to them now," Cal said. "I think once they know they have someone like Smoke on their side, that'll give them all the resolve they need."

"I've never met anyone like Mr. Jensen," Rusty said.

Cal smiled. "That's because there isn't anyone like Smoke Jensen."

The two were just finishing their lunch at the Palace Café when Sue Ellen came over to the table to visit with them.

"We made apple pie today, boys," Sue Ellen said. "Would you like a piece?"

"I'll say!" Cal replied. "With a piece of cheese on top, if you don't mind."

"Cheese, on apple pie?" Rusty said.

"You mean you've never tried it?"

"No."

"Miss Sue Ellen, put a slice of cheese on his pie as well," Cal said.

"What if I don't like it?" Rusty asked.

"Don't worry. If you don't like it, it won't go to waste. I'll just eat it for you," Cal offered.

Sue Ellen laughed. "Careful, Rusty, it may be that he's just setting you up so he can eat your pie, as well as his own."

"Ha! That won't happen," Rusty said.

A few minutes later the pie was delivered, and from the beginning, there was no question but that Rusty would eat it. He did so with relish, complimenting Cal on the suggestion and swearing that from now on, he would eat every piece of apple pie in just such a way.

They had just finished their pie when two of Willis's deputies came into the restaurant. Sue Ellen started toward them.

"Deputies Creech and Walker, can I help you gentlemen?"

"We've come to collect the tax," Creech said.

"Tax? What do you mean you are here to collect the tax? All my taxes are paid."

"We're talking about the new tax."

"A new tax? What is the tax for?"

"It's the Law Enforcement Capitalization tax," one of the deputies said. "You see, the town has added more lawmen for the protection of the citizens, 'n we're havin' to raise taxes to pay for it. Are you sayin' you ain't even heard of the new taxes?"

"Well, yes, I had heard that the taxes would be increased, but I assumed that would be from an addition to the sales and business taxes. I had no idea anyone would be coming around to ask for a direct payment. How much is this new tax?"

"It's ten dollars a week."

"Ten dollars a week?" Sue Ellen gasped in shock. "Why, that is insane! That would more than double the taxes I already pay. There is no way my restaurant can make enough to pay that kind of money!"

"Are you saying you aren't going to pay the taxes?" one of them asked gruffly.

"It's not so much that I won't pay them, as it is I can't pay them," Sue Ellen replied.

"You'll either pay the tax, or you're going to jail," the deputy said, reaching out to grab her.

"Let me go!"

"Let her go," Cal said.

"You stay out of this, cowboy. This woman is in debt, and what I do to her ain't none of your concern."

"You can't put someone in prison for debt."

"Who says I can't?"

"The Constitution says you can't. It's against the law."

"You know about the Constitution, do you?"

"I know enough to know that you can't put someone into prison for debt," Cal said. "Miz Sally taught me that."

"Yeah? Well, all I know is that Judge Boykin sent us to collect the money, or put her in jail, one or the other, and that's what I intend to do."

"Which one are you? Creech, or Walker?"

"Creech, but that would be Deputy Creech to you, cowboy. Who are you?"

"The name is Wood. Cal Wood."

"You're one of them that come with Smoke Jensen, ain't you?"

"Yes, I work for Smoke Jensen, and I consider him a good friend."

"You folks have caused nothin' but trouble ever since you got here," Creech said.

"Deputy Creech, I believe you said that you have come for ten dollars?" Cal said. He took a ten-dollar bill from his wallet and held it up. "Well, here it is."

"It don't do no good for you to pay it. It's got to come from her," Creech said.

"It will be coming from her. Miss Sue Ellen, this is for the dinner my friend and I just had."

"Wait a minute, you're givin' her ten dollars? I know

damn well there ain't no meal served in here that cost that much," Creech said.

"It was a very good meal, wasn't it, Rusty?" Cal asked.

"It was a very good meal. Especially the pie," Rusty answered. "Miss Sue Ellen, here's my ten dollars as well."

"I don't know what's goin' on here, but I don't like it," Creech said.

"It doesn't matter whether you like it or not," Cal replied. "You came here to collect a tax, didn't you? Well, here it is."

Sue Ellen came over to retrieve the money from Cal and Rusty, forming a silent "thank you" with her lips.

"Now, give these men their ten dollars, Miss Sue Ellen, so they can be on their way."

Sue Ellen walked back to where the two deputies were standing, and she held out a ten-dollar bill toward Creech.

"Here is your blood money," she said.

Creech started to reach for the money with his right hand, but he lowered his right hand and held his left out toward Sue Ellen. It was that gesture, using his left hand, and lowering his right hand so that it hovered just over his pistol, that put Cal on the alert. Suddenly, Creech gave Sue Ellen a shove, as his right hand dipped down to his side to draw his pistol.

Creech had a broad smile on his face, thinking he had put one over on Cal, but that smile left when he saw that Cal had beaten him to the draw. Both pistols fired at the same time, but Cal's bullet found its mark. Creech's didn't.

Creech collapsed to the floor, took a couple of gasping breaths, then died. Cal swung his pistol toward Walker.

"Hold it! Hold it!" Walker shouted, stretching his empty hands out toward Cal. "I ain't goin' for my gun!"

The shooting had happened so fast that none of the diners had had time to react. There were nine others in the restaurant, and they had been watching all the talk about the taxes, but when the shooting started, all were still sitting at their tables, shocked at the sudden turn of events.

"You . . . you're goin' to go to jail! You shot a deputy!" Walker said, pointing at Cal.

"Creech drew first, Walker, and you know it," one of the diners said.

"We all know it," another added.

"You wait till Willis hears about this. You'll be goin' to jail, 'n that's for sure," Walker said.

"Go get 'im. I'll wait here," Cal said.

"We'll all wait here," a third diner said.

Walker left at a dead run.

"Oh!" Sue Ellen said, putting her hand to her mouth. "This is all my fault!"

"Nonsense," Cal said. "They came in here to demand a tax . . . a tax which you paid, regardless of whether it was fair or not. Anyway, I'm the one who killed him, so I'm the one at fault."

"You aren't at fault, young man," one of the other diners said. "Everyone in here saw what happened."

"Yeah," another said. "Creech drew on you and he didn't leave you any choice."

At that moment Walker returned with Marshal Willis.

"He's the one, Marshal," Walker said, pointing to Cal. "He shot Creech down while Creech warn't doin' nothin' no more'n collectin' the tax like we was told to do."

"You're under arrest for murder!" Willis said to Cal.

"It wasn't murder, it was self-defense. He drew on me," Cal replied.

"He's telling the truth, Marshal," Sue Ellen said. "I was in the process of paying the tax when Mr. Creech shoved me, rather violently I might add, to one side and drew his pistol. This gentleman," she pointed to Cal, "was forced to defend himself."

"That's right, Marshal," another said. "Everything this man and Miss Sue Ellen told you is the gospel truth."

"Yeah? We'll just see about that," Willis said. He moved his hand toward his pistol, but stopped when he saw how quickly Cal had drawn his own gun.

"You know what, Marshal? I would feel a lot more comfortable if you and your deputy would just use two fingers on the butt of your pistols, take them from the holsters, and lay them on the table there."

"Look here, you can't take our guns!" Willis said angrily.

"I don't intend to keep them," Cal replied. "Just leave them on the table there. In a few minutes, after we're gone, you can send one of your deputies in to pick them up."

"Yes, I got a visit as well," Kate said when Cal and Rusty returned to the Pretty Girl and Happy Cowboy to tell what happened. "Deputy Clark has just informed me that we are to add a fifty percent tax to every drink we sell, plus a twenty-dollar per week business tax."

"Twenty dollars a week? We can't afford that, can we, Mom?" Rusty asked.

"Not for very long," Kate said. "I paid him this time, but I won't be able to keep those payments up, especially as the fifty percent sales tax is going to wind up driving business away."

"What about the Bull and Heifer?" Rusty asked.

Kate nodded. "Yes, I spoke with Bull Blackwell, he has been hit with the same taxes. So have all the other businesses in town, from Buckner-Ragsdale Emporium to White's Apothecary."

"It's just another way of Atwood trying to take over our place, isn't it?" Rusty asked.

"Yes, but he won't get it. I'll burn the place to the ground before I let him have it."

"What do we do now, Marshal?" Clark asked after he retrieved the pistols Willis and Walker had been forced to leave at the Palace Café. "We can't just let that feller walk free, can we? He killed Creech."

"We goin' to tell Atwood 'bout this?" Walker asked.

"We're goin' to have to tell him," Willis replied. "There's no way we can avoid it."

"He ain't goin' to like it. He ain't goin' to like it none a-tall. Especially since we ain't made no arrest," Clark said.

"There wasn't no way I coulda arrested him. He got the drop on us when I wasn't expectin' it," Willis said.

"I think right now he's over at the Pretty Girl most by hisself," Clark said. "We could go get 'im, all of us. There ain't no way he could do anythin' against all of us, against just one of him."

"Yeah," Willis said. "Yeah, you're right. And this time, we'll make sure we have the law on our side. I'll get us a warrant from the judge."

CHAPTER 32

"Didn't you just say that there were nine witnesses in the restaurant at the time of the shooting who would testify that Creech drew first?" Judge Boykin asked when Willis told him he wanted a warrant.

"Yeah, but what does that matter? You can just keep 'em from testifyin', like you did when Rusty was tried for killin' Jeb Calley."

"If we do that, Judge Turner will simply free him just as he did Rusty Abernathy. And I could wind up being removed from the bench. What good would I be, either to Atwood or you, if I'm no longer the judge?"

"What good are you now, if you say I can't arrest someone for shootin' one of my deputies?" Willis asked.

"Next time one of your deputies decides to try and kill someone, tell them to make certain they don't do it in front of a lot of witnesses."

"It just don't seem right," Willis said.

"If I were you, I would tell my deputies to continue to collect taxes from the businessmen, and cause as little trouble as you can."

"Atwood ain't goin' to like it," Willis said.

* * *

Smoke, Sally, and Cal were having breakfast in the hotel dining room the next morning, discussing the run-in Cal and Rusty had had with the two deputies the day before.

"I hope it doesn't wind up causing even more trouble for Miz Kate," Cal said.

"How could it cause any more trouble than my killing Atwood's man Pardeen, or Critchlow, or Conroy?" Smoke replied.

"Or Warren or Reed, who also rode for Atwood," Sally added.

"Yes, Creech is just one more."

Sally chuckled. "It may be that Atwood will be defeated by attrition. He can't have that many more men who are willing to die for him, can he?"

"Well, he still has the marshal and all his deputies," Smoke said. "That is, the ones that are left," he added, smiling across the table toward Cal. "And Slim Pollard says he has at least ten more of what he calls his special cadre out at the ranch. And if that's so, that means that attrition has taken out less than half of them."

"Oh, there's Kate," Sally said with a broad smile.

"And Mayor Cravens," Cal added.

"May we join you?" Kate asked as they approached.

"Of course," Smoke replied as he stood. Cal stood as well.

"Smoke, Sally, I brought Mayor Cravens to talk to you this morning, because he may need some help in the special election he is planning."

"You're planning to recall the city council?" Sally asked.

Mayor Cravens shook his head. "Unfortunately, we don't have the right of recall in Texas. But we *can* override the city council to repeal these new taxes they've put on the town. We can repeal them by veto referendum."

"By what?" Smoke asked.

"Veto referendum," Mayor Cravens repeated. "Our state constitution allows the citizens to call an election and vote on laws and ordinances passed by the state legislature, the county board of commissioners, or, and this is what pertains to us, city councils. The people can either vote to initiate a new law, or vote to repeal a law that's already on the books. In that case it would be called a veto referendum, and that's what we are going to do."

"Oh, that sounds wonderful!" Sally said.

"I just wished that women had the right to vote so I could vote for it," Kate said.

"Even if we can't vote for it, we can work for it," Sally said.

"Oh, I intend to do that," Kate said. "I plan to go around to see as many people as I can, to tell them of the election."

"Or you could have them come see you," Sally suggested with a smile.

"What do you mean?"

"You could have a meeting at the Pretty Girl."

"Yes, but I'm not sure we could get enough people to show up."

"Sure you can," Sally said. "If you had Rusty play the piano. And I don't mean just saloon tunes, I mean . . ."

"Yes! I know exactly what you mean!" Kate said enthusiastically. "Oh, yes, that's a wonderful idea. See, Mayor, I know they would be able to help."

By word of mouth, news was circulated that there was going to be an attempt to call a special election. At first, only those who could be fully trusted, and counted on to help with the process, were made aware of the plans. By mid-afternoon enough people had been notified that Mayor Cravens, who was behind the movement, suggested that the meeting be held.

At two o'clock that afternoon a sign was put up on the Pretty Girl and Happy Cowboy Saloon informing the public that it would be closed until four o'clock that evening. That didn't turn away too much business because it tended to be quiet in the afternoons anyway.

"Hey, Willis, somethin' is goin' on down at the Pretty Girl," Clark said.

"What do you mean?"

"I was goin' to go in 'n have me a beer, only they've got a sign up sayin' that it's closed."

"Closed? Ha! Maybe we've run her out of business. That should make Atwood happy."

"No, I don't think she's shuttin' down for good. Like I said, somethin' is goin' on down there."

"I'll check it out," Willis said, reaching for his hat.

As Willis approached the Pretty Girl and Happy Cowboy Saloon he saw that Peterson, the bartender, was standing just in front of the locked door. A couple of men approached the saloon, spoke briefly with Peterson, then left. Then, a third man approached and after a brief conversation, Peterson unlocked the door to let him in. Clark was right . . . there was something going on.

Willis watched for a moment or two longer, and he saw Peterson allow two men and two women to go inside. His curiosity getting the best of him, he decided this called for a closer investigation.

"Hello, Marshal," Peterson said, greeting Willis with a friendly smile. "Here for the concert, are you?"

"The what?"

"The concert. You know, Rusty isn't just a piano player, he is a concert pianist, and this afternoon he's going to be playing classical music."

"Why is the door locked?"

"To keep people from just coming in, in the middle of the concert," Peterson said. He held up the key. "If you are in there, you wouldn't want your enjoyment of music to be interrupted like that, would you? Here, I'll open the door for you."

"No, no, never mind," Willis said, holding up his hand. "I heard him playing some of that highfalutin stuff before, and it makes drops of sweat break out on me as big as my thumbnail."

"Oh, that's too bad. Rusty is quite talented, you know. We are very lucky to have a musician of his caliber here, in Etholen."

"I can't understand how anyone could like that."

"You're sure you don't want to attend the concert," Peterson said. "Why don't you come on in, I know Miz Kate would be happy to have you. I'm sure she can get you a seat right down front."

"How long do you plan to keep the saloon closed?"

"Oh, the concert should last for about two hours, I suppose."

"Two hours? Two hours of that caterwauling noise?"

"We'll be open for business again by four o'clock," Peterson said.

At that moment Barney Easter, who was the manager of the stagecoach depot, arrived with his wife. Easter glanced toward Willis, his face showing his curiosity, and just a little concern as to why the marshal was here.

"Hello, Mr. Easter," Peterson said in welcome.

"Hello, Ray. We're here for the concert," Easter said. Those who had been specifically invited to the meeting had been told to use this as their password.

"I'm glad you brought the missus with you. I'm sure she is going to enjoy the music," Peterson said. He opened the door, then glanced toward Willis. "Marshal, you're sure you don't want to attend?"

Willis waved his hand dismissively. "I'll be back when it's all over," he said, and turning, he walked away.

Easter chuckled. "I was concerned for a moment, there. You handled that very well."

"There ain't nothin' goin' on down at the Pretty Girl except a concert," Willis said when he got back to the marshal's office. "Rusty Abernathy is goin' to be playin' some of that highfalutin music this afternoon."

"And you mean they's actually some people that will come to listen to that of a pure purpose?" Clark replied.

Willis laughed. "You'd have to tie me to a chair to keep me in there this afternoon."

Inside the saloon Mayor Cravens greeted those who had come, and explained how the meeting would be conducted.

"For reasons I'm sure I don't have to explain, we need to keep this meeting secret," Cravens said. "That's why we are using the concert as our cover, and we'll actually conduct our business between each song."

"They aren't 'songs.' 'My Wild Irish Rose' is a 'song.' I will be playing opuses, symphonies, and sonatas, all compositions of renowned composers," Rusty said with a chuckle.

Many of those present laughed.

"All right, then, between each, would it be correct to say musical offering?"

"Yes, that would be correct," Rusty said.

"Very well, between each musical offering, we will discuss our business," Cravens said. He looked toward Rusty. "If you would, maestro, play your first, uh, selection."

Rusty's first number was Prelude Number 15 Opus 28 by Chopin. The conclusion was met with a round of applause, then Cravens stepped up to conduct the first bit of business.

"I want to thank all of you for being here," he said. "What we do at this meeting may be the first step in getting our town back."

"Mayor, as I understand it, we are going to have some kind of an election," Fred Matthews said. Matthews was one of the partners of Foster and Matthews Freighting.

"That's right. We're going to have a special election."

"How are we going to get an election called without the city council approval?" Matthews asked. "I know every one of those men, and I know that none of them are going with this."

"We don't need the approval of the city council," Mayor Cravens replied. "All we need to call, and to establish, a special election is a petition signed by ten percent of those who voted in the last election. There are forty-nine people present in this room right now. Three hundred and ten voted in the last election, so that means we'll need at least thirty-one of you to sign the petition. And while you are thinking about that, Rusty will play something else for us. What are you going to play this time?"

"My next presentation will be Symphony Ninety-Four by Haydn," Rusty said.

Just as Rusty began to play, Willis walked by the front of the saloon and, hearing the music, shrugged, then walked away. If there were some people in town who actually wanted to spend time listening to such boring music, let them. He walked down to the Bull and Heifer Saloon, which seemed to be a little fuller than normal this afternoon.

"You're doin' a good business today," Willis said.

"Yeah, well, with the damn taxes you people have put on us, I need to," Blackwell said. "Don't know why I'm so busy though."

"It's 'cause they're havin' a concert down at the Pretty

Girl," Willis said. "Rusty Abernathy is playin' some of that kind of music that just seems to go on forever. I reckon he's drivin' some of their customers away."

Blackwell laughed. "Well, I hope he plays all afternoon then."

Back at the Pretty Girl, the meeting continued.

"Tell me, Mayor, what do we do with this petition, once it's signed?" Barney Easter asked.

"We'll file it with Judge Boykin, and he will have no choice but to schedule the election," Cravens explained.

"Ha! A lot of good that will do. He's on Atwood's payroll, same as Willis."

"That doesn't matter," Cravens said. "We are going to make a certified copy of the petition and file that with Judge Turner, in the federal court. Since the right to vote is a federal law, he will be able to exercise authority over Boykin if Boykin denies the vote."

"How do we get a certified copy?" someone asked.

"It will be certified when Miss Delores Weathers signs it," Kate said.

"When who signs it? Who is Delores Weathers, and why would it be certified just because she signs it?"

"That would be me," Dolly said.

Everyone looked toward Dolly, who was sitting to one side with the other Pretty Girls that gave the saloon its name. And, as the other four Pretty Girls, Dolly was dressed in a way that emphasized her feminine attributes.

"You? How does your signing it have anything to do with it?"

"I'm a notary public. The petition will be certified as soon as I notarize it."

Mayor Cravens smiled and nodded. "That is true, ladies and gentlemen. Miss Weathers is, indeed, a notary public. If we are successful here, we can hold a vote next Tuesday that will repeal every tax applied to our citizenry since Willis became marshal. Rusty, you'd better start playing again, just in case Willis sends someone over here to check on us."

"All right," Rusty agreed.

Rusty's next selection was Symphony Number 6, Opus 68, by Beethoven.

The music not only provided cover for the meeting, it provided entertainment, and even those who were not used to listening to such classical selections found themselves enjoying the musical interludes between the business part of the meetings.

"Mayor, a moment ago you mentioned Willis. What about Willis and all his deputies?" Pete Malone asked.

Allen Blanton chuckled. "Tell me, Pete, do you really think those men have such a devotion to civic duty that they will continue to serve if they aren't getting paid?"

"They'll still be gettin' paid," Cletus Murphy said. "They'll be gettin' paid same way they are now, by Silas Atwood."

"Yes, but it must be putting a drain on him, or they wouldn't have introduced this draconian tax schedule," Blanton said.

"What kind of tax schedule?" Cletus asked.

"Did you read my editorial?" Blanton asked.

"Yeah, and you used that word in there, too. What does it mean?"

"Burdensome," Blanton explained.

"Well, why didn't you say so?"

"So, what you're sayin' is, all we have to do is sign our names on a piece of paper, have that pretty little girl over there sign it, too, 'n we can call this election?" one of the men said.

"That's all we have to do," Cravens said. "And by my count, there are forty-nine of us here, so there shouldn't be any problem."

"Mayor, didn't you say you need ten percent of the people who voted in the last election?" Smoke asked.

"Yes."

"Well you can't count Pearlie, Cal, or me."

"Oh, that's right," Cravens said. "Nor can I count women who are here." Cravens made another quick count. "There are fifteen women, and you three, that means there are eighteen here who can't vote, and that leaves . . . oh, my, we are right up against it, folks. That means that every one of you who is eligible to vote is going to have to sign. We can't leave anyone out."

CHAPTER 33

"Say, Joe, I hate to bring this up . . . but supposin' we sign this petition 'n get the election called, but it don't pass. That'll mean that Willis 'n his deputies is all still deputyin', 'n they're likely to come after those of us that sign, ain't they?" The questioner was Dave Vance, who worked at the R.D. Clayton stock barn.

"I won't lie to you, Dave," Cravens replied. "We may all be taking some risk in signing this."

"Some risk? Seems to me like we'll be takin' a lot of risk if we sign it."

"Dave, you've got to sign it," Cletus said. "You heard what the mayor said. We need thirty-one people to sign it, 'n thirty-one is all we got here."

"Just 'cause we all sign it, that don't mean it'll pass," Vance said. "If I was for sure it was goin' to pass oncet we hold the election, why I wouldn't think nothin' a-tall 'bout signin' it. But it seems to me like iffen it was goin' to pass, there ought to be more people here at the meetin'."

"Not necessarily," Blanton said. "This meeting was called on a spur of the moment, and we got nearly everyone we were able to contact. Besides which, the ballot will be secret, which means nobody will know how anyone voted, and can you think of anyone who might decide that they would want to vote *for* more taxes?"

"Yeah, well, that's all well 'n good 'bout it bein' a secret ballot 'n all. But oncet we put our names on this here petition the mayor is trying to get, why, that won't be no secret. Anybody who wants to know who signed it can just see our names there."

"They won't have to look up the petition to know who signed it," Blanton said. "I intend to publish every name in the paper."

"Why would you do a damn-fool thing like that?"

"Because I think it is a way of honoring those who are willing to do it."

"But puttin' our names on the thing means we are puttin' ourselves on the line, don't it?"

"Are you familiar with the Declaration of Independence?" Blanton asked.

"Well, yeah. Fourth of July and all that."

"The men who signed that document mutually pledged to each other their lives, their fortunes, and their sacred honor. Can we do any less?"

"No, by damn!" Cletus shouted.

"Dave, I know your history. I know that you put your life on the line at Antietam. You were there, weren't you?"

"Yes, but this ain't like that," Vance replied. "Then we had an army. We wasn't alone."

"You aren't alone here, Mr. Vance," Smoke said. "My friends and I have no intention of leaving here until Atwood and his men are no longer a threat to the town."

"There's your army, right there," Cletus said. "They've done took down seven of Atwood's men, all by themselves. Come on, I'll sign my name right next to yours, 'n I'll make my name bigger."

Vance paused for a moment, then he chuckled. "I didn't say I wasn't goin' to sign it. I was just commentin' on it is all."

"Rusty, perhaps you could honor us with another song . . . uh, I mean opus, while everyone is signing," Mayor Cravens suggested.

"Symphony Number Five, Opus Ninety-Five, by Antonín Dvořák," Rusty said.

As the music filled the saloon, Mayor Cravens sat behind a table and invited all the men to come up and sign the petition. Vance was the last one to sign, and several stared at him accusingly until he signed, making the total of signatories thirty-one, the minimum amount needed to bring about the desired result.

Mayor Cravens had them sign three copies: one to file with Judge Boykin, one to file with the state, and one to keep back, "just in case Boykin or Willis decided to destroy the petition."

Once Rusty's final presentation was completed, a smiling Mayor Craven held up the piece of paper.

"Gentlemen, enough signatures have been collected for the election to be held on Tuesday next," Mayor Cravens said when all had signed. "And this is the amendment for which you will be voting."

Clearing his throat, the mayor began to read:

"The ordinances and laws establishing the taxes created by the Law Enforcement Capitalization Act are hereby repealed. Only such taxes as the sales and property taxes that were enacted on August 1, 1877, concurrent with the establishment of the community of Etholen, will stay in force.

"This repeal will take effect immediately following the ballot count upon the day of the election."

"Yes!" someone shouted, and again there was loud and enthusiastic applause.

"Now, gentlemen, your task will be to contact as many

men as you possibly can, tell them of the election coming up next Tuesday, and make certain that they vote for it."

"Why do you address only the gentlemen present? And why do you limit the contact to the men only?" Kate asked.

"Mrs. Abernathy, I don't mean to be exclusive," Mayor Cravens replied. "But, in the interest of expediency, we must concentrate only on those who can vote."

"Joe Cravens, do you really think that the women of this community have no influence over the men who do vote?" Kate asked.

Cravens laughed, then raised his finger. "You have made an excellent point, Kate," he said. He looked back out over those gathered. *"Ladies,"* he said, coming down hard on the word 'ladies' "and gentlemen, contact everyone in town, men and women alike, tell them of the election, and suggest, strongly, that they vote for this amendment."

"Mayor Cravens," Blanton called out to get attention. "I will write an article about the meeting for the *Standard,* but in order to be assured of maximum publicity, I think I should also print off circulars advertising the election and post them around town."

"I think that would be a great idea, Allen. Tell me how much that would cost and I'll have the city . . . no, wait, there is no way we'll be able to get the city council to approve it. I'll pay for it out of my own pocket."

"We can take up a collection here to pay for it," Dave Vance said. "I'll put in my part."

Blanton shook his head and held out his hands. "Gentlemen, it isn't going to cost you anything. The cost of the paper and ink is negligible. All I need from this august body of community-oriented souls is your permission."

"I think, without fear of objection, that you have the universal approval of all of us," Cravens said. "As well as our appreciation."

"Hear! Hear!" several of the others called out.

* * *

As soon at the meeting and concert was over, Allen Blanton hurried back to the newspaper. The first thing he did, was print the circular he had spoken of at the meeting.

IMPORTANT NOTICE
to the CITIZENS OF ETHOLEN:

A SPECIAL ELECTION
TO REPEAL TAXES !
will be held on
TUESDAY, JUNE 8.

VOTE <u>YES</u> TO APPROVE THE MOTION.

With the circular printed, Blanton turned his attention to the story he intended to run in his newspaper. The next issue was due on the following day, and it had already been put to bed, but this story was important enough that he pulled the Associate Press article about the fire that burned the Whitney Opera House in Syracuse, New York.

Blanton didn't even attempt to write the story first before setting it. Instead he wrote the story and set the type at the same time. Then, the story having been set, he read over it to satisfy himself that he had caught the mood of the concert and the meeting.

OF GREAT CIVIC INTEREST
TO OUR COMMUNITY

Several concerned citizens of Etholen gathered at the Pretty Girl and Happy Cowboy Saloon today to hear a concert of classical music brilliantly performed by Rusty Abernathy. Mr. Abernathy, who is a concert pianist of exceptional talent, was in perfect form as he played selections by Beethoven.

But as it turned out, as great an event as the concert was, there was even more afoot. During the concert, a proposal was made that there be an effort to call a special election. The proposal was met with enthusiasm and support, and enough signatures were gathered on a petition to authorize . . . no to demand . . . that an election be held on Tuesday June 8. The election will be on a proposed amendment, which will have the immediate effect of rescinding the Law Enforcement Capitalization Act, thus relieving the citizens of Etholen from the crippling burden of taxes, which have been levied upon us by the city council.

In affixing their names to the petition, these brave men have assured a spot for themselves in the history of our city . . . and no doubt schoolchildren far into the twentieth century will be able to recite the names, which I now list:

Roy Beck, Lonnie Bivins, Allen Blanton, Rusty Abernathy, Arnold Carter, Mayor Joe Cravens, Andrew Dawson, Lou Dobbins, Dan Dunnigan, Barney Easter, Benjamin Evans, Ken Freeman, McKinley Garrison, Ron Gelbman, Bert Graham, Cole Gunter, Ed Haycox, Doodle Higgins, Michael Holloway, Roy Houston, Ed James, Robert Jamison, Gerald Kelly, Ray Kincaid, Luke Knowles, David Lewis, Pete Malone, Jim Martin, Ray Peterson, Cletus Murphy, and David Vance.

These thirty-one names are enough to guarantee the election will be held. They have done their part to free Etholen from the yoke

of oppressive taxes. Now, this newspaper
urges every citizen to do his civic duty and
vote "yes" on the amendment.

"What?" Judge Boykin said when Mayor Cravens put the
petition before him. "What is this?"

"It is a *mandamus* that an election be held on Tuesday
week, to vote on this act," Cravens said.

"What do you mean it is a *mandamus?* A *mandamus* can
only come from a superior court!"

"In this case . . . Your Honor"—Cravens set "Your
Honor" aside so that the words dripped with sarcasm—"it
is a *mandamus* from the people, and, as I'm sure you know,
in our form of government the people are our superior. This
is a petition with the required number of names, calling for
a special election. You have no choice . . . the election must
be held."

Boykin looked over toward Smoke, who had come to the
office with Cravens to deliver the petition.

"Is your name on here? This is your doing, isn't it?"

"Why, Judge Boykin, you know I'm not a resident of this
town. I can't vote, so if my signature was on there, it would
be invalid," Smoke replied.

Judge Boykin smiled smugly.

"I could just tear this up, you know. Then where would
you be?"

"We would be just fine," Smoke said. "We have sent a
copy to the state, and we have an extra copy. On the other
hand, if you would do something so foolish as to tear up
this petition of the people, you will be dead."

"What do you mean I would be dead?"

"Let me explain it to you. If you tear up that petition, I
will kill you where you stand," Smoke said calmly.

"What? You would say something like that to me? I am

a sitting judge, sir! A sitting judge! You wouldn't dare threaten me, sir! You wouldn't dare!"

Smoke chuckled dryly. "I didn't threaten you," he said.

"What do you call that, if not a threat?"

"I would call it a promise."

"Cravens, you heard him! You are my witness! I intend to serve him with a warrant for threatening to kill me. That is a ten-year sentence!"

"What are you talking about?" Mayor Cravens asked. "I didn't hear any such threat."

"That you, an elected mayor, would countenance such a thing as a threat against a sitting judge is unconscionable."

"Where are you going?" Smoke asked.

"I'm going to get someone to come in here as a material witness."

"No, you aren't," Smoke said. "You are going to sit back down and listen to what Mayor Cravens has to say."

"Well I . . . I never . . ." Judge Boykin sputtered.

"Sit down," Smoke repeated, but he didn't raise his voice. It wasn't necessary for him to do so.

"Go ahead, Mr. Mayor," Smoke said to Cravens.

"Judge Boykin, I am also serving you with a court order, setting aside the Law Enforcement Capitalization Act until its status can be determined by the election next Tuesday," Mayor Cravens said.

"Court order? What court order? I've issued no such order."

"Oh, I'm sorry, I should have been more specific. This order comes from Judge Turner of the West Texas Federal Court. And that means you will do it, sir," Cravens said.

"See here, you have no right to do this!"

"How is it that you are a sitting judge, and yet you know so little about the law?" Smoke asked.

"Don't you presume to lecture me about the law, sir," Judge Boykin said.

"I am a member of the bar, as you know, but don't worry, I won't. I could no more get you to see your duty than I could teach a pig to sing."

"I . . . I . . ." Boykin sputtered.

"We'll be going now, Judge," Mayor Cravens said. "We have a campaign to run." Cravens smiled. "Come to think of it, I suppose you have the same campaign to run. I expect we had all better get busy and let our republic form of government work its course."

Atwood held up the newspaper. "Are you telling me that the nonsense Blanton has printed in his newspaper is true? Is there actually going to be a vote against the taxes?"

Atwood was sitting in the parlor of his house, along with Willis, Clark, Judge Boykin, and Jay Kinder, Speaker of the City Council.

"I'm afraid so," Judge Boykin said.

"Can't you stop it?"

"How?"

"I don't know. Issue an order or something."

"If I did, Turner would just issue an order that would override it."

"Maybe if we conduct a rigorous enough campaign, we can convince the people that we need this tax base to keep them safe," Kinder said.

Atwood glared at him. "Are you serious? We are going to be able to convince people to pay more taxes? Why the hell did I select you as the speaker of the city council? My God, you are dumber than a day-old mule."

"Mr. Atwood, you have no right to talk to me like that," Kinder said, obviously stung by the harsh comment.

"I put you and the entire city council in office, Kinder. You belong to me. And that means I can talk to you any way I want."

"Well, what are we going to do?" Judge Boykin asked. "You're right, we aren't going to be able to convince them to vote against their own best interests."

"It depends on what you mean when you say convince them," Kinder said.

Boykin glanced over toward him. "What do you mean?"

"If they are frightened enough, perhaps they'll vote the way we want them to vote."

"We aren't going to be able to frighten them," Judge Boykin said. "Not as long as Smoke Jensen is here."

Atwood smiled. "My point, exactly."

CHAPTER 34

In all the time he had been in the newspaper business, Allen Blanton had only put out two "Extra" editions; one when Custer and his men were killed, and one when President Garfield was shot. Now he was about to put out his third.

EXTRA ! EXTRA ! EXTRA !

By court order the taxes demanded by the Law Enforcement Capitalization Act have been set aside. That means that, already, businesses that have been crippled by the taxes can reopen, and the additional tax burden upon the citizen has been lifted.

It is important to understand, though, that this relief is temporary, pending the outcome of the election on Tuesday. Therefore it is incumbent upon each of us to use the power of the ballot to make this relief permanent.

When the deputies learned that they would no longer be able to collect taxes, they saw it as an end to their gravy train, and they returned to the marshal's office to complain to Willis.

"I'll tell you right now, Willis," Booker said. "If the money is shut off, I don't intend to be a deputy anymore."

"Who said the money is goin' to be shut off?" Willis asked.

"Well, if we can't collect the taxes no more, just where do you expect the money to come from?"

"Mr. Atwood said not to worry, that he has come up with an idea. So let's wait and see what his idea is."

"You mean like his idea of havin' someone kill Jensen?" Clark asked. "Because that idea sure hasn't worked out, has it?"

"Just wait a while, and see what he has in mind."

Everyone responded to the upcoming election, as well as the court order setting aside taxes, by posting signs outside their places of business.

OPEN *for* BUSINESS *as before*
NO TAXES

The result was a flurry of business activity all over town, but no business bounced back as far as the Palace Café. It was so crowded that there was a waiting line to get a table. It wasn't just the businesspeople who celebrated the suspension of taxes, the mood of the town had greatly changed, and men and women strolled up and down the boardwalks, recognizing each other with smiles and friendly greetings.

Pearlie and Cal were nailing up election circulars all over town:

VOTE: **YES !**
to repeal taxes!

TUESDAY, JUNE 8

"How many more of these things do we have to put up?" Cal asked.

"I've only got about four or five more," Pearlie replied. "Why do you ask? Do you want to go get a beer?"

"Yeah," Cal said. "Let's go over to your sister's place."

Pearlie chuckled. "You're not fooling me, Cal. It's not a beer you're after. You just want to talk to some of the Pretty Girls."

"Well, that's why your sister named her place the way she did, isn't it?"

The two laughed as, with all the election circulars now put up, they started back to the saloon.

When they stepped inside, they saw Rusty and Dolly sitting together.

"Well now, Rusty, just how is this young lady supposed to earn her keep if she spends all her time with you instead of visiting with the cowboys?" Pearlie asked.

"She doesn't spend all her time with me," Rusty replied.

"Well, you can't prove that by me. Seems like every time I look up, I see the two of you together."

"Oh, she visits with the cowboys. But she spends her quality time with me," Rusty said with a broad smile.

"Would you like Linda Sue and Peggy Ann to join us?" Dolly asked, flashing a smile at Pearlie and Cal.

"Yeah, that would be nice. We'd like some quality time, too," Cal replied with a laugh.

Smoke and Sally were also in the Pretty Girl, sharing a table with Kate and Mayor Cravens. A burst of laughter came from the table where Pearlie and Cal were holding court.

"It's good to see people laughing again. I've not seen a mood this ebullient since Atwood started taking over everything," Cravens said.

"It's because of Smoke," Kate said. "He, my brother, and Cal came riding in on white horses, dressed in shining armor, and nothing has been the same since."

"And don't forget Mrs. Jensen," Mayor Cravens said. "She is the one who has taken our fight to the courts."

"There's no way I'm going to leave Sally out of this," Kate said. "If Smoke, Pearlie, and Cal are knights in shining armor, Sally is the crown princess they serve."

"Let's not celebrate too early," Smoke said. "We've had a few victories against Atwood, but I don't think he's ready to give up just yet."

"Oh, believe me, I know you are right," Mayor Cravens said. "But we have had so few victories against this . . . tyrant, is the only way I can think of him, that it is good to celebrate the ones that we do have."

Unlike Kate Abernathy, Silas Atwood didn't see Smoke Jensen as a knight in shining armor. But like the owner of the Pretty Girl and Happy Cowboy Saloon, he did see Jensen as the architect of the resistance that he was now facing. The court-ordered revocation of the Law Enforcement Capitalization Act, and the upcoming election, which would surely overturn it, was the latest setback.

From shortly after Jensen arrived, Atwood had correctly assessed him as a problem and had tried to eliminate the problem by eliminating Jensen. And the only way to eliminate Jensen was to kill him. So far every effort had failed, and Atwood was beginning to believe all he had heard about Smoke Jensen. Jensen wasn't a man who could be bested in a gunfight. If he was going to be killed, Atwood was going to have to come up with another way, but just what way would that be?

* * *

José Bustamante was a killer, but he was not a gunman in the classic sense. He was an assassin, pure and simple. When Bustamante learned there was a wealthy Texan who was willing to pay well to have someone killed, he started to contact him but decided instead to just go see him. Thus it was that, when he arrived at Atwood's house, he was unexpected. Dismounting in front of Atwood's house, one that Bustamante would call *casa grande,* he didn't bother to knock on the door. Instead, he sat on the porch swing and remained there for well over half an hour before Atwood, who had no idea that Bustamante was there, came outside.

"Who are you?" Atwood gasped when he saw a Mexican sitting cross-legged on his swing, a *sombrero* resting on his knee.

"I am Bustamante."

"How dare you sit on my front porch without permission. What are you doing here?"

"You sent for me, señor."

"What are you talking about? I didn't send for you."

Bustamante took a piece of paper from his pocket and showed it to Atwood. It was a letter Atwood had written to an acquaintance, an acquaintance he could trust.

> *From time to time in my business, I may have occasion to use a person who is possessed of a particular talent, as well as the predilection to use it without question or compunction. If you know such a person I would be most anxious to hire him.*

Atwood had sent the letter, but he had sent it six months earlier, long before Smoke Jensen had arrived on the scene. As it turned out, this was exactly one of those "times" he had mentioned in the letter. If this Mexican really was such a man, it was an unexpected and fortuitous piece of good luck that he should arrive here, now, when Atwood's need was even greater than it had ever been.

"Where did you get this letter?" Atwood asked.

"A man I did a job for gave me the letter," Bustamante said.

"Are you good with a gun?"

"I do not have a gun."

"You don't have a gun?"

"No, señor."

"Then there has been some misunderstanding here. Apparently you don't know what I am looking for."

"Do you want someone keeled, señor?"

"That's a hell of a question to ask."

"Do you want someone keeled?" Bustamante asked again.

"What if I do? How are you going to do that without a gun?"

"I do not need to be good with a gun, because I do not use a gun. For me, señor, killing is not a sport, it is a *profesión*," Bustamante said.

Atwood stroked his chin as he stared into the dark, obsidian eyes of the Mexican who had not yet risen from the swing.

"There have been others who have tried to kill Smoke Jensen. But they have all failed."

"I am not like the others."

"Yeah, maybe you'll do after all. All right, put your tack in the bunkhouse. Use that one," he said, pointing to the smaller of the two buildings. "The other one is for the cowboys. This one is for men who do . . . special jobs for me."

Bustamante nodded but said nothing. He led his horse into the barn, removed the saddle, found an empty stall, then he took the blanket in which he kept his tack with him to the bunkhouse Atwood had pointed out to him.

Clinton and two other men were in the bunkhouse. Bustamante saw a bunk on which the mattress was in an "S" roll, and he dropped his blanket there.

"Hey you, Mex!" Clinton called. "What are you doing in here?"

Bustamante didn't answer.

"I'm talkin' to you, Mex. You're in the wrong building. If you've just signed on, you need to be in the other bunkhouse."

"I seen 'im talkin' to Mr. Atwood a couple of minutes ago, Clinton," one of the other men said. "If he come in here, I reckon it's 'cause Atwood told 'im to."

"Is that right, Mex? Did Atwood tell you to come in here?"

Again, Bustamante didn't answer.

"What's the matter with you? Don't you speak English? *No habla Inglés?*"

Bustamante stared at him but said nothing.

"You know what I think? I think maybe he's deaf," one of the other two men said, and the others laughed.

Clinton pulled his pistol and pointed it at Bustamante. "Let's find out. Mex, here's what I'm going to do. I'm going to count to three, 'n if you don't say somethin' to me before I get to three, I'm goin' to shoot you dead. You *comprender*, Mex?"

"I am Bustamante."

A wide grin spread across Clinton's face, and he put the gun back in his holster. "Well now, Loomis, Hicks, what do you think of that? Our little brown friend can talk after all. Bustamante, is it?"

"*Si.*"

"I don't know what Mr. Atwood was thinkin' when he hired a Mex, but let me tell you how it's goin' to be. As long as you are in this bunkhouse, with us, you stay the hell out of my way. I don't like Mexicans. *Comprender* that, Bustamante?"

"*Sí.*"

It may have been close to midnight, Bustamante had no way of knowing, though he knew it was quite late. And, because of the chorus of snoring coming from the others, he knew that everyone was asleep. Getting up from bed, Bustamante removed his knife from its scabbard, then lit a candle. By the wavering light of the candle, he walked quietly across the wide, unfinished plank floor until he reached Clinton's bunk. Clinton was lying on his back, his mouth open, and snoring loudly.

Holding the candle in his left hand, and the knife in his right, Bustamante made a quick slice, with the blade cutting halfway through Clinton's neck. Clinton's eye popped open, and he remained conscious just long enough to be aware of what happened to him. He opened his mouth wider, as if to cry out, but because the larynx had been destroyed, he could make no sound. Blood gushed from the wound and began to pool on both sides as Clinton's eyes glazed over.

Bustamante went back to his own bed.

CHAPTER 35

"**W**hat the hell!" Loomis shouted the next morning. "Hicks! Boyle! Jones! Come here! Look at this!"

Loomis was standing over Clinton's bunk, looking down at his cut throat, his open, but unseeing eyes, and his blood-soaked pillow and blanket.

"Son of a bitch! Who did this?" Boyle asked.

"I don't know. Someone must've come in here last night," Jones said.

"I think it was the Mex," Loomis said.

"The Mex?" Boyle asked. "Who are you talkin' about?"

"That's right, you 'n Jones wasn't here when he come in yesterday. He says his name is Bustamante."

"It couldn'ta been him," Hicks said. "Hell, look down there! He's still here, lyin' in his bunk. He wouldn' still be here iffen he had done this."

"Then who did do it?"

"Did you hear about Clinton?" Slim Pollard asked Hog Jaw Lambert. Like Slim, Hog Jaw was one of the working cowboys on Eagle Shire. The two of them were riding fence line.

"Clinton? Ain't he one o' them gunmen that Atwood's brought onto the place? What about 'im?"

"He was found dead in his bunk this morning."

"Damn! You mean he died in his sleep?"

Slim chuckled, a macabre laugh. "Yeah, if you call gettin' your throat cut dying in your sleep."

"Someone cut his throat?"

"He didn't cut it himself."

"Who did it?"

"Nobody knows."

"That's a hell of a way to die," Hog Jaw said.

"Yeah, I suppose it is. But I'll be honest with you, Hog Jaw. I don't feel one bit sorry for the son of a bitch."

Hog Jaw looked around quickly to make sure that there was no one close enough to overhear them.

"No," he agreed. "I don't feel sorry for 'im, either. I wonder if it has somethin' to do with what's goin' on between Atwood and town right now?"

"It could be. You know he, Reed, Clinton, and Warren went to town together the other night. Clinton was the only one who come back."

"Yeah," Hog Jaw said. "They say that fella Smoke Jensen kilt 'em. I wonder if he come out here in the middle of the night 'n kilt Clinton?"

"I doubt it," Slim said. "So far ever'body Jensen has kilt has been face to face. It ain't like him to sneak up in the middle of the night 'n kill someone."

Atwood was certain that Bustamante was the one who killed Clinton, but he didn't ask him about it. And, if he was being honest with himself, he didn't really care. He had sent Clinton into town with two other men for what should have been an easy job . . . to kill Jensen in the middle of the night. Clinton and the other two had failed. If Bustamante could kill Clinton, in a bunkhouse that was filled with Clinton's friends, and neither be caught nor discovered, then this might just be the man he needed.

"You're right," Atwood said to Bustamante after sending for him. "I do want someone killed. His name is Smoke Jensen, and you will find him in town."

Smoke was in the Bull and Heifer Saloon, campaigning for the election.

"Hell, yeah, I'll vote against the taxes," someone said. "I don't like payin' extra for my drinks."

"And for ever'thing else you have to buy, too," another added.

"Mr. Jensen, have a beer on the house," Bull Blackwell said. "I think the best thing that's happened to this town is you comin' here."

"Hell, I think he ain't done nothin' but bring trouble to the town," someone said.

"You would say that, Hicks, you're ridin' for Atwood."

"Yeah? So, what if I do?"

"He ain't really ridin' for 'im. He ain't a cowboy," Slim Pollard said.

"If you mean I don't walk around with cow dung on my boots the way you 'n the others do, then yeah, I ain't a cowboy," Hicks replied. "But there's other jobs Mr. Atwood needs done besides cowboyin', and he hires special people for that."

"I think I've run across some of these special people you're talking about," Smoke said. "As a matter of fact three of them came into my hotel room the other night intent upon killing my wife and me."

"Yeah, well, I wouldn't know nothin' about that," Hicks said.

"No, I'm sure that you don't. Mr. Blackwell, thank you

for the beer," Smoke said, lifting the empty glass toward the bartender.

It was very dark outside with only the moon and dim squares of light around the few lampposts keeping it from being as black as the inside of a pit.

From the other end of the street Smoke could hear Rusty playing the piano, and he recognized the song "Lorena."

From the shadows of the Mexican quarters on the south side of the tracks, Smoke could hear a guitar and trumpet. They were playing different songs, yet, somehow it all seemed to blend into a melody that was distinctly here and now.

A dog barked.

Somewhere a baby cried.

Smoke could see the lights of the Milner Hotel and started toward them. Sally was already there, probably reading, and he was anxious to get back to her. He knew that most wives, being displaced from home for as long as Sally had been, would probably start showing their displeasure. But Sally was supportive in every way, and he was glad she had made such good friends with Pearlie's sister. It was almost as if Kate, like Pearlie, had been invited into the family.

He felt the assassin coming for him before he heard him, and he heard him before he saw him. A man, obviously a Mexican, suddenly materialized from the dark shadows between the buildings and sprang toward him, making a wide slash with his knife. Only that innate sense that allowed him to perceive danger when there was no other sign had saved his life, for he was moving out of the way at the exact moment the man started his attack. Otherwise the attacker's knife, swinging in a low, vicious arc, would have disemboweled him.

Despite the quickness of his reaction, however, the attacker did manage to cut him, and as Smoke went down into the dirt, rolling to get away, the flashing blade opened up a long wound in his side. The knife was so sharp and wielded so adroitly that Smoke barely felt it. He knew, however, that the knife had drawn blood.

The Mexican moved in quickly, thinking to finish Smoke off before he could recover, but Smoke twisted around on the ground, then thrust his feet out, catching the assailant in the chest with a powerful kick and driving him back several feet. But the Mexican was good, skilled and agile, and he recovered quickly, so that by the time Smoke was back on his feet, he was once again facing the knife wielder.

Smoke reached for his pistol, then realized with a shock that his holster was empty! The gun had fallen out while he was on the ground! He was unarmed and having to face someone who obviously knew how to use a knife.

The attacker, realizing that Smoke was defenseless, flashed a self-satisfied smile and made another swipe with his knife. Smoke managed to avoid the knife and thrusting out with the heel of his hand, he hit the man in the forehead, driving him back a few feet.

Smoke looked around on the ground to try to find his pistol as his attacker charged him again. Then Smoke heard a gunshot, and he saw a black hole appear in the forehead of his assailant. The Mexican went down, and Smoke turned to see Sally standing behind him, holding a smoking gun.

"I was getting tired of waiting," Sally said. "So I decided to come see what was keeping you."

"You mean you were actually going to go into the Bull and Heifer?"

"If necessary," Sally said, putting her gun back in the holster. "It looks like I made a good move."

"What? You mean this little fracas? Ahh, I was handling it all right."

"Yeah, I could tell," Sally replied with a chuckle. "You're bleeding like a stuck pig. We'd better get that taken care of."

"Nothing to it, I just need . . ."

"Smoke? Smoke? Smoke? Are you all right?"

When Smoke opened his eyes he saw Sally, Pearlie, and Cal looking down at him.

"Why are you asking me if I'm all right?"

Sally's smile was one of relief. "Because you are lying on your back in the middle of the street."

Pearlie, Cal, Kate, Rusty, Dolly, and Mayor Cravens were at Dr. Pinkstaff's office as he treated the wound in Smoke's side.

"How is he, Doc?" Pearlie asked.

"Well, he lost a lot of blood; that's why he fainted," Dr. Pinkstaff replied.

"I didn't faint," Smoke replied. "That's what women do when they see a mouse, or something."

"Well, if you didn't faint, what were you doing lying in the middle of the street?" Sally asked.

"I just . . . I just went to sleep rapidly," Smoke said.

Dr. Pinkstaff laughed. "If he's still got a sense of humor, he'll be just fine. I'm giving him a saline transfusion and he's going to need some rest until his blood builds back up. And you'll need to keep the wound clean."

"What do you mean by rest?" Smoke asked.

"By rest, I mean rest. I don't want you on your feet just yet. I'm going to keep you here for a while."

"How long is a while? I plan to be up and about by Tuesday."

"If you do what I tell you, I think I can promise you that

you'll be back on your feet by then. I'm going to give you a solution of chloral hydrate to help you sleep tonight."

"Wait a minute," Smoke said. "That stuff will knock me out, won't it?"

"Yes, but I think it is necessary. At least for tonight."

"I'm not going to take it."

"Yes, you are," Sally insisted.

"Bustamante is dead?" Atwood said.

"Yeah," Hicks said. "Welch has him down at the undertakin' place now, and he wants to know if you are goin' to pay for his buryin'."

"No, why should I pay for it?"

"I guess he thinks you should pay for it 'cause he worked for you."

"I paid for Pardeen, Creech, Warren, Reed, and Clinton because they were good men who had worked for me for a long time. Bustamante was only here for a few days, and he did nothing while he was here except possibly kill Clinton. I see no reason to pay for his burying."

Hicks laughed. "Yeah, that's what I told Welch."

"How is Jensen?"

"From what I hear he was cut up pretty bad," Hicks said. "He's most likely goin' to spend the night in the doctor's office."

Hick's words caused a broad smile to spread across Atwood's face, and he struck his open hand with his fist.

"We've got 'im!" he said. "If he is in the doctor's office tonight, he is helpless!"

"Want me to take care of 'im?" Hicks asked.

"Yes, and if you are successful, I guarantee you, you will be amply rewarded."

* * *

It was two o'clock when Cal came to relieve Pearlie at the doctor's office. Sally had stood watch until midnight, and Pearlie from midnight until two.

"How's he doing?" Cal asked.

"He's in there sleeping like a baby," Pearlie said.

"It's probably the first good night's sleep he's had since we left home," Cal said.

"There's coffee on the stove," Pearlie said as he left.

Cal looked in on Smoke, then took a seat. After several minutes he started getting very sleepy, and remembering Pearlie's reminder of the coffee, he went into the other room to pour himself a cup. He took a sip, then walked back to his guard position and saw someone standing over Smoke's bed.

"Pearlie, what are you . . . ?" It wasn't Pearlie!

The intruder turned and fired at Cal, who had leaped to one side as soon as he realized it wasn't Pearlie. Cal fired back, and the intruder went down. Hurrying to him, Cal looked down, then kicked the weapon away.

That action wasn't necessary. The man Cal shot was dead.

CHAPTER 36

Smoke was fully recovered by election day, and he, Pearlie, and Cal were watching the polling place to make certain that there was no intimidation of the voters. Sally, Kate, Sue Ellen, Dolly, and the Pretty Girls had set up a table near the polling booth, and they were serving lemonade and cookies. Cletus and Doodle, having just voted, were availing themselves of the refreshments offered.

"These cookies is so good, I think I'll vote two or three times," Cletus said.

"Don't even joke about that, Cletus," Mayor Cravens said. "We're going to win this election, hands down, and I don't want even a whisper that could give them a challenge."

"No, sir, I won't say nothin' like that no more," Cletus said. "Long as I can have me some more of these cookies."

"Of course you can, Cletus," Kate said. "But leave enough for the others to be able to enjoy as well."

"What about them fellas?" Doodle asked, pointing to a group of men. "You aren't going to give them any cookies and lemonade, are you?"

Doodle was pointing toward Marshal Willis and his deputies.

"Of course we will," Sally said with a broad smile.

"These refreshments are for everyone who votes. Would you like a cookie, Marshal?"

"Yeah," Clark said, starting toward the table.

"Clark!" Willis said sharply, shaking his head.

"No," Clark said. "We don't want none of your damn cookies."

"That would be 'we don't want any of your damn cookies,' to be correct about it," Pearlie said.

"Why, yes, Pearlie, that's very good," Sally said with an approving smile.

Willis, Clark, Booker, and Walker voted, then walked back down to the marshal's office. A few minutes later, the four men were seen riding out of town.

"Ha!" Rusty said. "Looks to me like Willis and his deputies have given up. They're leaving town!"

"They're goin' to win that election, Mr. Atwood," Willis was saying half an hour later. "There ain't no way they ain't goin' to win."

"What time will the voting poll close?" Atwood asked.

"They said they're goin' to keep it open till five o'clock."

"Then we haven't lost the election."

"Yeah, we have, you don't have no idea how many has already voted. And you know damn well they're votin' to get rid of the taxes."

"The votes have to be counted to make the election official, don't they?"

"Well yeah, but . . ."

"All we have to do is see to it that they aren't counted."

"How are we goin' to do that?"

"You let me worry about that."

* * *

When Slim Pollard dismounted, he walked over to the refreshment table where Smoke stood talking with some of the townspeople.

"You can't vote, Slim," Cletus said, "on account of you don't live in town. I wish you could, though, I've got a feelin' you'd do the right thing."

"Yeah, well, I hope I'm doin' the right thing now," Slim said. "I'm leavin'; I can't ride for the Eagle Shire no more. Atwood just ain't a man I can work for."

Doodle laughed. "Hell, Slim, you just now learnin' that?"

"Well, I don't know, maybe I have know'd about it for a while, 'n always before I kinda turned my head away from it. But I can't look away from what he's got planned now."

"What he has planned now? And just what would that be?" Smoke asked.

"He plans to come into town to stop the election."

"Stop it? How does he expect to do that?" Smoke asked. "The election is half over already."

"He plans to kill as many townspeople as he can, then he's goin' to steal the ballot box before the votes can be counted."

"Why, he's insane if he thinks he can razz an entire town," Peterson said.

"That's not as far-fetched as you might think," Smoke said. "Remember what Quantrill did with Lawrence."

"Yeah, that's right," Mayor Cravens said. "Mr. Pollard, how many men will Atwood have with him?"

"He'll have Willis an' his deputies, that's four, plus at least ten others from the ranch, and maybe a few more."

"I know he has a bunch of gun hands," Cletus said. "I didn't know he had that many."

"Some of the cowboys may ride with him," Slim said. "Not many, but a few."

"Why would they do that?" Mayor Cravens asked.

"Some will because cowboys just naturally have a loyalty to the brand they ride for, and some will because if you want to be a cowboy in this part of the county, now, Eagle Shire is the only job there is."

"What will we do, Mayor?" Doodle asked.

"I don't know," the mayor replied. "If there are that many of them coming into town, I don't see how we can possibly stand up to them. When it comes down to it, they will just about have us outnumbered . . . at least as far as young, fighting age men are concerned. And most of them know how to use guns. I'd be willing to say that there aren't more than nine or ten in all of Etholen who have ever used a gun before, let alone in battle."

"Smoke, we aren't just going to give in to them, are we?" Kate asked.

"Not by a long shot are we going to give in to them," Smoke replied. "Actually, it's good that this is all going to come to a head now. I said I wasn't going to leave until this business with Atwood was settled, and I meant it. I figure that, before nightfall, it will be settled."

"Do you really think we can hold him off?" Doodle asked.

"I'm not interested in just holding them off. We need to finish this business with Atwood, once and for all."

"But how are we going to do this? He's probably got us outnumbered, and all of his men are experienced fighting men."

Smoke glanced toward the courthouse and smiled.

"That may be. But we've got something he doesn't have."

Cletus Murphy, Roy Beck, Lonnie Bivins, Allen Blanton, Rusty Abernathy, Arnold Carter, Andrew Dawson, Barney Easter, Ken Freeman, Ron Gelbman, Bert Graham, Cole

Gunter, Doodle Higgins, Michael Holloway, Ed James, Robert Jamison, and Gerald Kelly dug the trench and rampart, and felled a couple of trees to add a revetment. The result was a defense position that was in place between the town and Eagle Shire.

"What do you think, Smoke?" Allen Blanton asked. "Looks to me like you could hold off an army." Blanton had been in charge of digging the fortification.

"I think you and the others did a great job," Smoke said.

"As long as they don't decide to circle around town and come in from the other side," Blanton suggested.

"Damn! If he does that we are in a peck of trouble," Cal said.

Blanton chuckled. "Don't worry about it, I know Atwood. He's not really all that smart, certainly not smart enough to think about going around the town."

"I hope you're right," Smoke said. "Cletus, Doodle, you two stay here with Pearlie, Cal, and me. The rest of you men can go on back into town now. I thank you very much for all the work you did in building this fort so quickly. You did a great job."

"I am the mayor of this town," Joe Cravens said. "I intend to stay as well. It wouldn't be right for me to desert my post now."

"All right, you can stay."

"And me," Rusty said.

"Rusty, if something happened to you, I'd never be able to face my sister again," Pearlie said.

"How is that any different from the last twenty years, Uncle Pearlie?" Rusty challenged.

Pearlie stared at Rusty for a long moment, then nodded. "You're right," he said. "You can stay."

"I don't have a gun," Rusty said.

Smoke pointed to the three cloth bags that Sally and Kate had sewn for them. "Yeah, you do," he said with a smile.

Fourteen men left Eagle Shire with Atwood. Calling upon his experience when he was a lieutenant in the Windsor Regiment during the war, Atwood rode at their head and had his men follow him, in a column of twos. When he was no more than a mile from town, he halted his men.

"Willis. Ride ahead and take a look around."

"You mean go by myself?"

"Of course go by yourself. You're the marshal of the town, you aren't going to attract any attention, especially if you are by yourself."

"All right," Willis agreed, though somewhat hesitantly.

Disengaging from the others, Willis rode ahead at a trot. He had just come around the last curve in the road, when he stopped. Ahead of him, and just to the side of the road, there appeared to be a couple of tree trunks, and he could see the head and shoulders of three men sticking up just above the improvised fortifications.

"Ha!" Willis said, a wide smile spreading across his face. Turning his horse around, he urged it into a rapid, ground-eating trot, until he got back to Atwood and the others.

"There's only three of 'em!" Willis said when he returned.

"Ha! Yes, that would be Jensen, Kate's brother, and the other man who came with them. I thought that might be the case," Atwood said, slapping his closed fist into his hand. "They've been so successful in dealing with my men before that they've grown arrogant and overconfident. Well, we are about to teach them a lesson. Unfortunately the lesson won't do them any good because they're going to die learning it."

* * *

"Smoke!" Cal called down from the tree he had climbed. He was holding a tin can in his hand, and a long string stretched from it to Smoke's position in the entrenchment. Smoke put the can to his ear.

"They are about a half mile away," Cal's tinny, but easily understood voice said.

Smoke put the can to his mouth. "Start giving me a countdown, by yards, when they are about fifty yards from the marked tree."

Smoke looked over toward Rusty. The first of the three cloth bags of powder had been pushed down into the breach of the gun, and a hollow cannon ball that had been filled with powder had been loaded. The cannon ball fuse protruded through the touchhole, and Rusty was holding a burning wick. The cannon was laid in on three selected targets, the marked tree being the first one.

"One hundred yards," Cal said, and he began counting down in ten-yard increments. When he got to twenty yards, Smoke called out to Rusty.

"Ready!"

Rusty moved the wick closer.

"Ten yards," Cal said.

"Fire!"

The cannon roared and belched fire. Quickly the barrel was sponged out, and a new sack of powder and a new cannon ball put in place.

"What the?" Atwood shouted when he heard the sound of the cannon being fired. He had heard such sounds before, but it had been more than twenty years in his past.

The preliminary explosion was followed by another

explosion, this one loud and ear-splitting, coming from the road behind him.

"Arghhhh!"

Men screamed in fear and pain.

"Forward at a gallop!" Atwood shouted, remembering enough of his battle experience to know that the best defense was to gallop out of the kill zone.

"Fifty yards from the double rock!" Cal said into the tin can, marking the second firing point.

"Fire!" Smoke shouted when Cal indicated that they were ten yards from the double rock.

This time the cannon ball exploded in the road far enough behind Atwood and the men who were advancing with him that no one was wounded.

"Yes! Faster, we can outrun them!" Atwood shouted.

Back at the entrenchment, Smoke had the gun moved up onto the rampart and the barrel depressed. This time, instead of being loaded with an explosive cannon ball, the barrel was filled with cut pieces of horseshoes that had been prepared by the blacksmith. Cal had come down from his position in the tree and he, Pearlie, Smoke, Cletus, and Doodle were in the trench, with rifles at the ready.

"Hold your fire until after the cannon has fired," Smoke told the others.

They could hear the sound of thundering hooves, then the riders came around the last bend in the road. Here, they spread out in a long front. Smoke had no idea how many they had started with, but he counted twelve. The twelve attackers started shooting, and Smoke and the others could hear the bullets whistling over their heads.

"Fire the cannon, Rusty!" Smoke shouted, and again, the cannon roared.

Smoke could see the bits of iron, hurtling toward Atwood and his men in a cloud of death. Four men went down under the fusillade.

"Now!" Smoke shouted, and he and the other four men began firing as rapidly as they could jack new rounds into the chambers. Within seconds, there wasn't one man left in the saddle.

EPILOGUE

Etholen, the following June

Smoke, Sally, Pearlie, and Cal were met at the depot by Allen Blanton, the newspaper publisher.

"I hope you don't mind being met by me instead of your sister or your nephew," Blanton said. "But, as I'm sure you can imagine, they're quite busy right now."

"Yes, I imagine they would be," Sally said.

"I know they're thrilled that you folks could come," Blanton said. "Actually, the entire town is. You folks are heroes around here, you know."

Smoke shook his head. "No more so than anyone else who took part that day . . . and that goes for the people who voted, and for people like you, Cletus, Doodle, and others who helped to turn out the vote."

"I've got something I want you to see before you go to the hotel," Blanton said.

A short while later, with their luggage loaded onto a small wagon that was being pulled behind a phaeton carriage, Blanton drove them to the Milner Hotel. But, before reaching the hotel, they stopped at the flagpole in front of the courthouse. The cannon was still there, but the sign beside it was much larger, and the name of the cannon had been changed.

THE CANNON
"SMOKE"

MANNED IN BATTLE
by Joe Cravens *and* Rusty Abernathy
under the COMMAND *of*
SMOKE JENSEN
and with the HEROIC SERVICE *of*
Wes "Pearlie" Fontaine, Cal Wood,
Cletus Murphy, *and* Doodle Higgins

**Brought FREEDOM *and* INDEPENDENCE
to Etholen, Texas**

"Well, I'm very honored, Mr. Blanton. And I know that Pearlie and Cal are as well."

"Yes, sir, we sure are," Pearlie said.

"So, Cletus is the new city marshal now?"

"Cletus is the new marshal, Doodle is his deputy, Mr. Peterson is our new mayor, Joe Cravens the judge, and Rusty, Bull Blackwell, Fred Matthews, Dave Vance, and I make up the new city council."

"My," Sally said. "It looks like the town has been reborn."

"Yes, ma'am, but not just the town," Blanton said. "The whole county. Atwood's ranch has been broken up. Some of it has been given back to the people he stole it from, and some of it was sold at auction. Slim Pollard and Miner Cobb bought some of it, with a bank loan, and they're doing just fine."

"Well, here we are," Blanton said a few minutes later when they stopped in front of the hotel. "I'll see you at the wedding tonight. I don't know who is the most excited, Miss Kate or Miss Dolly."

* * *

The wedding was held at the Pretty Girl and Happy Cowboy Saloon, which was well decorated for the event. All the tables had been taken out, and the chairs arranged so that there was an aisle down the center.

The priest, Mr. Peterson, the groomsman, and Joe Cravens, the groom, were standing at the front, where an altar had been constructed. Rusty was sitting at the piano.

After the bride's maids processed up the aisle and took their position, Rusty began playing Mendelsohn's Bridal March.

Smoke, Sally, and Cal turned to watch the bride, Kate, being escorted up the aisle by her brother, Pearlie. When they reached the altar, Kate moved over to stand next to Cravens, while Pearlie hurried back down the aisle where he met Dolly and escorted her up the aisle as well, all the while Rusty continued to play the Bridal March.

Then, when Dolly reached the altar, Rusty got up from the piano and hurried over to join her.

"Dearly Beloved, we are gathered here in the sight of God and these witnesses to join this man Joseph Cravens to this woman, Katherine Abernathy, and this man Rusty Abernathy, with this woman Delores Weathers in holy matrimony."

The next day

Smoke, Sally, Pearlie, and Cal were sitting at a table in the dining car on the train, on the way back to Colorado. They had ordered their food, but it hadn't yet been delivered.

"I thought the wedding was just beautiful," Sally said. "And, Pearlie, you looked so cute, escorting your sister and Dolly down the aisle."

Cal laughed. "Yeah, you were cute," he teased.

"And I'm so glad you have a family now," she added.

Pearlie reached across the table to take Sally's hand, then he took Cal's hand. At a nod from Pearlie, Cal reached across the table to take Smoke's hand, and he took Sally's other hand in his.

"Heck, Miz Sally," Pearlie said. "I've had a family all along."

"Yes, you have," Sally said, raising Pearlie's hand to kiss it.

"Lord, Smoke, you're not goin' to kiss my hand now, are you?" Cal asked.

Their laughter drowned out the train's whistle.

VENOM
OF THE MOUNTAIN MAN

CHAPTER 1

Salcedo, Wyoming Territory

The hooves of Smoke Jensen's horse Seven made a dry clatter on the rocks as Smoke made a rather steep descent down from a seldom-used trail. Seeing the road below, he felt a sense of relief. "There it is, Seven, there's the road. Taking the cutoff wasn't all that good an idea. I was beginning to think we never would see that road again."

Seven whickered.

"No, I wasn't lost. You know I don't get lost. I just get a little disoriented every now and then."

Seven whickered again.

"Ah, so now you're making fun of me, are you?"

On long rides, Smoke often talked to his horse because he wanted to hear a voice, even if it was his own. Talking to his horse seemed a step above talking to himself.

Smoke dismounted and reached up to squeeze Seven's ear. Seven dipped his head in appreciation of the gesture.

"Yeah, I know you like this. Tell you what. Why don't I walk the rest of the way down this hill? That way you won't have to be working as hard. And when we get on the road, we'll have a little breather."

Before they reached the road, Seven suddenly let out an

anxious whinny, and using his head, pushed Smoke aside so violently that he fell painfully onto the rocks.

"What was that all about?" Smoke said angrily.

Seven whinnied again and began backing away, lifting his forelegs high and bobbing his head up and down.

Smoke saw the rattler, coiled and bobbing its head, ready to strike. He drew his pistol and fired. There was a mist of blood where the snake's head had been, the head now at least five feet away from the reptile's still coiled and decapitated body.

"Are you all right?" Smoke asked anxiously as he began examining Seven's forelegs and feet. He found no indication that the snake had bitten him. He wrapped his arms around Seven's neck. "Good boy. Oh, wait. I know what you really want."

Again, he began squeezing Seven's ear. "Well, as much as you like this, we can't hang around here all day. We need to get going."

Smoke led Seven on down the rocky incline, then just before he reached the road, his foot slipped off a rock, and he felt the heel of his boot break off. "Damn," he said, picking up the heel. "Don't worry. I'm not going to remount right away, but probably a little earlier than I previously intended."

He limped along for at least two more miles. When he was certain Seven was well rested, he swung back into the saddle. "All right, boy. Let's go." He started Seven forward at a trot that was comfortable for both of them.

"We'll be coming into Salcedo soon. Tell me, Seven, do you think this bustling community will have a shoe store?"

Seven dipped his head.

"Oh, yeah, you would say that. You always are the optimist."

* * *

Salcedo was the result of what had once been a trading post, then a saloon, then a couple houses and a general store until, gradually, it became a town along the banks of the Platte River. The river was not navigable for steamboats, and even flatboats had a difficult time because of the shallowness of the water and the many sandbars and rocks along the route.

A sign at the town limits, exaggerting somewhat, stated

SALCEDO
POP 210

Smoke had been to Rawlins and was on his way back to his Sugarloaf ranch when he broke the heel. He found a boot and shoe store on Main Street, and the cobbler said that he could fix the boot. As Smoke stood at the window of the shoe repair shop, his attention was drawn to a stagecoach parked at the depot just across the street.

"Swan, Mule Gap, and Douglas!" the driver shouted. "If you're goin' to Swan, Mule Gap, or Douglas, get aboard now!"

Five passengers responded to the driver's call—two men, and a woman with two children. The coach had a shotgun guard, and as soon as he was in position, the driver popped his whip, the six horses strained in their harness, and the coach pulled away.

"Your boot is ready," George Friegh, the shoemaker, said as he stepped up beside Smoke watching the coach leave. "It's carryin' five thousand dollars in cash money."

"You mean that's common knowledge?" Smoke replied. "I thought stagecoach companies didn't want it known when they were carrying a sizeable cash shipment."

"Yeah, most of the time they do try 'n keep it quiet. But you can't do that with Emile Taylor."

"Who is Emile Taylor?" Smoke asked.

"Taylor's the shotgun guard. He's an old soldier, and like a lot of old soldiers, he's a drinkin' man. I heard him carryin' on last night while he was getting' hisself snockered at the Trail's End."

The Trail's End was the only saloon in Salcedo.

"He started talkin' about the money shipment they're takin' down to Douglas. Five thousand dollars he said it was."

"He told you that?"

"Not just me. Hell, mister, he was talkin' loud enough that ever'one in the saloon heard him."

Smoke examined the boot, then paid for the work. "You did a good job," he said, slipping the boot back on. "I'd better be getting back on the road."

Five miles south of Salcedo on the Douglas Pike

Four men were waiting on the side of the road, their horses ground hobbled behind them.

"You're sure it's carryin' five thousand dollars?" one of them asked.

"Yeah, I'm sure. I heard the shotgun guard braggin' about it."

"The reason I ask if you're sure is the last time we held up a stage we didn't get nothin' but thirty-seven dollars, 'n that's what we got from the passengers. Hell, you could get shot holdin' up a stage, and thirty-seven dollars ain't worth it."

"This here stagecoach has five thousand dollars. You can trust me on this."

"Here it comes," one of the other men said as the coach crested the hill and came into view.

"All right. You three get mounted and get your guns out. Gabe, you hold my horse. I'll have 'em throw the money bag down to me. Get your hoods on," he added as he pulled a hood down over his own head.

Smoke heard the unmistakable sound of a gunshot in the distance before him. There was only one shot, and it could have been a hunter, but he didn't think so. There was a sharp flatness to the sound—more like that of a pistol rather than a rifle. He wondered about it, but there was only one shot, and it could have been anything, so he didn't give it that much of a thought.

When he reached the top of the hill he saw the stagecoach stopped on the road in front of him. It was the same stagecoach he had watched leave Salcedo, and the passengers, including the woman and children, were standing outside the coach with their hands up. The driver had his hands up as well. For just a second he wondered about the shotgun guard, then he saw a body lying in the road beside the front wheel of the coach.

Four armed men, all but one mounted, were all wearing hoods that covered their faces. There was no doubt that Smoke had come upon a robbery.

Pulling his pistol, he urged Seven into a gallop and quickly closed the distance between himself and the stagecoach robbers. "Drop your guns!" he shouted.

"What the hell?" one of the robbers yelled, and all four of them shot at Smoke.

Smoke shot back, and the dismounted robber went down. There was another exchange of gunfire, and one of the mounted robbers went down as well.

"Let's get out of here!" one of the two remaining robbers shouted, and they galloped off.

Smoke reached the coach, then dismounted to check on

the two fallen robbers to make certain they presented no further danger to the coach. They didn't. Both were dead.

A quick examination of the shotgun guard determined that he, too, was dead.

"Mister, I don't know who you are," the driver said, "but you sure come along in time to save our bacon."

"The name is Jensen. Smoke Jensen. Are all of you all right? Was anyone hurt?"

"We're fine, Mr. Jensen, thanks to you," the woman passenger said.

From the *Douglas Budget*:

> Smoke Jensen is best known as the owner of Sugarloaf, a successful ranch near Big Rock, Colorado. He is also well-known as a paladin, a man whose skillful employment of a pistol has, on many occasions, defended the endangered from harm being visited upon them by evil-doers.
>
> Such was the case a few days ago when fate, in the form of the fortuitous arrival of Mr. Jensen, foiled an attempted stagecoach robbery, and perhaps saved the lives of the driver and passengers. The incident occurred on Douglas Pike Road, some five miles south of Salcedo, and five miles north of Mule Gap.
>
> Although Mr. Jensen called out to the road agents, offering them the opportunity to drop their guns, the four outlaws refused to do so, choosing instead to engage Jensen in a gunfight. This was a fatal decision for Lucas Monroe and Asa Briggs, both of whom were killed in the ensuing gunplay. Two of the men, already mounted, were able to escape.
>
> Although the bandits were wearing hoods

during the entire exchange, it is widely believed that one of the men who got away was Gabe Briggs, as he and his brother, Asa, like the James and Dalton brothers, rode the outlaw trail together.

Wiregrass Ranch, adjacent to Sugarloaf

Wiregrass Ranch had once belonged to Ned and Molly Condon. When they were murdered, Sam Condon, Ned's brother, came west from St. Louis. Sam had been a successful lawyer in that city, and everyone had thought he was coming to arrange for the sale of the ranch. Instead, he'd decided to stay, and he brought his wife, Sara Sue, and their then twelve-year-old son Thad with him. Both adjusted to their new surroundings quickly and easily. Thad not only adjusted, he thrived in the new environment.

Sam had made the conscious decision to sell off all the cattle Ned had owned and replaced them with two highly regarded registered Hereford bulls and ten registered Hereford cows. Within two years he had a herd of fifty, composed of ten bulls and forty cows.

Keeping his herd small, he was able to keep down expenses by having no permanent cowboys. Although not yet fourteen, Thad had become a very good hand.

Sam Condon's approach to ranching paid off well, and he earned a rather substantial income by selling registered cattle, both bulls and cows, to ranchers who wanted to improve their stock.

Sam and Sara Sue were celebrating their seventeenth wedding anniversary, and they had invited Smoke and Sally, their neighbors from the adjacent ranch, to have a celebratory dinner with them.

"Chicken and dumplin's, Missouri style," Sara Sue said.

"Oh, you don't have to educate me, Sara Sue," Smoke

said as his hostess spooned the pastry onto his plate. "It's been a while, but I'm a Missouri boy, too."

"Well, I'm from the Northeast, but I've learned to enjoy chicken and dumplings as well," Sally said. "Smoke loves them so, that I had to learn how to make the flat dumplings."

"She learned how to make them all right," Smoke said. "She just hasn't learned how to say *dumplin's*, without adding that last *g*," he teased.

The others laughed.

"Mr. Jensen, I read about you in the paper," Thad said.

"Oh?"

"Yes, sir. I read how you stopped a stagecoach holdup, 'n how you kilt two men."

"Thad," Sam said. "That's hardly a subject fit for discussion over the dinner table."

"But that is what you done, ain't it? You kilt two men?"

"That's what you did, isn't it?" Sara Sue said, correcting Thad's grammar.

"Sec, Pa, even Ma is talking about it," Thad said.

The others at the table laughed.

"I'll tell you what," Sam said. "We'll talk about it after dinner. That is, if Smoke is amenable to it."

"*Amenable*. Oh, a good lawyer's word," Sally said with a smile.

After dinner, Smoke, Sam, and Thad sat out on the front porch while Sally helped Sara Sue clean up from the meal. In the west, Red Table Mountain was living up to its name by glowing red in the setting sun.

"The newspaper said that one of the men who got away was Gabe Briggs," Sam said.

"He probably was, but they never removed their masks, so there is no way of knowing," Smoke replied.

"Would you have recognized him if he hadn't been wearing a mask?"

Smoke shook his head. "No, I don't think I would have.

I've heard of the Briggs Brothers, but then, who in this part of the country hasn't? But I've never seen either of them before that little fracas on the road."

"But he did see you," Sam said.

"Yes."

"Doesn't that worry you a little? I mean, he knows what you look like, but you don't know what he looks like. If he is bent upon revenging his brother you could be in serious danger."

"I appreciate your concern," Smoke said, "but my life has been such that I have made as many enemies as I have friends. I never know when some unknown enemy is going to call me out or, even worse, try and shoot me from ambush. I've lived with that for many years. Gabe Briggs will be just one more."

"How many men have you kilt, Mr. Jensen?" Thad asked.

"Thad! That's not a question you should ever ask anyone!" Sam scolded.

"I'm sorry," Thad said contritely. "I didn't mean it in a bad way. I think Mr. Jensen is a hero."

Smoke chuckled softly. "I'm not a hero, Thad, but I have always tried to do the right thing. I'm not proud of the number of men I've killed. No one should ever kill someone as a matter of pride. But I will tell you this. I've never killed anyone who wasn't trying to kill me."

CHAPTER 2

New York, New York

In operations such as gambling, prostitution, protection, and robbery, the Irish Assembly and the Five Points Gang had been competitors for the last three years. For a while they had been able to establish individual territories, and thus avoid any direct confrontation, but over the last couple months, the Irish Assembly had been expanding the area of their franchise and they and the Five Points Gang had renewed their hostilities.

It had come to a head two days ago when a member of the Five Points Gang was killed by the Irish Assembly.

Both gangs were currently gathered under the Second Street El. They had started their confrontation by shouting insults at each other, but the insults had grown sharper until a shot was fired.

For fifteen minutes guns blazed and bullets flew as merchants and citizens along Second Street stayed inside to avoid being shot. When it was over, the Five Points gang hauled away their dead and wounded, and the Irish Assembly did the same.

"Three killed," Gallagher said. "We lost three good men!"

"So did the Five Points Gang," Kelly said.

"Aye, well, they can afford it, for 'tis a lot more people they have than we do. Would someone be for tellin' me what good did it do?"

"Here now, Ian, you wouldn't be for lettin' them be runnin' over us, would you?" Kelly asked.

"Gallagher's right. I think the time has come for us to change," one of the others said.

"And give up ever'thing we've built up?" Ian asked.

"We've built nothing 'n if we don't change, we'll be for losin' it all."

"In what way would you be for changing? I'm asking that," Gallagher said.

"I'd say come to an accommodation with the Five Points gang," Kelly said.

"You'd be for givin' up to 'em?"

"Aye. Let's face facts. 'Tis time to realize that we can't beat them. The only thing we can do is find some way to work with them."

Sugarloaf Ranch

"You're sure you want to do this now?" Pearlie asked.

"Yes," Thad said.

"Maybe we ought to ask your mama before you do something like this."

"No, Pearlie, don't do that. She would just say no."

Smoke had recently bought five new, unbroken horses. Pearlie and Cal always broke the new horses, and so far Cal had broken two, and Pearlie two. There was one horse remaining, and Thad, who had come over to Sugarloaf Ranch with his parents, had left them visiting with Smoke and Sally while he went out to watch. It was just before

Pearlie was about to mount the horse that Thad had asked to be allowed to do it.

"I'm thirteen years old. I'm not a baby."

"All right," Pearlie said. "I guess this is as good a time as any to learn."

"What do I do?"

"Keep a hard seat and keep your heels down. Watch his ears. That'll help tell you when it's coming. Keep his head up. As long as his head is up, he can't do all that much."

Pearlie pointed to a loop. "Put your right hand in here and grab a fistful of mane with your left hand. And don't be afraid to haul back on the mane. That'll let 'im know who is in control."

"All right," Thad said somewhat tentatively.

"You gettin' a little nervous? You want to back out? Nobody is goin' to say anything to you if you do back out. Ridin' a buckin' horse is not an easy thing to do." Pearlie chuckled. "And there's most that'll tell you, it's not exactly a smart thing to do, either."

"I'm a little scared," Thad said. "But I want to do it anyway."

A broad smile spread across Pearlie's mouth. "Good for you. If you weren't scared, I would say that you are too dumb to ride. If you admit that you are scared, but you are still willing to do it, then you may have just enough sense and courage to have what it takes to do this. Climb up here, and let's get it done."

Thad climbed up onto the side of the stall where, a few minutes earlier, Cal had brought the already-saddled horse. Thad paused for a moment, then he dropped down into the saddle just as Cal opened the gate.

The horse exploded out of the stall, leaping up, then coming down on four stiffened legs. The first leap almost threw Thad from the saddle.

"Pull back on his mane!" Pearlie shouted.

"Hang on tight!" Cal added.

The horse kicked its hind legs into the air, but Thad hung on. It tried to lower its head, but following Pearlie's instructions, Thad pulled back on the mane and prevented the horse from doing so. It began whirling around, but it was unable to throw its rider.

"Yahoo!" Cal shouted.

"Thata boy, Thad! Hang on!" Pearlie called.

"THAD!" Sara Sue screamed, coming out with the others to see what was going on.

"Watch, Ma! Watch!" Thad shouted excitedly.

The horse tried for another several seconds then, unable to rid itself of its rider, began trotting around the corral under Thad's complete control.

"What are you doing?"

"Well, Sara Sue, it looks to me like he's just broken a horse," Sam said with a big smile.

"And you approve of that? He could have broken his neck."

"He didn't break his neck, but he did break the horse. I not only approve of it, I'm proud of him. In fact, Smoke, if you would be willing to sell him, I would like to buy that horse from you. Seems to me that any boy who can break a horse ought to own the horse that he broke."

"I'm sorry, Sam, but that horse isn't for sale," Smoke said.

"Oh? Well, I'm disappointed, but I understand."

"He isn't for sale because I'm giving him to Thad," Smoke said with a big smile.

"Really? This horse is mine?" Thad said while still in the saddle of the now docile horse.

"He's yours."

"Oh, thank you!" Thad shouted.

"Yes, Smoke, thank you very much. That's very nice of you," Sam said.

"What are you going to name him?" Pearlie asked.

Thad bent forward to pat the horse on his neck. "I'm going to name him Fire, because I got him from Mr. Smoke Jensen. Smoke and fire. Do you get it?"

"I get it. And I think it's a great name," Pearlie said, "because this horse also has fire in his belly."

"Open the gate to the corral so I can ride him around," Thad said.

"Cal, open the gate," Pearlie called.

Cal opened the gate.

"Now, watch us run!" Thad slapped his legs against Fire's sides, and the horse burst forth like a cannonball. Thad leaned forward but an inch above Fire's neck. He galloped to the far end of the lane, about a quarter of a mile away, then turning on a dime, raced back before he dismounted.

"Ma, when we go home, can I sleep in the stable with Fire tonight?"

"You most certainly cannot."

Sam laughed. "I guess we're lucky he doesn't want to bring Fire in to sleep in bed with him tonight."

Sara Sue laughed as well, then ran her hand through her son's hair. "Come on in. Mrs. Jensen has supper on the table."

"What are we havin'?" Thad asked.

"Thad! We are guests! A guest never asks the hostess what is being served," Sara Sue scolded.

"I just wanted to make sure she wasn't serving cauliflower. I hate cauliflower."

Smoke laughed. "Then you are safe, young man. Sally never serves cauliflower, because I don't like it, either."

New York City

"Mule Gap? And is it serious that you be, Warren Kennedy, that you would be going to a place called Mule Gap?"

"Aye, Clooney, 'tis serious I am," Kennedy replied.

The two men were in Grand Central Depot, awaiting the departure of the next transcontinental train. Clooney had come to see Kennedy off.

"And would you be for tellin' me, why you would pick a place with the name of Mule Fart, Wyoming?"

Kennedy laughed. "Mule Gap, not Mule Fart. And the why of it is because there is nothing left for me here in New York. Our last adventure was too costly. I have studied Mule Gap, 'n 'tis my thinking that such a wee place can provide opportunity for someone with an adventurous spirit 'n a willingness to apply himself to the possibilities offered."

"I've read about the West," Clooney said. "There are crazy men who walk around out there with guns strapped around their waists. They say that such men would as soon shoot you as look at you."

"'N are you for tellin' me, Ryan Clooney, that in this very city the people who lived along Second Street weren't dodging the bullets that were flying through the street? Aye, 'n we as well."

"That was different. There was a war bein' fought between the Five Points Gang and the Irish Assembly, 'n we just happened to be caught up in it," Clooney insisted.

"Aye, that may be true. But I'd just as soon not be caught up in such a thing again. 'N before someone decides to start another war, 'tis my intention to be well out of here."

"I can't believe you would leave New York 'n all your friends 'n family behind."

"I have no family but m' father, 'n he has said he wants nothing to do with me. I can make new friends."

"Still, it'll be strange havin' you gone."

"All aboard for the Western Flyer!" someone shouted through a megaphone. "Track number nine. All aboard."

"That's my train," Kennedy said, starting to the door that led to the tracks. "If you think you'd like to come out, let me know, and I'll find a place for you."

"Find a place for me? Find a place doin' what?"

"Same as before. Doin' whatever I tell you to do," Kennedy said with a little chuckle.

He boarded the train, then settled back into his seat. Born in Ireland, he had lived in New York from the time he was four years old. He knew nothing but New York, yet he was leaving it all behind him.

And he didn't feel so much as one twinge of regret.

Walcott, Wyoming

Seven days later, after just under two thousand miles of cities and small towns, farmland and ranches, rich cropland and bare plains, desert and mountain, the train pulled into the small town of Walcott, Wyoming. When the train rolled away, continuing its journey on to the coast, Kennedy had a moment of indecision. He was used to big buildings, sidewalks crowded with people, all of whom were in a hurry, streets filled with carriages, trolley cars, and elevated trains. The entire town of Walcott could be fitted into one city block.

He went into the depot to claim his luggage.

"This here luggage says it was checked in at New York City," the baggage master said. "Are you from New York?"

"Aye, that I am," Kennedy replied.

"I've never been to New York, but I've read about it. Is it true what they say as to how big it is?"

"Two million people."

"Two million people? I can hardly think about such a

number. Tell me, are you just visitin' or are you plannin' on settlin' down here?"

"Neither. I'm headed for Mule Gap. I plan to make that my residence."

To Kennedy's surprise, the baggage master laughed.

"What is it? What's so funny?"

"I can't imagine a New York feller like you wantin' to live in a little ol' place like Mule Gap. Walcott, maybe, I mean, bein' as we're a pretty big town our ownselves, but a little ol' place like Mule Gap? Now that, I've got to see."

Kennedy was beginning to have even more reservations about the wisdom of moving to Mule Gap. If a resident of Walcott thought it was small, it must be miniscule indeed.

"In for a penny, in for a pound," he said.

"Now, mister, I don't have the slightest idea what it is you just said, but here's your luggage."

Carrying his luggage with him, Kennedy walked to the stagecoach depot, which was just next door. There, he bought a ticket for Mule Gap.

Warm Springs, Wyoming

"These are good-looking horses," Dooley Lewis said. "They'll make a fine addition to my string. But I thought you said you had five horses you were going to sell me."

"One of them got waylaid by a thirteen-year-old boy," Smoke replied with a smile.

"Well, never let it be said that I would step in between a boy and his horse. I'll take these and be proud to have 'em." Lewis owned DL Ranch, just outside Warm Springs.

"How'd you fare the winter?" Lewis asked.

"We got through it just fine," Smoke said. "You?"

"We had a pretty severe storm, but we was fortunate. None of the ranchers lost many cows. I did lose a couple horses, though, which is why I'm grateful to you for selling me these four. By the way, you wouldn't want to sell that horse you're ridin', would you?"

With a chuckle, Smoke reached up and grabbed one of Seven's ears and began squeezing it gently. "Don't you listen to him, Seven. You know I would never sell you."

Seven dipped his head, then pressed his forehead against Smoke's chest.

"Set much a store by that horse, do you?" Lewis asked.

"He's more than just a horse," Smoke said. "He's same as flesh and blood."

Lewis nodded. "I reckon I can see that. I've had a few critters I've felt about like that, myself.

"Glad you understand. I'll be getting on, then." Smoke swung into the saddle and started the long ride back to Sugarloaf Ranch.

CHAPTER 3

Mule Gap

By stagecoach from Walcott, one didn't approach Mule Gap as much as one descended into it. Kennedy's first sight of the town was from the road several hundred feet high that hugged the edge of the Rattlesnake Mountain range. From there, he could see the entire town, each and every building, both commercial properties and private homes. The town consisted of probably no more than forty structures laid out along four roads that formed a cross with two legs and two arms. The tallest structure in town was a church steeple, and the largest building appeared to be the livery stable.

"Hold on back there, folks!" the driver called to his three passengers. "We're about to go into Mule Gap and the road down is a little steep, so sometimes the teams get to runnin' 'n its hard to hold 'em back!"

True to the driver's warning, the coach began going faster and jerking back and forth, which had the effect of tossing the passengers around.

Kennedy couldn't help but notice the stoicism with which the other two passengers, a drummer and a middle-aged woman, accepted the rapid and dangerous run down from

Rattlesnake Mountain. He held on tightly and attempted, to the degree possible, to exhibit an equal amount of stoicism.

Smoke looped Seven's reins around the hitching rail in front of Rafferty's General Store. Seeing the stagecoach coming rapidly down the long grade from the mountain ridge road, he smiled as he thought of the passengers inside. Some enjoyed the thrill of the rapid descent, some were terrified of it, but all would be treated to a very rough ride.

He entered the store and quickly made his selections. It had been three months since the last time Smoke was in Wyoming. Having completed his business with Dooley Lewis, he'd decided to stop in Mule Gap. The small town had been built on the promise of a railroad that never materialized.

Being on the North Platte River meant an ample supply of water, good grazing land nearby, and daily stagecoach service, which provided transportation up to Walcott, the nearest access to the railroad, and south to Douglas. It was those assets that allowed the town to survive.

Gil Rafferty was putting Smoke's purchases in a bag when the little bell on the door signaled the entrance of another customer. "Emma, we have another customer," he called out to his wife.

"I'll be right with you, sir," a woman called from the back of the store.

"'Tis no hurry I'm in, ma'am. Take your time," the customer replied.

Smoke glanced toward him and saw a man of average height and build, whose most distinguishing feature was his piercing hazel eyes. Unlike the denim trousers and cotton shirts worn by most Westerners, this man was wearing a blue suit, a white shirt covered by a red vest, and a black bowtie. As Smoke examined him more closely, he saw that the clothing was of the finest cut and most expensive material. The quality of the material and the cut of the suit, however, did nothing to deter the dust. His suit was covered with it. Smoke noticed that he was not wearing a pistol belt.

"Hello, friend," the man said to Smoke. Smiling, he extended his hand. "Kennedy is the name. Warren Kennedy."

"Smoke Jensen," Smoke replied, accepting the proffered hand. He smiled. "How did you like the last half mile of your ride on the stagecoach?"

"Ha. And 'tis thinkin' I am, that you would be talkin' about the rapid descent down the road."

"Yes."

"And how would you be for knowin' that I was on the coach?" Kennedy asked.

Smoke chuckled. "It's not hard, Mr. Kennedy."

With a laugh, Kennedy patted his hands against the jacket he was wearing. That action was answered by a cloud of dust. "No, I don't suppose it would be hard to tell. As to the answer for your question, 'twas exciting, I'll say that. But sure 'n what better way could I ask to arrive in what will be my new hometown?"

"Mr. Kennedy, I'm Emma Rafferty," an attractive middle-aged woman said. "My husband and I own this store. Mule Gap is to be your new hometown?"

"Aye, for 'tis my intention to settle here."

"Then let me be the first to welcome you. Now, what can I do for you?"

"I'll be for buying a house as soon as I can, 'n I've made out a list of things I think I'll be needin'." He handed Emma a piece of paper. "I would like for to be making the purchases now, 'n payin' you for them, but I'll be wantin' you to be for holding them for me till I have a house where I can put them."

"We'll be glad to do that for you, Mr. Kennedy. And for

now you can just look around the store to see if there's anything you may have forgotten," Emma said.

"I thank you for your service, Mrs. Rafferty." In accordance with Emma's suggestion, Kennedy began drifting around the store.

A moment later, three men came into the store. All three men had hoods pulled down over their faces.

"This is a holdup!" one of the men shouted, then he pointed to Smoke. "That's the son of a bitch that kilt my brother! Kill 'im!"

As soon the order was given, the man carrying a double-barreled shotgun swung it toward Smoke.

Smoke drew his own gun, but even as he was drawing, a shot rang out and the man wielding the scattergun went down.

Two more shots were fired, only one of them coming from Smoke's pistol, and the remaining two men went down.

When Smoke looked around to see who had saved his life, he saw a smiling Warren Kennedy standing near one of the display tables. A thin wisp of gun smoke curled up from the barrel of a gun Kennedy was holding.

Because he wasn't wearing a pistol belt, Smoke wondered where the gun had come from.

"Well, that was a bit of excitement, wasn't it? 'Tis a foine welcome I received," Kennedy said with a broad smile. He returned the pistol to a shoulder holster that had been hidden by his jacket, and the mystery of where the gun had come from was solved.

"Mister Kennedy, I'm glad you came around when you did," Rafferty said. "You sure saved our bacon."

"Yeah, I guess I could say that as well." Smoke pulled the hoods from their faces.

"Do you know any of them, Mr. Jensen?" Rafferty asked.

"I've never actually seen this man," Smoke said, standing

over the one who had recognized him. "But from what he yelled out just before the shooting started, I would make a guess that this would be Gabe Briggs."

"Briggs?" Rafferty said. "Yes, I remember the story from the newspaper. A man named Briggs was one of the ones who'd tried to hold up the stagecoach. You stopped the holdup, as I recall."

"Yes, Asa Briggs was the man's name." Smoke turned toward the well-dressed man who, having just arrived on the stagecoach, had also taken part in stopping this robbery. "Mr. Kennedy—"

"It's Warren, please. I'd like to be for considering you the first new friend I've made in my new hometown."

"Well, I have to say Mist . . . Warren . . . that saving my life is a way to get on my good side really fast."

Kennedy laughed. "Aye, 'twould be a way of makin' a new friend, I would think."

"Warren, why don't you come down to the saloon with me and let me buy you a drink? Mr. Rafferty, you can hold my groceries here until I come back for them, can't you?"

"I sure can."

"Thanks for the offer of a drink," Kennedy said. "'Twould be good to get a bit o' the dust out of my mouth, I'm thinking."

By the time they reached the saloon, word of the would-be robbery and shoot-out had already spread. Both men were greeted with accolades, and though Smoke had offered to buy Kennedy's drinks, he wasn't allowed to pay for them, as the saloon keeper said they were "on the house."

The two men took a table in the back of the Silver Dollar Saloon.

"Those three robbers knew you," Kennedy said. "But when their hoods were removed, you said you didn't know them."

"No, I'd never seen any of them before."

"Sure now, and 'tis not that rather odd? 'Twas knowin' you they did, but you weren't for knowin' them."

"Where are you from, Warren?"

"I'm from New York."

Smoke smiled. "Well then, that explains it. I've been out here for quite a while now, and over the years I've made a few enemies. As a matter of fact I've made a lot of enemies . . . but I'm glad to say that I have made more friends than enemies."

"Aye, 'n a new one today."

"A new one today," Smoke repeated, holding his glass of beer up to Kennedy's Irish whiskey.

During the ensuing conversation Kennedy learned that Smoke owned a rather large ranch down in Colorado.

"What do you do, Warren? And what has brought you to a place like Mule Gap?"

"I've made my living for many years being involved in various business ventures," Kennedy said. "Some have been profitable, some have been costly. I recently ran into some business difficulty in New York and decided it would be a good idea to leave the city 'n start somewhere else, so I decided to take what funds I had left and come West in search of new opportunity." He laughed. "And the reason I chose Mule Gap was because I was intrigued by the name."

Smoke laughed. "Are you telling me that you would invest in something because you like the name?"

"Aye," Kennedy replied with a sheepish grin. "Maybe that's the mistake I made in New York . . . investing in something because of its name."

"I think you're pulling my leg a bit," Smoke said.

"Perhaps just a bit," Kennedy replied, his smile growing broader. "I have studied Mule Gap. I think it is bound to grow, and I intend to grow with it."

"Well, I wish you luck, Warren," Smoke said, once

more lifting his drink in an informal toast. "Here's mud in your eye."

Warren made a toast of his own. "'N I'll be replyin' with an old Irish toast, taught to me by m' sainted mither, may she rest in peace." He held his glass up. "May we get what we want, may we get what we need, but may we never get what we deserve."

With a chuckle, Smoke joined him in the drink.

Two months later, the *Mule Gap Ledger* carried a story about Kennedy.

Warren Kennedy to Start Bank

Mule Gap to Become a Commercial City

Our readers will no doubt recognize Warren Kennedy, Mule Gap's newest citizen, as a hero for stopping a robbery and saving the lives of Mr. and Mrs. Gilbert Rafferty. What many may not know is Mr. Kennedy's entrepreneurial spirit. He has announced his intention to build a much-needed bank in our fair community and to that end has begun construction in the empty lot next to McGee's Boot and Shoe store.

With the addition of a bank, Mule Gap will be able to take its rightful place among the more progressive cities and towns of Wyoming. All citizens of Mule Gap should be thankful that this fine man has chosen our community as his new home.

* * *

A full year passed before Smoke made another visit to Mule Gap. As he approached the little town from the south, he heard gunfire and, slapping his legs against Seven's sides, pulled his pistol and proceeded toward the sound of shooting at a full gallop. He eased up, though, when he heard more shots fired, this time followed by shouts of excitement, not fear.

"Yahoo!" someone shouted, and again there were gunshots. "Yahoo!"

As Smoke came into town he saw that many of the buildings of the town were festooned with colorful streamers. He saw, also, that at least three of the businesses he had known before were now partnerships. The grocery store was now Rafferty and Kennedy. The boot store was sporting the sign MCGEE AND KENNEDY, and Warren Kennedy had built a new saloon to compete with the Silver Dollar.

Smoke saw, then, the source of the shouting and gunshots, for a rider was galloping down the middle of First Street, shooting into the air, and yelling at the top of his voice.

"Yahoo! Three cheers for his honor the mayor, Warren Kennedy! Yahoo!"

Smoke dismounted in front of Kennedy's Saloon, and looped the reins around the hitching rail, knowing full well that Seven would make no effort to leave even if he had just dropped the reins on the ground in front of the horse.

When he stepped into the saloon it was crowded with cheering men and laughing bar girls. A sign was stretched out across the wall behind the bar. *TO CELEBRATE HIS ELECTION, DRINKS ARE ON THE HOUSE TODAY!*

"I remember you," Warren Kennedy called. "'N I know you to be Smoke Jensen if memory serves."

"Smoke Jensen it is. You have a good memory."

"Well, Smoke Jensen, 'n would you be for havin' a drink with the new mayor of Mule Gap?"

Smoke smiled and walked over to take Kennedy's extended hand. "I'd be glad to have a drink with you. And, congratulations, Mayor. I knew you were an ambitious fellow, but I never thought you would get involved with politics."

"Believe me, 'twas never my intention," Kennedy said. "But the damndest thing . . . people kept after me and kept after me to run until I felt it wouldn't be fair to just keep saying no all the time. So, I broke down and said aye, and now here I am . . . the new mayor."

"I wish you luck."

"I've already been lucky. I ran against Gil Rafferty, and, as you know, he is as fine a man as you would hope to meet. Gil and I are business partners now."

"Yes, I saw the sign on his store."

"Even though many were asking me to run, 'tis surprised I am that I, being a citizen of Mule Gap for barely over a year, would have prevailed over someone like m' friend Gil Rafferty, who has been here for as long as the town has been in existence. But tell me, Smoke, what brings you to town?"

"Your bank," Smoke said. "I do a lot of business in Wyoming, so I thought it might be a good idea to have a local account."

"Well, I'll be very happy to have your business. After we have a drink together, come on down to the bank and I'll personally open your account."

Half an hour later, Smoke was sitting across the desk from Kennedy. "Warren, looking around town, I can't help but notice that you have expanded your business interests considerably beyond just banking."

"That's true," he said. "As Mule Gap began to grow, many of the businessmen and -women wanted their businesses to expand with it. They came to me for investment money, and if it seemed propitious for me to do so, I made the investment." Kennedy chuckled. "It seems that I now own almost half the town. That wasn't my intention. My intention was just to help the town grow. But, as they say, good things come from good deeds."

"Yes," Smoke said. "You came to Mule Gap to do good, and you have done very well."

Kennedy laughed out loud. "That is one way of putting it, my friend. But don't be fooled by what you see."

"Not sure I understand."

"I've made loans, 'n I've made investments to the degree that I've found myself overextended. I think the investments have been wise, 'n I think there is a great future in Mule Gap. But I'll have to be limiting any future investments until I'm able to accumulate a little more money."

"Warren, are you . . . ?" Smoke started to ask, but Kennedy held out his hand to interrupt the question.

"Smoke, if it was a loan of money you were about to offer, I thank you for that. But I'll not be for needing a loan. I've recently gone into a business venture with some new acquaintances, 'n 'tis thinking I am that it is one that will be very lucrative. And there is no competition in the endeavor."

"Oh? What is it?"

Kennedy held up his finger and wagged it back and forth gently. "Please don't ask me to tell you. Bein' Irish, as I am, I have many superstitions, 'n I fear that if I tell too many people of my plans, it'll bring me bad luck."

Smoke chuckled. "Far be it from me to want to bring you bad luck. So . . . if it isn't bad luck to wish you good luck, I'll do just that."

"I'll take yer good wishes, 'n then some," Kennedy replied.

CHAPTER 4

Stinking Water, Wyoming

The man dressed all in black dismounted in front of the Nippy Jones Saloon. Before he reached the step, he was confronted by a big man with a prominent scar on his face. The man was holding a pistol.

"Where do you think you're agoin'?" the scar-faced man asked.

"Not that it is any of your business, sir, but it is my intention to drink a beer, have dinner, then get a hotel room so I can spend the night."

"You're the one they call The Professor, ain't you? I've heard of you. Always dressed in black, they say."

"My name is Frank Bodine."

"But you're called The Professor?"

"Actually, I would be more properly called Professor Bodine, but yes, there are some who call me The Professor."

"Well, you ain't comin' in here, Professor."

"And just why wouldn't I be entering that establishment?"

"Because I said you ain't."

"Tell me, sir, do you have any particular grievance with

me? I am unaware of our paths ever having crossed in the past."

"I've heard of you."

"Evidently you have, as a moment ago you used the sobriquet that is so often attached to me."

"I done what?" the scar-faced man replied.

"You have heard of me," The Professor said.

"Yeah, that's what I said. I've heard of you," Scarface repeated.

"Merely having heard of me, does not, in itself, give you a reason to behave in such a contemptible fashion," The Professor said. "Now, please, sir, if you would, step aside."

Scarface shook his head. "Uh-uh. Come this time tomorrow, ever'one is goin' to know that The Professor has been kilt, 'n they're goin' to know who done it."

"I think you are making a big mistake, sir. Now, I'm going to ask you very politely to step aside and allow me to enter this saloon so that I can have myself dinner and a beer."

"You ain't goin' nowhere, you fancy-talkin' son of a bitch!" Scarface made his move, bringing the pistol up as quickly as a striking rattlesnake.

Even though Scarface had the advantage, the reaction of The Professor was not what he thought it would be. Instead of seeing fear in his eyes, Scarface saw complete confidence. Even worse, Scarface saw the faintest suggestion of a smile on The Professor's face.

Scarface was very good with a gun, and in most of his encounters, he had the advantage because his very reputation instilled fear in his adversaries. But there was no fear in the face of the man facing him, and it was Scarface who suddenly felt fear.

He wasn't frightened for very long. The Professor's draw was smooth and instantaneous, and his practiced thumb came back on the hammer in one fluid motion. He put the slightest pressure on the hair trigger of his Colt, causing a blossom of flame, followed by a booming thunderclap as the gun jumped in his hand.

Scarface tried to shoot the pistol he was holding, but the .44 slug from The Professor's pistol caught him in the middle of his chest. He dropped his own pistol unfired, then staggered backward, crashing through the batwing doors and backpedaling into a table before coming down onto it with a crash that turned the table into firewood. He landed flat on his back on the floor, his mouth open and a little sliver of blood oozing down his chin. His body was still jerking a bit, but his eyes were open and unseeing. He was already dead, the muscles continuing to respond as if waiting for signals that could no longer be sent.

The Professor holstered his pistol, then pushed through the batwing doors, following the outlaw's body inside. Without so much as a second glance at the man he had just killed, he stepped calmly up to the bar. "Beer," he said, aware that everyone in the saloon was shifting their gaze from the outlaw's body to the man dressed in black standing at the bar. Most had been caught by surprise at the sudden turn of events. They stood there, staring awestruck at the lawman lying in the V of the broken table.

"Mister, do you know who you just shot?" one of the men in the saloon asked.

"I'm afraid we didn't have time to get acquainted," The Professor replied.

"His name is Barton. Billy Barton. I never figured anyone would be good enough to beat him. What do they call you?"

"I'll tell you what they call him," another man said. "They call him The Professor."

Upon hearing the name, there was a collective gasp in the room. The Professor drank his beer without looking around.

Mule Gap

It was the first time The Professor had ever been in Mule Gap, but his reputation had preceded him. Several citizens saw the man sitting tall in the saddle and dressed all in black. They knew who he was, and they were aware of his deadly skill with a handgun.

As he rode through the center of town, heading for Kennedy's Saloon, he passed by a large white house that, at first glance, could be taken as the residence of one of the town's wealthier citizens. A second glance toward the establishment disclosed a square brown sign with the name of the establishment in gold script. *The Delilah House.* It billed itself as a "Sporting House for Gentlemen."

Like several other businesses in town, the Delilah House was half owned by Warren Kennedy, though this was one business that did not sport his name on the front of the building as its co-owner. In fact, his participation in the house of ill repute was kept secret for political purposes. As far as anyone knew, the business was owned and run by Delilah Dupree, a beautiful woman who had arrived two years earlier from New Orleans. She had no reservations about the avocation she followed. She believed that, because of the overall shortage of women in Carbon County, she was actually providing a service. And to that end, she proudly promoted her services by advertising in the local newspaper, *The Mule Gap Ledger.*

~ *The Delilah House* ~
A Sporting House for Gentlemen
WHERE
BEAUTIFUL *and* CULTURED
LADIES
will provide you with every
PLEASURE.

"Why should I be ashamed of it?" she would reply to anyone who questioned her. "I give my girls a clean place to stay, and I insist that the gentlemen callers be on their best behavior. If they are not well behaved, I don't let them return."

Three men who had come into her establishment a short while earlier were behaving in any way but gentlemanly. At the moment, the three visitors were in the parlor, where they were being loud and obnoxious. One of the men was sitting on the silk-covered sofa, with his boots up on a carved table. He had a droopy eyelid and a broken and misshapen nose. He was watching the other two men who had come with him. One was large and clean-shaven, the other was of medium build and had a sweeping handlebar mustache.

Delilah kept her staff small, believing that four girls specifically chosen for their beauty and charm would be preferable to a larger staff of women who had less to offer. Three of the young women, Fancy Bliss, Joy Love, and Candy Sweet, had welcomed the three visitors with practiced smiles when they first arrived. However, as the behavior of the men became more and more disturbing, the women became apprehensive, and their interaction with the men was cautious.

"Hey, Turley," one of the two men said to the other. "Which one of 'em are you goin' to choose?"

"I can't make up my mind. What about you, Gibbons?"

"I ain't made up my mind, neither," Gibbons responded. "Hey, I know what. Why don't you whores show us your goodies? How are we s'posed to know which one of you we want to take up to your room, lessen we can see 'em and decide?"

"Why no, we couldn't do that," one of the women said.

"What do you mean, you can't do that? Iffen we choose one of you, why, you'll have to get nekkid when we take you to bed, won't you? So what's the difference 'bout us seein' you nekkid then, or a-lookin' at your titties now?"

Because Delilah was in her office at the moment, she was unaware of the boorish behavior of the three men, but Fancy Bliss had managed to slip away.

When she went into the office there was an agitated expression on her face. "Miss Dupree?"

"Yes, Fancy, what is it?"

"There are three gentlemen in the parlor that . . . well, they are not being very gentlemanly."

"Thank you, Fancy. I'll take care of it."

"Yes, ma'am."

Delilah stepped up front to the parlor and saw immediately what Fancy was talking about. "Ladies, please withdraw to your rooms now."

"Yes, ma'am," they all replied, and quickly left.

"Hey, what did you do that for?" Gibbons asked. "What good is a whorehouse without whores? I was just fixin' to pick one of 'em out."

"Please leave," Delilah said. "This house is closed."

"What do you mean, *closed*?" Turley asked. "I know they's someone upstairs with one of your whores now, on account of I seen 'em go up."

"I will soon be sending him on his way, as well. This house is now closed. Please leave."

"The hell I will. I ain't goin' nowhere till . . ."

"Please do what Miss Dupree asked you to do." Fancy had stepped back into Delilah's office and had come out holding a sawed-off shotgun."

"Let's go, Turley," the man sitting on the sofa said. "We don't want to be where we aren't wanted, now, do we?"

"Come on. We ain't even—" Turley started to say, but again his comment was interrupted by Gibbons.

"I said let's go."

"All right, all right, I'm a-goin'."

The man who had issued the order turned toward Delilah, and she took a quick intake of breath when she saw the scar. She had heard of this man, and she realized that she was walking on thin ice, ordering them around as she did.

"We'll be goin' now," he said.

"Thank you. You are welcome back anytime your . . . friends . . . can exhibit less boorish behavior."

The scar-faced man chuckled. "You hear that Gibbons, Turley? We're boring. I been called lots of things, but I ain't never been accused of borin' nobody.

"Boorish, not boring," Delilah said, but even as she made the correction, she realized that none of the three had the slightest understanding of the word. She made no further effort to enlighten them, remaining silent, except for the sigh of relief when they left her establishment.

"Joy?" Delilah said.

"Yes, ma'am?"

"As unobtrusively as you can, go upstairs and try to determine how long it will be before Jasmine is finished with her gentleman visitor."

"Yes, ma'am."

Jasmine Delight was a beautiful octoroon with golden-hued skin and emerald eyes. She had come from New Orleans with Delilah.

Joy didn't have to check on Jasmine. Even as she started to, they could hear Jasmine's voice as she came downstairs with her client, Abner Wilson. A frequent visitor from Rawlins, he was a member of the territorial legislature.

"I do hope your visit with us was a pleasant one, Mr. Wilson," Delilah said as the distinguished-looking middle-aged man stepped out into the lobby."

"How can it not be a pleasant visit when one can spend company with a young lady as delightful as Jasmine?" Wilson replied. "And may I also say that I appreciate your discretion? If word of my visits were to reach the wrong ears, it would, I fear, be the end of my political career."

"You are always the perfect gentleman, sir, and you are always welcome at the Delilah House, where discretion is as important to us as any pleasure we can provide."

Just down the street from the Delilah House, a recent arrival in town was playing poker in Kennedy's Saloon. "I'll take three," said the man dressed in all black.

The dealer gave the man in black three cards, then looked over at the next player.

"What about you, Maloney?" the dealer asked. "How many cards?"

"One," Win said.

"Drawing to an inside straight, are you?" the dealer joked, slapping a new card down in front of Maloney.

Maloney was actually trying to fill a heart flush, but when he saw that the card was a spade, he folded.

"Well, mister, it's going to cost you five bucks to see what I've got," one of the other players said to the man in black.

The man in black looked at his cards, thought about it for a moment, then, with a shrug, folded.

One of the other players who had bet heavily on the hand lost, then pushed his chair back from the table. "Boys, I'd better give this game up while I still got enough to buy myself a beer."

Just as he was leaving the game, three men were coming into the saloon. One of them, seeing an open chair, came over to the table and, without being asked, sat down.

"A person with manners would have asked if he could join," the man in black said.

"Mister, you got 'ny idea who you're talkin' to?" the new man asked.

"Obviously, I'm talking to someone who is sans manners," the man in black replied.

"Sans manners? What does that mean?"

"It means your demeanor is boorish."

"Damn, that's the second time today, I've been called a bore."

The man in black smiled patronizingly.

"You really don't know who I am, do you?" asked the man with the drooping eyelid and misshapen nose.

"So far there's nothing about your personality that would lead me to *want* to know who you are."

"Well, I damn sure know you. You're the one folks call The Professor. My name is Puckett. Billy Bob Puckett. Does that name mean anything to you?"

The Professor recognized the name but gave no indication he did. "No, I don't think I've ever heard of you. Are you someone I should know?"

The other players around the table readily recognized the name, and realizing that a showdown between two well-known gunfighters was about to occur, they reacted in apprehension.

"Mister, Professor," the player who had just won the hand said. "Maybe you ain't never heard of him, but Billy Bob Puckett is . . . uh—" he stopped in midsentence, not wanting to agitate Puckett in any way.

"You can say it," Puckett said. "You can tell The Professor here that I ain't the kind of man a feller is goin' to want to rile. That is, not if he wants to live any longer."

"Well then, Mr. Puckett, I don't want to rile you because I certainly do plan to live longer . . . so please, do join us," The Professor said. "I have to admit that I have been admiring your hat. Perhaps, if there is a fortuitous fall of the pasteboards, I might just win it tonight."

Puckett took off his hat, a low-crowned black hat surrounded by a band of silver conchas. "You ain't gettin' my hat." He pulled a stack of bills from his pocket and put them on the table in front of him. "On the other hand, after I take all your money, I might just buy me a fancy brocaded vest to go with my hat."

The Professor chuckled. "We'll see, Mr. Puckett. We'll just see."

CHAPTER 5

The Professor won the first hand, and the next hand as well, and with that hand was a few dollars ahead.

"You're a pretty lucky fella, ain't you?" Puckett said.

"Sometimes it happens," The Professor replied as he raked in his winnings. "But luck is only effective when one has the skill to best employ it."

"Yeah, like what happened last week. Was you lucky or skillful?"

"Last week?"

"Yeah, last week in Stinking Water. Are you tryin' to tell me that you don't know what I'm talkin' about? You are the one they call The Professor, ain't you?"

"I am."

"You kilt Billy Barton."

"I did."

"Well, Mr. Professor, Billy Barton was a good friend of mine. And me 'n you is goin' to have an accountin' over that."

"Wait a minute," one of the other card players said, recognizing immediately that this raw-edged conversation might well lead to gunplay. "Are you sure you two want—"

"Stay out of this, friend," Puckett said.

First that player, then the others got up and walked away,

leaving only Puckett and The Professor. They were facing each other across a table upon which lay a spread of cards, some faceup, some facedown. There also remained on the table little personal banks of money in front of where each of the players had been sitting.

"Now you've done it," The Professor said. "Your ill-mannered behavior has ruined a perfectly good card game."

"Yeah? Well, they can always find another card game, but Barton can't, can he? He can't never play cards again, and he can't never have no women again, he can't never do nothin' again, on account of he's dead. I guess maybe you didn't know at the time that he was a good friend of mine, did you?" Puckett asked.

"No, but even if I had known, it wouldn't have made any difference. By the way, your grammar is atrocious," The Professor said.

"My gran'ma is what? Look here, you ain't got no business talkin' 'bout my gran'ma! She was a fine woman!"

"I'm sure she was."

"Now that you can think back on it, I'll just bet you wish you hadn'ta shot my friend, don't you?"

"No, I would've killed him anyway," The Professor said. "He was clearly a man who needed killing."

"You see them two fellas standin' over at the bar?" Puckett asked.

When The Professor looked in the direction pointed out by Puckett, he saw two men; one large and clean-shaven, the other of medium build, with a handlebar mustache. Both were looking toward the table.

"Them two boys is Gibbons and Turley. It turns out that Billy Barton was a friend of theirs, too. Me 'n them is just all broke up over losin' a good friend like we done."

"Yes, I could tell just how upset you gentlemen must have been over the demise of your friend by the grief you expressed at his funeral," The Professor said. "Oh, wait. That's right. There was no funeral, was there?"

"We was plannin' one," Puckett said.

"Really? Apparently, you didn't mention that little detail to the undertaker. Mr. Barton was laid out in a plain pine box, then buried on the far side of Boot Hill without even a marker."

"How do you know?"

"Because I was there," The Professor answered. "And I was the only one, except for the two grave diggers."

"You always go to the buryin' of men you kill?" Puckett asked.

The Professor flashed a cold look at Puckett. "When I can," he answered pointedly. "Sometimes I bury them myself."

"Just how many men have you killed?" Puckett asked.

"As many as I needed to."

"Is that right? Well, you won't be killin' no more."

"And why would you say that?"

"Because I'm about to kill you."

"And would that be just you, Mr. Puckett? Or do your two friends intend to cut themselves in to the dance?"

"Well now, that don't really matter none, does it? I mean, as long as you'll be dead."

Puckett started to draw his pistol, unaware that The Professor had already drawn his gun and was holding it under the table. The Professor fired, and Puckett's eyes opened in surprise as the bullet plowed into him before he could even clear leather.

The Professor turned his gun toward the two men at the bar . . . and though the odds had been three to one, he had the advantage. He already had his gun out, and Gibbons and Turley had been given no advance warning as to when Puckett intended to make his move. The Professor shot two more times. Gibbons, who was able to draw and point his gun toward The Professor, managed to take two steps before he fell. Turley had gone down in place.

"Son of a bitch! Did you all see that?" someone said. "The Professor took on three of 'em 'n kilt all three! 'N one of 'em he kilt was Billy Bob Puckett!"

Warren Kennedy poured cognac from a cut-glass decanter into two crystal snifters. "This is vintage 1858. I think you will find it more than adequate."

The Professor lifted the glass to his nose and took a whiff. "It has a very good nose."

The Professor and Kennedy held their glasses toward each other, though they didn't actually clink them together.

"Your real name is Frank Bodine?" Kennedy asked.

"Yes."

"Tell me, Mr. Bodine. Why do they call you the Professor?"

"I am called that because I actually am a professor. I have a PhD in English and taught that subject at the College of William and Mary."

Kennedy looked surprised. "Begorra! And are you for telling me you really were a professor? I thought perhaps they called you that because—"

"Of my skill with a pistol?" The Professor interrupted the observation with his reply. I suppose there is some justification for having that opinion."

"Yes. How did you . . . that is . . . a college professor as a professional gunman? You have to admit that 'tis a strange combination. How is that you be here in the West, following your . . . uh . . . particular line of work, rather than bein' a professor back at William and Mary?"

"I should have been promoted to head of the department," The Professor said. "I had the most seniority and I had the best record. But I was passed over in favor of the dean's nephew."

"That explains why you are no longer teaching, but not your skill with a pistol."

"The art of the fast draw and pistol marksmanship had always been a hobby of mine. I practiced until I was quite proficient, then I began to give demonstrations. I know there could be nothing more contrary to expectation than someone in the staid profession of academia being extraordinarily skilled in the use of a pistol, but I think that was, at least in part, what drew me to the practice. When I gave up my professorship, I decided to see if I could convert my hobby into a profession, and I realized that the best place to do that would be in the West. And that is what I have done for the last few years."

"Converting your hobby into a profession? That is an interesting choice of words," Kennedy said. "What you mean is you have been selling your gun to the highest bidder."

"Yes. Except, of course, when I am challenged by someone for a real or manufactured reason, such as the incident involving Billy Barton. I must confess that in contemplating my new profession, I had not considered the idea that there would be people wanting to kill me for the simple reason of enhancing their own reputation. I am quite certain that is what Billy Barton had in mind when he forced the encounter with me back in Stinking Water. And, despite Puckett's claim of revenge over the loss of his friend, I have no doubt but that his challenge was inspired by the same desire to enhance his reputation by killing The Professor."

"How would you like to get out of that business and use your gun only for legitimate purposes?"

"You mean become a lawman?"

"Aye."

The Professor shook his head. "I got five hundred dollars for killing Billy Barton. I'll be getting a like amount for killing Billy Bob Puckett. I don't know yet if there was any reward on either Gibbons or Turley, but I expect there is."

"There is. One hundred and fifty dollars on each of them," Kennedy said.

"Well then, there's thirteen hundred dollars I have earned legitimately just in the last two weeks. When I say that I have been selling my guns, that is true . . . but so far I have employed them only in the pursuit of wanted men for which bounties have been posted. No law position can pay that much."

"It can, if you combine the salary of being the city marshal for Mule Gap and my personal bodyguard," Kennedy said. "I can pay you a thousand dollars per month, and you won't have to be riding all over the territory, looking for elusive wanted men. However should you, in the pursuit of your duty, happen to kill a wanted man, we can put a caveat in your employment contract that would authorize you to keep any reward offered."

"Why would you need a bodyguard?"

"I have gotten involved in several business operations since arriving in Mule Gap," Kennedy said. "And in so doing, I have also made some enemies. I am quite proficient myself in the use of a pistol, though I'm sure I'm not as good as you are. 'Tis thinkin' I am that with my own efficacy, augmented by your even more formidable skill, my position as mayor and as a businessman would be practically unassailable."

"A thousand dollars per month?"

"Yes."

"Are your businesses doing that well that you can afford to pay me a thousand dollars a month?"

"Oh, I won't be paying you from my own pocket. I'll impose a special protection tax that will cover your salary." Kennedy laughed. "Like you, Professor Bodine, I also had a life before I came west, and in New York one of my particular specialties was in collecting a protection tax from businessmen, even if they didn't particularly want to buy the insurance."

The Professor extended his hand. "In that case, I think that from now on, *Marshal Bodine* would be a more appropriate sobriquet than *The Professor*. I accept your most generous offer."

"Thank you, Marshal Bodine. Go ahead and set up your office. Please feel free to come to me with anything that you might need."

"Deputies?"

"Yes, I'm glad you brought that up. I think you should have at least ten deputies. Pick out ten men who are particularly good with guns."

"Ten? For a town this small, why would I need any deputies at all?"

"I have plans," Kennedy said without being more specific. "Do you think you can find ten good men?"

"It depends on what you mean by *good*. 'Good' and 'good with guns' are not always compatible concepts. If you are talking about good with guns, I don't think they would be particularly interested in being deputy city marshals."

"You can offer them two hundred dollars a month and promise them extra sources of income that would pay even more than their salaries."

"What sources of income would those be?"

Kennedy finished his cognac before he replied. "As I told you, I'm a businessman, Marshal Bodine. And as it so happens, I'm a very good businessman. You let me worry about the additional sources of income."

"Just so that you understand, the deputies I hire will be of somewhat unsavory character."

"In the pursuit of peace, I am prepared to close my eyes to any such iniquities as your deputies might bring with them."

The Professor smiled. "Then I shall assemble my police force."

Sugarloaf Ranch

"Guess who I got a letter from today?" Sally said when Smoke came into the house.

"The Queen of England?"

"No, that was yesterday," Sally said, laughing. "Today I got a letter from Rosanna MacCallister. She and Andrew are opening a new play next week, and she's invited you and me."

"Sally, you know I can't go. I'm going up to Mule Gap."

"For two days," Sally said. "You would be back in plenty of time. I know you very well, Kirby Jensen. It isn't that you can't go, it's that you don't want to go."

"You're right. I don't want to go. I've been to New York. It's too crowded. But that doesn't mean you can't go."

"I don't want to go without you. I wouldn't enjoy it without you."

"You would enjoy it even more, and you know it. I would just be complaining and finding fault with everything."

Sally chuckled. "Yes, you would be doing that. You don't mind if I go by myself, do you?"

"No, I don't mind. Go, enjoy yourself, and give my excuses to Andrew and Rosanna."

"What excuse will I give?"

"You're the smartest person I know, Sally. You'll be able to come up with something."

"How about, Smoke sends his regrets, but he is auditioning for the ballet in San Francisco?"

Smoke laughed. "Yes, that ought to work."

Big Rock, Colorado

The ticket agent began stamping his authorization block, first on the inkpad, then on one of the ticket stubs, doing it several times so quickly that it sounded almost like beating a drum. When he was finished, he attached the tickets into two bundles with a couple spring clamps, smiled, and handed them to Sally. "There you are, Mrs. Jensen. This first batch of tickets will allow you to change trains in Denver, Kansas City, St. Louis, Chicago, Cleveland, and New York. Well, of course you won't change trains in New York until you start back home again. Then you use the second batch of tickets to change trains in—"

"Let me guess," Sally said. "Cleveland, Chicago, St. Louis, Kansas City, and Denver."

"Yes, that's it exactly."

"Thank you, Mr. Peabody. I'll try and remember that."

"You might want to make a note," Peabody suggested.

"Thank you," Sally said again.

CHAPTER 6

Sally had come to town, not only to buy tickets for her upcoming trip to New York, but also to shop for some new clothes. She had come with Smoke and they had taken the surrey rather than riding into town. Before they left, Smoke had apologized to Seven for leaving him behind.

"Smoke, for heaven's sake, Seven isn't a dog who misses his master," Sally had told him. "He's a horse."

"Yes, but he isn't just any horse, and you know it."

Sally laughed. "You're right. He is a magnificent horse, but the surrey is best for bringing my purchases back home."

Once they'd reached town, Smoke had announced that he would get a haircut, then wait for her at Longmont's Saloon.

He was in Earl's Barbershop when Sam Condon came in.

"Hello, neighbor," Smoke said.

"Hi, Smoke. I was just down to the bank and heard that you would be going up to Mule Gap tomorrow."

"That's right."

"Do you know a rancher there named Jim Harris? He owns Cross Trail, a ranch that's just outside Mule Gap."

"Yes, I know Jim. He's a good man."

"I just sold him Yankee Star."

"Yankee Star, huh? That's a damn fine bull," Smoke said.

"He is indeed, and I sort of hate to see him go, but Mr.

Harris made a very generous offer, and I don't feel I can turn him down. But, here's the thing. There's no bank in Mule Gap, and Harris is holding twenty-five hundred dollars in cash for me, the rest to be paid when the bull is delivered. I was going to go up and get it myself, but I heard you were going up, and if you could pick the money up for me, it would save me a trip, seeing as I will have to go up again when Thad and I deliver the bull."

"I'd be glad to, Sam, but there is a bank in Mule Gap. I do a lot of business in the Wyoming Territory, and I thought it would be good to have an account there. As a matter of fact, that's why I'm going up."

"Hmm. Well, maybe I misunderstood him. Anyway he's holding the money for me in cash, and I'd be pleased if you would pick it up for me."

"All right. If he wants to do a cash business, I'll pick up the money for you."

Earl chuckled.

"What are you laughing about?" Smoke asked.

"Well, think about it, Smoke. How many men would trust another man to bring him two thousand five hundred dollars in cash money?"

"Anyone who has a good friend who is also an honest man," Sam replied, answering the question even though it had been posed to Smoke.

Earl nodded. "I reckon you're right, at that."

"So, Thad's going to help you deliver the bull?" Smoke asked.

"Yes, he's looking forward to riding Fire up there. It will be the longest he's ever ridden him. You have no idea how much he and Fire have taken to each other. That was quite a wonderful thing you did when you gave him that horse."

"Thad's become quite a good hand for you, hasn't he?"

"Yes, he has, for all that he is only fourteen years old.

He's a good enough worker that I have no need for any hired hands."

"You do pay him, don't you?" Earl asked.

"Oh yes, he insists upon it, and I do pay him. But I'm making him put one half of it in a special savings account so that he'll have enough money to go to college when he comes of age. I have to admit he complains about that a little."

"That's a good idea to make him save like that. He may complain now, but he'll thank you someday," Earl said.

Sam chuckled. "Yeah, I'll tell him that."

"Sam, I'll need a letter from you to Jim, authorizing me to pick up the money," Smoke said.

"If you'll stop by Longmont's after you're finished here, I'll write the letter out for you," Sam promised.

"By coincidence, that's just where I planned to go next. I'll be down soon as Earl finishes up with me."

With a parting wave, Sam left the barbershop.

"Mr. Condon seems like a good man," Earl said. "When he came here after Ned and Molly were murdered, most of us thought he would just sell Wiregrass 'n go back to St. Louis. I mean, him bein' a lawyer 'n all. Who would have thought that a lawyer would want to run a ranch?"

"He's a good businessman, and even though Wiregrass is a small ranch, Sam has found a way to make it very successful," Smoke said. "He doesn't need hired hands because he's never had more than twenty to fifty head at any given time. He has specialized in raising only purebred Herefords, and he gets good money for them. Well, you heard him. He wants me to pick up twenty-five hundred dollars from Jim Harris for Yankee Star, and that's only half the money."

"I've had ranchers in here feeling good when their cows bring forty dollars a head." Earl pulled the barber's cape from Smoke, then turned the chair around so Smoke could examine himself in the mirror. "All finished, young man. What do you think?"

"Considering what you started with, I'd say you did a good job." Smoke gave the barber forty cents, a sum that included a fifteen-cent tip. "I guess I'll go have my beer now."

Louis Longmont was a Frenchman from New Orleans, and he was quick to point out that he was truly French, not Cajun. The difference, he explained, was that his parents moved to Louisiana directly from France, and not from Acadia. Louis owned Longmont's, which was one of two saloons in Big Rock, the other saloon being the Brown Dirt Cowboy Saloon

The Brown Dirt tended to cater to cowboys and working-men, and it provided not only alcoholic beverages and a limited menu, but also bar girls who did more than just provide drinks. Longmont's, on the other hand, was more like a club in which ladies not only felt welcome, but were assured there would be no stigma to their frequenting the establishment.

When Smoke stepped into the saloon he saw Sam sitting at Louis Longmont's private table. Access to Louis's private table was limited to those people he invited or those who he classified as personal friends. Smoke had been in the latter category for a number of years now, and Sam had been included shortly after he arrived.

"Stop by the bar and grab your beer," Sam said. "It's already paid for."

A moment later, with beer in hand, Smoke joined Sam and Louis at Louis's table.

"Sam was telling me all about Yankee Star," Louis said.

"I offered to draw high card for him, but he said he wasn't interested."

"I don't blame him," Smoke said. "Who would gamble a bull like Yankee Star on one card?"

"But think of it this way. If he won, he'd have the price of the bull and he'd still have the bull."

"You and I both know he wouldn't have won," Smoke said.

"Wait a minute. It's too big a gamble for me to take, but how do you know I wouldn't have won? The odds would be fifty-fifty that I would win."

"No, the odds would be one hundred percent that you wouldn't win. Let me show you why you were smart not to take him up on his offer," Smoke said. Smoke put a gold double eagle on the table. "All right, Louis. Let's cut."

"You first," Louis replied.

Smoke smiled. "He always has his sucker go first so he knows what card he *will* draw to win."

"You don't mean what he will draw to win. You mean what he *has* to draw to win, don't you?" Sam replied.

"No, I mean what he *will* draw to win. Watch."

Smoke drew a nine. Louis drew a jack.

"Double or nothing?" Louis asked with a smile.

Smoke drew a five. Louis drew a seven.

"Wait. That's just dumb luck, isn't it?" Sam asked.

With a laugh, Louis slid the gold coin back toward Smoke, then put the deck down in front of Sam. "Draw a card, Sam," he invited. "No bet."

Sam drew a king, then smiled. "Beat that."

Louis drew an ace.

"What the hell? How are you doing that? And you wanted to draw high card for Yankee Star?"

"I would have given him back," Louis said.

"You mean if you had won. What am I talking about? Of course you would have won."

"I was just teaching you an object lesson," Louis said. "Never gamble when all the odds are against you."

"I've got a feeling that if anyone gambles with you, the odds are always against them."

"That's why I never gamble," Louis said. He paused for a moment. "At least, not anymore."

"May I join you? Or is this a gentlemen-only club?"

All three men stood when Sally approached the table, and Smoke pulled out a chair for her.

"Did you get everything done?" Smoke asked.

"Yes, train tickets and a new dress to wear to the opening of the play."

"Madam Jensen, as beautiful as you will be in a new dress, all eyes in the audience will be on you, and I fear the poor players will strut and fret their hour upon the stage and be heard no more," Longmont said.

Sally laughed and clapped her hands. "Louis, you are wonderful the way compliments roll trippingly from the tongue."

"Are you two just going to trade Shakespeare with each other, or are we going to eat dinner?" Smoke said.

"Lunch, not dinner," Sally replied.

"All right, lunch. And, Louis no disrespect for the meals you serve, but I'm in the mood for a big thick, steak, so we'll be taking our dinner—"

"Lunch," Sally corrected again.

"Lunch at Lamberts."

"Just don't get hit by a throwed roll," Sam said.

"Thrown," Sally said. "And, yes, I know what the sign on the false front of the building says, but I just refuse to see it."

"Perhaps I should throw bottles of wine to my customers," Louis suggested. He laughed. "Every now and then I'm tempted to do just that, only I wouldn't be throwing a bottle to them, as much as it would be at them."

Moniel, Wyoming

When Duly Plappert dismounted in front of the Ace High Saloon, he pulled his pistol, rotated the cylinder so that a loaded chamber was under the firing pin, then pushed in through the batwing doors. Plappert was a bounty hunter, and the man he was looking for, Don Ingles, was standing at the far end of the bar.

"All you folks standing at the bar, step away," Plappert called.

"Who the hell are you to tell us to step—" Recognizing Plappert, the man who spoke swallowed the rest of his question, grabbed his drink, and left the bar. The others did the same, but when Ingles started to leave the bar, Plappert called out to him.

"Not you, Ingles. Me 'n you got business to settle."

"I ain't goin' to fight you, Plappert," Ingles said. "If you want to take me in, go ahead. But I ain't goin' to fight you."

"You got no choice," Plappert said. "You're worth two hunnert 'n fifty dollars to me, dead or alive. So if you don't draw on me, I'll just kill you anyway, then step down to the marshal's office to collect my reward."

"I ain't goin' to draw ag'in you. I told you that."

Plappert smiled a slow, evil smile. "And I told you, I don't care whether you draw on me or not. I can kill you, 'n it'll all be legal."

With a shout of fear, Ingles made a frantic grab for his pistol. Plappert's smile grew broader. He was actually enjoying the moment. He drew his pistol in a quick, smooth draw, then fired, his bullet catching Ingles in the chest. Then, even as Ingles lay dying on the floor, Plappert walked down to City Marshal Coleman's office to claim his prize.

Plappert waited in the office while Marshal Coleman walked down to the saloon to make certain that the man Plappert shot really was Don Ingles. As Plappert waited, he started looking through the marshal's wanted posters for his next job. That was when he saw a recruiting poster from Mule Gap.

—WANTED—

Men to Serve as
SPECIAL DEPUTIES

· HIGH SALARY ! *and* ADDITIONAL REWARDS !

☞ *See* The Professor
MULE GAP, WYOMING

Plappert was intrigued by the offer of "high salary and additional rewards." He was also intrigued by the fact that the person offering the job was the man known as The Professor. Plappert knew The Professor, and he knew that he wouldn't be involved in anything like this unless the pay was very good.

Coleman came back into the office.

"You satisfied that it's Ingles?" Plappert asked.

"He ain't dead yet," Coleman said.

"But you seen that it's Ingles, right?"

"He's dyin' hard."

"Marshal, I don't give damn how hard he's dyin' or how long it takes for the son of a bitch to die. All I need from you is to say that the man lying on the floor back in the saloon is Don Ingles, 'n that they's people in the saloon will tell you that I'm the one that shot 'im."

"It's Ingles," Marshal Coleman said.

"Now I'll need you to authorize payment of the two hunnert 'n fifty dollars."

"Two hundred fifty dollars seems an awfully small amount of money for a man's life," Coleman said.

"Hell, it ain't my fault that it's no higher, Marshal. I don't set the rewards," Plappert said.

One hour later and two hundred and fifty dollars richer, Plappert rode out of town. Folded up in his pocket was the recruiting poster he had seen in the marshal's office. He was heading toward Mule Gap.

CHAPTER 7

Mule Gap

Smoke was visiting Warren Kennedy in the mayor's office.

"None of my people gave you any trouble in making your deposit, did they?" Kennedy asked.

Smoke chuckled. "Warren, have you ever heard of a bank that *didn't* want to take your money?"

Kennedy laughed as well. "I guess you have a point there. I'm disappointed you didn't bring Sally with you. I would have enjoyed taking the two of you out to dinner."

"In your restaurant," Smoke said.

"I only own half of it," Kennedy replied

"Which means what? That you would have only had to pay for half the meal?"

Kennedy laughed again.

"Sally is at home, getting ready for her trip."

"Her trip? What trip?"

"Three days from now she'll be boarding the train to go to New York."

"Do you mean to tell me that she's going to New York, and you aren't going with her?"

"There's nothing in New York that I need to see," Smoke said.

"I agree with you there. I see no need for me to return to New York."

"Well," Smoke said, standing. "I'd better be going. I have to stop by Cross Trail before I start back."

"Harris's ranch? What are you doing out there?"

"A friend of mine sold a very expensive bull to Harris. I'm picking up twenty-five hundred dollars in cash, which is the first half of the purchase price. The other half is to be paid when the bull is delivered. To be honest, it seems a little strange to me. I don't know why Harris wants to deal in cash, when he has a bank here."

"I don't understand that, either," Kennedy said. "Who is your friend that sold the bull?"

"His name is Sam Condon. He runs Wiregrass, a small ranch next to mine."

Kennedy laughed. "He owns a *small* ranch next to yours? Smoke, from what I've heard about Sugarloaf, by comparison, just about *every* ranch is small."

Smoke nodded. "I do have a lot of acres. But in this case, Wiregrass really is small. Sam raises only purebred cattle, and the only help he has is his son."

"Can he make a living, raising just purebred cattle?"

"Are you kidding?" Smoke asked. "Do you really have no idea how much money purebred bulls can bring in? Sam Conrad is doing exceptionally well. He lives modestly, no hired hands, just him, his wife, and their boy. But he is a very wealthy man."

"How old is the boy?"

"If you would have asked me that a week ago, I wouldn't have been able to tell you. But he's fourteen. I know, because Sam just told me the other day."

"Well, I'm happy for anyone who is successful," Kennedy replied. "Come. I'll walk you to the door."

"No need to do that." Smoke laughed. "I'm sure that someone who owns half a town, as well as being the mayor, can find more things to keep him busy than to walk a visitor to the door."

"Ah, but you aren't just any visitor," Kennedy said. "You're a special visitor, and someday I'll find a way to get you to transfer all your money from the Bank of Big Rock to my bank."

"I don't think you'll be able to do that unless you move your bank at least twenty miles closer to Sugarloaf."

"Well, you've got me there," Kennedy said. "Next time you come to Mule Gap, be sure and bring Sally with you. I'll take both of you out to dinner."

"Maybe, when she gets back from New York, we'll do just that."

Fort Laramie, Wyoming

Clem Bates, Dan Cooper, Henry Barnes, and Slim Gibson were civilian scouts riding with the Second Cavalry. The great battles with the Northern Plains Indians had mostly passed, but there were still isolated raids against neighboring ranches, freight wagons, remote stores, and trading posts. One recent raid, led by Stone Eagle, had looted a store, then burned the building down.

Captain Neil Lewis of D Troop, 2nd Cavalry, led his troop in pursuit, and they caught up with three of the warriors on Horseshoe Creek, just north of the Laramie Peaks.

"Bates—you, Cooper, Barnes, and Gibson take these three back to the fort," Captain Lewis said. "I'm sure Stone Eagle is in one of the canyons in Laramie Peaks, and I think I know which one. We're going after him, and the ones with him."

Bates waited until the soldiers were out of sight, then he turned to the others. "I'm all for goin' back to the fort and havin' a beer, but I see no reason to take these heathen bastards along with us."

"What do you have in mind?" Barnes asked.

Bates looked at the three Indians who were standing with their hands tied in front of them. The Indians were staring sullenly at the four white men who had been left in charge.

"You are not Long Knives?" one of the Indians asked, referring to the term used by the Indians when speaking of soldiers.

"Nah," Barnes said. "We are civilians. We work for the army, but we ain't army."

"You will take us to the fort?"

Barnes shook his head. "We ain't takin' you to the fort. We're goin' to let you go."

The Indian translated for the other two, and all three smiled. The English-speaking Indian held out his hands. "You untie, and give us our guns?"

"No, I ain't goin' that far with you. I'm lettin' you go. Ain't that enough?"

"Yes, that is enough."

The Indians started toward their ponies, but Barnes called out to them.

"Uh-uh. You walk. If I give you your horses, like as not you'd join back up with Stone Eagle. You walk."

With a nod of understanding, the Indians turned and started to walk away.

Barnes drew his pistol and signaled for the others to do the same. He fired the first shot, shots from the other three coming quickly behind his shot. For the next few seconds the valley ran with gunshots as all three Indians went down.

Gibson was the first to get to them.

"Are they dead?" Barnes called out.

"Deader 'n a doornail," Gibson replied.

It was three days later when Colonel Roxbury called the four scouts into his office. "You say that the Indians were trying to run away, and I can't prove that they weren't, but there were a total of eighteen bullet holes in those three men, every one of them in the back."

"Yes, sir, well, when someone is running from you, their back is all you see," Barnes said.

Roxbury stroked his chin. "I'm lettin' you boys go. Every one of you. We have a hard enough time maintaining peace with the Indians as it is. It is people like you that make things even harder. I want you off this fort within the next fifteen minutes."

It was in the North Pass Saloon in Millersburg, later that afternoon, that they learned that a marshal they called The Professor was looking for men to be his deputies. The unusual aspect of the call was that he was willing to pay well and offered additional inducements.

"Come on, boys," Barnes said. "We're goin' to be deputies."

The Blackwell residence, Mule Gap

Lorena Coy was sitting in the swing on the front porch, keeping an eye on seven-year-old Eddie Blackwell, who, because he was small even for a seven-year-old, was called "Wee." His father Richard owned the Blackwell Emporium and was the wealthiest man in Mule Gap, even wealthier than Warren Kennedy. His store was successful enough that, unlike several other business owners in town, he was able to resist offers of partnership with Kennedy. And because he had loaned a few of his friends and fellow businessmen money when they needed it, he helped them stave off Kennedy's offer of partnership as well.

As a result not only of Blackwell's independence but also of his role in helping other businesses maintain their autonomy, he and Kennedy became business competitors, though they treated their adversarial relationship in a gentlemanly manner.

Richard Blackwell owned a brick house just outside the city limits, saying that he preferred country living to city living.

"City? What city? Surely you aren't calling Mule Gap a city, are you?" one of his friends had teased.

"Any place that has houses no more than fifty feet apart is a city," Richard had insisted.

Lorena was a fourteen-year-old-girl who lived with her mother. Since her father had died two years earlier, it had been difficult for the Coy family. Lorena's mother Sandra had to give up the house and move her and Lorena into a three-room apartment in Welsh's Boarding House. She then went to work as a clerk in the Blackwell Emporium, while Lorena took on the job of watching out for Wee, as both Richard and Edna Blackwell worked in the emporium.

At the moment, Wee was sitting on the ground under a tree.

"Wee, stay in the grass," Lorena called out to him. "Don't get in the mud and get all dirty. If you do, your mama would be really upset with you."

"She'd be upset with you, too, for letting me get all dirty," Wee said.

Lorena chuckled. "Yes, she would. And you don't want me getting in trouble, do you?"

"I'll stay out of the dirt," Wee promised.

Lorena turned her attention back to reading the book, only to be interrupted a few minutes later by a buckboard being driven into the front yard. There were two men in the buckboard, and both of them climbed down.

"If you've come to see Mr. Blackwell, he isn't here," Lorena said.

"That's good, because we didn't come to see either one of them," one of the men said.

"Oh? Then, what can I do for you?"

"You can come get into the buckboard," one of the men said.

"What? Why on earth would I want to do that?"

One of the men pointed his pistol at Wee. "Because you are going with us."

"What do you mean, go with you? Go where?"

"You'll go where we take you, and quit asking so damn many questions. Because if you don't come, we're goin' to kill this kid."

"Lorena, don't let them kill me!" Wee called out.

"All right, all right. I'll go with you," Lorena said. "Please, don't hurt him."

Lorena walked out to the buckboard, then she hesitated. "I can't go with you. There's no one to look after Wee. I can't leave him by himself."

"Oh, you don't have to worry none about that, girly. He'll be comin' with us, as well."

One of the two men walked up to the front porch and, using a knife, pinned a note to the front door of the house.

*We have your boy and the girl. You will be
contacted with instructions as to how much money it
will cost you and where to leave it. If you ever want
to see your boy again, you will do as you are told.*

A few miles north of the Blackwell residence, and unaware of the drama that was being played out there, Smoke Jensen was enjoying an after-lunch cup of coffee at Cross Trail Ranch. "Mrs. Harris, that was a great dinner."

"There's plenty left," Mrs. Harris said.

"Thank you, but I don't think I could eat another bite."

"Well, then, I shall leave you men to your business," she said.

Jim poured another cup of coffee, then slid it across the table to Smoke. "If you'll just sit there, I'll go get the money, then come back and count out the twenty-five hundred dollars. I had the bank in Douglas give it to me, all in twenty-dollar bills."

"All right," Smoke agreed, taking a swallow of his coffee as Jim left the room. He returned a moment later, holding a bundle of money. He began counting it out, making five stacks of twenty-dollar bills, twenty-five of them in each stack.

"Have you seen Yankee Star?" Jim asked as he counted out the money.

"Yes, I have. He's a fine bull, and you are getting your money's worth. But then, any bull Sam sells is worth the money. He is one smart man, finding a way to make such a small spread as profitable as he has."

"Yes, from my dealings with him I figured out long ago that he was a smart man."

"Jim, I'm curious. Why are you dealing in cash? The bank in Big Rock will certainly recognize drafts drawn on the bank of Mule Gap."

Jim chuckled. "They won't honor my draft if I have no money in Kennedy's bank to back it up."

"You said you had the bank in Douglas issue the money in twenty-dollar bills. But you are a lot closer to Mule Gap than Douglas. Why not use the bank in Mule Gap?"

"You've seen how things are in town, haven't you? Hell, Kennedy has his finger in just about every business in Mule Gap. I don't want to wind up with him owning half of Cross Trail."

"There's no way he could do that unless you sell half of

it to him, or borrow against the ranch and are unable to pay it back."

"You don't have to worry any about that. I have no intention of selling any of my ranch to him, nor do I ever intend to borrow money from him. I just don't trust him."

"I think you have him all wrong. Don't confuse being an astute and opportunistic businessman with dishonesty."

"As far as I know, cash is still negotiable, is it not?" Harris replied.

"Indeed it is."

"Then, as long as I don't need to borrow any money, I have no need for a bank."

"I suppose not." Smoke replied with a chuckle. He picked up the first of the five stacks of bills, all of which were bound by ribbons Mrs. Harris had provided for that purpose. He had brought his saddle bags into the house and put the stacks into the bag. "I'd better get started. I've a long ride ahead of me."

"Take care, Smoke, and thank you for doing this for us."

"No problem," Smoke said, tossing a wave over his shoulder as he started toward Seven, who had been waiting patiently for him.

CHAPTER 8

On the road to Mule Gap

"Hey Beamus. You see anythin' yet?"

The man named Beamus was lying on a rock, looking north toward Mule Gap. "No, I ain't seen nothin' yet. Listen, Quince, are you sure this fella is goin' to have twenty-five hunnert dollars on 'im?"

"Yeah, I'm sure. Twenty-five hunnert dollars in cash money."

Though at the moment only Beamus and Quince were talking, there were actually three men waiting at North Gate Canyon, which was just south of the line that separated Wyoming from Colorado. The third man was taking a leak.

"Hey, Parker, how long does it take you to piss, anyway?" Quince asked. "You want to be standin' there with your pecker in your hand when Jensen shows up?"

"You heard what Beamus said. He said he ain't seen nothin' yet," Parker replied, buttoning up his pants. "Hey, you're good at cipherin', Beamus. Oncet we get a-holt of this money, how much will that be for each of us?"

"Five hunnert dollars apiece."

"Five hunnert? Hell, they's only three of us. Even I know

that a third of twenty-five hunnert dollars is more 'n five hunnert."

"A thousand dollars goes to the feller that set this up for us," Beamus said.

"Wait. He gets a thousand dollars, 'n he don't take no risk a-tall? That ain't right," Parker said.

"We wouldn'ta even knowed about it iffen he hadn't told us. Besides, when was the last time you had five hunnert dollars that was all your'n?"

"That's a easy question to answer, on account of I ain't never had five hunnert dollars all at the same time."

"Well then, what's your complaint?"

"It just don't seem right, is all. Hey, I've got a idea. Why don't we keep all the money for our ownself, 'n just ride outta here?"

Beamus shook his head. "You ever hear tell of killin' the golden goose?"

"What golden goose?"

"Never mind. The reason we ain't goin' to just keep the money 'n ride outta here, is on account of cause he'll be comin' up with a lot of other jobs for us, just like this. We can make a lot of money if we just stick with him."

"Someone's a-comin'," Quince called down to the two men.

"All right. Let's get ready for 'im," Beamus ordered.

Smoke had been riding for a little over two hours. Behind him, like a line drawn down through the middle of the road, the darker color of hoof-churned earth stood out against the lighter, sunbaked ground. The way before him stretched out in motionless waves, one right after another. As each wave was crested, another was exposed and beyond that another still. The ride was a symphony of sound—the jangle of the horse's bit and harness, the squeaking leather as he shifted his weight upon the saddle, and the dull thud of hoofbeats.

Seven knew the way back home, and Smoke, who had had a long day, was so relaxed in the saddle that he was taking quick, short naps. The lack of attention to detail meant a man was able to leap out in front of him.

"Stop right there, mister!" the man shouted. He held a double-barreled shotgun leveled at Smoke

"Now, why do I get the idea you didn't stop me to ask for directions?" Smoke asked.

"Ha-ha. Did you hear that, Quince? Parker? We've got the drop on him, 'n he's makin' jokes."

The two other men walked out from behind an out-cropping of rocks adjacent to the road. Neither of them had drawn their pistols, depending on the shotgun to be all the cover they needed.

"Yeah, Beamus," Quince said. "He's just real funny."

"Get down off that horse," Beamus ordered.

Smoke could barely contain the smile as he slid out of the saddle. His chances against the three men were greatly improved by being dismounted.

"Now, mister, if you want to live, you'll hand over the money," Beamus said.

"What money?"

"Don't give us none o' that," Beamus said. "The twenty-five hunnert dollars in cash that you're a-carryin'."

"How do you know I'm carrying exactly two thousand five hundred dollars? To know the specific amount requires previous knowledge."

"It don't matter how we know. The point is you're about to hand that money over to us."

"I'm afraid I can't do that. If you know about the money, you also know that the money doesn't belong to me."

"Well, hell. If it ain't your money, then it ought not to bother you none to give it over to us," Quince said.

"Besides which, if you don't give us the money we'll just kill you and take it anyway," Parker added.

"Speaking of killing . . . isn't it funny how people will wake up in the morning with no idea that they won't be alive to see nightfall?" Smoke said.

"Well, hell, mister, you can still be alive come nightfall. All you have to do is hand over the money like we told you to."

"Oh, I wasn't talking about me not being alive," Smoke said. "I was talking about the three of you. I'll bet that when you three woke up this morning, you had no idea this would be the day you'd die."

"Are you crazy, mister? There's three of us," Parker said.

"That's all right. I've got three bullets."

"Damn, Beamus, shoot the son of a bitch!" Quince shouted as first he and then Parker sent their hands darting toward their pistols.

Beamus put his thumb on the hammers of the shotgun, but before he could pull them back, Smoke drew and fired. His second and third shots were so close upon the heels of the first that it sounded as if only one shot had been fired. Quince and Parker had barely cleared their holsters and were already collapsing before Beamus hit the ground.

Smoke checked the three men, ascertaining what he already knew . . . that they were dead. It took him but a few minutes to find the horses they had staked out. He didn't know which horse belonged to whom, but under the circumstances, he didn't think it mattered. He draped a body across each horse, then tying the reins of the two trailing horses to the saddle horn before them, he took the reins of the first horse and led them three miles until he reached the next town, Walden. He was acquainted with the sheriff there.

A single rider leading three horses, each containing a body thrown across the saddle, attracted a lot of attention. Though the townspeople didn't follow him down the street, the boardwalks on each side of Main Street quickly filled with the morbidly curious.

Smoke stopped and called out to one of the men, "Where's the undertaker?"

"He's on this street down at the corner of Fifth 'n Main. He's got his place in the back of the Adam's Feed 'n Seed store."

"Thanks. Would you mind stopping at the sheriff's office and asking him to come down?"

"You *want* the sheriff?" the man asked, surprised by the request.

For a moment, Smoke wondered why there was such a tone of surprise in the man's response, then he realized that the man might think he had murdered the three men.

"Yes, tell Sheriff Rand that Smoke Jensen would like to see him down at the mortuary."

That seemed to assuage the man's concern, and with a nod, he hurried to his task.

"Yeah, I know all three of these boys," Sheriff Rand said a few minutes later after he had examined the bodies. "They've been hopping back and forth across the Wyoming and Colorado line for the last five years, causin' trouble in both places."

"I'm transporting twenty-five hundred dollars in cash," Smoke said, "and these three knew the exact amount I was carrying."

"Well now, how would they know that?" the sheriff asked.

"That's a very good question," Smoke replied. "Just how did they know not only that I was carrying money, but the exact amount I was carrying?"

"Someone had to tell them," the sheriff said. "Who knew about it?"

"I don't know. The people in the bank at Douglas. Maybe someone who just happened to be in the bank when Mr. Harris got the money. Could be some of the hands who worked on Cross Trail knew about it," Smoke said.

"Yes, well, thanks to you, the money is still there. By the way, I think there's a couple hundred dollars reward on each of these boys."

"Collect the reward and give it to the county," Smoke said.

"That's real generous of you, Smoke. The county appreciates that."

"You can do the same thing with their horses."

"All three of the horses is more 'n likely stoled," the sheriff said, "but if we don't find the owners, we'll do just that."

With the sheriff informed and the bodies taken care of, Smoke left the mortuary and walked out to Seven.

"What about Pearlie and Cal?" Sheriff Rand asked. "Those two boys stayin' out of trouble?"

"About the only trouble they ever get into is with Sally," Smoke replied with a little laugh, "and almost all of it starts and ends in her kitchen."

"Ha!" Sheriff Rand replied. "I'll bet it doesn't take much for her to whip them into shape, either, does it."

"Not much," Smoke agreed.

"Yes well, I'm glad you stopped by. Just between us, I'm glad you put those three ne'er-do-wells out of business."

Smoke swung into the saddle. Lifting his hand, he turned Seven back into the street and continued his ride south.

Cheyenne, Wyoming

Everything had gone wrong when Chubb Slago, Lute Cruthis, Boots Zimmerman, and two others had attempted a bank robbery in Hutchinson County, Texas, a month ago. Right from the very beginning the would-be bank robbery had turned into a shoot-out. It began in the bank when the teller with more courage than sense produced a gun and began shooting. His act got him killed, but it also kept the robbers from getting any money. The shooting had alerted the rest of the town, and when the unsuccessful robbers left the bank, it seemed that everyone in Windom had a gun of some sort—pistol, rifle, or shotgun.

The five riders rode through the gauntlet of fire, losing two of their number.

Cruthis, Slago, and Zimmerman left Texas. One month and two small robberies later, they found themselves in Cheyenne, Wyoming, with very little money and no prospects, having escaped the Texas authorities. Boots had gone into the post office to see if they were on any wanted posters in Wyoming—they weren't—and he discovered the flyer from Mule Gap looking for deputies.

"Are you out of your mind?" Cruthis asked. "We run from deputies, not to them."

"Wait, Cruthis," Slago said. "Boots may have a good idea here."

"I'd like to know what would be so good about being a deputy city marshal," Cruthis said.

"Well for one thing, if any paper ever showed up with our names on it, it would be kinda good to be able to get to it first and get rid of it, wouldn't it?"

"Yeah." Cruthis smiled. "Yeah! That would be damn good."

"And it says well paying and other rewards," Slago said. "I don't know what it means by well paid, and I don't know what other rewards it is talking about, but no matter what it is, you have to admit that it is better than we've got now."

"Hey Boots, how do you think I'd look with a star?" Cruthis asked.

Zimmerman laughed. "I think you'd look damn fine."

Mule Gap

Clem Bates, Dan Cooper, Henry Barnes, and Slim Gibson were standing around in various poses in Marshal Bodine's office. Duly Plappert, whom Bodine had made his chief deputy, was sitting at the only other desk in the room. Chubb Slago, Lute Cruthis, and Boots Zimmerman were there as well, and so was Angus Delmer. They were watching Bodine swear in Boney Walls, the tenth and last deputy that Bodine intended to hire.

"All right, gentlemen, our little constabulary is complete," Bodine said, addressing the others. "From now on you will begin earning the generous stipend that is being offered for services rendered, so it is time you begin rendering said services."

"What the hell did he just say?" Zimmerman asked Slago.

"I'm not sure, but I think he said it was time we started working."

From that point forward, the deputies became a ubiquitous presence in Mule Gap. They patrolled the streets, strictly enforcing draconian laws against being drunk, being disorderly, spitting, tossing away a cigar butt, and anything else a deputy decided should be enforced. Each infraction of the laws, even if it was against a law no one had heard of, resulted in fines. In addition, every business in town saw additional taxes applied.

"I lived through reconstruction," said Albert Kirkland, who owned the gun shop. "And I swear, this is just as bad."

"Well, they have to police the entire county," Bud Coleman said. He owned the wagon freighting service. "And seeing as my wagons are out there, I don't mind tellin' you that I appreciate having that protection."

"Then why aren't they out there policing?" another asked.

"And while they're at it, they might also try and find some of them kids that have been took," still another added.

"You're talking about the Blackwell boy and the Coy girl, are you?" Kirkland asked.

"My drivers tell me there's at least three more missing," Coleman said. "A couple boys from Warm Springs 'n another girl."

"I thought they was let go."

"No, that was an earlier group they had. Their folks paid the ransom on them, 'n they was sent home."

"Hell, couldn't they tell the law where they was bein' held?"

"They did, but when Bodine sent a couple of his deputies out there to check up on 'em, they said there warn't nobody there."

"I'm surprised he even let the deputies go check it out," Kirkland said. "Seems to me like all he has them doin' is collecting money."

CHAPTER 9

Wiregrass

Sam Condon had invited Smoke and Sally to dinner as sort of a repayment for Smoke having brought him the twenty-five hundred dollars that was the down payment on the bull, Yankee Star.

"Do you want another piece of pie, Mrs. Jensen? I'll get it for you," Thad offered.

"Thank you, Thad, but I think I'll pass this time," Sally said.

"You sure you don't want another piece? I'll be glad to get it."

"Thad, Mrs. Jensen said no," Sara Sue said to her son.

Sam chuckled. "Thad is just trying to wrangle a second piece of pie for himself."

"Well, he didn't ask me," Smoke said. "I'll take another piece as long as it is very small."

A wide smile spread across Thad's face. "I'll get it!" he said, standing up from the table. He returned a moment later with a small piece of pie for Smoke, and a much larger piece for himself.

"Thad," Sara Sue scolded.

"Well, Ma, you always tell me I should be polite, and it

wouldn't be polite for Mr. Jensen to have to take seconds all by himself, would it? And he said he only wanted a small piece."

Sam laughed. "He's got you there, Sara Sue."

"Sally, is it true that you are going to New York?" Sara Sue asked.

"Yes. Andrew and Rosanna MacCallister have a new play in New York, and they sent me an invitation."

"Andrew and Rosanna MacCallister? Why, they are famous," Sara Sue said. "They personally sent you an invitation? Do you know them?"

"It is more a case of me knowing their brother, Falcon MacCallister. He is a very good friend of ours," Sally said. "I met Rosanna and Andrew through him. I must say that for all their fame and success, they are exceptionally nice people."

"Will you be going as well, Smoke?" Sam asked.

"No. Sally has an old college friend that she wants to visit as well, and that's an *opportunity* I can afford to miss."

The others laughed at his emphasis on the word *opportunity*.

"Cal is going with me," Sally said.

"Cal Wood?" Sara Sue asked. "Isn't he one of your hired hands?"

"I suppose you could say that," Sally said, "though he is much more than a hired hand."

Smoke chuckled. "We've practically adopted him . . . ever since he tried to rob Sally at gunpoint."

"What?" Sara Sue gasped.

"He was very young and very desperate," Sally said. "I knew then that he had no real intention of hurting me. I brought him home, gave him his first good meal in no telling how long, then talked Smoke into hiring him."

"He and Pearlie are more like a part of our family than hired hands," Smoke said.

"I can believe that," Sam said. "I've seen the way you are when you're together. It's not like they're hired hands at all. Don't get me wrong, they respect you, but it is more like you're family."

"Is Pearlie going to New York, as well?" Sara Sue asked.

"No. Pearlie has been there before, but Cal has never seen New York, and I would like to broaden his experience at least once."

"Sounds to me like that young man was dealt four aces when he ran into you two," Sam said.

"I expect he was." Smoke reached over, took Sally's hand, and smiled at her. "But then, I can say that as well, because I was dealt the same hand when I ran into Sally."

They continued their visit after dinner, going into the parlor to listen to music on the Symphonion disc player, and enjoying three-dimensional photographs of the wonders of the world on the stereopticon. By the time they were finished with their visit, it had grown dark.

"Oh my, look at the time," Sally said. "We didn't intend to impose upon your hospitality for so long."

"Nonsense, it was no imposition at all," Sara Sue replied. "We have greatly enjoyed your company."

"Thad, go outside and light the lanterns on the surrey for them so they can see to drive home," Sam directed.

"All right, Pa," Thad said, eager to help.

"Thad is a fine young man," Smoke said after Thad left. "I can see where he is such a help to you in running your operation here."

"Yes, he is." Sam chuckled. "But I'm glad you waited until he was out of the house before you said that. He has a big enough head as it is."

Smoke laughed.

"I'll tell you this—he has taken to Fire the way you have to Seven," Sam said. "He and that horse are as close as any boy would be with a dog."

"A good horse is like that," Smoke replied.

"I can't tell you how appreciative we are for that gift, and as far as Thad is concerned, you've made a friend for life."

"A good investment, I would say."

When Smoke and Sally went out to the surrey, both running lanterns were lit and the polished mirror behind the flames cast twin beams of light that joined a few feet in front of them to light their way.

"Thank you, Thad," Smoke said as he helped Sally in, then climbed up behind her. "Sam, Sara Sue, it was a wonderful evening, and we thank you for the invitation."

"It was great having you. Sally, do have a safe and most enjoyable trip," Sara Sue said.

With waves of good-bye, Smoke snapped the reins, and the team started out for the six-mile trip back to the Sugarloaf.

"I didn't know Cal had agreed to go with you," Smoke said as the surrey moved swiftly down the road.

"He hasn't yet, but the only reason he hasn't is because he thinks it wouldn't be fair to Pearlie for him to go and Pearlie to stay behind."

"I'm pretty sure Pearlie doesn't want to go."

"Are you kidding? He told me, and I quote, 'Miss Sally, the only way you're going to ever get me to go to someplace like New York is if you hog-tie me and drag me there.' I took that to mean that he didn't want to go."

Smoke laughed. "Yes, I'd say that is a pretty good indication of his lack of interest."

Though they didn't always do so, Pearlie and Cal had breakfast with Smoke and Sally the next morning. She had invited the two, sweetening the invitation with the promise of a freshly made batch of bear sign.

"I'll tell you what, Miss Sally, if God ever made anything

on earth that was any better than your bear sign, He sure did keep them for Himself," Pearlie said.

"You got that right," Cal added. "I'll bet you can't get anything like that in New York."

"No, but you can get a *tarte aux pommes* that will make your mouth water," Sally said.

"What's that?" Cal asked.

"Think about a flaky piecrust covered with a coat of sugar-glazed cake. Inside are honey-sweetened apples baked so soft that you can eat them with a spoon."

"When do we leave?" Cal asked.

"You mean you are no longer worried about leaving Pearlie behind?"

"Let him get his own trip to New York, and his own torty poms," Cal said with a broad smile. "I'm going with you."

French Creek Canyon in the Medicine Bow Mountains, Wyoming

It had been eight days since Lorena Coy and Eddie "Wee" Blackwell were taken in the back of a buckboard. When they'd arrived they saw that three other children were already there, and now all five shared the same cabin. Lorena, at fourteen, was the oldest. There was one other girl and two other boys. Except for Lorena and Eddie Blackwell, none of the others had ever met one another until they were together in the cabin. Circumstances had made them brothers and sisters. Marilyn Grant, who was twelve, was the other girl. The other boys were Burt Rowe, also twelve, and Travis Calhoun, who was thirteen.

"I want to go home," Wee said.

"We all want to go home, sweetheart," Lorena said, trying to comfort the boy. "And someday, we will."

"Why won't they let me go home?"

"Because they are mean men," Lorena said.

"They'll let us go home as soon as our folks pay the ransom," Travis said. "The problem is, I don't think my pa has as much money as they are asking for."

"My mother lives all alone and has no money at all," Lorena said.

"Why did they kidnap you?" Burt asked.

"Because I was looking after Wee when they kidnapped him. I don't know how this is all going to work out. If Mr. Blackwell pays for Wee, then perhaps they will let me go as well."

"Here comes Weasel," Burt said. He had been looking through the window.

"Is he bringing food?" Travis asked.

"Yeah, it looks like it. That is, if you can call that soup they been servin' us *food*," Burt said.

The door opened and Andy Whitman, called Weasel by everyone, stepped inside carrying a pot by its handle. He set the pot down on the table. The clear, hot broth in the pot had little substance to it.

"All right, boys and girls, get your bowls out. It's time for breakfast."

"I don't want any," Marilyn said.

"Yes, you do," Lorena insisted.

"It's not soup. It's nothing but hot water."

"It's a broth. It isn't very good, I admit, but you have to eat, Marilyn, even if you don't want to," Lorena said. "Please at least try."

"All right," Marilyn said reluctantly. She picked up her bowl. "I'll try."

"Mr. Weasel, have you heard anything from my pa?" Burt asked. "Has he got the money yet?"

"I ain't heard," Weasel said as he spooned the broth into the bowls. "Somebody else will be handlin' that. All I'm s'posed to do is keep an eye on you 'n feed you."

"Where's everyone else?" Lorena asked.

"They're gone," Weasel said without further explanation.

"You mean you're the only one here that's guardin' us right now?" Travis asked.

"Yeah. Why do you ask? Do you think you can get away from me?"

"Maybe," Travis said.

"Why don't you try it?" Weasel asked.

"Where are the others?" Marilyn asked.

"Who knows where they are? Perhaps they've gone to get you another brother," Weasel said with an evil laugh.

Red and White Mountain, Eagle County, Colorado

Fred Keefer, Elmer Reece, and Clyde Sanders had spent the night camped out just below the Red and White Mountain. Although it was light, the sun had not yet climbed above Bald Mountain silhouetted against a brightening dawn to the east.

"How far is it from here?" Reece asked.

"Not far. Only about another couple miles," Keefer said. "We'll be there before they finish their breakfast."

"Who are we pickin' up? A boy or a girl?"

"It's a boy. The chief said this one will pay well."

"He says that about all of 'em," Sanders said, "but we still got a cabin full of brats that we ain't yet got us so much as one dollar from."

"We made good money from that first batch," Sanders said.

"Except for one," Reece said.

"They prob'ly woulda paid for her, too, if she hadn't tried to escape 'n got herself kilt," Sanders said.

"Yeah well, it ain't our job to be a-worryin' none about things like that," Keefer said. "It's our job to grab 'em, 'n it's the chief's job to get the money for 'em. He says that the ones we've already got is the same as havin' money in the bank."

"Yeah well, it wouldn't be so bad them bein' there if the chief wasn't such a damn fuddy-duddy 'bout the girls that's there. I mean, we could at least be havin' a little fun with 'em," Reece said. "Now you take the one that escaped 'n got herself kilt? She was a looker. Almost as good lookin' as the two we got now."

"What do you mean, have fun with 'em?" Keefer asked. "They ain't nothin' but girls."

"Yeah? Well, one of 'em, Lorena, is tittied up just real good, 'n I wouldn't mind at all showin' her what it's all about."

"Then we would have damaged goods," Keefer said. "And you can't get much money for damaged goods. Besides, we got a little money now. You can always go to that whorehouse in Mule Gap. Them whores is all good lookin', 'n whores is much better anyway, on account of they don't need no teachin'."

"The whores there is all right, except they're kinda hoity-toity about things."

"Yeah well, that's 'cause Delilah is all hoity-toity her ownself," Keefer replied.

"I don't see how we're goin' to get any money for Lorena at all, on account of her mama don't hardly have no money. I don't even know why we're keepin' her," Sanders said.

"She come with that little one, 'n his pa has got lots of money. The chief says that the little one's pa will pay for both of 'em."

"Yeah well, I still can't see why we can't have a little fun with 'er before we turn 'er loose. That is, if we ever turn 'em loose," Reece said.

CHAPTER 10

Wiregrass

Sara Sue had been the first to rise this morning and she was in the kitchen preparing breakfast when her son came in. He was still yawning and stretching, and his hair looked like a haystack. She had long ago given up trying to make Thad comb his hair before breakfast.

"Thad, you'd better get out there and milk Ada. I can hear her bawling."

"All right, Ma." He grabbed a couple biscuits that his mother had just removed from the oven and took a bite from one. "You goin' to make gravy this mornin', Ma?"

"Yes. So you'd better leave enough biscuits."

"Good!" Thad said enthusiastically. He put one of the biscuits back.

Sara Sue laughed. "Thaddeus Condon, you and your father are two peas in the same pod . . . except he will at least comb his hair when he gets out of bed." She ran her hand through Thad's disheveled hair.

With the pail in one hand and the biscuit in the other, Thad started toward the barn.

Sara Sue watched him through the kitchen window. "My

goodness, you are growing so fast I can't keep you in clothes," she said quietly.

"Talking to yourself are you, woman?" Sam teased, coming into the kitchen at that moment.

"I was just noticing how big Thad is getting," she replied, making no effort to apologize for talking aloud.

"He's a fine boy, and he's going to be a big help in taking Yankee Star up to Cross Trail. We'll get started right after breakfast."

"How long do you think you'll be gone?"

"Oh, no more than a couple days, I wouldn't think. Smoke said that Pearlie will come over at least once a day to keep an eye on the rest of the cattle."

"That's good of him to do so. Oh, I'm going to need some water to clean up after breakfast. Would you get some, please?"

"Sure," Sam replied as he grabbed the water bucket. "Someday I'm going to connect a pipe from the windmill pump to the kitchen. Then we'll have running water without having to go outside."

Sara Sue laughed. "You've been saying that ever since we got here."

"I'm going to do it someday. You'll see." Sam snatched a biscuit.

"Sam, can't you wait for breakfast? I swear, you are as bad as your son," Sara Sue scolded, though she was smiling as she chastised him.

As Sam began pumping water, he could hear Thad singing from the barn while he was milking the cow.

> *"Oh, the years creep slowly by, Lorena,*
> *the snow is on the ground again."*

"Lorena" was a song Sam had learned while he was a soldier during the war. He had taught it to Thad, who actually had a pretty good voice.

With the bucket full, Sam returned to the kitchen. "He's singing to Ada again," he said with a little chuckle.

"He says Ada gives more milk when he sings to her," Sara Sue replied.

"Maybe he's right. They say that music has charms to soothe a savage beast."

"Sam, are you calling Ada a savage beast?"

"And are you telling me you've never seen Ada mad?" Sam replied with a laugh.

"Pa! Pa, help!"

Thad's call came from outside the house and both Sara Sue and Sam could hear the panic in his voice. They rushed out onto the back porch just in time to see that there were three horsemen surrounding their son. Thad was struggling to free himself from the rope that was looped around him, and the pail he had been carrying was turned over beside him with the milk spilled out on the ground.

A second rope was thrown over Thad, and one of the three horsemen dismounted and started toward him.

"Let him go, you son of a bitch!" Sam shouted, running toward the man who was closest to Thad.

One of the riders raised his pistol and fired, and Sam went down.

"Sam!" Sara Sue called hurrying toward him.

The same gunman who had shot Sam aimed at Sara Sue.

"No, don't shoot her!" another shouted. "Don't shoot her. If we kill both of 'em, who'll pay the ransom?"

Knowing she could do nothing for Thad right now, Sara Sue knelt by Sam, who was still alive and taking labored breaths.

"Thad," Sam said.

Sara Sue looked toward her son and saw that the rope was wrapped around him many times so that his arms were bound to his side. Two men lifted him up onto a horse ridden by the third man.

"They're taking him, Sam. Oh, they are taking him."

"Read this!" one of the men shouted, dropping a piece of paper on the ground just before the three men, with Thad as their prisoner, galloped away.

"Thad! We'll come for you!" Sara Sue shouted at the galloping horses. "We'll come for you!"

"Did they . . . did they take him?" Sam asked, barely able to speak."

"Yes. Oh, Sam, they took our son."

He sat up. "Help me saddle a horse."

"You're in no condition to ride. I've got to get you in town to the doctor. If I hitch up the buckboard, do you think you can help me get you into it?"

"Yeah," Sam replied. "I can do that."

Sara Sue started toward the barn.

"Sara Sue," Sam called. "Don't try and connect a team. Just use Harry. He's all we'll need."

Big Rock Railroad Depot

Smoke, Sally, Cal, and Pearlie were standing on the depot platform alongside the train that had already pulled into the station. The engine relief valve was opening and closing, venting steam in great gasping breaths. The overheated wheel bearings and journals were snapping and popping as they cooled.

"I'll bring you a souvenir from New York," Cal promised Pearlie.

"Yeah? Tell you what. Bring me a picture of you 'n Miz Sally standin' in Central Park."

"Oh, I think we can do better than that," Sally said. "We'll come up with something."

"All aboard!" the conductor shouted as he checked his watch.

Sally gave Smoke a kiss, and Pearlie a hug. Cal started toward Pearlie.

"Now, hold on there," Pearlie said, holding his hands out in front of him. "You aren't fixin' to give me a hug, too, are you?"

Cal chuckled. "Well, I was just going to shake your hand, but if you want a hug . . ." he teased.

"A handshake will be fine, thank you," Pearlie replied.

Cal shook Smoke's hand as well, then he followed Sally onto the train. A moment later, Sally's face appeared in the window, then almost as soon as she was seated, the engineer blew the whistle and there was a huge puff of steam as he opened the throttle. That was followed by a chain reaction of creaks and rattles as the slack was taken up from the connectors between the cars and the train started forward. Smoke walked along, keeping pace with Sally until he reached the end of the platform. By that time the train had picked up so much speed that even if the platform had gone on farther, he would not have been able to stay with it.

Smoke and Pearlie stood at the end of the platform as the remaining cars passed. Not until the final car sped by them did they turn away.

"Hey Smoke, you think maybe we could get something to eat before we go back out to the ranch?" Pearlie asked. "I'd hate to come into town and waste the opportunity."

"I was just thinking the same thing," Smoke said.

Delmonico's Fine Dining was only four buildings down from the depot, and Smoke and Pearlie stepped inside just before Sara Sue reached town, urging the horse into a rapid trot as she drove the buckboard east on Front Street. She was going so fast that the buckboard skidded a little as she turned right onto Sikes Street then pulled Harry to a stop in front of the single-story, unimposing building between the Big Rock Theater and the Brown Dirt Cowboy that was Dr. Urban's office.

"Doc! Dr. Urban, come quick!" Sara Sue called. Hopping down from the buckboard, she ran into the office repeating her call. "Come quick, please. Come quick!"

Dr. Urban was an exceptionally skinny man with a protruding Adam's apple. He pushed his glasses up his nose as he came into the front in response to Sara Sue's call. "Mrs. Condon! What is it? What's wrong?"

"It's Sam, Doctor. I've got him in the buckboard out front. He's been shot!"

"You say he's been shot?"

"Yes. Please, come quick!"

Delmonico's restaurant

"Ha!" Pearlie said. "I'd like to see the expression on Cal's face the first time he sees all those people in New York. He thinks Denver is a big city."

"It'll be a good experience for him," Smoke said.

"He'll be a babe in the woods."

"Sally knows New York well. She'll look out for him."

A few minutes later, Dick DeWeese, owner of Delmonico's restaurant, came out of the kitchen pushing a wheeled cart toward Smoke and Pearlie's table. The meal they had ordered was on a large round tray and covered by a silver dome. Ignoring a squeaking wheel, Dick reached the table and lifted the cover, releasing the delicious aroma.

"Here are your lamb chops, Mr. Jensen, cooked to absolute

perfection. I know that because I cooked them myself, and I'm delivering them personally to avoid any embarrassment."

"Embarrassment?" Smoke replied. "What embarrassment are you talking about?"

"Why, the embarrassment of one of the top ranchers in the entire state eating lamb. If someone like Tim Murchison or Ed Gillespie, or even Sheriff Carson, got wind of the fact that you are actually eating lamb, they would never let you live it down."

"Yeah well, you notice I ain't eatin' lamb," Pearlie said. "I ordered beefsteak 'n I hope that's what you brought me."

"Indeed I did. My remarks were addressed to Mr. Jensen."

Smoke laughed. "You can blame Sally for that. I had never tasted lamb in my life until she and I were married. Turns out this is what they eat where she came from." Smoke carved a piece of meat off, put it in his mouth, and smiled. "And it also turns out that I love it."

Having just finished a piece of chocolate cake, Smoke and Pearlie were enjoying a cup of coffee when a woman came into the restaurant and started toward their table.

"That's Mrs. Condon, isn't it?" Pearlie asked.

Smoke looked over toward the woman approaching the table. "Yes, it is." As she got closer, Smoke was shocked to see that tears were streaming down her face. He and Pearlie stood. "Sara Sue, what is it? What's wrong?"

"They've got Thad," Sara Sue sobbed. "They shot Sam, and they've got my child! Dr. Urban is with Sam now. Oh, Smoke, Sam might die!"

"Who has Thad?" Smoke asked. "And who shot Sam?"

"After they rode away, they left this note." She handed Smoke the piece of paper the riders had left behind.

*If you want to see your boy alive again, come to the
Del Rey Hotel in Mule Gap, Wyoming, with fifteen
thousand dollars. You have one week from today to
raise the money. You will be contacted at the hotel and
told where to deliver the money and pick up your boy.
<u>Come alone</u>.*

Leaving the restaurant, Smoke and Pearlie accompanied
Sara Sue back to Dr. Urban's office. Sam Condon was lying
on the bed, naked from the waist up. His trousers were
pulled as low as they could go, while still preserving some
modesty. A large bandage covered the lower right side of his
abdomen.

"How is he doing?" Smoke asked.

"He hasn't awakened yet from the anesthetic, but right
now that is the best thing for him. The less he moves around,
the better off he will be," Dr. Urban said. "The bullet was
low . . . too low to hit anything vital. I got it out. Now all we
have to worry about is infection."

"Do you think that will be a problem?" Smoke asked.

"Mrs. Condon did a good job of getting him here quickly.
We've got a really good start on it, so I think we'll be able
to hold it back."

Sara Sue told Smoke and Pearlie about the three men
who'd ridden in and snatched Thad. "I can get the fifteen
thousand dollars, but to tell the truth, I'm a little frightened
to go meet them by myself. When I found out you were
in town at the restaurant, I came to see you to ask if—"

Smoke held out his hand. "There is no need for you to ask
anything, Sara Sue. You know I will go with you."

"I am a little worried, though. The note said tell nobody.
If they saw us together, I wouldn't want to take any chances
on them doing anything to harm Thad."

"You don't need to worry about that. Thad is worth money to them only as long as he is alive and well."

"I pray that you are right. That he is still alive and unhurt," Sara Sue said.

"Prayer is always good," Smoke replied.

CHAPTER 11

French Creek Canyon

"Get down, boy,"

"Tied up like this, you'll have to help me down," Thad replied.

"Help 'im down, Sanders."

Sanders, the rider with whom Thad had ridden double for the entire morning, dismounted first then reached up to help Thad down from the horse. The boy examined his surroundings. Two cabins were backed up against French Creek. The larger of the two looked fairly well-kept and appeared to have been recently painted. The smaller one was constructed of wide weather-grayed planking.

A fourth man came out of the larger house.

"Any trouble while we were gone, Whitman?" Keefer asked.

"No, they have been calm as a passel of puppies. This is the one you was talkin' about?" Whitman asked, staring at Thad. "The one whose papa raises registered bulls?"

"Yeah."

"He's bigger 'n the others," Whitman said. "Hope he don't give us no trouble."

"He ain't goin' to give us no trouble, are you, boy?" Keefer asked as one of the men loosened the rope that was wrapped around Thad.

"Now I know Keefer, Sanders, and Whitman," Thad said. He looked at the fourth man. "What's your name?"

"What's it to you, what my name is?"

"I want to know your name because you're the one that shot Pa. And if he dies, I plan to kill you."

Sanders laughed. "Damn, Reece! How does it feel to have a fourteen-year-old after you?"

"Yeah, I'm only fourteen," Thad said. "But how old do you have to be to kill someone? I'll remember your name, Reece."

Reece walked up to Thad and slapped him hard. Thad retaliated by kicking Reece in the groin. Reece doubled over with pain as the others laughed.

"Why, you little shit!' Reece said when he straightened up again. He pulled his pistol then brought it down hard on Thad's head.

Thad went down.

"Here, Reece! Don't be damagin' the merchandise!" Keefer said, dismounting and hurrying over as Sanders knelt down to examine Thad. "If you've killed this boy you've just pissed away fifteen thousand dollars, and the chief ain't goin' to like that. He ain't goin' to like it at all."

"I ain't puttin' up with no mouthin'-off from a kid. He needs to learn how to respect his elders," Reece said.

"He's alive. He's just knocked out, is all," Sanders said, rising up from his quick examination.

"It's a good thing for you, Reece, that he is alive," Keefer said. "Get 'im inside with the others."

Whitman and Sanders picked Thad up then carried him into the smaller of the two cabins where they dropped him on the floor. Thad had regained consciousness, but barely, and was aware only of the sensation of being moved. When he was dropped on the floor, his head spun so that the only thing he could do, for the moment, was lie there.

"Are you all right?"

Thad opened his eyes and saw the face of a young girl hovering over him. He wasn't sure if he was actually seeing her or if it was some sort of an illusion brought on by the blow to his head.

"Are you all right?" the girl asked again.

Thad reached up to put his hand on her face, and she pulled away from his touch.

"You're real," he said.

"What?" the girl responded. "Yes, of course I'm real."

Thad sat up and his head began to spin so that he wasn't sure he could even sit there. He put his hand to his head, then winced in pain when his hand found the lump. "Wow, they must have hit me a lick."

"Yes, we were watching through the window. We saw Reece hit you."

"We?"

"There are five of us here," the girl said.

Looking around, Thad saw not only the young girl who was talking to him, but four others—another girl and three boys. A quick appraisal of them suggested that he might be the oldest one in the room. He wasn't sure about the girl who had just questioned him, though. She might be older than he was.

"How old are you?" Thad asked.

"What?" the girl responded, surprised by the question. She laughed. "You are hit on the head, dropped in here nearly as much dead as you are alive, but do you ask my name or where or what this place is? No, you ask me how old I am. Lord have mercy, that blow to your head must have made you daft."

"How old are you?" he asked again.

"I'm fourteen. Why?"

"When will you be fifteen?"

"Not until November."

Thad smiled. "I'll be fifteen in August. That makes me older."

Despite the seriousness of the situation, the girl laughed. "You are a strange boy. We are all prisoners, and the only thing you are worried about is who is the oldest."

"Someone has to make plans," Thad said. "And it is obvious that the best person to make the plans would be the one who is the oldest."

"Make plans for what?" the girl asked.

"Escape," Thad replied in a single clipped word.

"Escape?"

"Yeah, I don't plan to stay here, and I'll take anyone with me who wants to go. You're right. I didn't ask you your name. What is it?"

"My name is Lorena."

"Lorena?" Thad said. "Really? Your name is Lorena?"

"Yes. Is there something wrong with my name?" the girl asked, a little piqued by his response to her name.

"No, nothing at all. I think it's great!" He began to sing. "'The sun's low down the sky, Lorena, the frost gleams where the flowers have been.'"

"Yes!" Lorena said, laughing. "Mama said that is how I got my name. She used to listen to people singing that song and—" She stopped in midsentence. Her eyes welled with tears and they began sliding down her cheeks. "I'm afraid I may never see Mama again."

"Yes, you will," Thad said. "We all will." He looked at the other girl and three boys. Not one of them had spoken since he arrived. "My name is Thad. I've met Lorena. What are your names?"

"My name is Marilyn Grant," the other girl said.

"How old are you, Marilyn?"

"I'm twelve."

Two boys were Travis Calhoun, who was thirteen, and Burt Rowe, who was eleven.

"And who are you?" Thad asked the smallest, who had not yet spoken.

"Wee."

"We? No, just you. The others have told me their names."

Lorena laughed. "Wee is his name. Actually, it's Eddie, but his mama and daddy started calling him Wee because he is so small."

Thad smiled and stuck out his hand. "It's nice to meet you, Wee."

Smiling back at Thad, Wee took his hand.

"We are sort of like brothers and sisters here," Lorena said. "That's how it has to be since we are all in the same boat."

"How long have you been here?" Thad asked.

Burt Rowe had been there the longest—six weeks. Next came Travis, then Marilyn Grant, then Lorena and Wee.

"Wee and I were taken together," Lorena said. "I was watching over him for his parents." She grew quiet, then her eyes welled with tears again. "I certainly wasn't doing a very good job of it, though, or those men wouldn't have taken us."

"Why do you say that?" Thad asked. "Was there really anything you could have done to prevent it?"

"No, but—"

"There are no buts to it. I wasn't able to keep them from getting me. How were you supposed to be able to stop them from getting you and Wee?"

"There wasn't any way," Lorena admitted.

"Then don't say you weren't doing a very good job."

"I want to go home," Wee said. "I want my mama." Tears slid down his cheeks, but he wasn't weeping aloud.

"You'll go home again, Wee. Marilyn, Travis, Burt, you will, too. I'll tell the four of you the same thing I told Lorena. You will see your ma and pa again."

"How?" Travis asked. "I know that the men who took us are asking for a whole lot of money. I don't think Pop even has that much money."

"If we all stick together and pay attention to what's going on around us, we'll find some way to get out of here, and it won't cost any of our folks anything. I promise you," Thad said.

He had thought they were only dealing with four men, but he learned from Lorena that there were more.

"How many are there?"

"I don't know. I've never seen anyone but the four who stay here all the time. Keefer is the leader of the ones here, but I know there's someone else who is in charge of all of them because I've heard them talk about him. But I've never heard the name," Lorena said.

"Why did Reece hit you in the head with a pistol?" Travis asked. "I don't think any of the rest of us were hit."

"It may be because I kicked him in the—" Because he didn't want to say the word in front of the two girls, Thad altered his sentence. "Uh, it was because I told him I was going to kill him."

Marilyn gasped. "You don't really mean that, do you?"

"Reece shot my pa. If I find out that Pa is dead, then, yes, I do mean it. I'll kill Reece."

"How are you going to do that?" Travis asked. "He's got a gun. All of them have guns. We don't."

"I haven't figured out yet how I'll do it." A determined expression showed on Thad's face as he responded to the question Travis had put to him. "But I will find a way."

"Here comes Sanders." Burt had been looking through the window.

"What do you suppose he wants?" Travis asked.

"It looks like he's bringin' us our dinner," Burt answered.

"Good. All I had for breakfast was a biscuit, and I'm hungry," Thad said.

"After you eat, you'll still be hungry," Travis said. "Believe me."

Travis was right. The "meal" consisted of a bowl of soup, though the soup was little more than hot water with a few globules of fat from the meat that had been its base but was missing from what was being served. There were also a few vegetables, small pieces of potato, and some cabbage.

"Is this what they serve every meal?" Thad asked, looking at his bowl in dismay.

"No," Travis said. "Sometimes it's worse."

"Do you really plan to try and escape?" Marilyn asked as the six ate their lunch.

"Yes, but not just me," Thad said. "Like I said, I plan for all of us to escape."

"How are we going to do that?" Travis asked.

"Simple. We'll just slip out the door in the middle of the night. They can't keep an eye on us twenty-four hours a day."

Travis shook his head. "There's only one door to this cabin, and they keep it locked, day and night. And as you can see, the window is too little for anyone but Wee to get through. Even with him, it would be a tight squeeze."

"I'll find some way," Thad said determinedly.

"We can't all of us escape. Even if we managed to get out of the house some way, Wee is too young. He wouldn't be able to keep up with the rest of us."

"Yes, I would," Wee insisted. "I can run fast."

"It probably wouldn't be running as much as it would be staying out of sight," Thad said.

Wee smiled. "I'm real good at playing hide-'n-seek. Sometimes me 'n Lorena used to play hide-'n-seek, 'n I can hide real good, can't I, Lorena?"

"Yes, honey, you are very good at hide-'n-seek," Lorena said, smiling at the boy.

"Can you keep real quiet when you have to?" Thad asked.

"Uh-huh. All I have to do is put a lock on my lips," Wee said, and the two girls chuckled.

"Don't worry," Thad said to the others. "When we go, Wee goes with us, and he won't be a problem."

"When are we going to go?" Burt asked.

"I don't know yet. I'll have to study things for a while until I can figure out the best thing to do. Do they ever let us out of the house?"

"Only to use the privy," Travis said. "They come unlock the door in the middle of the morning and in the middle of the afternoon so we can use the privy, but they only let us out one at a time."

"Except for the girls," Lorena said. "We always go together so one of us can be outside to let the others know it's being used."

"And all the time we're using the privy, whoever it was that unlocked the door for us is standing on the front porch, waiting for us to all get back in the cabin," Burt said.

"It's sort of creepy," Lorena said.

"Yes, it is," Marilyn agreed. "I don't like the way Reece looks at us."

"Me, neither," Lorena said. "The way he looks at us makes my skin crawl."

"You won't have to worry about how he looks at you much longer," Thad promised.

"Why do you say that? Are you coming up with a plan?" Lorena asked.

"Not yet. But I will."

CHAPTER 12

Big Rock

Five days after Sara Sue took Sam to the doctor, Dr. Urban declared that the immediate danger was over and Sam could go home.

"I intend to do more than just go home," Sam said. "I want you to wrap me up good and tight. I'm going after my son."

"You do, and you'll more than likely be dead within a week," Dr. Urban replied. "You need rest, and you need to drink a lot of beef broth to restore your blood."

Smoke had come to town with Sara Sue to help her take Sam back home. Smoke actually had a fine, well-sprung carriage which he very rarely used, but it was perfect for giving Sam a gentle ride back to Wiregrass Ranch. Once there, with Pearlie on one side and Smoke on the other, they were able to help Sam walk into his house.

"You rest easy, Sam. I'll go after Thad," Smoke promised.

"I appreciate that, but I want you to deliver the bull to Mr. Harris."

"I intend to do both," Smoke said. "The note said for Sara

Sue to come alone. I'll be with her, but I'll have the cover of delivering the bull."

"Yes," Sam said. "Yes, I hadn't thought of that. That might work. Smoke, please, bring my son back."

"Don't worry. I'll get him safely home to you."

"Thank you, Smoke. From the bottom of my heart, thank you."

"Is Mr. Condon actually going to pay those bastards?" Pearlie asked as they drove back to Sugarloaf. "I hate to see him have to do that."

"I feel the same way," Smoke replied. "But right now the most important thing to Sam and Sara Sue is the safe return of their son, and I agree with them. Thad's safety is the number one priority. So the first thing I intend to do is to get young Thad back alive and unharmed. If that means paying the ransom, we'll do that. After that, will be time to deal with the kidnappers."

"When do we start?" Pearlie asked.

"We'll start in a few days by delivering the bull to Jim Harris."

Three days later Smoke and Pearlie returned to Wiregrass. They were glad to see that Sam was able to move around on his own, though he had to do so very slowly and be careful not to open up the wound.

"When will you be going up to Mule Gap, Sara Sue?" Smoke asked.

"I'll ride into town tomorrow morning and take the coach up," she replied.

"All right. We'll see you there."

Smoke and Pearlie went out into the corral to get Yankee Star.

"That's him, Seven," Smoke said to his horse. "Go get him and bring him to me."

Smoke and Pearlie leaned against the corral fence and watched as Seven moved through the half-dozen cows until he reached the bull. Moving first to one side of the bull, then the other, Seven herded Yankee Star back to the corral gate and held him there as Smoke dropped the lead rope over the cow's head.

"Heck, Smoke, why do we even have to go?" Pearlie teased. "Just tell Seven to take him up there."

Smoke laughed. "I don't doubt but that he could do it."

"Is this your favorite Seven? I know he is number three."

"Oh, I don't know that he is my favorite," Smoke replied. "They have all had their own unique personality, and I've been really close to every one of them. But I do think this Seven may be the smartest of all of them. I can talk to him like a person, and I swear he can follow the conversation."

"He's one fine horse, all right," Pearlie agreed.

Chicago, Illinois

It was nine o'clock in the evening when the train from St. Louis carrying Sally and Cal rolled into the Central Depot located in the middle of Chicago. They would change trains for the last time before continuing on to New York.

Leaving the train, they walked up a long concrete walkway that separated the tracks, as well as the trains already sitting in the station. As they walked by a sitting train, Cal glanced into the window and saw a very beautiful young woman. They made eye contact, and she smiled shyly, but held his gaze as long as she could.

"Ships in the night," Sally said.

"Ma'am?" Cal replied.

Sally chuckled. "I saw you and the young lady exchange long glances. It was a sweet moment, but poignant as well, for that train will be going to Atlanta, and we're going on to New York . . . like ships passing in the night. It's from a poem by Longfellow."

Sally recited the poem.

"Ships that pass in the night, and speak each other in passing,
Only a signal shown and a distant voice in the darkness;
So on the ocean of life we pass and speak one another,
Only a look and a voice, then darkness again and a silence."

"Wow. You know what?" Cal said. "I think I actually understand that. It means that the girl I looked at on the train and I will never see each other again, doesn't it?"

Sally chuckled "Very astute, Cal."

Inside the depot they found a curious mix of architectural styles with several restaurants and spacious waiting rooms.

"I wish we could stay here long enough for me to see Chicago," Cal said. "I've heard about it a lot, and I would really like to see it."

"Maybe we can see it on the way back home," Sally suggested. "Now, we have to get to New York in time for the play, but on the way back home, there will be no time constraints imposed upon us."

As they waited for the train, Cal saw a copy of the *New York Evening World* and bought it to read.

WILLIAM DOOLIN FREED TODAY

William Doolin, one-time member of the Irish Assembly, a gang of ruffians who ply

their trade in the Bridgetown section of the
city, has been released. Sometimes using
the alias Brockway, he served six years for
armed robbery. He has been cautioned not to
return to his old pursuits, but he seems most
likely to do so.

"Cal," Sally said, returning to the bench where he was
seated, reading the newspaper. "The Hummer will depart on
track nine at six o'clock tomorrow morning. We'll be in
New York by two o'clock the following day." She smiled
broadly. "Are you getting excited?"

"A little, I guess," Cal said.

"Do you think you can rest on the benches here in the
waiting room? If we got a hotel room it would be at least an
hour and a half before we got in bed, and I would be so
frightened that we would miss the train, that I would want
us up by three o'clock in the morning. We would wind up
with no more than four hours in the hotel."

"This will be fine, Miz Sally." Cal laughed. "Maybe
you're forgettin' how many times I've had to throw my
blanket out on the ground, sometimes in the snow, even. I
don't think we'll be getting any snow in here."

Sally laughed. "It isn't very likely."

Cal wasn't sure what awakened him, but he woke in the
middle of the night and lay there with his eyes open, staring
at the vaulted ceiling far above. The room was illuminated
by dozens of hanging chandeliers, as well of scores of
sconce lanterns attached either to the wall or to the many
supporting columns. He lifted his head to check on Sally,
and that's when he saw a man reaching carefully, ever so
carefully, for Sally's purse that lay between her and the
seat back.

The man was startled midreach by the clicking sound of a hammer being pulled back and a cylinder rotating to bring a bullet in alignment, both with the barrel and the firing pin. The would-be purse snatcher looked in the direction from which the sound had come.

"Yeah, you heard right," Cal said, smiling broadly over the .44 Colt he was holding, pointed directly at the intruder. "That was the sound of me cocking the pistol. And if you don't pull your hand away from that purse, the next and last sound you hear will be when I pull the trigger and blow your head half off." He spoke the words calmly and with a cool detachment that frightened the thief, even more than if the words had been spit out in anger.

"Go away," Cal said. "Stay away."

"Y-yes sir!" the would-be thief said, making a hasty departure.

"Cal?" Sally mumbled in a sleepy voice. "Is everything all right? I thought I heard you talking."

"Yes, ma'am, everything is just fine," Cal said.

CHAPTER 13

New York City

Even though the Irish Assembly was no more, Ian Gallagher was still very active, controlling all the action in the Bay Ridge neighborhood of Brooklyn. Prostitution, gambling, and protection all came under his purview, and nobody dared to begin operating without his permission and without giving him his cut.

At the moment, Gallagher was ensconced at "his" table in the back of Paddy's Pub, playing the game of Brandubh with Paddy Boyle, who owned the pub. Reaching down to the board, he moved one of his pieces.

"That's the third time you've made that same move, Gallagher," Boyle said. "Repetitive moves mean you lose."

"I haven't made the move yet, Paddy, I was just studyin' where to move next," Gallagher replied, returning the piece to its original position.

If Boyle had been playing anyone else, he would have insisted that the game had just been forfeited to him. But this wasn't anyone else. This was Ian Gallagher, and people didn't argue with Ian Gallagher. That is, not if they wanted to stay alive.

"All right. I was just warnin' you in case you did decide to make that move."

"Mr. Gallagher? Is Mr. Gallagher in here?" The questioner was a young boy wearing a cap sporting the words WESTERN UNION.

"I'm back here, boy," Gallagher called out.

"I have a telegram for you, sir." The boy hurried back to the table and presented the telegram. "The telegrapher said there wasn't no name on who sent it." He waited for the expected tip.

"All right, you've delivered the telegram 'n told me there wasn't no name, so what is it that you're waiting on?" Gallagher asked the boy as he tore open the envelope.

"Most usually whenever someone gets a telegram, what they do is give the one what brung it to 'em a tip, sir."

"You get paid by Western Union, don't you?"

"Yes, sir."

"And they pay you to deliver telegrams?"

"Yes sir, but—"

"There ain't no buts," Gallagher said with a dismissive wave of his hand. "So be gone with you, now."

"Yes, sir," the boy replied, intimidated by the gruff voice of someone the boy knew was not to be crossed.

MRS KIRBY JENSEN ARRIVING
GRAND CENTRAL DEPOT ON BOARD
TRANSCONTINENTAL TRAIN HUMMER
TWO PM THIS DAY STOP ARRANGE FOR HER
TO BE YOUR GUEST UNTIL FURTHER NOTICE
STOP YOU WILL BE WELL COMPENSATED
FOR HER STAY WITH YOU STOP

Gallagher folded the telegram over and stuck it in his pocket.

"Now, that don't make any sense at all. There ain't no

name on the telegram." Doolin, recently released from prison, had been kibitzing the game. "The boy said there wouldn't be a name. Do you know who sent it?"

"Yeah," Gallagher replied without giving any further information.

"Anythin' serious?" Boyle asked.

"No, nothing serious. It's my move, I believe."

"Aye," Boyle said, overlooking the disqualifying move Gallagher had made just before the arrival of the telegram. "It's your move, that's for sure and certain."

Half an hour later, Gallagher and Brockway were meeting with Kelly and O'Leary, two of the men in his gang, for that is truly what men who worked with him could be called.

"What do we do with her when we snatch her?" Kelly asked.

"Hold her until someone pays us to let her go," Gallagher said.

"How will we recognize who she is?"

"You know she won't be coming here without baggage," Gallagher said. "We've got people in the depot. When she claims her baggage, we'll know who she is."

On board the Hummer

Six days and five trains after leaving the Big Rock Depot, the transcontinental train called the Hummer rolled into New York. From the moment the train crossed the Hudson River, Cal had been glued to the window, beholding sights like nothing he had ever seen before. Then the train stopped.

"Why did we stop?" he asked.

"We've reached Grand Central Depot," Sally answered.

"Where? I don't see a depot."

Sally chuckled. "You will. Just wait."

The train began backing up and Cal, who was more confused now than he had been before, studied the sights outside. He saw that they were backing toward a huge, sprawling, five-story building. Projecting out from the building was a network of tracks, most of which were occupied by trains. He continued to watch as they backed into the station, and a moment later, saw that they were slipping in between two trains that were already in place. This train and the one closest to it were separated by a long, narrow, brick path. He realized then, that they had also passed under an overhead roof of some sort. He stared at the windows of the adjacent train, realizing he couldn't possibly see again the young woman he had seen in the train window in Chicago, but thinking it might be nice to have another 'ships that pass in the night' moment . . . but no such moment occurred.

"All right, folks. This is Grand Central Depot," the conductor said, coming through the car. "Please watch your step as you leave the train."

Cal followed Sally and the other passengers through the aisle of the car, then down the steps, and onto the brick platform. Other trains were arriving and departing, and the roof high overhead seemed to capture the sounds. Chugging engines, vented steam, rolling wheels, clattering connectors, squeaking brakes, clanging bells, and hundreds of voices cast the cacophonous clamor back down.

"I'm sure it'll be a few minutes before we'll be able to claim our luggage, so we may as well get something to eat," Sally said once they stepped into the depot.

"Yes, ma'am," Cal replied with a broad smile. "You know me, Miss Sally. I'm always ready to eat."

Gallagher and Brockway were waiting in the baggage claim area of the depot. Gallagher was leaning up against the wall with his arms folded across his chest. A few minutes earlier he had given Guido Sarducci a five-dollar bill, and all Sarducci had to do was identify the luggage belonging to Mrs. Kirby Jensen.

"It's that piece there," Sarducci told Gallagher as he pointed to a large, maroon leather case.

"Set it aside from the other pieces of luggage so I can see who comes for it," Gallagher ordered.

"Yes, sir."

Gallagher watched as men and women came to claim their luggage, but the maroon piece Sarducci had pointed out remained unclaimed until an attractive woman and a man considerably younger step up to the open window.

"Yes, ma'am, Mrs. Jensen. I have your luggage right here," Sarducci said, speaking loudly enough for Gallagher to hear the exchange.

Gallagher watched as first Mrs. Jensen claimed her luggage, then the young man with her.

"Cal Wood," the young man said to Sarducci.

There had been no mention of a Cal Wood in the telegram, so Gallagher didn't know if they were traveling together or if they just happened to arrive at the baggage claim at the same time. When he saw a red-cap take both pieces, though, he realized that they must be together.

Gallagher and Brockway followed them outside, heard the Jensen woman tell the cabdriver that they wished to go to the Fifth Avenue Hotel, and got into the cab behind the one that she and Cal had taken.

"Fifth Avenue Hotel," Gallagher said.

Reaching their destination, he paid the driver, then he and Brockway followed Sally and Cal into the hotel. Brockway stayed in the lobby as Gallagher stepped up to the front desk and stood to one side as if waiting to register. His intention was to find out what room they would be staying in.

"Mrs. Jensen, yes," the desk clerk said with a smile. "I

believe I would be holding two tickets for you, for opening night of the play *Bold Lady* at the Rex Theater."

"Yes, thank you."

"Enjoy the play, the clerk said. "If Andrew and Rosanna MacCallister are going to be in it, I know it will be great."

As first Sally and then Cal signed the registration book, Gallagher's plans changed. It no longer mattered what room she was staying in. She would be going to a play the next night. That was all the information he needed.

He turned and gave a brief nod to Brockway, and they left the hotel.

CHAPTER 14

Cross Trails Ranch

"Oh now, that is a fine-looking bull," Jim Harris said as he examined Yankee Star.

Smoke and Pearlie had arrived with the bull a few minutes earlier, and he was turned out in the reinforced cattle pen that Harris had constructed just for him.

"He is a good-looking bull, and he comes from a champion sire and dam," Smoke said.

"I'm curious. Why didn't Sam Condon deliver the bull himself?"

"Haven't you heard? Sam was shot last week," Smoke said.

"No, I hadn't heard! Was he killed?"

"No. He's recovering now."

"Thank God for that. What happened?"

Smoke described what had taken place at Wiregrass Ranch, ending with the fact that Sam's son, Thad, had been abducted. "It looks like Sam is going to pull through being shot all right, but he and Sara Sue are both very worried about their son."

"Oh, Lord, I didn't know that was going on down in Colorado, as well," Harris replied.

"What do you mean, going on in Colorado *as well*?" Smoke asked, surprised by the comment.

"We've had a rash of abductions around here," Harris said. "There have been at least ten that I know of."

"Ten children are missing?"

"No, only five of them are still missing. Four have been returned, but it cost their folks a lot of money to get them back."

"You said you knew of ten, five still missing and four returned. What about the tenth one?"

"Oh, that was Lucy Blair." Harris shook his head. "Sadly, she was found dead on the banks of Savery Creek."

"How was she killed?" Pearlie asked.

"Somebody had cut her throat. Some folks say it was because she was too much for the outlaws to handle. Sixteen, she was, and a real pretty thing, too."

"What about the sheriff?" Smoke asked.

"The sheriff's up in Rawlins. He's over sixty years old and has no deputies. His office is pretty much just a political position. Nobody ever really depends on him for any real law."

"Where do you get your law support?"

"There's a marshal in town, 'n there's some talk of comin' up with a way for him to be able to operate out of town. I don't know if that's happened yet, but I hope they can get it done."

After delivering the bull to Jim Harris, Smoke and Pearlie rode on into Mule Gap. This was one full day before Sara Sue was supposed to meet with someone representing the kidnappers of her son. They had come a day earlier so that it would not appear as if they were with her. The early arrival also allowed them to have a look around the town to determine whether or not any danger faced the woman when she came to keep her appointment.

The meeting was to take place in the Del Rey Hotel on the next day, but Smoke and Pearlie planned to spend this night camping out just south of town on the Pinkhampton Pike. Sara Sue would be coming in by stagecoach, the next day, and the coach would have to come by way of that road.

The two men stopped in front of Kennedy's Saloon, looped the reins around the hitching rail, then stepped inside.

"Smoke!" a friendly voice called.

Looking toward the sound of the voice, Smoke saw Warren Kennedy. A man dressed all in black was sitting at the table with Kennedy.

"Ethan," Kennedy called out to the bartender, "Smoke Jensen's money is no good in my saloon. Find out what he and the gentleman with him want, then have one of the girls bring it to our table."

"Yes, gentlemen, what will it be?" Ethan asked as Smoke and Pearlie reached the bar.

"I'll have a beer," Smoke said.

"And I'll have the same," Pearlie added.

"Who's with you?" Kennedy asked as Smoke and Pearlie joined the two men at the table.

"This is my ranch foreman," Smoke said. "Pearlie."

"Pearlie . . ." Kennedy repeated, dragging it out, obviously looking for a last name.

"Pearlie," he replied without giving a last name. That finished the inquisition.

"Pearlie, this is Warren Kennedy," Smoke said. "Or perhaps I should say, His Honor, since Mr. Kennedy is also the mayor of Mule Gap."

"Pleased to meet you, Mayor," Pearlie said.

Smoke turned his attention to the man dressed in black, who, unlike Kennedy, had not stood at their approach. He was staring at Smoke with eyes that could best be described as flat and featureless.

"And this fearsome-looking gentleman is City Marshal Frank Bodine," Smoke said, continuing the introductions.

"County Marshal Bodine," Kennedy said.

"County Marshal?" Smoke replied, unfamiliar with the term.

"We have a sheriff, but he never leaves his office in Rawlins, and he has no deputies. The result of the sheriff's inactivity is that the residents of Carbon County are left without any type of law enforcement."

"Yes, come to think of it, that's exactly what Jim Harris said," Smoke replied. "He said you were trying to come up with a way to extend the town marshal's jurisdiction."

"And I have done so. I didn't want to make Marshal Bodine a deputy sheriff and thus subservient to the sheriff up in Rawlins, so I made him the county marshal."

"How were you able to do that? Legally, I mean."

"I have filed with the territorial capital in Cheyenne our intention to incorporate the entire county, except for the towns of Rawlins, Douglas, and Warm Springs, into the town of Mule Gap."

"And they have approved that?"

"It hasn't been disapproved," Kennedy replied with a smile.

Smoke laughed. "I have to give you credit, Warren, you do seem to have a way of getting things done. And I agree that the citizens of the county do need some protection by the law. But this is an awfully large area for one man to handle."

"That's why Marshal Bodine has recruited so many deputies," Kennedy replied. "I have—that is, the town of Mule Gap has—authorized a strength of ten deputy marshals."

"That's quite a sizeable police force."

"Yes, but as you say, Carbon County is a large area to cover."

Smoke turned his attention to the man in black. "So tell me, Marshal Bodine. Are you working on finding the kidnapped children and getting them returned to their families?"

"You know about the kidnappings?" Kennedy asked.

"Yes. A few days ago a boy was taken from a neighboring ranch. In trying to defend him, his father was shot."

"Oh," Kennedy replied. "Was he killed?"

"No, he survived the shooting."

"That is good to hear. What is he doing about recovering his son?" Kennedy asked. "I mean, I hope he is going to pay the ransom."

"Why would you say that?"

"We have been experiencing a rash of these kidnappings. The ransom has been paid on four of the children, and they have been returned safely to their families. That is a favorable outcome for all concerned."

"Except the families who may be out their life savings," Smoke said.

"Surely, Smoke, you aren't putting mere money above the life of the child, are you?" Kennedy challenged.

"No, of course I'm not doing that, but it does seem to me that the most favorable outcome would be to catch the men who are doing this, free the children, and put the men in prison."

"Yes, of course that would be the most favorable outcome, and I believe that, in time, Marshal Bodine will be able to do just that. But until then, don't you agree with me that the best thing for these families to do is pay the ransom?"

"Under the circumstances, yes," Smoke replied. "I do believe it is Sam Condon's intention to pay the ransom."

"Yes, well, if Mr. Condon can afford it, that is no doubt the best and safest way to have his son released without harm," Kennedy said. "But I am interested. What brings you to my town? Does it have anything to do with the kidnapping of the Condon boy?"

"No, our visit has nothing to do with that. Pearlie and I just delivered a bull to Jim Harris. Being here at the time of the boy's kidnapping is purely coincidental."

"I see. Harris, no doubt, paid you in cash again because he won't use my bank."

"You know him well," Smoke said.

"Evidently I don't know him well enough. I have been totally incapable of talking him into using my bank."

"Jim Harris is a stubborn man, all right."

"Will you be staying with us tonight?" Kennedy asked. "You know, I own half of the Del Rey Hotel, and I think I can promise you a comfortable stay."

"We have somewhere else we have to be tonight, but we'll be back tomorrow and will probably spend one or two nights," Smoke said.

"Oh? Why so long? Not that you aren't welcome," Kennedy added with a smile. "As you have no doubt learned by now, I am a businessman, and having a couple guests in my hotel for a few nights is always a good thing."

"Warren Kennedy looking for every way he can to make another dollar? You don't say," Smoke teased. "As you may know, Sally is in New York now, so I've no real reason to get back home so quickly. Pearlie and I thought we might take advantage of our time up here to get in a little hunting."

"For the kidnapped boy?" Bodine asked.

"No, that would be your job, so I'll leave that up to you," Smoke said. "I was thinking more along the lines of pronghorn deer."

CHAPTER 15

Rex Theater, New York City

Rosanna MacCallister as Dame Sara stood in the light at center stage, holding a dagger before her. "Oh noble sire, that you would have given your life in defense of my honor—honor which I do not have—has left me prostrate with grief and shame. Grief, because I cannot imagine a world without you, and shame because the honor for which you gave your life does not exist.

"Yes, Albert, it shames me to say that I have long hidden the truth from you. For you see, I am a woman debased. I am not, as you believe, the daughter of nobility. I was to a lowly servant woman born, my birth killing the very woman who had given me life. I was taken as their own by the nobles whom my mother served, Lord and Lady Montjoy. Would but the blood from the thrust of this dagger wash clean the stain on my soul." She raised the dagger above her breast.

Andrew MacCallister as Lord Albert Cairns rushed in from stage left. "Wait. Do not harm yourself because of foolish pride and wrong intelligence! The news that I was slain was inaccurately reported. I live yet, and I have long known of your humble origins. Do you not believe that your noble upbringing has made you as noble as one to the manor born? It is not who you were, but who you are that has earned my love."

Dame Sara dropped the dirk and the two embraced at center stage.

As the curtain closed, the theater erupted with applause and cheers. Sally and Cal had been given seats in the orchestra section of the theater, and they rose with the others to give the two actors upon the stage a standing ovation.

The curtains opened again, and all the secondary players rushed out to take their curtain call, their appearances on stage in inverse order of the significance of their roles. After taking their bows, the actors moved to either side of the stage and held their arms out toward the two principals of the show, Andrew and Rosanna MacCallister. The stage manager hurried onto the stage carrying a large bouquet of yellow roses, which he presented to Rosanna.

Again, the applause swelled.

Across the street from the theater, Gallagher, Brockway, Kelly, and O'Leary watched as the patrons left the theater. The theatergoers were talking about the play they had just seen.

"Isn't Rosanna MacCallister just the most beautiful woman you ever saw?"

"It is the skill of the stage makeup artist that causes her to look so beautiful."

"If she wasn't already beautiful, no makeup artistry could make her so."

"We're a-lookin' for the same woman we saw gettin' off the train, right?" Brockway asked.

"Yes."

"I don't see her."

"She was sitting down front. She will be one of the last to leave," Gallagher said as he handed a small brown bottle and a handkerchief to Brockway. "Do you know how to use this?"

"Yeah, I know," Brockway replied.

"I'm goin' on ahead," Gallagher said. "When she comes out, you three follow her."

"All right."

He left the other three and hurried on ahead, positioning himself between the Rex Theater and the Fifth Avenue Hotel.

"Mrs. Jensen?" one of the theater ushers asked, approaching Sally and Cal just as they were rising from their seats.

"Yes?" Sally replied.

"Mr. MacCallister has issued an invitation for you two to join the company backstage."

"Oh, how nice of him," Sally said.

"If you would come with me, please, madam."

Sally and Cal followed the usher through a small door just to the left of the stage, then wandered through the labyrinth of flats, props, ropes, and miscellaneous components that were necessary to stage a major play before a sophisticated New York audience.

"Ah!" Cal gasped, jumping back in shock when he saw a severed human head. "What's that?"

"Do not be concerned, sir," the usher replied. "That is the head of Yorick."

"Who? Well, what's his head doing here?"

Sally chuckled, then reached for the head and holding it in front of her, began reciting. "'Alas, poor Yorick! I knew him, Horatio; a fellow of infinite jest, of most excellent fancy; he hath borne me on his back a thousand times; and now, how abhorred in my imagination it is! My gorge rises at it. Here hung those lips that I have kissed I know not how oft. Where be your gibes now? Your gambols? Your songs?

Your flashes of merriment, that were wont to set the table on a roar.'"

"Oh, most excellent, madam!" the theater usher said, clapping his hands. "You know your Shakespeare."

"Not really. A few lines from *Hamlet, Macbeth, Romeo and Juliet* is all. Just enough to allow me to show off from time to time."

As they were talking, Cal was making a closer examination of the head. "Oh," he said with an understanding smile. "This isn't real."

"They used to use real heads, but they didn't last long," Sally said.

"What?" Cal gasped.

Sally laughed out loud. "I'm teasing you, Cal."

As they continued to explore, they came to an area that was reserved for the players—a large common room with mirrors and dressing screens for the "bit actors" and dressing rooms for those with larger roles. The doors leading to the dressing rooms for Andrew and Rosanna each had a star and their name, but at the moment the two stars of the play were sharing the common room with the others.

Everyone was still keyed up from the performance, and they were laughing and talking excitedly. Andrew called for attention, and everyone grew quiet.

"I would like to congratulate each and every one of you," he said. "You did well as you strutted and fretted your hour upon the stage."

"But," Rosanna interrupted, holding up her finger, "unlike the next line in the bard's famous soliloquy, I predict that all of you will be heard again."

"Who could not do well when playing with the two best thespians in New York theater, Andrew and Rosanna MacCallister?" one of the supporting actors declared, holding his arm out toward the brother and sister.

The other actors applauded.

"Sally, how wonderful of you and your friend to come to our opening night," Rosanna said when she saw Sally and Cal.

"Are you kidding? Who could resist such an invitation?" Sally replied.

"Yes, if you are living in the city. But, my goodness, you came two thousand miles."

"It was a good excuse to visit New York again," Sally replied. "And to show the city to a young man that Smoke and I have come to regard as family."

"Yes, seeing the city through the eyes of someone who is seeing it for the first time can be quite exhilarating," Rosanna replied

"Sally, will you be taking dinner tonight with Rosanna, me, and some of the others?" Andrew asked.

"We would be most happy to," Sally said.

"We'll gather at Delmonico's at midnight," Andrew said. "The restaurant will be closed then to all except our private party. I will give the maître d' your names so that you may be assured entry."

"At midnight?"

"Yes. If that is too late for you, I understand."

"No, that'll be fine," Sally said. "It will give Cal and me time to stop by our rooms at the hotel."

"Good. We'll see you then."

"What the hell?" O'Leary asked. "How come she ain't come out yet? You think maybe there's a back door to that place?"

"I don't know, there might be but . . . wait. That's her comin' out right now," Brockway said.

"Who's that man with her?" O'Leary said."

"I don't know, but he was on the train with her," Brockway replied.

"So what?" Kelly asked.

"So, what are we going to do with him? I mean, he'll be in the way, won't he?"

"He won't be in the way."

"What do you mean, 'he won't be in the way'? He's there, ain't he?"

"He won't be in the way, 'cause we'll kill 'im."

"Your friends are good people," Cal said as he and Sally started the ten-block walk from the theater to the hotel. "They don't seem like New York people at all."

Sally laughed. "What do you mean, 'they don't seem like New York people'? What are New York people like?"

"I've seen them in Denver before. They're just sort of very full of themselves."

"Well, Rosanna and Andrew may live in New York now, but they're from Colorado. Don't forget, they are Falcon MacCallister's brother and sister."

"Yeah, that's true, isn't it? I forgot."

"Did you enjoy the play?"

"Oh, yes, ma'am, I sure did. Why, that was about the most wonderful thing I've ever seen. I mean, the way ever'one was upon that stage, why, it was like we was"—Cal paused, then, with a smile, corrected his grammar—"like we were right there in the same room with them, just watching ever'thing that was going on."

"That's the illusion brilliant thespians can create," Sally replied. "And thank you for correcting your grammar."

"Yes, ma'am. Well, bein' that you"—he paused for a second—"were once a schoolteacher, I know what a store you put in proper English, so I try to use good grammar whenever I can."

"Very good, Cal, very good," Sally said.

"I think it's funny that we're goin' to be eatin' with them at the Delmonico restaurant," Cal said.

"Funny? Why do you say that? What's funny about having a late dinner at Delmonico's?"

"Well, think about it, Miz Sally. There's a Delmonico's in Big Rock 'n there's one here in New York. I mean, when we go back 'n tell Mr. DeWeese that there's a restaurant in New York that's got the same name as his, why, he'll more 'n likely be proud of that, don't you think?"

Sally laughed. "He more than likely will be."

As the two continued their walk back to the hotel, Cal happened to notice in the window of a closed store the reflection of three men following them. It seemed too late for any casual pedestrians, but there had been a full house for the play. Also there were other theaters nearby, and their audiences had turned out onto the street at about the same time, so it was possible that those men were part of the theater crowd.

Using that reasoning, Cal discounted the three men, but a little later he caught another glimpse of them and something in their actions alerted him. It looked to him as if the men might be trying to avoid being seen. Why would that be, unless they were up to no good?

"Miz Sally, I think maybe we ought to step it up a bit," Cal said.

"What do you mean?"

"There are some men on the street behind us."

Sally chuckled. "Cal, it isn't unusual that there would be people on the street. Over two million people live in New York."

"Yes, ma'am, but it's not the rest of the two million

people I'm worryin' about. It's the three men that are behind us. They're actin' kind of funny."

"Funny how?"

"Like they don't want to be seen."

Sally looked back and as she did, the two men stepped into an alcove. It might have been a coincidence, but Cal might also be right. She got the same feeling of apprehension that he was experiencing. "All right. If it'll make you feel better . . ."

"I'd feel just a whole lot better if I had my gun with me," Cal said.

"So would I," Sally agreed.

As they approached the end of the block, a man suddenly stepped in front of them. He was holding a pistol, and Cal automatically went for his own gun. But there was no gun there. His gun was back in his suitcase in the hotel room.

"Just hold it right there." The man smiled, though it was a smile without humor.

"You don't really expect us to be carrying around a great deal of money, do you?" Sally asked. "If this is a holdup, I'm afraid you are going to be quite disappointed."

"Oh, this isn't a holdup. No ma'am, we have something else in mind for you, Mrs. Jensen."

"What?" Sally replied, shocked to be addressed by name.

Many people back in Colorado knew her, even in Denver. That could be expected as she was married to one of the biggest ranchers in the state. Smoke Jensen's fame went considerably further than the mere fact that he was a successful rancher. His skill with a gun was unmatched.

But she wasn't in Colorado. She was in New York. And what were the chances of someone in New York knowing her by name? "How is it that you know my name?"

"We have plans for you," the man said.

"The hell you do," Cal said. "If you hurt—" That was as

far as he got before he was hit just above his right ear by something hard and heavy. He went down.

"Cal!" Sally started to bend down to see to him when powerful arms were wrapped around her. She felt a cloth being pressed over her nose and mouth. She fought against it and couldn't help but take several deep breaths. She was aware of a cloying, sweet smell . . . then nothing.

CHAPTER 16

Mule Gap

Lute Cruthis and Boots Zimmerman were patrolling First Street when they saw someone coming out of the Silver Dollar Saloon.

"Hey, Boots. Ain't that Melvin Varner?"

"I don't know," Zimmerman said. "I ain't never seen 'im before."

"I have. Me 'n him 'n some others done a job together back in Kansas a couple years ago. He got caught for it 'n when to jail, but I heard he escaped, 'n here he is."

"Think they's a reward on 'im?"

"Yeah, I know there is."

Varner had just rolled himself a cigarette and was lighting it. He was unaware of the two deputies approaching him.

"Hello, Varner," Cruthis said.

Varner looked up in surprise at being addressed by name. At first there was an expression of concern on his face until he recognized Cruthis. Then he smiled. "Lute! I'll be damned. It's been a coon's age since I last seen you. What are you doing in these—" Varner paused in midsentence when he saw what was on the front of Cruthis's shirt. "You're a star packer now?"

"That's right. 'N you're under arrest."

Varner held his hand out. "No, now, you don't want to do that to an old friend. What you might not know is I kilt me a guard when I broke outta jail back in Kansas. If I go back there I'll more 'n likely hang."

"I know. That's why they's a thousand-dollar reward out for you," Cruthis said.

"Reward? What would that mean to you? If you're the law, you can't collect."

"Yeah, we can. We got us a special deal," Cruthis said. "Draw, Varner."

Even as Cruthis said the word, he was already reaching for his gun.

"No!" Varner shouted, but seeing Cruthis start his draw, Varner had no choice. He went for his gun and though Cruthis beat him, he waited for a second to let Varner clear leather before he shot.

Varner went down with the gun in his hand.

At the sound of the shot, several people rushed out of the saloon, and a couple men on the other side of the street crossed over to the scene.

"What happened?" someone asked.

"This is Melvin Varner," Cruthis said, still holding the smoking gun in his hand. "He's wanted for murder. When I tried to arrest him, he drew his gun." Cruthis pointed to the gun in Varner's hand.

"Damn, Deputy, you was lucky you beat 'im," another said.

"I seen the whole thing," Zimmerman said. "It's just like Lute said. He told Varner he was under arrest, 'n next thing you know, Varner was drawing on 'im."

On the Pinkhampton Pike, four miles south of Mule Gap

Smoke and Pearlie had camped alongside the South Platte River, about one hundred yards off the Pinkhampton Pike. The coffee had already been made, and as Smoke washed his face in water dipped from the river, Pearlie was looking after six pieces of bacon twitching in the pan over the fire. There were no eggs, but yesterday they had bought a loaf of bread and it would be fried up in the bacon grease to complete their breakfast meal.

"What time will the stage be comin' through?" Pearlie asked.

"The way station is halfway between here and Douglas, and I expect they got underway by seven this morning," Smoke said. "They should be coming by here at about eight.

"Mrs. Condon is carrying fifteen thousand dollars in cash, is she?"

"No, she's carrying a draft from the bank of Big Rock for that amount. It wouldn't do anyone else any good to steal it."

Pearlie nodded. "That's good."

Taking the bacon out, Smoke dropped some bread slices into the grease, then he laughed.

"What is it?"

"Can you imagine what Sally would say if she saw me eating something like this? She's convinced that bacon grease is bad for you."

"Now, how can anything that tastes that good be bad for you?" Pearlie asked.

They ate in silence for a moment.

"I hope Cal is havin' hisself a fine time up there in New York," Pearlie said.

"I expect he is. For someone like Cal, seeing the city for the first time, it has to be exciting for him."

New York City

"Get up!"

Cal felt someone kicking him in the side.

"Get up. I'll not be havin' it said that Mickey Muldoon has drunks sleepin' on the streets on his beat. Get up."

Cal was kicked again: "Ow! Stop kicking me! What are you kicking me for?" He raised up on his hands and knees and saw that it was daylight.

What was he doing on the sidewalk like this?

"Are you still drunk? Do you think you can for findin' your way home? Or do I need to put ye in jail?"

"What do you mean, put me in jail? Put me in jail for what?" Cal stood up and saw that the obnoxious man yelling at him was a police officer. He noticed a tenderness just above his ear, and putting his hand there, winced with pain from the contact. "I'm not drunk." He pulled his hand away and looked at it. Blood showed on the tips of his fingers.

"Here, let me take a look, lad," the policeman asked, his entire demeanor changing at the sight of the blood. "Aye, 'tis a good lick you have there. Who done it?"

"I don't know," Cal said. "They came up behind me an' . . . Mrs. Jensen! Where is Mrs. Jensen?"

"Who? Lad, when I came upon you a few minutes ago, you were layin' there all alone. 'Twas thinkin', I was, that you be drunk. Who is the lady you be askin' about?"

"Mrs. Jensen. She was with me, and we were goin' back to the hotel when—" He stopped in midsentence. "The man with the gun knew her. How did he know her? And what did he mean when he said he had plans for her?"

"A man with a gun? Begorra, 'n you said nothing about a man with a gun. He knew the lady, you say? I think you said her name was Jensen?"

"Yes, sir. Mrs. Kirby Jensen. Her husband is one of the

biggest ranchers in all of Colorado, is all," Cal said. "But we're in New York, so how did he know Miz Sally's name?"

"Mrs. Sally? Here now 'n 'twas the name *Jensen* you told me."

"Yes, Mrs. Jensen. But her first name is Sally, 'n that's what me 'n Pearlie call her. Only, to be respectful, we call her Miz Sally."

"If this Mrs. Jensen is a rich woman from Colorado, what is she doin' in New York?"

"She come here to see some old friends, 'n she brought me with her 'cause I had never been to New York before."

"So, where is this lady now?" Officer Muldoon asked. "How come it is that she left you lyin' on the sidewalk?"

"That's just it, Deputy. Miz Sally would never just leave me there, lessen somethin' happened to her."

The policeman shook his head. "What's your name?"

"Cal. Uh, Cal Wood."

"Sure 'n tell me now, Mr. Wood, would you be for havin' any way of collaboratin' this story you're tellin' me?"

"Collaboratin'? What does that mean?"

"Is there any way you can prove to me what you're saying? My first thought is that you was drunk last night. All right. I can see that you was hit in the head, but how do I know you didn't just get drunk 'n get into a fight?"

"Because I'm tellin' you I wasn't drunk."

"Is there any way you can prove that story to me?"

"No, I told you, we aren't from here. We're from Colorado 'n I don't know anyone here who can—" Cal paused in midsentence again. "Wait a minute. Andrew MacCallister."

"Who?"

"Andrew MacCallister 'n his sister Rosanna. They're famous actors, and we went to see their play last night. They can tell you about Mrs. Jensen."

Officer Muldoon laughed. "Lad, are you tryin' to tell me now, that just because you was in the audience of a play they was in, that they can verify your story? Sure 'n there must've been two or three hundred people watchin' the play last night. How are they goin' to be able to pick you out like that?"

"Miz Sally 'n I went backstage after the play to see them."

"You went backstage to see them, did you? Well then, maybe they can and maybe they can't. I expect lots of people go backstage after a play," the policeman replied. He shook his head. "But 'tis tellin' you right now, I'll not be for botherin' those people."

"You've got to, Deputy! Don't you see? The men who did this to me have captured Mrs. Jensen! I don't know what they have in mind for her, but it can't be good."

"All right. Come with me, then, 'n I'll be for lettin' you tell yer story to the desk sergeant. He'll be the one makin' the decision as to what should be done with you."

Still a little dizzy and with the knot above his ear still very painful, Cal followed the policeman back to the Midtown South Precinct.

"Sergeant, I'll be for turnin' this man over to you," the policeman who had awakened Cal said. "Passed out on the street, he was, when I found 'im, 'n I was thinkin' that he was drunk. Turns out he was hit on the head 'n knocked out."

"That may be, Muldoon, but why are you bringin' 'im to me? Are you plannin' on puttin' 'im in jail?"

"No, but he's got 'im a story I think maybe you ought to hear. Tell the sergeant your story, Mr. Wood."

Cal told the story of coming to New York for Mrs. Jensen to visit with some old friends and Cal to see the city for the first time.

"What is about New York that would make a man

come all the way from Texas, just to pay us a visit?" the desk sergeant asked.

"Colorado," Cal corrected. "And I just wanted to see the big city."

"Well, last night 'twould appear that you saw more than you wanted."

"Lad, tell the sergeant about them famous actors," Muldoon said.

"Wait," the desk sergeant said. "'Tis thinkin' I am that we should get Lieutenant Kilpatrick to listen to the lad's story."

After a short wait, Lieutenant Kilpatrick joined the discussion. He was a big man with red hair and a red mustache.

"All right, Mr. Wood, go on with your story," the lieutenant said when he was told why he was summoned.

Cal told about seeing the play and going backstage to meet all the actors and actresses afterward.

"And you're saying that if we talk to the MacCallisters, they'll collaborate everything you're telling us?" Lieutenant Kilpatrick asked.

There was that word again . . . *collaborate*. "Yeah," Cal said. "They will."

"Just because you happened to go backstage to see them after the play?"

"Yes, sir. Well, not just that. Andrew and Rosanna Mac-Callister are very good friends of Miz Sally's. They're the ones that gave us the tickets to see the play. We were supposed to have supper with 'em last night, only we got attacked by the four men before we could do it."

"Four men, you say?"

"Yes, sir. There was one man in front of us. He was holdin' a gun. And three who had been trailin' us."

"Lieutenant, if there were four men, I'd say it be a bit more than a mere street burglary," Muldoon said.

"I think you may be right, Muldoon."

"It must've been one of them that hit me. And when I came to this morning, Miz Sally was gone. They took her."

"Do you have any idea why they would take her?"

"No, sir, I don't. But I do remember that the man with the gun called her by name."

"Did this woman, Mrs. Sally . . ."

"Jensen," Cal corrected. "Miz Jensen."

"Yes. Did Mrs. Jensen know the man?"

"No, sir, she didn't."

Lieutenant Kilpatrick, who was the watch commander, stroked his chin. "Hmm, how would someone in New York know someone from Colorado?"

"She isn't from Colorado," Cal said. "I think she's originally from someplace like Boston or something. And she's even lived here in New York."

"I thought you said she was from Colorado," the desk sergeant said, confused by Cal's response.

"Yes, sir, she is. That is, she is now. She's married to Smoke Jensen, who is one of the biggest ranchers in the whole state."

"If her husband is a rich man, maybe somebody grabbed her to hold her for ransom," Muldoon suggested.

"And would you be for tellin' me, Mickey Muldoon, how 'tis that any of our brigands would be knowin' that?" the desk sergeant replied.

"The lad said that the man with the gun knew her name," Muldoon said. "If he was for knowin' her name, don't you think, Sergeant Keogh, that he might also know that her husband was rich?"

"Aye, that could be the case," Lieutenant Kilpatrick said. "But before we go any further with this, I want to hear from the actors if they verify the lad's story."

CHAPTER 17

When Sally awakened, she found herself on a bed with her arms stretched over her head and tied by her wrists to the headboard. She didn't know where she was, but she was fairly certain that she was in the middle of a business district. She could smell cabbage and corned beef and had been smelling it all day as if it was being cooked for a restaurant, rather than in someone's personal kitchen. She had also heard passing trains on elevated tracks, as well as the hollow clopping sound of hooves on the paver blocks of the street.

She had come to in the middle of the night, realizing then that she had been put out by chloroform being applied over her nose and mouth. She had not been hurt, but she was very uncomfortable and her back hurt because she couldn't change positions. Rags had been stuffed into her mouth in order to keep her from screaming.

She had no idea what time it was, but based on the way sunshine was streaming in through an incredibly dirty window, she believed it had to be midmorning. She had not eaten since lunch the previous day, but being hungry was not her greatest concern at the moment.

The door opened, and someone came in. This, she knew, was Kelly, because he had been in to check on her before.

"How are you getting along, Mrs. Jensen?"

Sally made a few sounds, but because of the gag, she couldn't actually talk.

"Oh, well now, you can't be for answerin' me with the gag in your mouth, can you?" Kelly said. "Would you like me to take it out?"

She nodded.

"You won't be for doin' a lot of screamin' now, will you? 'Cause to tell you the truth, in this neighborhood screamin' won't do you no good, 'n it'll just piss off Gallagher. He ain't no one you want to be for pissin' off. Do you promise not to scream?"

Sally nodded again, and Kelly removed the gag, then took the rag from her mouth. She took several gasping breaths, then tried to spit out the few pieces of cloth that had gotten into her mouth.

"Would you like a drink of water?" Kelly asked.

"Yes, please."

He held a cup of water to her lips, but she drank with some difficulty, unable to lift her head very far from the bed.

"'Tis thinkin' I am, that you might be a bit hungry. Would you be for wanting some cabbage, Mrs. Jensen?"

"How am I going to eat if I'm tied to the bed like this?"

"Aye now, 'tis a good question. I'll be for fetchin' you some food 'n then I'll be right back to untie the ropes."

As Sally waited for Kelly to return, she heard an elevated train pass by outside. It seemed to be on the same relative level, and she realized that she was on one of the upper floors of the building. She had no idea what her captors wanted with her. They had not robbed her, nor had they mistreated her in any way, other than in keeping her as a prisoner. She was also worried about Cal. What had happened to him? Was he also a prisoner?

"Here you are, Mrs. Jensen," Kelly said, coming back into the room. He was carrying a plate. "Cabbage 'n boiled potatoes for you." He set the plate on a small table then leaned over the bed to untie the ropes.

"Thank you," Sally said. Sitting up on the edge of the bed, she began rubbing her wrists. "How do you know my name? And why am I here?"

"The reason we know your name is 'cause Gallagher told me 'n O'Leary 'n Brockway what it was. Only, I'm not for knowin' why 'tis that we're for holdin' you here."

"You mean you are holding me prisoner for no reason?"

"I wouldn't be for sayin' that now, Mrs. Jensen. 'Tis just that I'm not for knowin' what the reason may be."

"Where is Cal?"

"Where is who?"

"Cal is the young man who was with me. Where is he?"

"I don't know where he is. We just left him there."

"Is he dead?"

"If he is, we ain't the ones that done it. All we done is give 'im a good knock on the head so as to keep him out of the way when we took you."

"Poor Cal. He must be worried sick."

Kelly laughed. "Here you be a prisoner, 'n 'tis the lad you was with that you be worried about."

Rex Theater

"Oh, heavens!" Rosanna MacCallister gasped. "Someone has taken Sally?"

"Yes, ma'am." Cal had been brought to the Rex Theater by Lieutenant Kilpatrick, who wanted to hear for himself if Cal's story could be verified. And, truth to tell, he also wanted to meet the famous brother-and-sister acting duo.

"So you are willing to corroborate this man's story?" the lieutenant asked.

"I can't speak to what has happened to her, because I wasn't there," Rosanna said. "But I will say that Sally

Jensen is a friend of mine . . . a very good friend. And Mr. Wood is correct in saying that she is one of the most prominent ladies in Colorado."

"And she and Mr. Wood were here last night?"

"Indeed they were," Rosanna said. "My brother and I had specifically provided them with tickets to the best seats in the house."

"And they were good seats, too. Me 'n Miz Sally . . . that is, Miz Sally and I," Cal corrected, "were just talkin' about it on the way back to the hotel. We were really lookin' forward to havin' supper with you at Delmonico's."

"Yes, we were wondering why you didn't show up. We thought perhaps you were just too tired from the long trip."

"No, ma'am. We didn't show up on account of what happened to Miz Sally."

"Officer, you've got to get her back," Rosanna said.

"I promise you, ma'am, we'll do all we can," Lieutenant Kilpatrick replied.

"I want to help," Cal said.

"You can help best by staying out of the way," Lieutenant Kilpatrick said.

"You would be making a big mistake if you exclude Cal Wood," Andrew said. "I know him to be quite helpful in situations like this. I have seen him in action before."

"He's a civilian. I have no authority to let him be involved."

"I'm not exactly a civilian," Cal said.

"What do you mean?"

"I'm a deputy sheriff in Eagle County, Colorado."

Kilpatrick laughed. "You're a deputy sheriff in Eagle County, Colorado? Why, you wouldn't even have any authority outside that county, let alone outside of the state. I'm afraid you would be a sheep among wolves, here in New York."

"Lieutenant, I've been among wolves before," Cal said.

"And grizzlies 'n mountain lions, bad outlaws, 'n even worsè . . . Indians. I'm pretty sure I can handle myself among the worst you have here."

"Yeah? Then tell me, Wood, how did you wind up face-down on the sidewalk last night?"

"I . . . guess you've got me on that one," Cal replied timorously.

"You go back to the hotel. If we are able to find anything out, we'll let you know."

Mayor Grace's office, New York City

"Your Honor, you have a couple visitors waiting to see you, sir," the mayor's administrative aide said.

Mayor Grace looked confused. "Visitors? I thought the appointment book was completed."

"Yes, sir, well, these two aren't on the appointment book. It's Andrew and Rosanna MacCallister."

"Are you talking about the actors?"

"Yes, sir."

The mayor smiled broadly. "Well, by all means, show them in." He stood to greet them when they entered.

"Mr. and Mrs. MacCallister, what an honor to have you call. Oh, wait. You aren't husband and wife. You are brother and sister, I believe."

"That is correct, Your Honor," Andrew said.

"Well, what can I do for you?"

"We need some help for a friend of ours," Andrew said.

"What sort of help?"

"First, let me show you this." Andrew showed the mayor a dime novel—*Smoke Jensen and the Rocky Mountain Gang* by Ned Buntline. "Have you ever heard of this person?"

"Ned Buntline?"

"No, Smoke Jensen."

"You mean a character in a book?"

"No, I mean Smoke Jensen. He is a real person," Andrew said. "True, these are made-up stories about him, but his real adventures would make an even more exciting story."

"Why are you showing me this? Does your request have something to do with Smoke Jensen?"

"It has to do with his wife," Rosanna said. "Sally Jensen is here in New York now."

Mayor Grace smiled. "Ah, you mean she wants to meet me. Of course, bring her in. I would be glad to meet her."

"I'm sure she would like to meet you, Mr. Mayor," Andrew said. "Right now I think she would be happy to meet anyone, but she can't. She has been taken prisoner."

"Taken prisoner? What do you mean? Who has taken her prisoner?"

"Lieutenant Kilpatrick thinks it might be the Irish Assembly," Andrew said.

Mayor Grace shook his head. "Impossible. There is no Irish Assembly anymore."

"True, but Kilpatrick thinks it might be some of the same men who were once a part of the Irish Assembly."

"All right," Mayor Grace said. "That could be, but I'm sure the police are doing all they can to find her. What do you want me to do?"

"Sally came to New York to see our new play," Rosanna said. "And she brought Cal Wood with her. Cal is a young man who works for Smoke and Sally on their ranch, Sugarloaf. He wants to help look for Sally, but the police say that he has no authority to do so."

"Well, that's silly. If all he wants to do is look for her, he doesn't need any authority."

"But we want you to give him authority to do more than just look," Andrew said. "We want him to have the same authority as a policeman."

"You want me to make him a policeman? All right. I can do that."

"No, we want him to work with the police, not be one. He is a deputy sheriff for Eagle County, Colorado, so it isn't as if he has no experience in working with the law. And he has been with Smoke for some time now, which means that many of the adventures Smoke is famous for have involved Cal."

"Suppose I make him a special New York deputy, answerable directly to me?" Mayor Grace suggested. "That will give him the authority to work with the police, but not limit him to being a beat policeman."

"Yes!" Andrew replied with a big smile. "That is exactly what we were hoping you would do!"

"If you would like to have coffee with me and tell me about your new play, I'll have the commission drawn up while we are waiting."

Cal, unaware that Andrew and Rosanna were arranging for his appointment as New York City deputy sheriff, was standing at the corner where the attack had taken place. Officer Mickey Muldoon was with him.

"'N you say that the brigand who attacked you came from here?" Muldoon pointed to the gap between the two buildings.

"Yes. No. That is, the fella with the gun come from there, but the three men who attacked Miz Sally and me came up from behind us."

"How is it that you know it was three men if they were behind you?"

"I saw them a couple times. At first I thought maybe they were just out on the street at the same time Miz Sally and I were, but then I saw that they were acting like they didn't want to be seen."

"And would you for be knowin' what time it was?"

"I'd say it was about ten o'clock," Cal said.

"Ten, was it?"

"Yes."

"Not many on the street at ten. 'Tis goin' to be hard findin' a witness, I'm afraid."

CHAPTER 18

Near Mule Gap

"Here comes the coach," Pearlie said, though his declaration wasn't necessary.

Even as Smoke was rolling up his blankets he could hear the coach approaching—the drum of hooves, the squeak and rattle of the coach, and the shouts of the driver.

Smoke and Pearlie stepped out to the side of the road and watched as the coach rolled by. Smoke was glad to see that Sara Sue was sitting next to the window, but though they made no overt acknowledgment, it was evident that they did see each other.

"What'll we do now? Are we goin' to follow the coach into town?" Pearlie asked.

"We won't exactly follow it, I mean, not to the degree that we can keep it in sight, but I think, after a few minutes, we will go on into town."

"Did you know them two cowboys, miss?" the man sitting on the seat across from her asked. He appeared to be in his late twenties or early thirties, and had a narrow face, a sharp nose, and a small mustache.

"What two cowboys?"

"The two men standing alongside the road. I saw you looking at them, and was wonderin' if, perhaps, you know'd 'em."

"No, why? Is there any reason I should?"

"No, ma'am, none that I can think of. It's just that they seemed to be payin' an awful lot of attention to you. 'Course, you bein' a seemly lookin' woman, I can see as how they mighta took a second look at you."

Before Sara Sue could respond, a sudden gust of wind came in through the open windows, carrying upon its breath a great and smothering billow of dust. For a moment the cloud of dust so filled the coach one couldn't see from one side to the other.

"Oh, heavens!" Sara Sue said, coughing and fanning herself.

"That's the trouble when you're a-travelin' on a real clear day," the narrow-faced passenger said. "But then, all things considered, I reckon I'd rather put up with a few clouds of dust, now 'n then, than a pourin' rain comin' in 'n gettin' ever' thing 'n ever'one soakin' wet."

"I suppose that's true."

"What's your business in comin' to Mule Gap?" the man asked.

"Sir! With all due respect, my business isn't any of your business," Sara Sue replied.

The other passenger chuckled. "No ma'am, I guess you're right. Anyhow, we're comin' into Mule Gap now."

Sara Sue looked through the window and saw the buildings passing by—at first a scattering of houses, then business buildings, until, finally, the coach came to a halt.

She exited the coach and checked in to the Del Rey Hotel, requesting that a bathtub and water be brought to her room.

* * *

"I don't know if she's got the money with her or not, but she come alone," the thin-faced, mustachioed man said.

"Very good."

"You said I'd get paid for it."

"If she has the money, we'll all enjoy a payday soon."

"All right. Just so's you know I done my part, even if I wasn't one o' them what went down into Colorado and took the boy."

One hour after the stagecoach rolled into Mule Gap, Sara Sue Condon, feeling much cleaner, presented herself at the Bank of Mule Gap.

"Yes, ma'am," the teller said.

"I should like to speak with Mr. Kennedy," Sara Sue said.

"May I tell him what it's about?"

"Yes, I intend to make a rather sizeable deposit."

"Why, ma'am, you don't need to see Mr. Kennedy to do that. I can take care of it for you."

"I would prefer to see—"

"It's all right, Mr. May, I'll see the young lady," Kennedy said. "Madam, would you like to speak in my office?"

"Yes, thank you," Sara Sue said, following the banker into an office that opened off the back of the room.

"Now, you said something about a rather sizeable deposit, I believe?"

"Yes, but I think I should tell you, I don't expect it to be here for very long."

"Oh? You are about to make a purchase in our town, perhaps?"

"No, Mr. Kennedy. I'm about to pay the ransom for the release of my son."

"Oh. You must be Mrs. Condon," Kennedy said. "Yes, I

heard about your unfortunate experience. You have my best wishes for the safe return of the boy."

"How did you know about it?" Sara Sue asked.

"Your neighbor, Mr. Jensen, told me."

"Oh, yes. He delivered a bull to Mr. Harris for us. And of course, he is aware of what happened."

"Are you disturbed that I know about it?" Kennedy asked solicitously.

"No, I suppose not. I guess it was only obvious that he might have said something about it. He wanted to offer his help in some way, but I told him no. In the first place, what, exactly could he do? And in the second place, the ransom note demanded that I be alone, and I've no doubt but that means I don't allow anyone else to get involved. My number one priority, Mr. Kennedy, and I'm sure you can understand, is to get my son back. I will do nothing to jeopardize that."

"I quite understand," Kennedy said. "So you will be depositing the full amount requested by the brigands who have taken your son?"

"Yes, I have a fifteen-thousand-dollar draft from the bank in Big Rock," Sara Sue said.

Kennedy nodded. "I will personally set up the account for you," he promised.

"We'd like two rooms, please," Smoke said to the desk clerk of the Del Rey Hotel.

"Yes, sir," the clerk replied, turning the registration book around to Smoke.

As Smoke signed in, he saw that the name just above his was *Mrs. Sam Condon.* He also took note of her room number, which was 207.

"How long will you gentlemen be staying with us?" the clerk asked, after Pearlie added his name to the book.

"I don't know for sure," Smoke replied. "It depends on how our business goes."

After he and Pearlie received their keys, they climbed the stairs to the second floor, then Smoke knocked on the door of Sara Sue's room.

"Yes, who is it?" a hesitant voice called from the other side of the door.

Smoke recognized the voice as belonging to Sara Sue. "Mrs. Smith?" he called. It was the signal that had been worked out between them.

"You have the wrong room," Sara Sue replied.

That, too, was a signal, and it told Smoke that she wasn't alone.

"I beg your pardon, ma'am." Smoke glanced at Pearlie, who was also aware of the meaning of the response.

Pearlie stepped down to one of the hall lights, a sconce lantern attached to the wall just by the head of the stairs. From that position he enjoyed a view of the door to Sara Sue's room, as well as the sofa in the lobby below. He removed the globe to the lantern as if working on it, and Smoke went down to the lobby and sat on the sofa. He picked up the newspaper and began to "read" it, though he kept an eye on the top of the stairs, ready to receive a signal from Pearlie.

Sara Sue was comforted to know that Smoke was there. She had responded in a way that let him know that she wasn't alone in her room. A man who had identified himself as Fred Keefer was in the room with her. He was the representative from the kidnappers.

"Who was that at the door?" Keefer asked.

"I don't know. You heard him. He was looking for someone named Smith."

"You didn't bring anyone with you, did you?"

"You were in the lobby of the hotel when I arrived," Sara Sue said. "I saw you sitting on the sofa. You know that I came alone."

"There could have been someone waiting outside."

"There could have been, but there wasn't."

"Did you bring the money?"

"Yes."

"Where is it?"

"It's in the bank."

"It ain't supposed to be in the bank. You're supposed to have the money with you," Keefer said, his tone of voice little more than a growl.

"My husband said that I shouldn't pay the money until I have proof that Thad is still alive and unharmed."

"I can tell you he is still alive, 'n he ain't been hurt none."

"I'm sorry, but your word isn't good enough," Sara Sue said. "I shall require more proof than that."

"What kind of proof? You want me to bring a piece of his shirt or somethin'?"

"No, I want a note from Thad written in his own hand, telling me that he is unharmed."

"I ain't got a note like that."

"When you can provide me with that note, I'll give you half the money," Sara Sue said.

"Half the money? What do you mean, *'half the money'*? If you want your boy back alive, you're goin' to have to come up with *all* the money."

"And I will," Sara Sue promised. "Half when I see a note from Thad, telling me he is all right, and the other half when my son is delivered safely to me."

"I don't think the chief is goin' to like that," Keefer said.

"I would think that it would depend upon how much he wants the money, wouldn't you?"

"Seems to me like you ain't in no position to be makin'

any demands," Keefer said. "Especially since we have your boy."

"Do you know how much reward money Bob Ford was paid for killing Jesse James?" Sara Sue asked.

Keefer shook his head. "What? No, I don't have no idea. Why would you ask such a fool question, anyway?"

"It was ten thousand dollars," Sara Sue said. "If we don't get my son back alive and unharmed, my husband and I will use this ransom money to establish a reward of five thousand dollars to be paid for each of you, Mr. Keefer—you and the other two men who took Thad. Oh, and this won't be a dead-or-alive reward. It will only be paid when we have proof that you are dead."

"Maybe there's somethin' you don't understand. The three of us ain't the only ones that's a part of this. Iffen we was to get kilt, your boy would still be a prisoner," Keefer said.

"What difference would that make to you?" Sara Sue challenged.

"What? What do you mean?"

"It's a simple question. If you are dead, then it won't make any difference to you whether my boy is still a prisoner or not, will it? And when you think about it, nothing in the entire world will make any difference to you, because you will be dead. On the other hand, if you deliver my son to me in as good health as he was when you took him, why, you and your friends will be fifteen thousand dollars richer. I would think it would be to your personal advantage to see that is done.

"Now, do you really want to pass up the seventy-five hundred dollars that I'll give you after I have proof that my son is alive and well, and the other seventy-five hundred dollars that will paid upon safe delivery of my son?"

"I'll . . . uh . . . see the others 'n see what they have to say," Keefer said.

"You do that."

"It might be a while before we get back to you."

"Don't be too long. As you know, I have a wounded husband that I want to get back to."

"I wasn't the one that shot 'im," Keefer said.

"But you did nothing to stop him from being shot," Sara Sue replied.

"If you remember, I kept you from bein' shot."

"I remember," Sara Sue said coolly.

"All right. Well, uh, I'll be goin' now," Keefer said. The meeting had not gone as planned, and he was unsure of what he should do next.

As he started down the stairs, he paid no attention to the man who seemed to be working on the hallway lantern. He did recognize the man who was reading a paper in the hotel lobby. It was Smoke Jensen. Keefer hadn't had any personal run-ins with Smoke Jensen, but he did know who he was. A few weeks ago, when he'd learned that Jensen would be carrying twenty-five hundred dollars in cash, he had given the information to Bemus, Parker, and Quince. He had thought it would be a quick way to earn a little money, and it seemed like a simple enough thing to do, especially with the odds of three men to one. But when they tried to hold up Jensen, the three of them wound up dead.

Keefer knew that Jensen and the Condons were friends. He didn't know why Smoke Jensen was there now, but he knew that he didn't like it.

Pearlie looked back toward Sara Sue's room and saw her step out into the hallway. "Are you all right, Miz Condon?"

"Yes," she answered. "I did just as Sam and Smoke suggested. I hope I didn't make a mistake."

"You didn't."

CHAPTER 19

French Creek Canyon

As Travis had pointed out, the door was securely locked all the time, keeping Thad and the others trapped inside. But every time Thad used the privy, he made as close an observation of their surroundings as he could. The little cabin where the captive children were staying was set considerably closer to the creek than the larger house that was being used by their guards. That meant that if they could escape through the back of the cabin, they couldn't be immediately seen from the house where the guards were staying. The task would be how to get out the back, as there was neither door nor window there.

A further examination of the cabin gave him an idea, and he smiled. The smaller of the two buildings was not only closer to the creek, it was also on uneven ground, with the back of the cabin on stilts that elevated it about two feet above the ground. The best way to escape would be through the floor.

"Travis," Thad said when he returned to the cabin. "Keep a lookout through the window, will you? Tell me if you see anyone coming."

"Why? What are you going to do?"

"I'm going to figure out a way for us to escape," Thad said as he got down on his hands and knees to look at the floor near the back wall. He saw right away that the problem was going to be in removing the nails. But even if he had a way of extracting them, they were so deep into the wood that he couldn't get to them. Sighing, he stood up. "I don't know how we are going to get the nails out."

"Why do you want the nails out?" Marilyn asked.

"Because I want to pull up the boards."

"Maybe you could use a nail to scratch around those nails," Lorena suggested. "The wood is old and dry-rotted. It shouldn't take much to scrape it away."

"Yes, but I would need a loose nail and something to pry the nails up."

"Here's a nail," Burt said, pointing to a nail that stuck halfway out of a wall stud.

Thad walked over to grab the nail and try to pull it out, but he couldn't make it budge. "It's no use. I'll have to come up with some other way."

"Maybe not," Lorena said. Walking over to the door, she reached above it, then took down the horseshoe that was hanging there. "Try this," she suggested with a smile.

Using the horseshoe, Thad was able to extract the nail. Then, using the nail to scratch around those on the floor, he was finally able to get purchase, and after a few tries was rewarded by seeing the nail come up about a quarter of an inch. A short while later, he had the nail completely out. "Yes! Yes, this will work!"

"Why do you want to pull the nails out of the floor?" Burt asked.

"When we get all the nails pulled, we can take up the boards and crawl through the floor and out back. We'll do it in the middle of the night, but they probably couldn't see us anyway. They can't see the back of the cabin from the house."

"It's going to take a long time to get all the nails out," Marilyn said.

"What else have we got to do?" Thad replied.

"It won't work," Travis said.

"Why not?"

"One of them is always comin' in. What if he sees holes in the floor where the nails have been?"

"How's he going to notice that? He'd have to be looking right at the floor," Burt said.

"No, Travis has a point," Thad said. "I'm not sure how we'll handle that."

"How about every time one of us goes out, we pick up a handful of dirt?" Lorena suggested. "Then, we can just drop the dirt over the nail hole."

"Yes!" Thad said. "That's a good idea, Lorena!"

Lorena beamed proudly as Thad started working on the next nail.

Mule Gap

Keefer was in the Silver Dollar Saloon sitting at a table with two other men.

"You didn't get the money?" Clyde Sanders asked.

"No," Keefer replied. "She said she would give us half of the money when we showed her proof that her boy was still alive 'n the other half when we turned him over to her. That is, if she even has the money."

"She has the money," the third man said.

"How do you know?"

"She made a deposit of that amount in the bank."

"All right," Sander said with a big smile. "Once we get the money for the Condon kid, the others will pay as well."

"Yeah, well, there may be a problem," Keefer suggested.

"What problem is that?" Sanders asked.

"Smoke Jensen."

"Who is Smoke Jensen?"

"He owns a ranch next to the Condon Ranch," Keefer said. "You might remember what happened when Bemus, Parker, and Quince tried to rob him."

"Oh, yeah," Sanders said. "He kilt all three of 'em."

"Well, he's here in town. I seen 'im sittin' in the lobby of the hotel."

"You think he might cause us some trouble?" Sanders asked.

"I don't know. It could just be a coincidence, but it's better to be safe than sorry," Keefer said. "I think we need to take care of the situation."

"What do you think we should do about it?" Sanders asked.

"You two do nothing," the third man said. "Keefer, I want you and Sanders to get back out to the cabin and keep an eye on those kids. Thanks to Marshal Bodine, we now have a town full of deputy marshals—gunmen, every one. All we have to do is put out a reward on Mr. Jensen, and the deputies will take care of the situation for us."

"How much of a reward?" Keefer asked.

"Five thousand dollars should be enough."

"Damn, do we have that much money?"

"We've gotten ten thousand in ransom payments for the first group that we took."

"And you think it's a good idea to use up half the money just to get rid of one man?"

"You said yourself, Keefer, Smoke Jensen could be a problem. I would rather pay five thousand dollars to take care of the problem than let him take care of all of us."

"Yeah," Keefer said. "Yeah, I see what you are saying."

"How do you think is the best way to handle it?" Pearlie asked as he and Smoke had lunch at the Purity Café.

"He's going to have to go to wherever they are keeping the boy to get the note. When he leaves town, we'll follow him."

"How do we know he hasn't already left town?"

Smoke nodded toward the window. "When he left the hotel, he went into the Silver Dollar Saloon. That bay on the right end of the hitching rail is his horse. He hasn't left yet."

Finishing their lunch, the two men killed time by drinking coffee as they waited for Keefer to leave.

Then Pearlie saw him. "There he is."

"We'll give him time to ride off, then we'll follow him," Smoke said.

The four streets in Mule Gap were laid out in such a way as to form a three-by-three grid. Keefer rode north to First Street, then turned west. Smoke and Pearlie finished their coffee, then left the café.

"Hello, Seven," Smoke said, greeting his horse as he unwrapped the reins from the hitching rail. "What do you say we go for a ride?"

Seven dipped his head.

"Yeah, I thought you might like—"

That was as far as he got before a shot rang out and Smoke saw a hole suddenly appear in Seven's neck. The horse went down.

"Seven!" Smoke shouted.

A second shot zipped by Smoke's ear so close that it popped as it went by.

Looking up from his downed horse, Smoke saw four men in the middle of the street, coming toward him and Pearlie. All four men had guns in their hands, and all four guns were blazing. Pearlie went down.

"Pearlie!"

"Get 'em, Smoke. Get 'em," Pearlie called out to him.

"You sons of bitches!" Smoke shouted. With pistol in hand, he moved to the middle of the street. The four men continued to fire, but not one of their bullets found Smoke. He fired only four times, and all four men went down. With the immediate danger over, he rushed back to check on Pearlie.

"Did you get the bastards?" Pearlie asked.

"Yeah. Where are you hit?"

"All over."

"You're hit all over?"

"Well, I hurt all over," Pearlie said.

Smoke made a quick examination and found the wound in Pearlie's hip, and he was bleeding profusely. Smoke tore off a piece of Pearlie's shirt, then stuffed it into the bullet hole to stop the bleeding. By then half the town had turned out to see what was going on. Very few had actually seen the gunfight—it had been over so fast—but the ones who had seen it were talking excitedly to the others about Smoke Jensen engaged in a gun battle with four men and shooting all four down.

Smoke looked up toward the people who were standing on the porch in front of the Purity Café. "Somebody get a doctor, please."

"He's out there lookin' at them four in the street," someone replied.

"There's no need for him to be looking at them," Smoke said. "They're all dead."

"How do you know they're dead, mister?"

"Because I didn't have time not to kill them."

"Smoke," Pearlie said. "You'd better see to Seven."

"When the doctor gets here, I'll see to Seven."

"Go ahead. See to him now," Pearlie said. "I'm not going anywhere."

Smoke nodded, then stepped over to his horse. The bullet that hit him in the neck had apparently cut his jugular vein. Seven's head was lying in an enormous pool of blood. His eyes were open, but they were already opaque with death.

Smoke closed his eyes and pinched the bridge of his nose. Not since his first wife Nicole and their son Art had been murdered had he come so close to crying. Though he felt like it, he fought against the tears and pushed the lump in his throat back down. He blinked a few times then reached out to put his hand on Seven's ear. He rubbed the ear as he so often had. Seven loved that, and even though Smoke knew Seven couldn't feel it . . . Smoke could. And he very much wanted . . . no, he very much *needed* to do it.

"I know horses go to heaven." His voice broke, but as he was talking so quietly, nobody heard him. "Heaven is supposed to be a place of total happiness, and I won't be happy unless I see you there. Run free, Seven, you've done your duty here on earth. Wait for me, old friend. Someday we'll ride together again."

Smoke left Seven lying there then hurried back over to Pearlie, reaching him just as the doctor arrived.

"Let me take a look here," the doctor said. He saw the little piece of shirt that was jammed into the bullet hole. "How the blazes did this cloth get in here?"

"I put it there," Smoke said. "He was bleeding quite a bit, and I figured I should stop it."

"Well, you are right about that," the doctor said, "but I wish you could have found something a little cleaner than this to use."

"Come on, Doc, my shirt is clean enough," Pearlie said. "It hasn't been more 'n a week since I washed it last."

"Well, he was right to stop the bleeding," the doctor said.

"How bad is it?" Smoke asked.

"Doesn't look like it's too bad."

"Who killed these men?" someone shouted from the middle of the street.

Looking toward the sound of the angry voice, Smoke saw the one they called The Professor, Frank Bodine. The badge of a marshal was prominent on the black shirt he was wearing.

"I did," Smoke said, rising up from the squatting position he had been in beside Pearlie.

"Do you want to tell me why you killed them?"

"Because the sons of bitches killed my horse," Smoke said in an angry, clipped voice.

"You killed four men over a horse?"

"It ain't quite like that, Marshal," one of the townspeople said. "I seen the whole thing. These two men, that one"—he pointed to Smoke—"and the feller on the ground come out of the café there, 'n them four that's lyin' out in the street commenced firin' without so much as a fare-thee-well. This feller was just fixin' to get on his horse when it was hit 'n went down. And that feller was hit at the same time." He pointed toward Pearlie. "So this man—"

"His name is Jensen," Bodine said. "Smoke Jensen."

"Yes, sir. Well, Mr. Jensen, he stepped into the street 'n shot back. He musta shot four times 'cause all four o' them men went down, but if he did shoot four times, he done it so fast I couldn't tell."

"Harvey Long is tellin' the truth, Marshal, 'cause I seen it, too. 'N it was just like Harvey said it was. Them men in the street commenced shootin' just as soon as Jensen 'n that other man started to mount up. Why, there weren't even no words spoke a-fore the shootin' started."

"These four men were my deputies," Bodine said. "I'm pretty sure they thought they were doing their duty."

"Was it their duty to ambush my friend and me?" Smoke asked.

"No, of course not. I would theorize that they saw the two of you in violation of some city ordinance or county law, and it was their intention to bring you in for questioning."

"They wanted us for questioning? Then why didn't they say so? Whatever possessed them to simply start shooting like that?" Smoke asked.

Bodine shook his head. "I don't know. Perhaps they

were coming to question you when they perceived danger and reacted without thinking it through. At any rate, the county has lost four good men."

"Will you be needing me for anything, Marshal?" Smoke asked pointedly.

"No, I can't say that I do. You're free to go."

"Thank you."

"Mr. Jensen?" the doctor said.

"Yes?"

"We need to get your friend down to my office so I can cleanse his wound and get him wrapped up with a sterile bandage."

"Yeah," Smoke said. "I had better make some arrangements for Seven, as well."

CHAPTER 20

French Creek Canyon

For two days Thad and the others had been pulling nails up from the floor. The work was painstaking. Enough of the wood had to be scraped away from each nail to get purchase on the nail head so it could be removed. Even then, it wasn't easy to pull the nail. The horseshoe could only catch one side of the nail head, and then not too securely. The horseshoe had to be worked around the nail a little on one side then a little on the other, lifting it about a quarter of an inch at a time with each effort.

Because it was so painstaking and time consuming, the effort was tiring and had to be spread out evenly among all of them except Wee. But even he did his part, often returning from his trips to the privy with a pocket full of dirt. Thad allowed Wee to cover the holes that had been opened as a result of the extracted nails.

To date, they had extracted thirty nails, which was enough to allow them to pull up three boards. Thad calculated that they would need at least three more boards in order to create an opening wide enough to enable them to slip down through the hole in the floor.

"Here comes Mr. Reece," Wee called from the window.

"Some of the newer holes can be seen," Thad said.

Lorena grabbed a broom and just as Reece came into the building, she began sweeping the dirt around over the area where they had been working.

"Well now, sweepin' are you? Can you cook, too? You're goin' to be a real looker soon," Reece said. "You could be a real man-pleaser one of these days. Especially if you would let me teach you a few things." His words dripped with sexual innuendo.

"You stay away from her, Reece," Thad said menacingly.

"Oh yes, you are the one who is goin' to kill me, ain't you?" Reece asked with a mocking laugh. "You her protector now? Boy, you pure-dee got me shakin' in my boots."

Thad glared at Reece, but didn't respond to his taunting challenge.

"How does it feel, girl, to know that you got someone that's goin' to protect you?" Reece asked.

"What do you want, Reece?" Thad asked.

"That would be Mr. Reece to you, boy."

"What do you want, Reece?" Thad repeated.

Reece grinned, though there was no humor in his smile. "I got good news for you, boy. It looks like your mama is goin' to pay the money for you to get out of here."

"That doesn't change anything," Thad replied.

"It doesn't change anything? Didn't you hear what I said? I said your mama is goin' to pay us to set you free."

"That doesn't change anything," Thad repeated.

"You mean you still plan to kill me?"

Thad glared at Reece, but he didn't respond.

"Well, I just come in to tell you the good news," Reece said. "Little lady, you just go back to sweepin'. From all the dirt on the floor in here, it looks like it needs it." He left, and the others turned to look at Thad.

"Are you going to go home?" Travis asked.

"Yeah, I'm going home," Thad replied. Then he smiled.

"We are all going home. I'm not leaving here until we all leave here."

"I knew you wouldn't leave us!" Burt said with a happy smile.

"We need to do this a little faster," Thad said. "Let's all work on the nails at the same time. We've pulled enough nails we can use them to scrape around the nails we haven't pulled yet.

"Me too?" Wee asked.

"No, you keep doing just what you were doing," Thad said. "You did a good job, Wee, warning us about Reece. I'm proud of you."

A pleased smile spread across Wee's face, and he went back over to stand on the box that let him look through the window.

"Let's get to work," Thad said to the others.

Fancy Bliss, Joy Love, and Candy Sweet were riding in the buckboard being driven by Clyde Sanders when it arrived at the house and cabin located on the bank of French Creek. Delilah Dupree had agreed to let them make a client visit, at double the cost of what their services would have been at the House of Pleasure.

As they arrived, they saw a young girl standing in front of a privy.

"Oh," Fancy said. "There are children here?"

"Don't worry none about it," Sanders said. "They're all stayin' in that little cabin. They won't have nothin' to do with our business."

"What do you mean, *all* are staying in that little cabin? How many are there?"

"They's six of 'em now, but if it all works out, there'll only be five pretty soon. Maybe we can get rid of the others, too."

"Get rid of them? What are you talking about? Why are the children here?" Fancy asked.

"You ask too many questions," Sanders said. "We ain't payin' you women to come out here just so we would have someone to talk to. Now, get on into the big house 'n let's get down to business."

A second girl came out of the privy as Fancy and the other two ladies climbed down from the buckboard. The two girls looked at Fancy, and she tried to study the expression on their faces.

Keefer, Reece, and Whitman were smiling broadly when Sanders and the three women went into the house.

"Well, now, ladies, we're goin' to have us a real fine time here," Keefer said.

"Oh my. There are four of you. It looks as if one of us will be doing double duty," Joy said.

"We're payin' you to spend the whole night with us," Keefer said. "I expect all of you will be doin' double duty."

"We done drawed high cards," Whitman said. "Reece is goin' to have to wait his turn. I got high card so I get my pick," he added with a broad, salacious smile.

"Hey Keefer, you left town too soon," Sanders said. "You missed the killin' ."

Keefer smiled. "Jensen got kilt, did he?"

"No. Four of the deputies tried to kill him, but he wound up killin' all four of them, shootin' 'em down in the street. It was the damndest thing I've ever seen."

"You talk like you're excited about it," Keefer scolded.

"Well, I don't like the way it turned out, that's for sure 'n certain," Sanders said. Inexplicably, a broad smile spread across his face. "But if that warn't the damndest thing I've ever seen, I don't know what else would be."

"Are you tellin' me that Jensen took on four of the deputies and kilt them all by hisself?" Keefer asked.

"He's right, honey," Candy said. "Why, the whole town is talking about it."

"Seein' as how Bates, Cooper, Barnes, and Gibson is all Bodine's deputies, how come he ain't put Jensen in jail?"

"On account of in the first place, it was self-defense 'n there was lots of people that seen it," Sanders said. "And in the second place, if you want to know the truth, I'm not just real sure that Bodine could handle Jensen."

"What are you talkin' about? Bodine is the best there is," Keefer insisted.

"Maybe not," Sanders said.

"I'll be damned," Keefer said. "We'd better keep an eye on Jensen. He's goin' to be trouble, you mark my words."

"Why are you so concerned about Smoke Jensen?" Fancy asked. "What do you mean there's going to be trouble? Is there bad blood between you?"

"No, I ain't never even met the man," Keefer replied.

"Does it have anything to do with the children who are staying out here?"

"What children?" Keefer asked, surprised by the question.

"I saw two little girls going from the privy to that little cabin. Mr. Sanders said there are six children staying in the cabin."

Keefer shot an angry glance toward Sanders before he looked back at Fancy, replacing the momentary flash of anger with a quick forced smile.

"Yeah, their parents are payin' us to keep 'em out here for a while. They thought it would be good for them to spend some time on the creek with friends. It's sort of a vacation for them."

"Oh, how wonderful! Maybe we can visit with them a while, later on," Joy suggested.

Keefer shook his head. "I don't think so. You're all whores.

Do you really think these kids' mamas and papas are goin' to want their kids spending any time with a whore?"

Joy's smile faded, replaced by a momentary look of shame. She smiled again, and if it was a practiced smile, it at least had the effect of lightening the mood and changing the subject. "I believe you said something about a party?"

"Did you see the three ladies?" Wee asked when Lorena and Marilyn returned to the cabin.

"We saw them," Lorena said, "but I don't think you could exactly call them ladies."

"What do you call them?" Wee asked, confused by Lorena's response.

Lorena smiled. "Never mind. You can call them ladies."

"Did they go into the house?" Thad asked.

"Yes."

"Good."

"Why good?"

"That means they won't be paying too much attention to us for a while. We should be able get a lot of work done today."

Mule Gap

"I'll buy your horse from you," Boyd Evans, the manager of the livery stable, said to Smoke as they were standing over Seven's body.

"You want to buy Seven? Whatever for? Why would you pay for a dead horse?"

"Horses have a lot of collagen, and the glue factories pay well for that."

"No!" Smoke said. "Seven is not going to be used to make glue! This is my third horse named Seven. Number one is dead, but number two has been turned out to pasture."

"You've had three horses named Seven?" Evans asked.

"I'm about to have another horse named Seven, and why not? If England can have eight kings named Henry I can have as many horses named Seven as I want."

"Wait. Are you telling me that England has eight kings, and all of them are named Henry?"

"No," Smoke replied in an exasperated tone of voice. "What I am telling you is that I want Seven to have a respectable burial."

"Where do you want him buried?"

"Where in Mule Gap are horses buried?"

"There's a place out behind the livery where some of 'em are buried. And some folks bury 'em on their own land."

"I can't take him back to Sugarloaf, so we'll have to bury him here."

Evans brought out a team of mules, connected a harness to Seven, and pulled his body to a place behind the livery stable. There, he hired four men to dig a hole big enough and deep enough to inter Seven.

Smoke watched until the grave was closed, then he went back into the livery to pay the bill. "And I want to rent a horse for the time I'm here."

"You want to rent one or buy one?" the stable owner said. "I have some fine horses for sale."

"No, my next horse is already back at my ranch. He's a two-year-old, the son of Seven, and he looks just like him."

"All right. You can pick out the one you want to rent."

Smoke chose a bay with four stockings and a blaze. He ran his hand over the horse, feeling for any abnormalities in its configuration, but found none. "All right. I'll take this one."

"For how long?"

"Until I bring him back."

"In that case, I'll take a hundred dollars to hold until you bring him back."

Smoke agreed.

He returned to the doctor's office a short while later and found Pearlie sitting up in a chair, fully dressed. "What are you doing up? I thought you would be in bed."

"I'm up, 'cause I wasn't really hurt."

"What do you mean you weren't hurt? You were shot. I saw the bullet wound."

"Well, yeah, I was shot, but like I said, I wasn't really hurt. The doctor himself said I wasn't hurt."

"I said no such thing," the doctor said, coming into the waiting room of his office. "I said that none of your vital organs were involved and that, if you are careful, this wound won't give you any trouble."

"You also said I could leave," Pearlie said.

"I did say that, but you may also recall that I said you couldn't leave until I saw Mr. Jensen and would be assured that he would take care of you."

"Well, he's here, 'n he's goin' to take me out of here. Aren't you, Smoke?"

Smoke laughed. "Yes, if you're up to leaving here, I'll take you with me."

"Let's go have supper," Pearlie suggested.

CHAPTER 21

"Mrs. Condon, imagine seeing you here," Smoke said when he and Pearlie stepped into the restaurant at the Del Rey Hotel.

"Why, Mr. Jensen," Sara Sue said, "won't the two of you join me?"

"You aren't expecting anyone else?"

"No, I'm here all alone," Sara Sue replied.

The exchange was loud enough for others in the dining room to hear, and it was specifically designed to make anyone who was paying particular attention to them think that the meeting was accidental. Not until Smoke and Pearlie joined her at the table, with Pearlie walking with a pronounced limp, did they speak quietly enough to be able to hold a private conversation.

"Have you heard anything yet?" Smoke asked.

"No, and I'm so worried."

"I wouldn't be worried yet. It's obvious that the man who visited you has no authority to make the decision himself. That has to come from someone else, and it is sure to be one or maybe two days before anyone contacts you."

"Oh, I just hate to think of Thad being held for two more days by those awful men," Sara Sue said.

"I know Thad," Smoke said. "He is a very tough and

resourceful young man. I have a feeling that he is more than holding his own against them."

"Oh!" Sara Sue said. "You were in a shooting today. And Pearlie, I heard that you were shot. I'm glad to see you up and about, and forgive me for not inquiring sooner about you."

"I'm doing just fine, Mrs. Condon. I've got a little bit of a limp is all. You might call it a hitch in my get-about," he added with a chuckle.

"I'm worried about the shooting," Sara Sue said. "Do you think it's because they know you are helping me?"

"It could be," Smoke admitted. "But it could just as likely be someone trying to settle an old score with me."

"Heavens, you mean there is someone out there who might actually want to shoot you?"

"More than one, I'm afraid," Smoke said.

"I knew you were . . . uh . . . rather well-known for your skill with a gun, and I knew that you had helped many people, but I didn't know there would actually be men who would want to shoot you."

"This isn't the first time, and they haven't gotten the job done yet."

"The worst thing," Pearlie said, "worse than me getting shot, is that they killed his horse."

"Seven?" Sara Sue said. "Oh, Smoke, no! I didn't hear about that. I'm so sorry. I know what store you set by that horse."

"It was tough to lose him, all right," Smoke said. "But I'm thankful I didn't lose Pearlie."

"Yes, as am I."

"What do you hear from Sam?"

"I got a telegram from him today. He says he's doing fine, he misses me, and he knows I will get—" Sara Sue paused in midsentence then, with a choke in her voice, she continued. "He said he knows I will get Thad back safely."

"We will get him back safely," Smoke said.

Sara Sue smiled through her tears. "I am so thankful to you for helping us."

"Smoke, you told a big one at the dinner table tonight, didn't you?" Pearlie said as the two men left the hotel.

"What was that?"

"You told Mrs. Condon that the shooting today coulda been someone tryin' to settle an old score. You know as well as I do that someone has figured out we're helpin' Mrs. Condon, and they was just tryin' to get us out of the way."

"You're right," Smoke said. "But she's worried enough as it is. If she thinks the kidnappers know we're helping her, she will be afraid they will follow through on their threat to harm Thad. I see no reason to give her anything more to worry about."

"Yeah, I guess you're right," Pearlie said. "She seemed real upset about Seven."

"Yes, she always had a few lumps of sugar for Seven anytime she saw him."

"I'm real sorry about Seven, Smoke. He was as good a horse as I've ever known."

"He was a good one, all right. I'm going to hate to have to tell Sally about it. She loved him as much as I did."

"She's going to take it hard, that's for sure," Pearlie said.

"We've obviously lost the trail on Keefer," Smoke said. "I think our best bet now is just to wait until they contact Mrs. Condon again. They'll do that because, so far, she hasn't paid them one red cent."

"Say, as long as we're going to wait until they contact Miz Condon again, you don't mind if we wait in the saloon, do you?" Pearlie asked as they walked by Kennedy's Saloon.

Smoke chuckled. "As a matter of fact, a saloon is a

perfect place to wait. You can sometimes pick up some good information in a saloon."

Kennedy wasn't in the saloon, but the bartender recognized Smoke and greeted him with a smile. Then he turned his attention to Pearlie.

"And how are you doin', young fella? The last time I seen you, you was lyin' in the dirt, bleedin' like a stuck pig."

"You saw that, did you?"

"Oh, I think most of the town saw it."

"Well, thanks to Smoke stoppin' the bleeding, and the doc cleaning out the wound, I'm getting along pretty well," Pearlie replied.

"Well, I must say, Smoke Jensen has certainly made our town famous. How many towns can say that Smoke Jensen faced down four men in the street?"

"Smoke Jensen?" another man said. He had been standing at the far end of the bar, nursing his drink. "Are you the . . . *great* . . . Smoke Jensen?" He set the word *great* apart in his question, twisting it in a way that indicated it was meant as a mockery and not as an accolade.

"Ethan, give the gentleman at the other end of the bar a drink on me," Smoke said easily. He had recognized the taunting in the man's voice and was trying to defuse the situation.

"I'll buy my own drink," the man said.

"Good, I like a man who pays his own way," Smoke said, purposely turning a deaf ear to the man's taunts.

"I seen the fight you was in today," the man said. "Them four was fools. They wan't a damn one of 'em what coulda hit a bull in the ass if they was ten foot from it. Oh, wait, they did kill your horse, though, didn't they?" He laughed. "Did you cry when your horse got shot?"

"I got a lump in my throat, yes," Smoke said.

"Well now, ain't that just too bad?" The heckler laughed again.

"Mr. Allison, you got no call to act like that about a man

losin' his horse," Ethan, the bartender, said. "You know how most men feel about their horses."

"Allison?" Smoke said. "Would you be the one they call Blackjack Allison?"

"Heard of me, have you?"

"Yeah." The only reason Smoke had heard of Blackjack Allison was because Sheriff Carson, down in Big Rock, had mentioned him no more than a week earlier. Smoke recalled what the sheriff had said.

"I just got another notice on someone named Blackjack Allison. He's been in seven or eight gunfights recently. But as they were all face-to-face gunfights, he hasn't been charged for any of them. From what I've heard, though, he's someone who is trying to build a reputation. On at least a few of the fights, it is said that he pushed the other man into drawing on him."

"Are you trying to push me into a gunfight, Allison?"

"I don't know," Allison said. "Are me 'n you, the *great* Smoke Jensen, about to have a gunfight?"

Most in the saloon, sensing there was about to be a gun-fight, began moving out of the way. Only Pearlie, standing just behind Smoke and certainly in the line of fire if shooting began, didn't move. He continued to drink his beer with as much nonchalance as if he had been sitting alone at a table.

"There's no need for us to fight," Smoke said.

"Oh, yes, there is. You see, you're worth five thousand dollars to me. Dead."

"Five thousand dollars? Mr. Allison, are you out of your mind? I don't have any paper out on me anywhere. What in the world makes you think I'm worth five thousand dollars?"

"I didn't say they was paper out on you," Allison replied. "All I said was you was worth five thousand dollars to me iffen I was to kill you."

"Who has made that offer?"

"It ain't none of your concern who has made that offer, seein' as you won't be around to do nothin' about it." Allison called to Pearlie, "Hey you, the one drinkin' the beer."

"The name is Pearlie." He spoke as calmly as if introducing himself at a friendly encounter.

"Yeah? Well, Pearlie, you done got shot oncet today. Iffen you don't want to get shot again, you'd better move out of the way."

"What do you mean, if I don't want to get shot?" Pearlie replied. "I thought Smoke is the one you're getting paid to shoot. Just how is it that I'm going to get shot?"

"What's the matter with you? Are you crazy? Me 'n Smoke Jensen here is about to have ourselves a little dance. And you bein' where you are could likely get shot."

"Oh, I see what you're saying, but there's no problem," Pearlie said. "Besides, I haven't finished my drink."

"Jensen, you'd better tell your friend here to get out of the way," Allison said.

"Oh, I think he's quite safe," Smoke replied.

Allison smiled. "Because you don't think I'll miss?"

"No, the truth is, Allison, you won't even get a shot off."

"The hell I won't!" Allison yelled as he started toward his gun.

In a lightning draw, Smoke had his pistol in his hand.

"No! Wait!" Allison shouted, letting his gun drop back into its holster and raising both arms over his head. "How? How the hell did you do that?"

The saloon patrons observing the unfolding scene from their vantage points within the room were as shocked as Allison, and the same question he had asked was on many of their lips. *How did he get his gun out so fast?*

"Look, I was just funnin' with you," Allison said. "I didn't have no real idea of drawin' ag'in you. What . . . what are you goin' to do?"

"Yes, Smoke, what *are* you going to do?" Warren Kennedy asked, having just stepped into the saloon that bore his name.

"I'm not sure what I'm going to do," Smoke said. "I think I'll just shoot him."

"You ain't goin' to shoot me," Allison said. "It would be murder."

"I'll leave it up to you, Warren," Smoke said easily. "This is your saloon. Do you want me to kill him? Or should I let him live?"

"I'm tempted to tell you to go ahead and shoot him." Kennedy smiled. "You're quite a well-known figure, Mr. Jensen. Why, if I put a sign on the wall behind the bar that said Smoke Jensen killed Blackjack Allison here, why, I've no doubt it would be good for business."

"You wouldn't do that," Allison said nervously. "Not after we—"

"Get out of here, Allison," Kennedy said with a contemptuous nod of his head toward the door. "And don't come back into my saloon picking a fight you can't handle."

"Can I put my hands back down?" Allison asked Smoke. "Yeah."

Allison dropped his hands then turned to leave.

"Wait a minute," Smoke called.

Allison stopped.

"Before you leave, shuck out of that gun belt. The pistol stays here," Smoke said.

"The hell it does!" Allison replied in one last attempt at bravado.

"Leave it," Smoke said coldly.

"Mister, you're crazy if you think I'm going to give up my gun."

Smoke pulled the hammer back on his pistol, and the deadly metallic click sounded loud in the room. "Oh, I think you will."

Allison paused for a moment longer, then, looking at

Smoke with an expression of intense anger, unbuckled his gun belt and let it drop to the floor.

"Now you can go," Smoke said.

"When do I get it back?" he asked.

"Not until my friend and I have left the saloon."

Kennedy laughed out loud after Allison left the saloon. "Ethan, drinks on the house . . . for everyone," Kennedy ordered.

"Yes, sir, Mr. Kennedy," Ethan replied.

With a happy shout, as much in relief of tension as appreciation for the drinks, all the patrons rushed to the bar with their orders.

"You son of a bitch!" Allison shouted, stepping back into the barroom, holding a rifle to his shoulder.

Many were now in Allison's line of fire. Shouts of surprise and fear erupted as everyone tried to get out of the way. The room filled with the sound of a gunshot . . . and Allison stood there for a moment with a look of shock on his face. "You? You shot me?"

He dropped the rifle and slapped his hand over a bleeding hole in his chest, standing there only long enough for people to see the blood streaming between his fingers before he pitched forward and landed facedown on the floor.

Not until then did everyone realize where the shot had come from. They all turned to see Warren Kennedy standing with a smoking pistol in his hand.

"That's the second time you've saved my life," Smoke said.

"Yes, it is, isn't it?" Kennedy replied with a self-assured smile.

CHAPTER 22

New York City

Officer Muldoon stepped up to the front desk at the Fifth Avenue Hotel.

"Yes, Officer, what can I do for you?" the desk clerk asked.

"Would you be for tellin' me please in what room I might find a Mr. Cal Wood?"

The desk clerk ran his fingers down the open pages of the registration book until he found the name. "He is in room four-oh-three. Officer, there is nothing wrong, is there? What I mean is only the most select people stay here, and I wouldn't want any kind of confrontation that would disturb our guests."

"There is nothing wrong, and the lad is in no trouble," Muldoon said. "All I'll be doing is talking with him."

"You may take the elevator," the clerk said.

A few moments later, the elevator operator opened the door onto the fourth floor. "You'll find four-oh-three that way, Officer. Just down the hall and on the left," the operator said.

"Thank you."

* * *

Cal was lying on his bed with his hands laced behind his head. He had not yet sent a telegram to Smoke, and he was wondering whether or not he should. He knew there was nothing Smoke could do, and he felt that there was no sense in worrying him. If the situation turned worse, he would tell him, but for now, Cal was absorbing all the worry himself. And he was literally sick with it, primarily because he wasn't doing anything about it.

A knock on the door jarred him from his melancholy, and remembering that the police lieutenant had promised to inform him of anything they might learn, he leaped up from the bed and hurried to open the door. "Officer Muldoon! Have you any news?"

"Nothing about your lady yet, but I've some news that might be to your liking."

"What is it?"

"Your friends . . . the famous actors?"

"Yes? What about them?"

"They've gone to see His Honor, the mayor. Would you be for believin' that Mayor Grace has made you a New York City deputy? You'll be workin' on the case with me."

"Oh!" Cal said as a huge smile spread across his face. "Oh, Officer Muldoon, that is great!"

"Come along. We'll walk my beat together."

"Wait for me in the lobby," Cal said. "I need to change clothes."

Cal went down to the lobby a few minutes later dressed as he would be if he had been back in Colorado. He was wearing boots, but no spurs, blue denim trousers, a yellow shirt, and a Stetson hat with a turquoise-studded hatband. He was also wearing a pistol belt, complete with filled bullet loops. His Colt .45 rode conspicuously on his hip.

"I don't know about the pistol, lad," Officer Muldoon said.

"Remember, I'm a deputy sheriff for Eagle County,

Colorado," Cal said. "And you said yourself that the mayor issued me a special license to act as a deputy here in New York."

Muldoon chuckled. "That's right, he did. Tell me, Deputy Wood, are you any good with that pistol?"

"I haven't shot myself in the leg yet," Cal replied.

Muldoon laughed. "Good enough. Come with me. I don't mind saying that, considerin' some o' the brigands we'll be seein', 'twill be good to have you along."

The first place they visited was Donovan's Pub, an Irish bar that was just across the street from where Cal and Sally were attacked. It was obvious Muldoon was a frequent visitor. Everyone in the pub gave him a hearty greeting.

"Who's the cowboy with you, Muldoon?" one of the customers asked.

"He is a deputy sheriff from Colorado," Muldoon said, using the information Cal had provided him, but withholding the fact that he was also a New York deputy. "Deputy Wood, he is."

"What's a deputy from Colorado doin' here in New York?" another asked.

"I'm looking for a woman that was taken last night," Cal said.

"Taken? Taken where?"

"That's what we're trying to find out . . . where she was taken."

"It happened right across the street, sometime between ten o'clock and eleven o'clock it was. 'Tis wondering, the deputy and I are, whether any of you might have seen somethin'," Muldoon said.

"Hey, cowboy," one of the patrons called out to Cal. "What are you doin' comin' into a man's drinkin' bar with cow shit on your shoes?"

"Damn, are you telling me I've got cow shit on my

boots?" Cal replied, holding one of them up to examine. "And here they are brand new, too."

"Ha! Darby, I think the lad has got you," the bartender said to the man who had challenged Cal.

"Aye," one of the other patrons said. "Sure 'n the only shit now is on Darby's face 'n not on the lad's shoes."

"Think you're smart, do you, cowboy?" Darby had been leaning against the bar, but when he stepped away from it, Cal saw how large he was—at least six-foot-three, with broad shoulders and powerful arms. He bent both arms at the elbow and made a beckoning sign with his curled fingers. "Here now, 'n why don't you show us just how smart you be."

"Easy enough to show you how smart I am," Cal replied with an easy smile. "I'm too smart to fight with a giant like you."

"Well now lad, this has done gone too far. You've got m' dander up, you have, 'n the only way I'm goin' to be pacified is if I teach you a little lesson."

"Leave the lad be, Darby," Muldoon said. "You touch 'im 'n you'll be windin' up in the Tombs."

"Won't be the first time I've been in jail. 'Twill be worth it to teach the cowboy a lesson," Darby said with a broad smile.

Cal knew that Darby was about to rush him, and he came up on his toes ready to deal with it.

With a yell that could almost be a growl, Darby bent over at the waist with his arms stretched out in front of him and charged Cal. Cal deftly stepped aside, drew his pistol, and brought it down as hard as he could on Darby's head. He put the gun back in its holster so quickly that no more than one or two of the witnesses even knew that a gun was used.

"Blimey now, 'n did you see that?" someone shouted.

Darby lay very still and for a moment Cal was afraid that he might have killed him.

He knelt quickly to check on him and was relieved to find that he was still alive. "Bartender, do you have a pitcher of water?"

"Aye." The bartender drew a pitcher of water and handed it to Cal, who poured it over Darby, standing ready in case any fight remained in the Irishman.

Darby came to, spitting and coughing. He got up on his hands and knees. "Begorra. Would someone be for tellin' me what I'm doin' on the floor?"

"Why, you tripped over yer own feet, you big galoot," the bartender said.

"I did?"

"Aye." The bartender drew a mug of beer. "Here, have a mug on the house. I can't be for havin' m' customers fall all over the place in the pub now, can I? How would that look for business?"

"I'll have a drink with you, Darby," one of the others said.

Soon several others made the same offer.

"What about you, lad?" Darby asked Cal. "Would you be for havin' a drink with ol' Darby?"

"Yes, thank you. I'd like that," Cal said.

The bartender drew a mug for Cal, who blew off the foam, then held his beer out toward the others as they all drank.

"You done well in there, Cal," Muldoon said when they left the pub a short while later. "I was wonderin' how you would handle it. If you backed away, you woulda lost face that you could never recover. But 'twas for sure 'n certain that you'd be no match for him."

"Thanks," Cal said, feeling good about the policeman's compliments.

Five Points, New York City

The buildings on Baxter Street were festooned with awnings stretched out over the sidewalks and clothes hanging to dry from the windows of the upper floors. Even though night had fallen, the street was well illuminated by corner lamps and the ambient light streaming from the windows of the buildings.

"I sure wish I had a picture of her," Cal said. "I think that would help."

"No, lad. If they snatched her in the middle of the night, 'tis not likely anyone saw her . . . so a picture would do you no good. 'Tis if someone has heard somethin' that we're hopin' for."

"Mickey, if something has happened to her, I'll not be able to face Smoke."

"Smoke?"

"Smoke is her husband."

"His name is Smoke?"

"His real name is Kirby, but I've never actually heard him called that. I've never seen two people who cared more about each other than those two. I've come close to gettin' married m'self, but it wasn't meant to be. If I ever do get married though, I would sure hope to have something like those two have."

"Aye, the missus 'n I were like that," Officer Muldoon said.

"Were?"

"Aye. She took the new-monia 'n died last year."

"Oh, I'm sorry," Cal said.

"Sure now, lad. 'Twas not yer fault. You don't have nothin' to be sorry for. 'Tis just hopin', I am, that we can find your friend."

"Yeah," Cal said. "I'm hoping that, too."

"We've a few more pubs to look into. Maybe something will turn up."

"Maybe," Cal said, but his response was weak.

The next pub they went into was called Cara.

"A woman owns this place?" Cal asked.

"What? No, 'n why would you be for sayin' such a thing?"

"It's got a woman's name. Cara."

Muldoon chuckled. "Here now, 'n that's nothin' o' the sort. The word *cara* is Gaelic for *friends*. You might say the place is called Friends."

"Friends. Yes, that would be a good name, I think."

Muldoon had decided that he might have better results if he spoke to the patrons individually, rather than making a public inquiry. He reasoned that some might be more open to tell what they knew in private, rather than to speak before everyone.

The individual questioning wasn't producing any more results, until Cal saw someone in the back of the room who looked familiar. He thought back to the few quick glances he had of the three men who had been following Sally and him and he was almost sure it was one of them.

"Mickey, that man in the back, the one in the brown jacket," Cal said. "I think he might have been one of the three men who were following Miz Sally and me."

"The one in in the brown jacket, you say?"

"Yes. I'm certain he was one of them."

Muldoon smiled. "Well, now, could be that our luck is about to change. His name is O'Leary, 'n he's of the sort to do such a blackhearted thing."

"You, O'Leary. I'd like to talk to you," Cal called out, pointing to the man who had caught his attention.

"We ain't got nothin' to talk about," O'Leary said.

"I think I've seen you before."

"I told you, I've got no wish to be for talkin' to you."

"It's just a friendly question, is all," Cal said.

"No it ain't. There ain't nothin' friendly about it," O'Leary replied. He turned away for just a moment, and when he turned back he had a gun in his hand.

"Look out, lad. He's got a gun!" Muldoon said as he unsnapped the cover to his own holster in an effort to get to his pistol.

O'Leary fired toward Cal and Muldoon.

Cal's mentor in the art of the fast draw was Smoke Jensen, the master, and Cal had his own gun out so quickly there was barely a separation between the two shots. The difference was the first shooter missed and Cal did not.

Holding the smoking gun in his hand for a moment longer, he ascertained no other imminent threat and put the pistol back in his holster.

"Damn!" someone said in awe. "Did you see that?"

"Yeah, Murphy, we all seen it," another bar patron replied.

Muldoon had not even gotten his holster open in the time it took for Cal and the shooter to exchange shots. He pulled his hand away sheepishly. "Here now, 'tis damn good with that gun that you be, lad. If I had to guess, I'd say you've had to do that before."

"A few times," Cal said. "Am I in trouble?"

"No trouble. For sure 'n certain O'Leary would have killed you. Aye, 'n me, too, I'm thinkin' . . . if you hadn't shot him. 'Tis my own life you saved. No, lad, 'tis a medal you deserve, not a charge."

"You said you know him."

"Aye, Ian Patrick O'Leary. He's been a troublemaker ever since I started walkin' this beat."

"I am absolutely positive he was one of the three men that followed Miz Sally and me."

"I think you be right. Otherwise O'Leary would not have tried to shoot you as he done. This'll give us an idea where to go next," Muldoon said. "We'll be for visitin' some o' the Irish Assembly now."

"What is the Irish Assembly?"

"At one time 'twas a gang o' Irish brigands who did nothin' but give Ireland a bad name. They got into a gun battle with the Five Points gang, 'n 'tis said they broke up soon after that. Broke up they may be, but many o' the same group o' hoodlums are still hangin' around 'n still gettin' into the same mischief they was gettin' into when they was a gang."

"Was O'Leary one of them?" Cal asked.

"Aye, O'Leary was one of them. I know a lot more who once wore the Assembly's shamrock, but since it is no more, a lot of 'em are tryin' to straighten their lives up 'n make a go of it. 'Tis them we'll be startin' with, and I'll be for askin' them what they know about Mrs. Jensen being taken like she was. I got a feelin' there'll be a lot o' folk who have heard about it, but are not for wantin' to have anything to do with it. I know a few boys who just might be able to help us out."

CHAPTER 23

Sally could tell by the lengthening shadows as well as the dimmer light in her room that it was getting late in the afternoon. The man she now knew as Kelly came into her room.

"I brought you some supper," Kelly said.

"Thank you."

"I'll be for untyin' you now so you can eat, if you'll give me yer promise not to try and escape."

"Mr. Kelly, how would I be able to do that? You appear to be a very strong man. There is no way I can overpower you. I can't jump out of the window. I'm quite certain that I'm not on the ground floor."

Kelly chuckled. "No ma'am, I don't reckon you can overpower me, and you ain't on a ground floor." He loosened the ties, and again, Sally began to rub her wrists.

"When can I see Mr. Gallagher again?" she asked.

"Why would you be wantin' ter see him?"

"You said that he is the one who gave you the instructions to capture me. I want to know why he did that. What is to be gained by holding me prisoner?"

"Yes ma'am, I reckon I can see as ter how you might be some considerable plexed by it. I'd tell you if I knew, but I don't have no idee a' tall."

"Is Mr. Gallagher here right now?"

"No, ma'am, he ain't."

"You mean, you are the only one watching me?"

"Aye."

"Let me go, Mr. Kelly."

Kelly shook his head. "I can't do that."

"Sure you can. You can simply tell Mr. Gallagher that I escaped."

"And how did you escape, would you be for tellin' me that? Sure 'n you've already pointed out how that ain't possible, bein' as you can't get by me."

"My husband is a very wealthy man. You could turn me over to the police, and I would see to it that you got quite a nice reward for it."

"'Tis tempted I am, Miz Jensen, but I'll not be goin' up against the likes o' Ian Gallagher. You've no idea how evil he is."

"Evil to the degree that I have to fear harm coming to me while I am your prisoner?"

"No, ma'am. I done asked him that, 'n he promised me you wouldn't be hurt none whilst we are keepin' you."

"Thank you, Mr. Kelly." As Sally ate her supper, potato soup, she thought about Kelly. His concern for her seemed genuine, and she couldn't help but think there may be some way to exploit that.

"Is your husband a famous man, Mrs. Jensen?" he asked.

"Famous? Oh, I don't know that I would say that . . . though he has certainly acquired quite a reputation in Colorado, as well as a few other western states. Why do you ask?"

"After we found out who you was, Brockway said that they was some books wrote about your husband. He said he read some of 'em while he was in prison."

"Oh, heavens, you must be talking about those dreadful dime novels written by Mr. Judson."

"Judson? No, I don't think that was the name."

"His real name is Edward Judson, but he writes many of his novels as Ned Buntline."

"Yeah!" Kelly said, smiling broadly. "That's it. Ned Buntline. Has he really wrote books about your husband?"

"He has."

"Wow, havin' them books wrote about him must've made your husband rich."

"My husband was not compensated in any way for the use of his name in any of Mr. Judson's books. They are, at best, the unauthorized appropriation of his name, and at worst, outright piracy."

"That don't seem fair," Kelly said.

Sally laughed.

"What are you laughin' at?"

"I am laughing at the ludicrousness of a situation in which you are concerned about whether my husband has been fairly treated for the appropriation of his name, while at the same time holding me in this place against my will."

"Aye," Kelly said sheepishly. "'Tis a foul deed I be doin', 'n I take no pride in it."

Mule Gap

The morning sun was streaming in through the window of her office, and Delilah was counting the take for the week, which had come to two hundred and fifty-five dollars, including the money paid in advance for the "visit" her girls had made the night before. She looked up to see Fancy standing at the door.

"Fancy, dear, come in, come in," Delilah invited. "How was your visit last night?"

"It was . . . all right," Fancy replied with a short hesitation before she said the words *all right*.

"What is it? What is wrong?" Delilah asked, concern

chasing the smile from her face. "Fancy, did any of those men hurt any of you?"

"No, ma'am, it isn't that. It's just that there's something going on out there, something to do with the children, that I've been thinking about."

"Children? What children?"

"There are a bunch of children out there."

"Good gracious. Are you telling me those men allowed children to be present while . . . uh, while you were . . . ?"

"No, ma'am, nothing like that. They are staying in a separate cabin, all by themselves. They said that the children's parents have sent them out there so they can spend some time on the creek . . . but if they were doing that, wouldn't they be running around outside, playing and such? I kept glancing through the window, and except for the two young girls I saw at the privy, the children never once left their cabin. And from the expression on the two girls' faces, it sure didn't seem like they were having fun. I just feel like something's not quite right there."

"Two little girls? How many children are there? Oh, wait. You wouldn't know, would you?"

"Yes ma'am, I do know. One of the men told me there are six children out there."

"Six, you say?"

"Yes, ma'am. Of course I can't vouch for that myself. Like I said, I only seen the two little girls. And I don't know if the remaining children are boys or girls. When I started asking about them, Keefer didn't want to talk about them anymore, and I sort of got the idea that he was upset with Sanders for telling me about them in the first place."

"How very odd," Delilah said.

"Yes, ma'am, that's what I thought, too. Do you think, maybe, it might be the children who have been kidnapped?"

"I don't know. I am aware of only five kidnapped children, but there could be more, I suppose."

"I hope I didn't do the wrong thing by coming in here to tell you this. I mean, if it really is just kids there on a vacation, I surely wouldn't want to get anyone in trouble."

"No, don't worry about it," Delilah said with a reassuring smile. "You did the right thing."

The worried expression on Fancy's face was replaced by a wide smile. "Good, I was hoping I was."

Delilah Dupree stepped into Marshal Bodine's office a few minutes later. The man called The Professor was sitting at his desk, reading *The Death of Ivan Ilyich* by Leo Tolstoy.

"That's a very good book," Delilah said.

Putting a bookmark to keep his page, Bodine set the book down. "Really? And how would you know? Are you just saying that as a matter of conversation, Miss Dupree? Or do you actually have any idea what this book is about?"

"No, I'm not just saying that, and yes, I have read the book. It's about a man facing his own death. But then, from what I have heard about you, facing death is something you do frequently."

"It is part of my chosen profession," Bodine replied.

"You mean your secondary profession . . . after you left teaching."

"What is it, Miss Dupree? What brings you here?"

"You are aware, are you not, Marshal, that there have been several children kidnapped?"

"Yes, of course I'm aware of that. Who, around here, isn't aware of it?"

"Have you been able to do anything about it?"

"I'm . . . working on a few leads," Bodine replied. "Why do the kidnappings concern you? Do you know any of the children involved?"

"No, but three of my girls spent last night in a house on French Creek. This morning one of my young ladies reported that there are several children in a cabin adjacent to the house where my young ladies were taken. When she asked about them, she was told their parents knew they were there, and had paid for their children to be there as a vacation on the lake."

"Do you have any reason to doubt that, Miss Dupree?" Bodine asked.

"Are you asking me if I doubt the story told me by Jill? No, I don't doubt it for a moment."

"Jill?"

"Fancy Bliss is her working name. Her real name is Jill Peterson. And no I have no reason to doubt her story."

"What I was asking is do you have any reason to doubt the story that was told to Miss"—Bodine paused for a long moment before he said the name—"Peterson."

"That story was told to her by Fred Keefer, and yes, I very much doubt it. I know Mr. Keefer, and he is not a very nice man. It would not surprise me one bit if he was involved in the kidnapping."

"That's quite an accusation you are making, Miss Dupree. And about someone you know, too. How well do you know him?"

"Keefer is a frequent guest at my house, and I have had many opportunities to observe him. He is a mean-spirited man, and he is no gentleman."

Bodine smiled. "Why, Miss Dupree. I thought everyone who came to your establishment was a gentleman. That is how you advertise yourself, isn't it?"

"Surely, Marshal, as a professor, you know the subtleties of advertising. If I suggest that only gentlemen are welcome at my house, then those who do come are more likely to *act* as gentlemen."

"You have a good point," Bodine said.

"What about Keefer?"

"What about him?"

"Well, aren't you going to arrest him?"

"How can I arrest him? I have no evidence that he has committed any sort of crime."

"But I told you what Fancy told me."

"Miss Dupree, why don't you just continue to run your house, which you obviously do very well, since I've never had any trouble with you, and leave the law enforcement up to me?"

"Do you mean to tell me that you aren't even going to look into it?" Delilah asked.

"Of course I'm going to look into it. I intend to follow every lead, but I don't intend to engage in precipitous action that would not only set my investigation back, it could also result in a lawsuit for unlawful arrest."

"But—"

"Good day, Miss Dupree," Bodine said. By way of dismissal he picked up his book and reopened it to the place of the marker.

Leaving the marshal's office, Delilah felt a sense of frustration. She had not gotten the reaction from the marshal that she had expected. How could he turn his back on information that had the potential to lead to the rescue of the kidnapped children?

Not content with being so summarily dismissed, she decided to go over the marshal's head and seek out Warren Kennedy. He was the mayor, which meant he had authority over the marshal. Delilah smiled. She should have gone to him in the first place. After all, she and the mayor had a rather special relationship.

As she walked toward the bank, she encountered two women coming toward her. When the two women recognized her, a sour expression crossed their faces.

"Come, Matilda," one of them said. "Let's cross the street so we don't have to share the walk with that woman."

"Hello, ladies. What a beautiful day it is, don't you think?" Delilah called out to them.

"Humph," one of them uttered in disgust.

Stepping into the bank, Delilah got the same reaction. A woman put her hands on her husband's arm and led him away as if she were frightened that he might succumb to Delilah's sex appeal, right there in the bank.

"Yes, Miss Dupree?" the bank teller asked as she approached the teller's cage.

"I would like to deposit last night's receipts."

"Very well," the teller said, taking the proffered bills from her.

"And I would like to speak to Mr. Kennedy," Delilah said.

"I'm afraid that isn't possible."

"Why isn't it possible?"

"Because Mr. Kennedy is busy right now."

"That's all right. I'll wait until he isn't busy."

"Do you mean . . . in the bank?" the teller asked, aghast.

"Of course in the bank. Where else would I wait to see the president of the bank? In the stable?"

"Very well. I'll see if he has time to visit with you," the teller said in a self-righteous huff.

"Thank you."

"I thought I told you never to come here," Kennedy said a moment later when Delilah was let into his office. "I thought you understood the whole idea of my being a silent partner is keeping secret any relation between us."

Delilah smiled. "Now, Warren, really. Mule Gap is a small town. Do you think there is anyone who doesn't know of our . . . relationship?"

"Still, it's nothing I want to flaunt. Now, what is it? What do you need?"

"I want to talk to you about the children who have been kidnapped," Delilah said.

"Kidnapped children? Why, what does that have to do with me? Or you, for that matter?"

"I think I know where they are. In a cabin on French Creek."

"What?" Kennedy replied in surprise. "Now, how on earth would you know that?"

"A few of my girls went out there yesterday and they saw them."

Kennedy drummed his fingers on his desk for a moment as he considered what Delilah had just said. "Have you told this to anybody?"

"Yes, I told Marshal Bodine."

"You haven't said anything to Mrs. Condon?"

"Mrs. Condon? No. Who is she, and why should I say anything to her?"

"She is in town now, staying at the hotel. And her son is one of the kidnap victims."

"That would be the sixth child," Delilah said.

"What?"

"I was aware of only five, but there are six children out there. Don't you see, Warren? There are six children who are kidnapped, and there are six children out there in a cabin on the lake. This isn't a mere coincidence. I'm convinced the children out there are the same ones that have been captured."

"Yes, you may be right. The evidence is too strong to be a mere coincidence. What did Marshal Bodine say when you told him?"

"He said he would look into it, but really, Warren, he didn't seem all that interested. He said something about being concerned over a possible lawsuit."

Kennedy smiled. "It's good to see that he's looking out for the town. I wouldn't want us to be facing a lawsuit. If there is anything to this, I'm sure he will get to the bottom of it. Why don't you just let him do his job?"

"All right," Delilah said. "I'll leave it up to him. It's just that I thought that, as you are the mayor, you might like to know."

"You were right to come to me, Delilah. Yes, I do want to know, and I will follow up on this with The Professor." He put his hand on her cheek. "And what I said earlier about you not coming here? I'm sorry if I sounded harsh. I didn't mean to."

"I know. You're the mayor of this town. You have an image to maintain. And believe me, I don't want to do anything that would jeopardize that position. It wouldn't be good for either of us."

"I'm glad that you understand. Let me walk you to the door. That is a wise decision, Miss Dupree," Kennedy said rather loudly as he and Delilah left his office and walked through the main lobby of the bank. "Transferring your funds into the savings account will assure that the money is working for you by earning interest."

"Thank you for your help," Delilah replied, going along with the game.

CHAPTER 24

When Delilah approached the front desk of the Del Rey Hotel a few minutes later, the clerk frowned when he saw her.

"Miss Dupree, you know that the hotel owners have banned you from doing any business in here."

"I am not here to do any business," Delilah replied.

"That may be so, but you aren't welcome in the hotel for any reason, so I'm going to have to ask you to leave. I'm sure you understand."

"No, Mr. Hodge, I don't understand. I told you I'm not here to conduct any business. I'm here to see one of the hotel residents."

Hodge shook his head. "I don't care why you are here. You're going to have to leave, now."

"If you force me to leave this hotel before I am able to visit with the person I'm looking for, then I will go directly to the *Mule Gap Ledger* and give Mr. Blanton a list of names of everyone who has been a guest at the House of Pleasure. Now that I think of it, Mr. Hodge, your name and the names of both sanctimonious owners of this hotel will be on that list."

"You wouldn't dare do a thing like that," Hodge said. "It would ruin you. You would have to close your business."

"My particular business is always in demand, and I have

enough money to go somewhere else and start all over again," Delilah said. "Do you?"

Hodge was silent for a moment. "Who do you want to see?"

"Mrs. Condon."

"It is room two-oh-seven."

Delilah flashed a smile, then reached across the desk to put her fingers on his cheek. "Thank you so much, Mr. Hodge. You've been a great help. Come around sometime and I'll have one of my girls express just how appreciative I am."

"If you are going to up to her room, please do so quickly. I wouldn't want someone to see you and get word back to the wrong people that you were here."

"Oh? Tell me, Sylvester, and just who would you say are the wrong people?"

"Please, go. Just go on up the stairs," a very agitated Hodge said.

With a little chuckle, Delilah strolled confidently across the lobby.

When Sara Sue heard the knock on her door, she grew tense. Was it the kidnappers getting in touch with her again or was it Smoke Jensen? "Who is it?" she called.

"Mrs. Condon, please, I'd like to speak to you. It's important." The voice was that of a woman.

Curious, Sara Sue walked over to open the door. The woman standing in the hall was a very attractive woman, but also a woman who wore more face paint than anyone Sara Sue had ever seen. Even the dress she wore seemed to be . . . the only word Sara Sue could think of was *provocative*.

"What do you want to talk about?" Sara Sue asked.

"I want to talk about the kidnapped children. And please, let me in. It isn't safe for me to be seen talking to you. I'm in great danger, standing here just outside your door." The expression on her face and the tone in her voice as she made the declaration of personal danger convinced Sara Sue that the woman was telling the truth.

"Yes, do come in," Sara Sue said, stepping aside to allow the woman to enter. She shut the door behind her visitor.

The woman smiled. "It's better for you as well. I'm not the kind of woman a good lady like you would want to be seen with."

"Oh?"

"My name is Delilah Dupree, Mrs. Condon. I am what they call a madam. I manage a house of ill repute."

"You said something about the kidnapped children," Sara Sue said.

"Thank you for not reacting to my, uh, profession."

"The children?" Sara Sue repeated.

"Yes. Last night three of my girls paid a . . . uh, professional visit to a house that is about eight miles west of here on French Creek. While they were there, they discovered that six children were there. The men my girls were visiting told them that the children's parents knew the children were there, that they were there on a vacation, and the men were just looking out for them."

"Six children?" Sara Sue frowned. Jim Harris had told Smoke the number of kidnapped children still unaccounted for would be six, counting Thad, and Smoke had shared that information with her. It was too close to be a mere coincidence. "That's how many are missing."

"I wasn't aware of the exact number until a short time ago," Delilah said. "But I knew there was something a little fishy about their story of six kids being on vacation."

"And you say they are in a cabin?"

"Yes, according to my girls there are two buildings there—a small house and an even smaller cabin."

"Have you told the sheriff?" Sara Sue asked.

Delilah's chuckle was derisive. "Mrs. Condon, our sheriff

never leaves Rawlins. You may as well shout it into the wind as tell him. I did tell Marshal Bodine, but he seemed almost dismissive about it. I'm telling you. Seeing as one of the kidnapped children is yours, you have a bona fide reason to know. Though, to be truthful, I have no idea what you can do about it."

Sara Sue smiled at Delilah. "Thank you, Miss Dupree. I very much appreciate your telling me this."

"Oh, you don't have to thank me, ma'am," Delilah said. "Lord knows, I'm a sinful woman, but even I know that what these men have done—taking kids from their mamas and papas—is wrong. I hope you are able to get your boy back all right."

"I pray that I will," Sara Sue said. "Miss Dupree, there is a gentleman in town, a neighbor. His name is Smoke Jensen, and I would like to see him, but, under the circumstances, it would be ill-advised for me to be seen with him. I wonder if I could prevail upon you to find him and ask him to call on me."

"I'll be happy to do it," Delilah said. "But now, I wonder if you would do me a favor and look out into the hallway? I don't want anyone to see me leaving your room."

"Of course," Sara Sue said. Opening the door, she looked both ways down the hallway and saw that it was empty. "There's nobody here."

Delilah stuck out her hand, but Sara Sue ignored the proffered handshake and impulsively embraced her instead. "Thank you," she said again.

Delilah stepped out into the hallway, moving quickly because she didn't want Mrs. Condon to see the tears that had formed in her eyes.

Arnold Fenton had been sent to follow Delilah, and he was standing just behind the turn in the wall at the top of the stairs when he saw the door open, and Mrs. Condon stick her head out. She glanced toward the other end of the hall first, which gave him a chance to pull his head back without being seen.

A moment later the door to her room opened again, and the woman who ran the whorehouse stepped out into the hallway. His information was accurate. She had met with the Condon woman.

Fenton pulled back and hurried down the stairs so he wouldn't be seen. The person who'd sent him would want to know.

When Delilah stepped into the Silver Dollar Saloon a few minutes later, she was met by one of the bar girls who worked there. "What are you doing here, Delilah? I hope you aren't here to steal any of the girls for your house."

"Hello, Belle," Delilah replied. "No, nothing like that. I'm looking for a man."

"Aren't we all?" Belle replied with a teasing smile.

Delilah smiled with her. "No, this is a particular man. His name is Smoke Jensen."

"Honey, you won't get nowhere with him," Belle said. "Believe me, because I have tried. All the girls have tried, but nobody has been able to get him to do nothin'. They say he's married, 'n if he is, his wife is one lucky woman 'cause he is as straight as an arrow."

"I want to try, anyway," Delilah said. "Is he in here?"

"Oh, he's here all right." Belle pointed to a table near the piano, where two men sat, drinking beer.

"Thanks," Delilah said as, with a toss of her head, she started toward the table.

"Here comes a new girl." Pearlie smiled. "I have to admit, she's prettier than the others."

"Don't let me hold you back," Smoke said.

"Mr. Jensen?" the girl said as she approached him.

Smoke was surprised that she had addressed him by name. Also, he noticed, her demeanor was different from that of the other girls. Hers was a direct business-like approach without the "come on" smile the others employed.

"Yes, I'm Smoke Jensen. What can I do for you?"

"My name is Delilah Dupree. Do you know a lady named Mrs. Condon?"

"Yes, I know her," Smoke said. "Has something happened to her?"

"No," Delilah replied quickly. "I'm sorry if I gave you a start." She looked around to make certain she could talk to him without being overheard. "I just came from a visit with her, and she asked me to ask you to come see her."

"Is she still in the hotel?" Smoke asked.

"Yes, room . . ."

"Two-oh-seven," Smoke said before she could get the number out,

"Yes, that's the room number."

"Thank you," Smoke said. "I . . . was going to offer to buy you a drink, but I have an idea that you don't work here."

"No, I don't. I have my own place of business, the Delilah House. You and your gentleman friend are welcome at any time, though Belle tells me that you are married and are very loyal to your wife."

"That's true," Smoke said.

"I'm not married," Pearlie said with a broad smile.

Delilah returned the smile. "Of course the invitation is for you as well."

"Come on, Pearlie," Smoke said, standing. "Mrs. Condon wouldn't be sending for us unless it was very important."

* * *

"You say she spent some time in the room with the Condon woman, then went from there directly to meet with Smoke Jensen?"

"Yeah," Fenton said, "that's exactly what she done."

"I'm afraid Miss Dupree has become a liability."

"What does that mean?"

"It means I'm going to have get someone to take care of her."

"How much will you pay?"

"One hundred dollars."

"Not good enough," Fenton said. "I don't like killin' women. I was thinking more along the lines of five hunnert dollars."

The two men settled on two hundred and fifty dollars, a sum that satisfied both.

Smoke knocked on the door. "Did you ask for fresh towels, ma'am?" he called.

The door opened quickly, and Smoke stepped inside, Pearlie having remained downstairs in the hotel lobby.

"What is it?" Smoke asked.

"I think I know where they are keeping Thad and the other children," Sara Sue said.

"Where?"

"In a cabin on French Creek, about eight miles west of here. Do you know where French Creek is?"

"I not only know where it is, the place I'm thinking about has two buildings there. They were abandoned the last time I saw them."

"Yes! That's it!" Sara Sue said excitedly. "Delilah said there was a small house and an even smaller cabin."

"Only one way to find out, and that is for me to go out there," he said.

"Oh, Smoke, do be careful," she said. "I want Thad back, safe and sound, but I do feel responsible for Pearlie getting shot and for that dear horse of yours getting killed. I wouldn't want to be responsible for anything else like that happening."

"Don't worry. We'll get Thad back, safe and sound. And the other children, as well," he promised.

CHAPTER 25

"What are you doing in my office?" Delilah asked. "Can't you read the signs? There are no gentlemen callers allowed in this part of the house. You have the parlor . . . and the upstairs rooms when you are invited by one of the ladies."

"You've been opening your big mouth, haven't you?"

"Opening my mouth? Opening my mouth about what? Arnold Fenton, what are you talking about?"

"I seen you goin' into the Condon woman's room. Then I seen you goin' down to the Silver Dollar to talk to Smoke Jensen. What did you tell 'em?"

"What did I tell them about what?"

"You know about what. What did you tell them about them kids that's bein' held out at French Creek?"

"It's true, isn't it?" Delilah replied. "The children who are being held out there are the kidnap victims! My God, Arnold, are you one of the kidnappers?"

Fenton took his gun out. "It's not that you know too much, Delilah. It's that you know too much and don't know enough to keep your mouth shut."

"Arnold! No!"

Delilah's office echoed with the sound of a gun being

fired. Delilah's head flopped back in her chair, blood coming from the bullet hole in her forehead.

"Delilah!" Joy Love shouted, rushing into the office. When she saw her friend and employer dead in her chair, she turned to Arnold Fenton, who was standing there, the smoking six-gun still in his hand. "Arnold! What did you do?"

Arnold turned his gun on Joy and pulled the trigger.

Jasmine was upstairs asleep. Fancy and Candy were in the kitchen when they heard the shots fired. As they rushed out of the kitchen they saw Fenton leaving by the front door. They hurried into Delilah's office and saw her with her head tossed back and her face covered with blood, and Joy lying dead on the floor.

"Delilah!" Candy shouted.

Fancy looked at both of them for a moment. "They're dead. Both of them are dead."

"What will we do?"

"That was Arnold Fenton, wasn't it? The man we saw running out the front door

"Yes, that was Fenton."

"He has to be the one who killed them."

"But why?" Candy asked. "Why would he kill them? Joy said he has always been nice to her."

"I don't know, but we need to tell the marshal about it.

The two women hurried down to the marshal's office.

"He killed them!" Fancy said breathlessly.

"He killed both of them!" Candy added.

The words were shouted simultaneously by both women so that they tumbled over each other in a way that neither could be understood.

"Here now, here!" Marshal Bodine said. "How do you expect me to hear anything or understand what you're saying if both of you are talking at once?"

"He killed Delilah," Fancy said.

"And Joy," Candy added.

"Who killed them?"

"Arnold Fenton," Candy said.

"We think," Fancy said.

"Do you think he killed them or do you know he killed them?"

"We know," Candy said.

"How do you know? Did you actually see him shooting them?"

"We think it was him, but it has to be. We saw him running out the front door," Fancy said.

"But you didn't actually see him shooting."

"No, but who else could it have been?"

"Perhaps Fenton heard the shot and ran away because he was frightened."

"Why was he in the house in the first place?" Fancy asked.

"Well, you tell me, Miss Bliss. Why would anyone visit the Delilah House? They certainly don't go there to have a photograph taken." Bodine chuckled.

"I can't believe this. We came here to tell you that Delilah and Joy have been killed, and you make a joke about it?" Candy said.

"You are right, and I apologize if my reaction seemed inappropriate. I meant no disrespect. But you must also see my point of view. Unless you actually saw Fenton in the act of shooting the two ladies, any connection between him and the murder is circumstantial at best."

"Let's go, Candy," Fancy said bitterly. "It's clear that the law doesn't care about women like us."

Bodine made no response as the two left his office.

By early morning of the next day, news of the double murder had spread quickly through the town, by word, and by the article in the *Mule Gap Ledger*.

TERRIBLE MURDER!

Two Women Shot Dead

Yesterday, Miss Delilah Dupree and Miss Suzie Fugate were both shot dead. Miss Dupree was the manager of the Delilah House, a business of ill repute, and Miss Fugate, a soiled dove in Miss Dupree's employ. Miss Fugate was better known to the clients of the house as Joy Love.

Motive for the shooting isn't known, but Marshal Bodine has suggested that the killing might be the result of a jilted client who wanted exclusive access to one of the two women.

As of this writing, the identity of the killer or killers is unknown, though it is believed that someone was seen running from the house immediately after the shots were fired. The identity of that person is being withheld as part of the ongoing investigation.

Although Miss Dupree was engaged in a business that is best practiced in the shadows, she was said to be a woman of education and mannerly bearing.

"I'm not surprised," a citizen of the town said. "The only thing that surprises me is that someone hasn't been murdered in that place before now."

"I've seen Miss Dupree around. She always seemed nice," another citizen replied.

"Nice or not, she was a whore, and when you run a whorehouse, you can expect things like that to happen."

* * *

"Oh, Smoke, do you think Miss Dupree's murder may have something to do with her visiting me?" Sara Sue asked.

She, Smoke, and Pearlie were sharing a table at breakfast in the hotel dining room. Pearlie ate heartily as he listened to the conversation.

"I don't know," Smoke replied. "But I won't lie to you. It could have been connected."

"I feel so guilty."

"There's nothing for you to feel guilty about. She came to you, you didn't go to her."

"That's true. But still, it would be very upsetting to me if I thought I'd had anything to do with her death."

"Even if her getting killed had something to do with her visiting you, the blame and the guilt belong to the person who actually killed her. Besides, two were killed. Both of them didn't come to see you."

"I suppose you're right," Sara Sue said, relieved by the thought.

"On the other hand, if her getting killed does have something to do with her visiting you, that means her story about the kids is true and someone is getting a little concerned about it."

"Yes, that's true, isn't it?"

"If that is true, they will also realize that you now know where the children are," Smoke said. "So I want you to leave."

"Smoke, I can't leave! Not until I get Thad back."

"You don't have to leave town. I just want you to leave the hotel. Too many people know you are here. I don't want you exposed to that danger."

"But this is the only hotel in town," Sara Sue said. "If I leave here, where will I go?"

"You'll be staying with Mrs. Coy."

"Who?"

"Sandra Coy. She has three rooms at Welsh's Boarding

House. We'll sneak you over there, and you can stay out of sight until we bring the children back."

"And Mrs. Coy approves of this plan?"

"Yes."

Sandra Coy was about the same age as Sara Sue. She had dark hair and emerald eyes, and the lithe form of the ballet dancer she once was.

"Mrs. Coy, this is the lady I told you about," Smoke said.

"How nice to meet you," Mrs. Coy said.

"I think it is wonderful of you to put me up like this," Sara Sue said. "I hope I am not too big of a burden."

"You aren't a burden at all," Mrs. Coy said. "This way, we can wait for our children together."

"Our children? You mean you have a child among the kidnapped children?"

"Yes, my daughter, Lorena." Mrs. Coy chuckled self-deprecatingly. "I know you are probably wondering why someone would kidnap a child from a widow who lives in a boardinghouse. Lorena had been hired by the Blackwells to sit with their son Eddie while they were running their place of business. Their son was the target of the kidnappers, and she was with him when he was taken, so they took her, as well."

"I'll tell you what I told Mrs. Condon," Smoke said. "We will get the children back . . . all of them . . . and we will get them back safely."

"Mrs. Coy—"

"Please, if we are going to live together for a while, can't we use first names? I'm Sandra."

Sara Sue smiled. "And I'm Sara Sue. Sandra, has Smoke told you why I need to stay with you rather than in the hotel?"

"Yes. He told me that your life may be in danger."

"And you do realize, don't you, that by my staying here with you, it also puts your life in danger?"

"Yes, I know. Do you like tea or coffee?"

For just a moment, Sara Sue was confused by the question, wondering what it had to do with her life being in danger. Then she smiled as she knew exactly what Sandra was telling her. She was making her feel welcome, despite any inherent danger in sharing her quarters.

Sara Sue smiled. "Coffee."

Sandra smiled as well. "Oh, that's wonderful. I was afraid you might be one of those tea drinkers."

Sara Sue laughed. "Sandra, I think you and I will get along quite well."

"So do I, Sara Sue."

Delilah Dupree was well-known in Mule Gap, and though her public persona was unsavory, many knew the better side of her. Father Than Pyron of St. Paul's Episcopal Church knew that side of her. Delilah didn't attend service on Sunday, giving the reason, "I'm afraid my presence would make the others uncomfortable." She took private communion shortly after the others left.

Delilah's church attendance was secret and so were her contributions, or so she thought. Whenever she gave money through the church to help out people in need, Father Pyron always made sure the recipients of her assistance knew from whence the money came.

As a result of Delilah's beneficence, a surprisingly large number of people turned out to attend her funeral. The same church that she feared would be offended by her presence was filled with mourners.

Sara Sue Condon, who believed that Delilah was murdered because she had come to see her, was there. So too were Smoke and Pearlie. Neither Frank Bodine nor Warren Kennedy attended.

Fancy Bliss and Candy Sweet, whose real names were Jill Peterson and Ann Bailey, were there as well, dressed in black with their faces covered by black veils. Jasmine Delight, whose real name was Lin Kwan, was also dressed in black. She sat beside her two friends—sisters in sin as they had called themselves in happier times.

Two coffins—one for Delilah and one for Suzie Fugate, which was Joy Love's real name—stood at the front of the church. The organist played a funereal fugue by Bach.

When the music was over, Father Pyron stepped up to the ambo. "Was Mary Magdalene a prostitute? She has the reputation in Western Christianity as being a repentant prostitute or loose woman, though some theologians believe that that the identity of Mary Magdalene may have been merged with the identity of the unnamed sinner who anoints Jesus' feet with her hair. Regardless of whether Mary Magdalene was a prostitute or not, we know that she found redemption in her love of the Lord and, indeed, was the first of His followers to see the risen Christ.

"Because Jesus found room in His heart and His kingdom for her, we know, too, that He has welcomed our sisters, Delilah and Suzie. I call them our sisters because many in here have benefited from Delilah's kind heart and her generous willingness to help others. And yes, I count myself in that number."

From the church, the mourners followed the hearse carrying both coffins to Boot Hill, where the two graves had already been opened. The canopy, which was normally reserved for the immediate family of the deceased, had been erected and Fancy, Candy, and Jasmine sat on the chairs provided, joined by all the bar girls of the Silver Dollar and Kennedy's Saloon.

It had been Fancy who'd invited them. "Girls like us have only each other. That makes us family."

"You dumb son of a bitch! You killed both of them! Why the hell did you kill both of them?"

"The other one came in while I was with Delilah. I didn't have no choice," Fenton said.

"Yes, you had a choice. You could have planned it better. Have you seen how many people have turned out for the funeral? Half the town is over in the cemetery right now. You think the town is going to just let this go?"

"Who would've thought there would be that many people for a whore's funeral?" Fenton asked.

"Here, take this money and go. Get out of town and don't come back."

"This . . . this is only a hunnert dollars. You said I would get two hunnert and fifty."

"That was for killing one person. You didn't do the job as contracted. You killed two."

"No, now, I ain't goin' to take that. You need to pay me what you told me you would."

"Or what? You will undo your job? How are you going to bring her back alive?"

"But this ain't right." Fenton heard the click of a hammer being drawn back as a pistol was cocked.

"I said go away."

Fenton stared at the pistol pointed toward him, then, with a shrug, he picked up the money and left. But instead of leaving town as he had been told to do, he went up the street to the Silver Dollar Saloon. "Whiskey."

The bartender poured the drink and slid the glass across the bar.

"Can you believe all the people that turned out for that whore's funeral?" Fenton asked.

"All of our girls went," the bartender said.

"She was a whore," Fenton said. "Nothin' but a damn whore." He tossed the drink down.

"You say she like there was only one. There were two of them, and even if they was whores, they didn't deserve to get murdered."

Fenton held his glass out for a refill. "Whores. They were whores."

"Whores are people, too," the bartender said.

Fenton tossed the second glass down, then held out his glass for another.

"I think maybe you should buy your whiskey somewhere else," the bartender said.

"You feelin' sorry for them whores, are you?" Fenton asked.

"Yeah, I am."

With a dismissive snort, Fenton left the saloon. As soon as he stepped outside, he saw a man dressed all in black standing in the middle of the street.

"Arnold Fenton, you are under arrest for the murder of Delilah Dupree and Suzie Fugate," Marshal Bodine called out to him.

"What? What do you mean, *murder*?"

"Come along," Bodine said.

"The hell I will!" Fenton made a desperate grab for his pistol, but before he could get the gun more than halfway out of his holster, a blazing pistol appeared in Bodine's hand.

Fenton fell facedown into the dirt and lay there without moving.

CHAPTER 26

As the funeral was wrapping up, nobody in the cemetery was aware that the killer of Delilah and Suzie had just been shot down.

As Fancy dropped dirt onto Delilah's coffin and Candy dropped dirt onto Suzie's coffin, Father Pyron read the concluding prayer. "Forasmuch as it hath pleased Almighty God of His great mercy to take unto Himself the soul of our dear sister here departed: we therefore commit her body to the ground; earth to earth, ashes to ashes, dust to dust; in sure and certain hope of the Resurrection to eternal life, through our Lord Jesus Christ; who shall change our vile body, that it may be like unto His glorious body, according to the mighty working, whereby He is able to subdue all things to himself."

As everyone began leaving the cemetery, Fancy walked over to talk to Sara Sue. "You've got a boy that's one of the kidnapped kids, don't you?"

"Yes, I do."

"Did Delilah tell you what we seen?"

"You were one of the ladies she was talking about?"

Fancy nodded her head. "Yes, ma'am, 'n I thank you for callin' me a lady, seein' as I ain't nothin' o' the kind. I wish now I hadn't a-told her nothin' 'bout us seein' them kids 'cause it was her knowin' about it that got 'er killed. I know it was."

"Oh!" Sara Sue said. "In that case, maybe you shouldn't be seen talking to me, either."

"I don't care now," Fancy said. "I want Arnold Fenton to pay for what he done. And I want those little children to go back to their mamas and papas."

"They will go back to their parents," Smoke said. "And safely."

"Who are you?" Fancy asked.

"The name is Smoke Jensen, ma'am. Mrs. Condon is my neighbor. Who is Arnold Fenton?"

"He's the one who killed Delilah and Joy."

"How do you know he's the one who did it?"

"I know, because me 'n Candy seen 'im runnin' out of the house just after we heard the shots. 'N besides us 'n Jasmine who was upstairs at the time, he was the only one in the house then."

"Did you tell the marshal this?"

"Yes, me 'n Candy both told 'im, but it didn't seem to make no difference to him. Ma'am, I hope you get your boy back safe."

"Thank you," Sara Sue said.

"Do you believe her, Smoke?" Pearlie asked as Fancy hurried away.

"Yes, I don't have any reason not to believe her. Pearlie, you see to it that Sara Sue gets safely back to the boarding-house. I'm going to have a talk with my friend the mayor. Maybe he can get The Professor to do something."

"He's already taken care of it," Kennedy said, replying to Smoke's inquiry. "If you'll go down to the undertaker's, you'll see that he has Fenton laid out on his embalming table, right now. We can thank our marshal for that."

"Bodine killed Fenton?"

"Aye, and 'tis glad I am to see that the son of a bitch paid for his brutal crime."

"I wish he hadn't killed him. I wish he had arrested him."

"Why? The brigand deserved to die."

"Oh, I don't disagree with you there," Smoke said. "But I'm sure Fenton killed Miss Dupree because she apparently had some information about the kidnapped children. And I doubt that he killed on his own. I'm sure he was paid to do it, and I would have liked to know who was really behind the killing."

"Aye, I see your point," Kennedy said. "But from what I've heard, the marshal had no choice in the matter. The brigand drew on him."

"Well, if that is the case, then, no, he didn't have any choice," Smoke said.

"What makes you think Delilah had information about the location of the children?" Kennedy asked.

"Oh, I don't know that she did have information about the location of the children, though she might have. Now that she is dead, we won't know, one way or the other." Smoke not only knew that Delilah did know where the children were, he knew that she had shared that information with Sara Sue. Even with a friend like Warren Kennedy, he thought it would be best to keep such information to himself.

"You know, I very much wanted to go to Delilah's funeral," Kennedy said. "Sure, 'n there's no way you would be for knowing this—in fact, I don't think anyone in town actually knew it—but Delilah and I"—he paused in the midst of his comment as if having difficulty continuing—"well, we had what you might call a relationship."

"No, I didn't know that," Smoke said. "If that is the case, why didn't you go to the funeral? It seemed that half the town was there."

"Aye, half the town was there 'tis exactly the reason why I couldn't go. I'm invested in businesses all over town, 'n it would not be good for business for all to know o' the feelin's Delilah 'n I had for one another. Not for me, you understand. "'Twould not bother me if people held it against me for lovin' Delilah as I did. But the people who are in business with me could have suffered, not for anything they have done, but for my own doing. 'N I couldn't be for hurting the business of others, now could I?"

"I can see how you might feel that way, Warren, but based upon the people that I saw at her funeral, I really don't think anyone in town would have thought any less of you if you had attended the funeral."

"Aye, perhaps that's right," Kennedy agreed. "But I'll be payin' my respects to her when I visit her grave."

After escorting Sara Sue safely to the boardinghouse, Pearlie hid outside for a while, just to make certain that no one showed up. Then he walked down to the Delilah House and went inside.

An elderly, white-haired woman was cleaning. "We're closed. Maybe you ain't heard nothin' about it, but Miss Dupree was kilt. I don't know if we're ever goin' to open again."

"I know," Pearlie said. "I'm real sorry about that. I was at her funeral."

"Then if you know about that, why are you here?"

"I'm here to see Miss Peterson."

The woman got a surprised look on her face. "You know Miss Fancy's real name?"

"Yes, is she here? I would like to see her."

"It won't do you no good. She's not takin' on any customers. What with Joy kilt, 'n Jasmine runnin' off after the funeral, there's only Fancy 'n Candy left. Neither one of 'em doin' that, 'n I don't know if anyone's ever goin' to do that again. Leastwise, not in this place."

Pearlie shook his head. "That's not why I want to see her. I just want to talk to her, is all. My name is Pearlie. Tell her I was with Smoke and Mrs. Condon, and we met at Miss Dupree's funeral."

"All right. Wait here," the maid said.

Fancy was sitting in Delilah's office, staring through the window. Delilah wasn't the first madam Fancy had ever worked for, but she was the first one Fancy had ever had a genuine affection for. Delilah treated everyone in the house as if they were part of her family, and though Fancy had shed tears during her funeral, she was still feeling the pain of her friend's loss.

"Miss Fancy?"

Fancy turned to the woman who had spoken.

"Yes, Rose?"

"There's a fella here who wants to see you."

"Didn't you tell him we were closed?"

"Yes, ma'am, I told him that, but he said all he wants to do is talk to you. He said you met him at the funeral."

Fancy stepped to the door and looked out into the parlor. She recognized him as one of the men she had met at the funeral. "All right. Tell him to come in."

A moment later, Pearlie knocked on the door

Almost automatically, Fancy smiled at him. "You're Pearlie, aren't you?"

"Yes, ma'am. Can I shut the door? I want to talk to you, and I don't want folks to hear."

"Well, there's no one here but Candy and Rose, but sure, shut the door if you want to."

Pearlie shut the door then, at Fancy's invitation, sat down. "Who have you told about seeing those kids?"

"Only Delilah, and then today, you, Mrs. Condon, and Smoke Jensen."

"I'm going to ask you not to tell anyone else."

"Why not? Don't you think people should know about it?"

"For one thing, Smoke and I plan to get those kids back home safely. If word gets back to the kidnappers that we know where the kids are, they may move them."

"Oh, yes. I hadn't thought of that."

"And for another thing, the more people who know that you saw them, the more dangerous it will be for you. Who else knows about them?"

"Right now, Candy is the only other person who knows."

"Tell her not to tell anyone else."

"The men out at the cabin—Keefer, Reece, Whitman, and Sanders—know that we know, but I haven't seen any of them in town since we came back."

"Smoke and I will take care of them. Do you and Candy have anyplace you could go to hide out for a while?"

Fancy smiled. "I'll bet we could go stay with Dewey Gimlin."

"Who is that?"

"He's an old trapper who lives out of town. He would never come to the house, but from time to time Candy or I would visit him."

"Who knows this?"

"Other than the three of us, nobody but Delilah knew. Mr. Gimlin is a very private man who doesn't want anyone knowin' any of his business. Truth to tell, I doubt there are half a dozen people in town who have ever even heard of him."

"You think he would put you and Candy up for a while?"

Fancy's smile grew even broader. "Are you teasing, Pearlie? I know he would."

When Smoke stepped into the marshal's office, three of his six remaining deputies were in the office with him.

Smoke had been in town long enough to learn all of the deputies by name, and he recognized Duly Plappert, Chug Slago, and Boney Walls.

"You're the fella that killed Bates, Cooper, Barnes, and Gibson, ain't you?" Plappert asked.

"I am."

"I guess you think you're pretty good with that gun."

"I'm good enough, I suppose."

"Don't you think there might be somebody out there that's better 'n you?"

"If there is, I haven't met him yet, or I wouldn't still be alive."

"Uh-huh. Tell me, Jensen, just how much longer do you think you're goin' to stay alive?" Plappert asked.

"I expect to be alive right up until the moment I'm dead."

"That might just come sooner 'n you think," Plappert said.

"That's enough, Plappert," The Professor said. "What is it, Jensen? What do you want?"

"I hear you killed Fenton," Smoke replied.

"Yes, I killed him."

"Why?"

"Because when I tried to arrest him, he tried to kill me. It was self-defense. Isn't that the way it was with you and my four deputies?"

"Something like that, yes. What I meant was when the two young ladies who worked for Delilah told you that Fenton was the one who killed Miss Dupree and Miss Fugate, you didn't pay any attention to them."

"They were whores, Jensen. I have no intention of conducting my investigations on the word of whores. To quote the great bard, 'Wisely, and slow. They stumble that run fast.'"

Smoke chuckled. "I know you were an English professor at William and Mary, but given your present reputation, I have a hard time connecting you with *Romeo and Juliet.*"

"And I have an even more difficult time believing that it is even a quote that you would recognize."

"You can thank my wife for that. But to get back to the subject, you came to believe that Fenton killed Miss Dupree and Miss Fugate, or you wouldn't have attempted to arrest him. What changed your mind?"

"Nothing changed my mind. I just thought I would talk to him and give him the opportunity to deny that he was in Delilah's establishment during the time of the shooting . . . or to explain why he was there if he didn't deny it."

"But you didn't get to ask him?"

"No, I didn't. Tell me, Jensen, why are you so interested in this case?"

"I believe that Miss Dupree knew the whereabouts of the kidnapped children. And I believe that Fenton's killing her had something to do with that."

"I see. So you are suggesting that Fenton was one of the kidnappers?"

"I would say either that or he was working for the kidnappers."

"Working for them in what way?"

"I think he was paid to kill Delilah in order to keep her from telling anyone where the kidnapped children are."

"You mean like someone offered to pay Allison to kill you?"

Smoke was surprised by the comment, but he was even more surprised by the next comment.

"Or how my deputies planned to collect that same reward by killing you?"

"Who is offering the reward?" Smoke asked.

The Professor shook his head. "I don't have any idea, and that is what makes the whole thing so fatuous. If one doesn't know from whom they are to collect the reward, why accomplish the mission, especially without guarantee of payment?"

"Did Delilah tell you where the children were being kept?" Smoke asked.

"No, why would you think she would do that?"

"Well, you are the law. It seems to me like you would be the logical place for her to go with the information."

"How do you know she even knew? Did she tell you where they were?"

Smoke smiled but didn't answer The Professor's question. "I'll be seeing you, Marshal." He turned and left.

"Plappert, I think you and Slago should keep an eye on Mr. Jensen," Bodine said.

"With pleasure," Plappert replied with a broad grin.

CHAPTER 27

New York City

Sally had still not been mistreated in any way, other than the fact that she was kept tied to the bed all the time. The only time she was untied was while she was eating or using the privy, and at this moment she was lying on the bed with her arms stretched out over her head, tied to the bedposts. Remaining in such a position for so long was very uncomfortable, and she tried, to the extent possible, to relieve the pressure on her back.

The door was open between the two rooms, and she could hear her captors talking in the other room.

"He's dead."

She had learned the identity of the three men who'd brought her to this place and recognized the speaker's voice. Gallagher was the one with the pistol, who had stepped out from the alley to confront them. The three men who had been following them, she now knew, were Kelly, Brockway, and O'Leary. One of them had hit Cal from behind, and the other had used chloroform to knock her out.

"Who's dead?" Kelly asked.

"O'Leary is dead. That damned cowboy killed him."

Cowboy? Sally thought. Smoke? A quick, happy thought flashed through her mind. Is Smoke here?

"We should have killed the son of a bitch when we had the chance," Brockway said.

Cal! They have to be talking about Cal. She realized almost instantly that her thought it might be Smoke was unreasonable. Even if he knew of her situation, he wouldn't have had time to get there yet. She was happy Cal was still alive.

"'Tis walkin' around the city he is, wearin' a pistol 'n a holster like he was ridin' the range," Brockway said.

"'N would you be for tellin' me how he can be doin' that?" Kelly asked. "Wouldn't Muldoon be for arresting him for doin' so?"

"Here's the thing," Gallagher said. "Turns out that the son of a bitch is a deputy sheriff back in Colorado, 'n now the mayor has made him a deputy in New York. He 'n Muldoon are workin' together."

"Lookin' for the woman, are they?" Brockway asked.

"Aye."

"Are we goin' to be for movin' her?" Brockway asked.

"I see no reason for doin' so," Gallagher said. "Only O'Leary knew she was here, 'n he's dead. There's two million people in this town. How are they goin' to find 'er now?"

"Aye, right you be."

"I'll be for tellin' you this, though. Our friend in Wyoming is goin' to be havin' to pay us well, seein' as this little job we're doin' for him has gotten one of us killed."

Friend in Wyoming? Who could that be? Sally wondered. And why would someone in Wyoming want me captured and held prisoner? What possible reason could there be for that?

Sally asked that question of Kelly when he came into her room an hour later, bringing her one of the two meals she was given each day.

"I don't know who it is," Kelly said. "Sure 'n all I know is that Gallagher got a telegram tellin' that you was comin', 'n we was to snatch you up."

"But why?" Sally asked. "Why did someone from Wyoming want me to be taken prisoner?"

"I don't know," Kelly said. "But I can tell you that it was for the money that we took you."

"What money?"

"'Tis a lot of questions you be askin', woman, when you should be usin' your mouth for eatin' now," Kelly scolded.

Sally asked no more questions, and after the meal, Kelly started to tie her to the headboard again.

"Mr. Kelly, please don't tie me to the bed again. You have done that every day, and the ropes are cutting off the circulation. I could wind up losing the use of my hands. Or losing them altogether."

Kelly looked back toward the door that opened into the other room. "Put your hands up there."

"Please?"

"I'll not be for tying you to the bed," Kelly said. "But keep yer hands there so that if Gallagher or Brockway looks in, they'll be for thinkin' that yer still tied up."

"Thank you, Mr. Kelly. Oh, thank you."

"'N if either of them happen to discover that you not be tied, I want you to tell 'im that you untied yourself."

"I will," she promised, stretching her hands up over her head toward the iron headboard.

Kelly wrapped the rope around them, but he didn't tie them.

Sally waited until Kelly left, then she got out of bed and walked over to the window. It was the first time she had been able to look outside since she was brought there, and her suspicion that she was very near an elevated railroad was confirmed. There, not fifty feet from the side of the building, was an elevated track. To her surprise, she wasn't on the second floor of the building as she had thought. She wasn't even with the elevated railroad, she was looking down on it. Gauging by the building across the street, she realized that she was on the fourth floor. She was much too high to escape through the window. With frustrated disappointment, she returned to the bed but didn't lie down with her hands over her head. She sat up on the bed and was still sitting there half an hour later when Gallagher came into the room.

"What are you doing sitting there like that?" Gallagher asked in a loud angry voice.

"My back was hurting from lying down, so . . ." Sally replied.

"You're supposed to be tied up."

"I got loose. Really, Mr. Gallagher, what is the advantage of keeping me tied up? Either you, or Mr. Kelly, or Mr. Brockway, and sometimes all of you are always in the other room. And because we are on the fourth floor, there's no way I can escape through the window. There is really no need to tie me."

Gallagher stared at her for a long moment, stroking his chin. "All right," he said with a nod. "I'll leave you untied."

"Thank you."

Gallagher turned to leave.

"Mr. Gallagher?"

He turned in acknowledgment of her call.

"What's going to happen to me?" Sally asked.

"I don't know."

"You don't know?"

"Whatever happens to you won't be for me to decide."

"Who is behind all this? Who wanted me taken like this, and for what reason?"

"Blimey, woman, you sure be one for askin' so many questions," Gallagher said.

"'N can you be for blamin' me, Mr. Gallagher? For sure,

'tis my ownself that's in danger here. 'N have I no right ter know about m' own fate?" Sally asked, affecting an Irish brogue.

"Is it Irish you be?"

"Aye, 'twas from Ireland m' own sweet mither came."

"He didn't say anything about you bein' Irish."

Sally wasn't Irish, but she had been around enough Irish in her youth to be able to perfectly mimic the brogue. She didn't know if it would do her any good, but she didn't think it would do her any harm.

"Would you be for tellin' me now, Mr. Gallagher, who is the blaggard that ordered you to cotch me so, 'n keep me like a wee bird in a cage?"

"'Tis an old friend is all I can say," Gallagher replied.

"'N how is it that an Irishman like you has a friend in Wyoming? Have you traveled in the West?"

"I've never been out of New York. 'Tis a friend I know from here."

"'N is he still a friend, seein' as one of yer own was killed?"

"I'll be for confessin' to you that 'twas not part o' the deal that one of us would be killed," Gallagher said. "When it comes to settlin' with the money, I'll be for askin' 'im to pay us well."

"And if he does not?"

"'Tis not for you to worry about such a thing," Gallagher replied as he turned to leave the room before Sally could ask any more questions.

Cal and Muldoon had found nothing the night before. Cal's "commission" limited him to working with a New York policeman, and Muldoon was the policeman who had been assigned to work with him. But Muldoon was available only during his watch, which had been changed from the day watch to the one from seven o'clock in the evening until three o'clock the next morning. It was Muldoon who had asked for the change. As he told Cal, most of the people they would need to see could be seen only at night. The bad thing was that Cal was too anxious to spend an entire day doing nothing while he waited for Muldoon's shift to start.

Cal wondered whether or not he should send a telegram to Smoke. He didn't want to—at least, not until he had some sort of news to report to him, hopefully positive news. It had been his hope to get Sally's kidnapping resolved quickly enough that Smoke would not have to be worried, but it was already too late for anything to be done quickly. Smoke had to be told.

Cal went to the nearest Western Union office to send the message. A little bell on the door dinged as he stepped inside, and the telegrapher looked up. Seeing a man openly wearing a pistol, the telegrapher reacted with fear.

"Oh, don't worry about the gun," Cal said, calming the telegrapher's nerves. "I'm a deputy, working with the police." He showed the telegrapher the commission paper signed by Mayor Grace.

"Indeed, sir," the telegrapher said, obviously relieved that Cal wasn't some outlaw there to do him harm. "What can I do for you, Officer?"

"I need to send a telegram to Big Rock, Colorado."

"Big Rock, Colorado? I've never heard of the place. Does Big Rock, Colorado, have a Western Union office?"

"We sure do. It's right next to the railroad depot," Cal said.

"All right. Let me look in the book and determine the routing procedures."

"Can't you just start tapping that thing to say To Big Rock?"

The telegrapher smiled. "No sir, it will have to be routed . . . I expect through Denver." He studied his book for a moment, then nodded. "Yes, just as I expected, it will go through Denver. Can you write, sir?"

"What? Yes, I can write."

The telegrapher gave him a tablet and a pencil. "Write your message for me."

Cal wrote: When Mrs. Sally and I were walking some men came up, knocked me out, and took Sally. She is missing now, but the police don't think she has been harmed because they have received no information about a woman being harmed. I have been made a deputy in the New York Police Department, and I am working with the police to try and find her. I will continue to look for her until we find her and I will keep you informed. If you want to send me a message you can reach me at the Fifth Avenue Hotel. Cal

When he was finished, he slid the message across the counter to the telegrapher.

"Oh, my. That is too bad about your friend, but this message is much too long. It will cost you a fortune. Suppose you let me rewrite it for you. I promise I will get the same information across."

"All right," Cal agreed.

SALLY MISSING STOP AM WORKING WITH POLICE TO FIND HER STOP POLICE BELIEVE SHE IS NOT HARMED AS THEY HAVE NO INFORMATION ANY WOMAN HURT STOP WILL CONTINUE TO LOOK FOR HER AND KEEP YOU INFORMED STOP REACH ME AT FIFTH AVENUE HOTEL STOP CAL

Cal examined the telegram just before it was sent. He saw that it said only that she was missing, rather than that she had actually been taken, and he was about to correct it when he decided that missing was enough.

"That will be five dollars and eighty cents," the telegrapher said.

Big Rock

A short while later the telegrapher in Big Rock took the message. "Oh," he said aloud. "Oh, dear me, this isn't good. This isn't good at all."

"What is it, Mr. Deckert?" the Western Union delivery boy asked.

"Missus Jensen is missing in New York."

"Miz Jensen? You mean Miz Smoke Jensen?"

"Yes." Quickly, Deckert printed out the message, put it in a yellow envelope, and handed it to the boy. "Here, Tommy, take this out to Sugarloaf and give it to Mr. Jensen. Ride as quickly as you can."

"Yes, sir," Tommy said.

"I'm sorry, son," Slim Taylor said when Tommy rode into Sugarloaf. In the absence of both Pearlie and Cal, Slim was acting as the foreman over the cowboys who were watching over the ranch. "Ever'one is gone right now. Mr. Jensen 'n Pearlie are up in Wyoming, and Miz Jensen 'n Cal are in New York City."

"Well, do you know how I can get ahold of Mr. Jensen?" Tommy asked. "I've got a telegram for him that's just real important."

"Well, I know he took a bull up for Mr. Condon. He said a-fore he left that if I had to get ahold of him to go see Condon."

"Where does Mr. Condon live?"

"He lives over on the Wiregrass Ranch. That's about ten miles east o' here."

"Thanks," Tommy said.

* * *

Sam Condon leaned against the post as he read the telegram. "Damn."

"Do you know how to get this telegram to Mr. Jensen?" Tommy asked.

"Yes. Send it to him in care of my wife at the Del Rey Hotel in Mule Gap, Wyoming," Sam said.

"It'll cost more to send the telegram a second time," Tommy said.

"I'll pay the fee," Sam said.

After getting his billfold, Sam gave Tommy a ten-dollar bill.

"Oh, it won't cost that much."

"You've had a long ride out here to find out how to deliver an important message," Sam said. "Young man, I admire your adherence to the pursuit of your duty. You keep the change."

"Gee, Mr. Condon, thank you!" Tommy said, smiling broadly at his good fortune.

"Get the message through, son. It's very important."

"Yes, sir, I will."

CHAPTER 28

French Creek Canyon

"Where's Whitman?" Keefer asked.

"We was plumb out of whiskey," Reece said, "so he went into town to get some."

"Not Mule Gap, I hope. Remember, we ain't s'posed to go into Mule Gap except on business, 'n whiskey ain't business."

"Don't worry. He went to Warm Springs."

"All right," Keefer said. "We could do with some whiskey around here. I'm goin' to get the Condon boy to write the note, then I'll be takin' it in to his mama and get the money. Sanders, I want you to come with me."

"All right," Sanders said.

"Reece, that'll leave you alone with the kids until Whitman gets back. Think you can handle that?"

"Hell, yes, I can handle it. What is there to handlin' a handful of snot-nosed brats?"

"Just don't both of you get drunk when Whitman gets back with the whiskey, is all," Keefer ordered. "Somebody needs to be sober to keep an eye on the kids."

Leaving the others in the bigger house, Keefer started toward the cabin.

"Mr. Keefer is coming," Wee said.

"I wonder what he wants," Burt said. "He don't normally come over here. It's always one of the others."

"Can you see any of the nail holes?" Thad asked anxiously.

"No, they're well covered," Lorena replied.

The six gathered in a group, looking toward the door as they heard the lock being opened.

Keefer stepped into the cabin. "What are you all standin' together like that for?"

"Because we're all real good friends," Thad replied.

"You got a smart mouth, you know that, kid?"

"I hope so. I've always considered being smart as a virtue," Thad replied.

Lorena laughed, and Keefer shot her an angry glance.

"Here," he said, handing a paper and pencil to Thad. "I need you to write a note to your mama so she'll know you are alive 'n well."

"No," Thad said.

"What do you mean, you won't do it?" Keefer asked. "Your mama is the one who asked for the note."

"I have a feeling you'll be using the note for more than just to let her know I'm alive."

"Write the note, boy," Keefer demanded,

"No."

"Thad, don't you think your mother might want to know that you are all right?" Lorena asked.

"Listen to the girl," Keefer said. "Remember, your mama is the one who asked for the note in the first place."

"All right. I'll do it," Thad said after a moment of consideration. "I guess you are right."

"Maybe you can put all our names in the note too,"

Lorena suggested. "That will let our parents know that we are all right, as well."

"Yeah, that would be a good idea," Thad agreed. "I'll do that."

"No, you ain't goin' to do nothin' like that," Keefer said. "Your mama said she wanted to see a note from you. She didn't say nothin' 'bout all the other kids we got here."

"If you expect a note from me, it will also have everybody else's name on it," Thad said. "Otherwise, I won't write it."

"Mr. Keefer, what will be the harm?" Lorena asked. "I'm sure that all Mrs. Condon wants is to know that Thad is alive and well. This note will tell her that. If you are expecting to collect money for the rest of us, don't you think our parents should also know that we are all right?"

"Yeah," Keefer finally agreed. "All right. You can put ever'body else's name in the note, too."

Taking the pencil and paper Keefer presented him, Thad began to write.

Ma, I am not hurt. I am worried about Pa. There are five others with me. Will you tell their parents they are all right, too? They are Lorena Coy and Marilyn Grant, those are the girls. The boys are Travis Calhoun, Burt Rowe, and Eddie Blackwell. I love you, Ma.

> *Sincerely,*
> *Your son,*
> *Thaddeus R. Condon*

Thad showed the note to Lorena, who read it, then giggled. "Why are you laughing?"

"Why did you sign your entire name to the note? Don't you think your mother knows your name?"

"When we learned how to write letters in school, the teacher said we should always sign our whole name so that the person we are writing to would know who the letter came from."

Lorena smiled. "I suppose you're right." She folded the note in half then ran her finger and thumb along the crease.

"Don't do that!" Thad said, cringing.

"Don't do what?" Lorena asked, surprised by Thad's outburst.

"Don't rub your fingers on paper!" he said. "I can't stand to rub my hands on paper, and I can't stand to watch anyone else do it."

Lorena laughed. "You're the strangest boy I've ever met." She handed the note to Keefer.

With the note stuck down in his shirt pocket, Keefer returned to the house, where Sanders had already saddled their horses. Reece was out on the front porch, watching.

"Reece, you keep an eye on the kids," Keefer said as he swung into the saddle. "I hate to leave only one person here—we've never done that before—but I'm goin' to have to. I'll be needin' Sanders with me when I go into town to get the money from the Condon woman."

"Don't you be worryin' none about me. I'll be just fine," Reece said. "Just go get the money."

"If she gives us the money, are we going to come back here and get the kid and take him to her?" Sanders asked.

"It depends on what the boss says," Keefer replied.

Reece stayed out on the front porch, watching them ride off. Once they were out of sight, he looked over toward the little cabin and unconsciously rubbed himself as he thought of the oldest girl. "Guess what, little girl," he said quietly. "Now that the others are gone, me 'n you are goin' to have us a little fun."

Mule Gap

"When are we going?" Pearlie asked.

"We aren't going. Only I am."

"You mean I'm not going? According to Fancy, there are four men out there watching the kids. You plan to take on all four of 'em by yourself?"

"Yes," Smoke said. "Look, Pearlie, you're still wounded. I'm afraid that if you go, you could open up the wound and start bleeding again."

"If I do, you can always stick a piece of my dirty shirt in the hole to stop the bleeding," Pearlie suggested.

Smoke chuckled. "That's true. I could do that, but I have something else I want you to do. Sara Sue is staying with Mrs. Coy. I want you to keep an eye on both of them today. They also know where the kids are located, and someone might decide that is a problem."

Pearlie nodded. "Yeah. Yeah, I can see how that might be. All right. I'll watch over them."

"Thanks. That'll make my job easier, knowing that you're looking out for them."

Astride a rented horse, Smoke started west along French Creek Road, so named because it ran parallel with French Creek, a rapid stream that made gurgling and bubbling sounds as the white water broke over the rocks and swept the smaller pebbles downstream. He was less than two miles out of town when he saw Deputy Plappert and Deputy Slago step into the middle of the road. Both deputies had already drawn their pistols from their holsters.

Plappert held up his hand. "Where do you think you're a-goin'?"

"Oh, I'm just goin' for a ride," Smoke replied.

"Do your ridin' back toward town," Plappert ordered.

"Why should I do that? I've seen town. I thought I'd just take a ride out in the country."

"Marshal Bodine don't trust you. He wants you to stay in town," Plappert said.

Slowly and unthreateningly, Smoke dismounted and glanced over toward Slago. "Can he talk?"

"Of course he can talk," Plappert replied.

Smoke was amused by the fact that it was Plappert, not Slago, who had responded.

"Are you planning on collecting that five-thousand-dollar reward that's been offered for me?"

"Could be," Plappert replied.

"Who are you planning to collect it from?"

"Seein' as how you ain't goin' to be the one collectin', that ain't none of your business," Plappert said.

Smoke chucked. "I guess you have a point there. But don't I have to be dead, first, before you can collect it?"

"Yeah, you do, don't you?" Plappert replied.

During the entire conversation, the two deputies had their guns in their hands. Though he was still holding the gun, Slago had lowered it so that it was no longer pointing at Smoke. Plappert's gun was pointed toward Smoke, but it wasn't cocked.

"What was it you said once? That you planned to live right up until the moment you died?" Plappert asked.

"That's what I said, all right."

An evil grin spread across Plappert's face. "This is that moment."

Smoke started his draw the instant he saw Plappert's thumb tighten on the hammer of his pistol. He drew and fired before Plappert could even cock his pistol.

"What the hell?" Slago shouted, bringing his pistol up and cocking it. But he was unable to get a shot off before Smoke's gun roared.

"How about that? Turns out you could speak, after all," Smoke said.

* * *

At the small cabin, Reece unlocked the door then stepped inside. "You," he said, pointing to Lorena. "Can you cook?"

"Yes, I can cook," she replied.

"We got a mess of fish. If you'll fry 'em up, you can have fish for dinner."

"Oh, goody!" Wee said. "I like fried fish."

"Why do you want me to cook, all of a sudden?" Lorena asked. "You've never asked me to cook before."

"We've never had a mess of fish before," Reece said. "Besides, ever'one else is gone. I'm the only one here, right now, 'n I don't plan on doin' the cookin'. Now, do you want some fried fish or not?"

"All right," Lorena said. "I'll go with you."

Lorena stepped onto the front porch with Reece, and waited as he, again, locked the door.

Thad stood at the window and watched as Reece led Lorena toward the house. He had a funny feeling about the man taking her over to the big house. Thad couldn't put his finger on just what was making him uneasy . . . but he didn't feel good about Lorena being alone in the house with Reece.

He stepped back to look at the boards they had been working on. Their efforts over the previous days had removed every nail from six of the floorboards, and it was time to pull them up. "Let's get these boards pulled up."

"I thought we weren't going to do it until tonight when nobody could see us," Travis said.

"There's nobody here now but Reece, and he's in the house with Lorena," Thad said. "He won't be paying any attention to us, and he won't see what's happening."

"I don't want to go and leave Lorena behind," Wee said.

"I promise you, Wee, we won't leave her behind," Thad

said. "As a matter of fact, as soon as we get the boards up, I'm going to go check on her."

"What if Mr. Reece sees you?" Marilyn asked.

"I'll be very careful," Thad promised.

They began working on the boards, but it wasn't as easy to pull them up as he had thought it would be. Even though they were no longer secured, the fit was so tight that they couldn't get a grip on the first one. Thad tried using a nail to get to the end of it, but that didn't work.

"Try a bunch of nails," Marilyn suggested.

Thad took her suggestion and with four nails stuck down between the end of the board and the wall, they were able to lift the end of the board up high enough to get a hand around it. Once they did that, the board came up easily.

They had no trouble with the remaining floorboards. As each board came up, the hole was widened, and it was easy to grab the next. It took but a few minutes to open the hole, and as Thad knelt down over it, he could smell the dirt beneath the cabin, and hear the sound of the flowing creek that was only a few feet away.

"All right," he said, giving the orders. "I'll go through first and check on Reece and Lorena. The rest of you wait here until I come back for you."

"I don't want to leave Lorena," Wee said again.

"I told you, Wee, aren't going to leave her," Thad promised.

"What if you are seen?" Burt asked.

"I'm just going to have to take that chance," Thad said. "Remember, wait here until I come back."

"What if you don't come back?" Travis asked.

"Then put the boards back over the hole and swear that you don't know how I got out." Thad went through the hole, dropped down onto his belly, and wriggled out from under the cabin. Staying on his stomach, he wriggled across the distance that separated the two buildings.

CHAPTER 29

Inside the main house neither Lorena nor Reece were aware that Thad had escaped from the cabin and was crawling toward the house. Busy rolling the fish in cornmeal, Lorena was also unaware of what was going on behind her. Reece had taken off his boots and shirt, removed his gun belt and holster, and was stepping out of his pants. He was staring at Lorena with a wide leering grin.

"I'll need some grease," Lorena said, turning back toward Reece. "Do you know where—" Seeing him standing behind her wearing only his underwear, Lorena gasped. "Mr. Reece, what are you doing?"

"I'm goin' to make a woman out of you, girl," he said. "'N when we're through, you're goin' to thank me."

"No! Get away, get away!"

Lorena's shout alerted Thad, and standing up quickly, he looked through the window. It took only one glance for him to realize what was going on.

Running to the front door, he jerked it open and shouted, "Get away from her, you son of a bitch!"

Reece grabbed a butcher knife lying on the kitchen counter. "How the hell did you get here? I'm going to split you open like gutting a hog!"

Thad felt a surge of fear, then saw Reece's pistol belt

draped over a chair. Moving quickly, he grabbed the gun and turned it toward Reece. "Drop the knife!"

"I will, after I use it on you," Reece said with a confident grin.

Thad pulled the trigger, but nothing happened. At the last minute, even as Reece was lunging toward him, he remembered to pull the hammer back. He did that and pulled the trigger. There was no danger of him missing the mark. Reece was so close to him the only way he could have missed would be to jerk the gun to one side.

The expression on Reece's face changed from one of confidence to one of total shock. With his eyes open wide, he took a couple steps back, dropped the knife, and slapped his hands over the bullet hole in his chest. "Why, you little . . ." Reece gasped. His eyes rolled up into his head, then he fell.

"Oh, Thad!" Lorena said. "He was going to . . . he was . . ."

"I know." Thad dropped down to one knee and made a closer examination of the man he had just shot. "Well, he won't bother you again. He'll never bother anyone again."

"Is he dead?"

"Yeah, he's dead." Thad stood up, then he walked over to get the pistol belt and strap it on. "We need to get out of here before the others come back."

"How did you get out of the cabin?"

"I went down through the hole. Did you see what he did with the key?"

"Yes, it's hanging on the nail next to the door."

Thad grabbed the key. "Good. This way, the others won't have to go through the floor."

When Thad unlocked the front door to the cabin a moment later, he saw the other four gathered fearfully in the corner. "What are you all doing over there?"

"We heard a shot," Travis said. "We thought Reece had killed you."

"No, I killed Reece," Thad replied, speaking as calmly as

if he had just said that the sun was shining. "Come on. Let's go."

The others joined him without hesitation, and a moment later all six were below the bank of French Creek. They could stand without breaking the skyline, and even if Keefer and Sanders returned at that very moment, they would not see them.

"Which way?" Travis asked.

"When Wee and I were brought here, we were coming west," Lorena said.

"Then we'll go east," Thad said.

"It'll be faster if we go on the road," Travis suggested.

Thad shook his head. "We can't do that. We'll have to stay down here by the creek. Keefer and Sanders were going into Mule Gap to deliver my note. We don't want to run into either of those bastards."

"Oh," Wee said. "You said a bad word."

"That's all right, Wee," Lorena said. "These sons of bitches are bastards."

The others chuckled.

"I think we'd better get going," Thad suggested. "I want to be a long way from here before the others come back."

The six started following the creek bed with Thad in front, then Lorena. Then Wee, and Marilyn, while Travis brought up the rear.

"I'm scared," Wee said. "Are you scared, Marilyn?"

"Yes."

"Are you scared, Burt?"

"No, I'm just glad to be out of there."

"Are you scared, Travis?"

"No, I'm like Burt. I'm just glad to get away from there."

"Are you afraid, Lorena?"

"No, I'm not afraid."

"Why aren't you afraid?"

Lorena looked at Thad and smiled. "As long as Thad is with us, I'm not afraid."

"Thad?" Wee said.

"What?"

"I think Lorena likes you," he said with a broad smile.

Welsh's Boarding House, Mule Gap

"I hope you like apple pie, Mr. Pearlie," Sandra Coy said. "I baked it last night."

"I love apple pie," Pearlie replied with an appreciative grin. "And you can just call me Pearlie. No *mister* is needed."

"All right. Pearlie it is," Sandra said as she cut three pieces of pie while Sara Sue was pouring three cups of coffee.

"Pearlie, do you think Smoke will be able to find the kids and bring them back?" Sandra asked.

"I don't think he will, I know he will," Pearlie said as he picked up a fork to dig into the pie.

"But won't men be there guarding the children?" Sara Sue asked.

"There are four men there," Pearlie said as he took his first bite. "Mrs. Coy—"

"Sandra."

Pearlie gave a brief nod. "Sandra, this is a mighty fine pie."

"Four? There is just Smoke against four men?" Sara Sue said.

"The odds are a bit uneven, I know. I mean, there just being four of them against Smoke. But they have nobody but themselves to thank for being put into such a position."

Sandra laughed. "Are you saying that the four men are in more danger than Mr. Jensen?"

"Yes," Pearlie replied without further explanation. "Do you think I could have another cup of coffee?"

Along French Creek

Smoke draped the bodies of Plappert and Slago over their horses, gave both horses a slap on the rump, and started them back at a trot. He knew they would return to the livery. It would be quite a shock to Evans, but he would, no doubt, get them back to the marshal to be taken care of.

Smoke had a pretty good idea where the kids were being kept. On a previous trip to Mule Gap, he had seen the deserted house and cabin and had examined them out of curiosity.

"Did you hear shootin'?" Keefer asked.

"I can't hardly hear nothin', loud as that damn creek is."

"I thought I heard gunfire, but I guess not."

"Hey, how come, do you think, that there ain't none of the other kids' parents offered to give us any money yet?" Sanders asked.

"That ain't our problem," Keefer said. "Right now our only job is to collect the money for the boy."

"We goin' to let the boy go?"

"We're goin' to do exactly what the chief tells us to do." Keefer said as they rounded the bend. Then he saw him. "Son of a bitch! It's Jensen!"

Smoke had heard the two men talking, so he wasn't as surprised to see them as they were to see him. "Where are the kids?" he called out.

The answer to Smoke's query was gunfire as both kidnappers drew their guns and began shooting.

Smoke had shouted the question with no real expectation of any kind of response other than what he had gotten. His

own gun was in his hand as quickly as Keefer's and Sanders's were in theirs. However, Smoke wasn't riding Seven. Seven had been a good and stable partner in any gunfight, but the rental horse was anything but. He reared up and twisted around, which had the positive effect of making Smoke a more difficult target. The negative effect was making it hard for Smoke to be effective in his own shooting.

For a few seconds, the valley echoed and reechoed with gunfire, then Smoke dismounted and was able, in but two more shots, to knock both Keefer and Sanders from their saddles. Their horses galloped away with empty saddles. Smoke's rental horse would have done the same thing if he hadn't been holding so securely on to the reins.

With his horse calmed down and his gun in hand, Smoke advanced cautiously to examine the two men he had just engaged. The man he didn't recognize was already dead, but Keefer was still breathing in labored gasps.

"Where are the kids?" Smoke asked.

"You go to hell," Keefer said.

"What a fine thing to say as you're dying," Smoke replied, but Keefer didn't hear him. He had already drawn his last breath.

Smoke saw a piece of paper sticking out of Keefer's pocket, and removing it, saw that it was the note Sara Sue had demanded. "All right. We know the kids are all alive and well." Having spoken the words aloud, however, he felt foolish for talking to himself. It had never seemed as if he had been talking to himself when he carried on such conversations with Seven. Then they were conversations, not soliloquies. Seven, invariably, had responded to Smoke's words by whickers, whinnies, or understanding shakes of his head.

Although he didn't like to leave the two men where they'd fallen, he didn't really have much choice in the matter as both their horses had run off. So, leaving the two

men, Smoke remounted and continued to follow the creek road. He wasn't looking for the cabin—he knew where it was—he was merely advancing toward it.

He heard the sound of voices ahead and pulled the horse to a halt in order to listen more intently. It sounded like kids' voices. Were they being brought out by their kidnappers? No, that didn't seem likely. The voices weren't coming from the road, but from below the bank on the creek itself.

Smoke headed the rental horse into a growth of trees, dismounted, then tied him there. Pulling his pistol, he moved back down closer to the creek, stood behind a tree, and waited. If the kids were being escorted against their will, he intended to take care of it.

"How much farther, Lorena?" That was definitely a very young voice.

"I don't think it's too much farther," a girl's voice said.

"Quit talking, Wee. We don't want anyone to hear us." That was definitely Thad's voice.

Smoke saw them then, six young people with Thad in the lead. There were no adults with them. They had to have had escaped.

"The only one hearing you is me, Thad," Smoke said, stepping out into the open.

"Thad!" Lorena said, her voice elevated by fright.

"It's all right, Lorena. That's my friend, Mr. Jensen!" Thad said happily.

Thad started running toward Smoke, and the others joined him. Without embarrassment, Thad embraced Smoke, then he introduced the others. "Mr. Jensen, how is my pa?"

"He's at home with bandages wrapped around him," Smoke said. "But Doctor Urban says he's going to be just fine. Come on up onto the road. It'll be easier walking up here. I'll go back to town with you."

"Where's Seven?" Thad asked, seeing the rental horse.

"Seven was killed, Thad."

"The kidnappers did it?"

"I don't think Seven's killers had anything to do with the kidnappers, but they were shooting at Pearlie and me, and they killed Seven and they shot Pearlie."

"Oh, Pearlie has been shot?"

"Yes, but like your pa, he'll be all right." Smoke smiled. "And your ma is in Mule Gap, waiting for you. I expect she's going to be one happy lady. I expect all your parents are going to be happy to see you," he added.

"I'll be glad to see my mama and papa," Wee said.

"All right, boys, I got the whiskey!" Whitman shouted, returning to the house and cabin. "I got us four bottles, that ought to hold us for a—" Whitman paused in midsentence when he noticed that the door to the cabin was standing wide open.

"What the hell? Hey! The cabin door is open," he shouted as he dismounted and hurried into the cabin. There he saw that the cabin was empty, and there was a big hole in the floor. *That's probably the way they escaped,* he thought, but then the door was standing wide open. Why would they go through a hole in the floor, if they could just go through the door?

Whitman hurried to the house to tell the others, but when he got there, he saw nothing but Reece's half-naked and fully dead body. Whitman didn't know where Keefer and Sanders were, but he figured they were probably in pursuit of the kids.

For a moment, he considered trying to catch up with them, but he figured they had too big a lead on him. The best thing to do, he decided, was to go into town and tell the boss.

Halfway to town, he came across the bodies of Keefer and Sanders.

CHAPTER 30

New York City

Cal had still heard nothing back from Smoke, and that confused and worried him. Why hadn't Smoke replied? He wondered if he should send another telegram, and if so, what should he say? Should he word the telegram in such a way as to make the situation more critical? Maybe Smoke didn't get the telegram. The telegrapher said he had never heard of Big Rock. Maybe they couldn't find it.

But no, that wasn't likely. Big Rock did have a Western Union, and they got telegrams all the time. Maybe he should send another one asking Smoke to come to New York.

No, Cal didn't want to do that. He'd been with Sally when she was taken. He was responsible for her, and he was the one who should get her back. Muldoon had said just last night that they were making progress, but Cal would like to know just what kind of progress they were making. It was certainly nothing that he could measure.

He went downstairs to check the clock. He had just enough time to eat his supper then go to the police precinct for the change of watch.

"Hello, Cal," the dining room waiter said. "Any word on Mrs. Jensen yet?"

"No, Charley, not yet," Cal replied. He and the waiter had become acquainted over the last few days.

Charley had been intrigued by Cal's Western garb, and confessed that he had always wanted to go west and be a cowboy. "I hope you find her, and that she is unharmed."

"I'll find her," Cal insisted as he picked up the menu.

"Don't eat the beef tonight," Charley said, speaking so quietly that no one but Cal could hear. "It isn't a very good cut and is quite tough."

"What do you suggest?"

"The pork roast is quite good."

"Thanks."

Cal had never actually seen a big city police department before, so he had never seen a watch change, either. He found the entire thing very fascinating but was glad he was an observer rather than a participant in the event.

It began with the police lining up like soldiers in a formation, then the watch commander spoke, giving them the latest information. "The Five Points Gang is giving us trouble again. Vito Costaconti got of jail last week, and word on the street is he's gone right back to his old ways. Keep an eye out for him.

"Also, Officer Muldoon is looking for a woman—"

"Does your wife know that, Mickey?" one of the policemen called out, and the others in the watch laughed.

"Here, now!" the watch commander said, scolding them by his tone of voice. "There will be none of that! It so happens that this is a fine lady of character, a visitor to our city when she got taken by person or persons unknown. And I'll also tell you this. Himself, His Honor, the mayor has taken an interest in this case.

"Muldoon and our new deputy, Cal Wood"—the watch commander looked toward Cal, nodded his head, and

smiled—"are the two assigned to looking for the lady, but I want all of you to keep your eyes and your ears open. And if you hear anything, let us know."

"Lieutenant, it might help us in the search if you could be for tellin' us the lady's name," one of the policeman said. "That is, if it's not being kept a secret."

"That would be Jensen," the lieutenant said. "Mrs. Kirby Jensen."

"What's her first name, Lieutenant?"

The watch commander looked toward Cal.

"Miz Sally," Cal said automatically, then he clarified it. "Sally is her first name."

"All right, gentlemen, you have the watch orders, turn out now, and remember"—the lieutenant held up his finger—"it's us against them."

The watch was dismissed, and Muldoon went over to join Cal.

"I'm sorry, lad, that we've no been successful so far. 'Tis sure I am that she's still alive or we woulda heard about it. The brigands are holding her as prisoner somewhere, but the why of it escapes me. It can't be for a ransom, for who would know that her husband is a rich man? And how would they be for getting in touch with him?"

"I sent Smoke a telegram telling him about Miz Sally, but I've not heard anything from him."

Mule Gap

"I wonder why we haven't heard anything from Smoke," Sara Sue said. "I'm beginning to get a little worried."

"Don't be worried," Pearlie said. "Smoke will be back with the children, all safe and sound."

"You say that with such confidence, Pearlie. How can you be so sure?"

"I've known Smoke for a long time now. I've seen him

in situations you would swear he could never escape, but he always does."

"I suppose that's why they write books about him," Sara Sue said with a smile."

"They write books about Smoke Jensen?" Sandra asked, surprised by the comment.

"Yeah, they sure do," Pearlie said, smiling. "But I tell you the truth. He's not too happy about being a character in a dime novel."

There was a knock on the door then, so loud that it made all three of them jump.

"Yes? Who is it?" Sandra called.

"Do you have Miz Condon in there?" a man called from the other side of the door.

Sandra looked over toward Pearlie.

"Who wants to know?" Pearlie replied.

"There's a man in there, Angus," a second voice said.

There was another knock. *"Open the door!"* The order was loud and insistent.

Pearlie took off his boots.

"What are you doing?" Sara Sue asked.

Pearlie held his finger over his lips, then signaled for Sara Sue to get under the bed.

"Open the door!" the voice was louder and more demanding. The knock was much louder, too, and so heavy it was causing the door to shake on its hinges.

"Sandra, get in the bed and pull the covers up to your chin," Pearlie said.

"What?"

"Just do it, please."

Sandra did so as the loud knocking continued.

"Open the door!"

"Just a minute, just a minute. Hold your horses. I'm coming," Pearlie said as he stripped out of his shirt, tossed it casually onto the foot of the bed, then tousled his hair. Bare

from the waist up, except for the part of the bandage that could be seen sticking up from his pants, he padded barefoot across the floor, unbuttoning the top three buttons of his trousers.

He opened the door, but only partway. "What do you want?" he demanded.

Deputies Zimmerman and Delmer pushed into the room. Sandra let out a little scream of alarm.

"Here!" Pearlie demanded angrily. "What do you think you are doing?"

"We're lookin' for Miz Condon," Zimmerman said.

"Well, as you can see, she isn't in here. Why are you looking for Miz Condon here, anyway? I believe you will find her at the hotel."

"She ain't there," Delmer said.

"Then I have no idea where she is. What do you want her for, anyway?" Pearlie asked.

"The Professor wants to put her into . . . what was that he said, Boots?"

"Protective custody," Zimmerman replied.

"Yes, well, I think she would appreciate that. But go look for her somewhere else. As you can clearly see, you have interrupted a rather delicate moment here."

Delmer laughed. "Yeah, I can see that you're . . . busy."

The two men left, and Sandra started to get out of bed. Pearlie held out his right hand and held the finger of his left hand over his lips in a signal to be quiet.

Sandra looked at him confused by his action, but a few seconds later Pearlie's action was validated when the door was jerked open again.

"Now what?" Pearlie demanded angrily.

Without actually coming into the room, the two men glanced around then left again.

Pearlie walked over to the window and looked out. Not until he saw the two deputies walking away did he say

anything. "All right, ladies, you can both come out now." He reached for his shirt.

"Oh, that was so frightening," Sandra said. "But I'm confused. Those were both deputies . . . why should we fear them?"

"It was deputies that shot me, remember," Pearlie said. "Smoke doesn't trust your marshal and his deputies, and neither do I."

"Oh!" Sandra said, lifting her hand to her mouth

"What is it?"

"Those men! They will tell everyone that we . . . that is . . . what they saw. I'll never be able to hold my head up in this town again."

"Then come to Big Rock," Sara Sue invited. "I know that Sam and I can find something much better for you than what you are doing now. And you can stay with us until you get settled."

Smoke and the six children were walking on the road.

When they came close to where he had left the bodies of Keefer and Sanders, he held up his hand. "Wait a minute. When we get around this next bend, you kids are likely to see something you've never seen before, and I want you to be ready for it."

"You mean dead people?" Thad asked.

"Yes."

"It's Keefer and Sanders, isn't it?"

"I expect so," Smoke said. "I left them there, but if you kids don't want to see the bodies, I can go up now and move them."

"I don't want you to leave us," Marilyn said.

"Me, either," Burt added.

"I saw my grandpa when he was dead," Wee said.

"Well, your grandpa was laid out in a coffin, nice and neat," Smoke said.

"No, he wasn't. He was on the porch swing with his head hanging down."

"All right," Smoke said. "Just so you know."

The two bodies were lying just where Smoke had left them. He had been concerned that the buzzards or coyotes might have gotten to them, which would have made a rather gory picture for the children to see, but the bodies were, thus far, undisturbed.

The children looked at the bodies with hesitant curiosity, then hurried on by.

"I'm tired," Wee said a while later. "Can we stop and rest?"

"No, I want to go home," Travis said.

"I do, too," Marilyn added.

"What if I picked you up and let you ride on the horse?" Smoke asked. "Would that be all right?"

"Yes!" Wee said enthusiastically. "I would like that!"

About half an hour after Smoke and the children had passed by the bodies of Keefer and Sanders, Whitman came across them. "What the hell?" he said aloud, pulling his horse to a stop.

First Reece was dead, and now he'd found Keefer and Sanders. Clearly there had been a rescue made of the children, and it had to be several men involved in order to kill all three of them.

Frightened that there might be someone close by waiting specifically for him, Whitman dismounted and led his horse off the road and into the trees. He snaked the Winchester out of the saddle sheath, jacked a round into the chamber, then lay down behind the rock in such a way as to afford him a view of the road in both directions.

If someone was coming after him, he would be ready for them.

When Smoke and the children came into town about two hours later, Smoke was leading the horse, and Wee was sitting in the saddle, holding on to the saddle horn. All the others were walking.

Bill Lewis was sweeping the porch in front of his drugstore when he saw the entourage coming into town. Not sure what he was seeing, he held the broom for a moment and stared at them.

"Hello, Mr. Lewis!" Wee called. "Do you see me riding this horse?"

"I'll be damned! It's the children," Lewis said. At first, he spoke the words quietly, then realizing the significance of it, he shouted the news at the top of his voice. "It's the children! The kidnapped children have been returned!"

The entrance of the little entourage raised quite a commotion in town, and word spread quickly The first of the parents to react were Richard and Millicent Blackwell, whose Emporium was right next to the Lewis Apothecary. Both came running out to meet their child

"Wee!" Mrs. Blackwell shouted.

"Mama!" Wee let go of the saddle horn and stretched his arms out toward his mother. The sudden action caused him to lose his balance, and he fell.

"Wee!" Mrs. Blackwell shouted again, but in alarm.

Thad, who was standing close by, caught the boy as he tumbled from the saddle.

By the time the children reached the middle of town, Sara Sue and Thad had made a happy reunion, as had Lorena and her mother Sandra.

"Thad saved us, Mama," Lorena said proudly. "He saved all of us."

"Thad did?" Sara Sue asked in surprise.

"That's right," Smoke said. "By the time I got there, they were already free. I found them walking along the side of a creek."

"Thad! You're wearing a pistol!" Sara Sue said, noticing it for the first time."

"Yes, ma'am," Thad replied. Taking the gun belt off, he handed it to Smoke. "I don't suppose I'll be needing this again."

Lorena noticed that her mother was standing next to Thad's mother. "Mama, do you know Thad's mother?"

"Oh, sweetheart, Sara Sue Condon and I are great friends," Sandra replied.

"Lorena likes Thad," Wee said.

"They're dead. All three of them are dead," Whitman was reporting. "First thing, I found Reece dead in the house, then I found Keefer 'n Sanders lying dead out on the creek 'bout halfway into town. 'N here's the thing . . . Reece was half-naked, he was. Half-naked with a bullet hole in his chest."

"Why weren't you there with them?"

"We was out of whiskey, 'n I went inter town to get it. It warn't my fault. I mean it was just a bunch of kids, 'n they was locked up in a cabin. Who woulda thought that three men couldn't look after six kids?"

"Half-naked you say? There's no doubt in my mind, but that Reece was going after one of the little girls and managed to lose control of the situation. The son of a bitch never could keep his pecker in his pants."

"His pecker was still in his pants," Whitman said.

"This has cost us fifty thousand dollars, fifteen thousand dollars for the boy, and another thirty-five for the rest of

them. All because you went into town to get whiskey, and Reece couldn't keep his pecker in his pants."

"His pecker was in his pants," Whitman repeated.

"The kids are all back safe, now. With Keefer, Sanders, and Reece dead, there's no way to connect us to the kidnapping."

"Except for me. The kids seen me lots of times."

"That's right, isn't it? My suggestion is that you get out of town and stay out of sight."

CHAPTER 31

As all the children began to reconnect with their parents, Smoke stepped into the marshal's office, where he found Bodine sitting behind his desk, playing a game of solitaire. "I'm a little surprised to see you setting in here, with all the kids returned."

"It is as you said. All the children have been returned. What purpose would it serve me to be out in the middle of it? After all, you are the White Knight himself, arriving on a prancing steed after having rescued the princess in distress," Bodine said sarcastically. "I wouldn't want to steal any of your glory."

Smoke chuckled, overlooking the sarcasm. "Wrong on both accounts, Bodine. I wasn't riding a prancing steed, I was walking. And I didn't rescue the children. They escaped by themselves."

"How did they manage that?"

"By taking advantage of the opportunity when it presented itself. I found them on the bank of French Creek, heading into town. Had I not seen them, they would have made it into town on their own."

"Apparently the kidnappers were unaware of the courage and ingenuity of the young people in their charge," Bodine said.

"Apparently so," Smoke replied.

"Why are you here, Jensen? Did you come to tell me that the children were freed? Obviously I already know that. Everyone in town is aware of that bit of information."

"No, I came to tell you there are two bodies lying on the bank of French Creek."

"Yes, I know that as well. That would be Fred Keefer and Clyde Sanders. Did you kill them?"

"Yes."

"I thought you said you had nothing to do with the children's escape."

"I didn't."

"Then why did you kill them?"

"Because they were trying to kill me. I happened onto them as I was going to the cabin where the children were being held."

"Wait a minute. You knew where the children were being held, and you didn't tell me?"

"It was my understanding, Bodine, that you knew as well. Delilah did tell you where the children were, didn't she?"

"Did you kill Elmer Reece as well?" Bodine asked, pointedly avoiding Smoke's question.

"Reece? No. Who is Reece, and why do you ask if I killed him?"

"He was found dead in the house where the kidnapped children were being held."

Smoke thought of Thad, and remembered that he had been wearing a pistol belt when they met on the creek bank. Had Thad killed the man Bodine was talking about? If so, he had said nothing about it. And Smoke was glad Thad hadn't spoken of it. Someone with less moral fiber would have, no doubt, bragged about it.

"How did you get that information so fast?" Smoke

asked. "We just got into town. And how did you know the names of the two men I killed?"

"A good citizen found all three of the bodies and made the report," Bodine said. "I've already got some of my deputies out to recover the bodies."

"What about Plappert and Slago? They were a couple of your deputies, weren't they?"

"*Were* is the operative word," The Professor said. "I sent them out on a routine scouting mission, and both of them returned draped over their horses. You wouldn't know anything about that, would you?"

"Apparently they were trying to collect on that five-thousand-dollar reward that someone, as yet unknown, has put out on me. That is, I think it is still a person unknown. Do you have any idea who it might be?"

"No idea at all," Bodine replied.

"Too bad. I would like to know what that reward is all about."

"Will there be anything else, Mr. Jensen?" Bodine asked, picking up the deck of cards, expressing his interest in continuing the game.

"No," Smoke replied. "There will be nothing else."

When Smoke stepped back out into the street, the rescued children, all now reunited with their parents, were the center of attention of a large and still growing crowd of people celebrating the return. Joining the gathering of the children, parents, and citizens, was the mayor of Mule Gap.

Kennedy held up his arms in a call for attention. "Ladies and gentleman, may I have your attention, please? I'd like to say a few words."

"Leave it to a politician to give a speech at the drop of a hat," Gil Rafferty said jokingly.

"Well, Gil, if you had been more of a speechifier, why, mayhaps you would be the mayor now," someone said. His comment was met with laughter, including that from both Rafferty and Kennedy.

"Ladies and gentlemen, in honor of our children being returned to us, I, Mayor Warren Kennedy, mayor of the great city of Mule Gap, do hereby declare this to be an official Welcome Home Day."

The crowd cheered.

"That's real good, Mayor, but what does that mean?" someone asked.

"Well, for one thing, it means that to celebrate the event I will provide one free drink to anyone who comes into Kennedy's Saloon during the next two hours."

Several cheered, but one of the women pointed out the obvious.

"Mr. Mayor, if we are celebrating the children, do you really think that giving away free drinks is the appropriate thing to do?"

"We all know that you are a prohibitionist, Miz Ragsdale," someone said. "If it was up to you, there wouldn't never be no drinks served nowhere, no time."

"No, Mr. Turner, Mrs. Ragsdale is right," Kennedy said, responding to the one who had challenged Mrs. Ragsdale. "Children have no business being in a saloon, so for the next hour there will be free candy at the Rafferty and Kennedy store for all the children."

"Is that for all the children, or just the ones that was captured?" a boy asked.

"Young man, that is for all the children," Kennedy said.

All the children present cheered.

"And Blackwell's Emporium will provide free ribbon for all the ladies," Richard Blackwell offered.

"I say we give three cheers for Smoke Jensen for bringing our children back to us," someone said.

But before the cheers could be organized, Smoke held up

his hand. "No! I had nothing to do with the rescue. These children escaped of their own initiative. If cheers are to be given, they should be given to the children."

"It was Thad!" Lorena shouted. "Thad is the one who saved us!"

"Then three cheers for Thad *and* the children," someone said, and as the cheers were given, Smoke noticed that Lorena was looking with adoration toward Thad.

Wee saw it as well. "Mama, Lorena likes Thad."

"Yes, dear, I think the whole town likes Thad," Mrs. Blackwell replied.

After the celebration, Smoke and Pearlie went into Kennedy's Saloon and took their free beer to a table.

"Are you ready to go back home?" Smoke asked.

"Well, yeah, I am, but how are we goin' to get there, you bein' without a horse?" Pearlie asked. "On account of, I've got an idea how we can do it."

"You're not going to tell me that we'll go all the way to Sugarloaf, riding double on your horse," Smoke said.

Pearlie laughed. "I wasn't thinkin' that, 'n I don't think Dandy would like it much, either. No, sir, I was thinkin' about goin' down to Sugarloaf, getting New Seven, and bringing him back up here for you."

"No, that is, for sure, too much riding for you right now. You could break that wound open again. If you did that, and started bleeding out on the trail, what would you do?"

"I'd stick a piece of dirty shirt in the bullet hole," Pearlie teased. "It worked the last time."

"You could do that, I suppose," Smoke replied. "Or I could rent a coach to take all four of us, Sara Sue, Thad, you and me, back home. You can tie your horse on behind the coach."

"Damn, a private coach, huh? Yeah, that will be nice. Will it be big enough to take Sandra and Lorena back with us?"

"Sandra and Lorena?" Smoke asked, curious about the additional people.

"Yeah, I think Sandra and her daughter would more 'n likely be more comfortable back in Big Rock than they would be if they had to stay here."

"Why is that?"

"Well, it's just something that . . . I mean, I couldn't come up with anything else that quick, and I didn't think about how it would look. Anyhow, I just think that Sandra would be more comfortable living in Big Rock than if she stayed here."

"Pearlie, why do I think there is more to this story?"

"Well, there is more to it, but Miz Condon was there when it happened, and she can tell you that nothin' happened."

Smoke laughed. "Sara Sue was there when it happened, but she can tell me that nothing happened? Pearlie, you aren't making one lick of sense."

Pearlie told Smoke about the two deputies Boots Zimmerman and Angus Delmer coming by Sandra Coy's apartment, and how he fooled them by making them think something was going on between him and Sandra. "Talk like that could get all over town. I wouldn't feel good about leaving her here with all that."

Smoke chuckled. "All right. I see what you are talking about now. If you want my opinion, you did a good job of looking out for her and I think what you did was clever. But yes, we can take them. Finish your beer. We'll go see Sara Sue and Thad."

"Yes?" Sara Sue called, responding to the knock on her door.

"Western Union, ma'am," a voice called from the other side.

"Oh, it must be from your father," Sara Sue said to Thad as she hurried to the door. She was taking the telegram from the delivery boy, just as Smoke and Pearlie were arriving.

"Smoke, Pearlie," Sara Sue said. "Come in, come in. It looks as if I have just gotten a telegram from Sam."

"No problem, I hope," Smoke said.

"I sent him a telegram telling him that Thad was safely back. He may just be responding to it, though I don't know how he could have done so, so quickly." She gave the boy a nickel, and with a touch to the tip of his hat, the boy left.

"Let's see what he has to say." With a big smile, she pulled the telegram from the envelope. As soon as she began reading, the smile faded, and her face was twisted into an expression of great concern. "Oh, no!"

"What is it? Ma, has something happened to Pa?"

"No, dear. This telegram is for Smoke."

"The telegram is for me?" Smoke asked, his voice laced with curiosity and concern.

"Here." Sara Sue handed him the telegram. "You had better read it."

SALLY MISSING STOP AM WORKING WITH POLICE TO FIND HER STOP POLICE BELIEVE SHE IS NOT HARMED AS THEY HAVE NO INFORMATION ANY WOMAN HURT STOP WILL CONTINUE TO LOOK FOR HER AND KEEP YOU INFORMED STOP REACH ME AT FIFTH AVENUE HOTEL STOP CAL

Smoke hurried from the hotel to the telegraph office. "When did you get this telegram from New York?" Smoke showed the telegrapher the telegram he had just read.

"Oh, about half an hour ago . . . but it didn't come from New York. It came from Big Rock, Colorado."

"Ah, yes, that makes sense. Cal has no way of knowing that I'm here, so of course he would have sent it to me there. Well, I want to send a telegram to him in New York."

"Yes sir, would that be in care of Ian Gallagher?"

"Ian Gallagher? No, why would it be? Who is Gallagher, and why would you think I would want to send a telegram to him?"

"Isn't Mrs. Jensen a guest of Mr. Gallagher while she is in New York?"

"Mister, what *are* you talking about?" Smoke asked.

"Just a minute, and I will show you." The telegrapher stepped back to a cabinet, opened a drawer, and shuffled through some papers until he found the one he was looking for. "Ah, here it is."

Returning to the front counter, he showed the telegram to Smoke. "I sent this message one week ago."

MRS KIRBY JENSEN ARRIVING
GRAND CENTRAL DEPOT ON BOARD
TRANSCONTINENTAL TRAIN HUMMER
TWO PM THIS DAY STOP
ARRANGE FOR HER TO BE YOUR GUEST
UNTIL FURTHER NOTICE STOP
YOU WILL BE WELL COMPENSATED FOR
HER STAY WITH YOU STOP

Smoke read the message, then shook his head. "I don't know anything about this. What does it mean? Who sent it?"

"Well, I assumed he was doing it for you, you know,

making arrangements for your wife to have accommodations while she was in New York? I thought he was doing it as a favor, since the two of you seem to be such good friends."

"Who sent the message?" Smoke asked again, more forcibly than before.

"Why, it was His Honor, Mayor Kennedy, forcefully who sent the message," the telegrapher said.

"That son of a bitch!" Smoke said angrily. He turned and left the telegraph office.

His first thought was to go directly to Kennedy's office, but he returned to the hotel instead. "It was Kennedy," he told Pearlie, Sara Sue, and Thad. "He is the one who had Sally kidnapped. The question is why did he do it?"

"Are you going after him?" Pearlie asked.

"Yes. I need to find out where Sally is, and right now he's the only one who can tell me."

"I'll come with you," Pearlie offered. He smiled. "If you have to beat it out of him, I want to watch."

"Do I have a telegram?" Marshal Bodine asked the Western Union telegrapher when he stepped into the office.

"No, sir."

"Then what is it? What are you doing here?"

"Marshal, I think there's going to be trouble between Mr. Jensen and the mayor."

"Why do you say that?"

"Mr. Jensen received a telegram saying his wife is missing. Then he found out that, about a week ago, the mayor had sent a telegram to New York about his wife. I'm not sure what this is all about, Marshal, but when Mr. Jensen left to see the mayor, he was very mad. I'm afraid there might be some trouble between them."

"You were right to come to me," the marshal said.

* * *

"Wait, sir, you can't just go into the mayor's office without being announced!" the clerk out front said.

"Is that so? Well, you just watch me," Smoke said.

"Smoke? What is it? What's wrong?" Kennedy asked when Smoke stepped into his office.

"What is this about?" Smoke demanded, dropping on the desk in front of Kennedy a copy of the telegram he had sent to Gallagher.

Kennedy looked at the telegram and his face turned white. "How did you get this? It is against the law for a telegrapher to disclose the contents of a private telegram."

"This telegram concerns my wife," Smoke said. "That gives me every right to know about it. Now, who is Gallagher?"

"He's a friend back in New York," Kennedy said. "I . . . I thought I was doing you a favor, making arrangements for Mrs. Jensen's accommodations."

"She is missing," Smoke said. "The police are trying to find her. I suppose you don't know anything about that."

"I . . . uh—" Whatever Kennedy was going to say was interrupted by the sound of a gunshot from outside the window, and he went down with a bullet hole in his chest.

Smoke ran to the window, but whoever had taken the shot was gone. He returned to the mayor lying on the floor. Pearlie was squatting behind him.

"Dead?" Smoke asked.

"Not yet," Pearlie said. "But he soon will be."

"Your wife . . . won't be hurt," Kennedy said, gasping the words out. "She was supposed to be . . . insurance to keep you . . . from going after the children until . . . the ransom was paid." Kennedy tried to laugh, but the effort brought blood bubbling from his lips. "Who would . . .

have thought . . . the children would . . . escape . . . on their own?"

"Who shot you, Warren," Smoke asked. "Do you have any idea?"

Kennedy's eyes were still open, but his gasping breaths had stopped.

CHAPTER 32

New York City

"How long are we goin' to keep Mrs. Jensen?" Kelly asked.

"As long as it takes," Gallagher replied.

"As long as what takes?"

"As long as it takes for Kennedy to send us the money," Gallagher replied.

"Warren Kennedy? He's the one that's behind all this?" Kelly asked, surprised to hear the name.

"Aye. 'N would you be for tellin' me who else we know who went West?"

"You shoulda tol' me it was Kennedy. I didn't like the son of a bitch when he was here. You might remember 'twas him who got us into a war with the Five Points gang 'n wound up gettin' a lot of our friends killed."

"Aye, but 'tis a sweet thing he has goin' now. He is the mayor of the town, 'n soon as he gets the money from somethin' he's workin' on, he'll be sendin' for me to come join him. You can go, too."

"No, thank you. I've no wish to leave New York. What if he don't send the money? What will we do with the woman?"

"What makes you think he won't be sendin' the money?"

"Do you know anythin' about this woman's husband?" Kelly asked.

"No."

"Well, I do. He's some kinda hero in the West. He's a gunfighter, 'n when he shoots someone, he never misses."

Gallagher laughed. "'N where would you be for getting that information?"

"From *Shootout at Sunset*," Kelly replied.

"What? What are you talkin' about?"

"I'm talkin' about Smoke Jensen, the legendary gunfighter." Kelly reached into his back pocket and pulled out the book, the title of which he had just mentioned. "You can read all about it in this book."

Gallagher looked at the book and laughed. "A dime novel? 'N am I to be worryin' 'bout some character in a book?"

"'Tis more than just a character in a book. He's a real person, 'n if he ever finds out it was Kennedy who had his wife took, there's goin' to be hell to pay," Kelly insisted.

"I'll send Kennedy a telegram 'n ask when he plans on sendin' the money," Gallagher said.

In the office of the Western Union, the telegrapher showed Gallagher the telegram he was about to send.

MRS JENSEN IS OUR GUEST AS REQUESTED
STOP WHEN WILL MONEY BE SENT STOP
GALLAGHER

"And this is to the mayor of Mule Gap?" the telegrapher asked.

"Aye."

"Very well, sir. That will be one dollar and ten cents."

* * *

Gallagher returned to the tenement building on West Third Street, just east of McDougal. From the chugging steam engine, the rumble of the cars, and the squeak and rattle of the elevated tracks, the site was loud with the sounds of a passing train. He could smell the horse manure coming from the Minetta Stable on the south side of the street. Standing out in front of St. Clement's Protestant Episcopal Church, Reverend Peabody nodded at Gallagher as he stepped down from the cab. Gallagher made no acknowledgment in response to the good pastor's greeting.

Hurrying up the stairs to the fourth-floor apartment, Gallagher saw Kelly reading a book. "Is it another book about Mrs. Jensen's husband that you're reading?"

"Aye." Kelly held up the book. "This one is called *Smoke Jensen and The Railroad Bandits.* He goes after ten railroad bandits all by his ownself, 'n he kills ever' one of 'em. It's a real excitin' story."

"Those are all made-up stories," Gallagher said.

"Aye, 'tis exactly what Mrs. Jensen said when I asked her about them. She said none of the books about her husband are true stories. But he must be like they say he is, or people wouldn't be for writin' books about him, would they?"

"Here now, Patrick Kelly, 'n 'tis beginnin' ter worry about you, I am. Would you be for tellin' me why 'tis so close to the women you are getting? The time may come when we'll have to take care of her. If you get too friendly with her, you may not be able to do what will need to be done."

"Take care of her?"

"Aye."

"What does that mean? Take care of her?"

"You know what it means."

"I thought you said Mrs. Jensen would no' be hurt."

"'Tis not my intention to do so. But if don't hear from Kennedy, and if we be cheated out o' the money, then we'll no be for keepin' 'er, 'n we won't be able to just let her go free now, will we?"

"Is it thinkin', you are, that we'll no' be getting the money?" Kelly asked.

"I don't know," Gallagher said. "I sent him a message, asking for the money, 'n I expect to be hearin' from him soon."

"What if he does send the money? What will we be doin' with the woman then? She'll still know who we are."

"Aye, 'tis a good point you have made. We'll see what Kennedy has in mind, 'n if he has nothin' to tell us, we'll have no choice but to take care of the woman our own-selves."

"I would no' be for killin' her," Kelly said.

"Don't you be for gettin' sweet on her now," Gallagher warned. "You knew when you came in with us, that there would be times when we might have to do somethin' like that. It's all a part of the business."

Mule Gap

As soon as Smoke and Pearlie left the mayor's office, they were met by Marshal Bodine and his four remaining deputies. All five of them had their guns drawn.

"What is this?" Smoke asked.

"You are under arrest," Bodine said.

"For what?"

"For the murder of Mayor Kennedy," Bodine said.

"Well, now, that's interesting," Smoke said. "What makes you think Mayor Kennedy is dead?"

"Well, isn't he?"

"Yes, he is. But how do you know?"

"Soon, the whole town is going to know," Bodine said.

"I have no doubt but that they will," Smoke replied, "but don't you think there should be a motive?"

"Apparently, Mr. Jensen, you discovered that it was Kennedy who was behind the five-thousand-dollar reward."

"No, I didn't know that, but now that I think about it, it makes sense."

"Get their guns," Bodine ordered. "Get the guns from both of them."

"Am I under arrest, too?" Pearlie asked.

"No. But I have no intention of leaving you armed while I incarcerate your friend."

Within moments, the town learned that Mayor Kennedy had been killed, and that Smoke had been arrested for murder. Reaction was mixed. Some who didn't actually know Smoke were ready to accept that he was guilty, but many who did know Smoke were positive there must be some sort of explanation. Smoke would not have murdered Kennedy. If he did shoot him, there would have had to be a very good reason for it.

It was the telegrapher who supplied the reason when he personally visited the marshal. "I just received this telegram from New York, intended for the mayor. Apparently someone in New York is holding Mr. Jensen's wife as a prisoner and is doing so at the behest of the mayor."

"What are you talking about?" Bodine asked after he read the telegram. "There is nothing here that says Mrs. Jensen is a prisoner."

"I spoke with Mr. Jensen earlier, and I told him about a telegram that Mayor Kennedy had sent, arranging for Mrs. Jensen to be met by this man, Gallagher. Mr. Jensen was unaware of any such arrangement."

Bodine's smile was little more than a ribald smirk. "Well, now, perhaps this was merely the arrangement of a tryst. In that case, of course Jensen wouldn't know about it. Thank you, Mr. Cox, I had previously thought that Jensen killed the mayor because of his belief that the mayor had posted a reward to anyone who would kill Jensen. But now I believe you have just supplied the actual motive. It is obvious that Jensen killed the mayor in a moment of jealous rage."

"No, I don't believe that is it at all!" Cox said. "If you will but read the previous telegram, you will see that the mayor offered Gallagher money for meeting and hosting Mrs. Jensen. I believe the word *hosting* is a cover word for asking Gallagher to take her as his prisoner."

Bodine chuckled. "That's what you believe, is it? Tell me, Cox, do you actually think a court would listen to you stating something you *believe*?"

"Well, it isn't hard to figure out," Cox said.

"Thank you, Mr. Cox. If you don't mind, I'll keep this message. And if you would, bring the other one to me as well."

"I don't know whether or not that would be proper," Cox said. "Telegrams are protected by the government as privileged communication. You can't see them without proper authorization."

"With the mayor dead, I am now the highest authority," Bodine said. "And that is all the authorization I need now. Bring me the telegrams in question. That is, unless you want to wind up sharing a cell with Mr. Jensen."

"No, I'll . . . uh . . . bring you the telegrams."

That same afternoon, Bodine authorized the building of a gallows, right in the middle of First Street. A newly printed sign was placed on an easel next to the gallows under construction, explaining the purpose of the gallows.

ON THESE GALLOWS TOMORROW
SMOKE JENSEN
Will Be Hanged
for the MURDER *of*
Our Beloved Mayor
WARREN KENNEDY

"You can't hang a man without a trial!" Gil Rafferty said.

"Oh, there will be an adjudication," Bodine replied. "We will try him, find him guilty, and hang him at high noon tomorrow. And these two telegrams will be all the evidence we will need to make the case."

Smoke Jensen was already considered by many of the citizens to be a hero for his role in bringing the kidnapped children back to Mule Gap. News that he was to be hanged spread through the town like wildfire.

"How are they going to hold a trial without a judge?"

"Rufus Gordon is a judge."

"Gordon is a drunk. He hasn't heard a case in five years."

"He's still a judge, and Bodine plans to use him."

"Why, how can that be, in any way, a fair trial? Gordon will do anything Bodine asks of him, ever'body knows that."

Visiting with Sara Sue, Thad, and Sandra, Pearlie said, "I'm not going to let them hang Smoke."

"How are you going to stop it?" Sara Sue asked.

"I can testify in court that the gunshot came through the window. I know, because I was there. We left to go tell the marshal, but Bodine and all his deputies were standing right in front of the mayor's office when we stepped out into the street. He arrested Smoke for murder before either one of us could say a word."

"Wait a minute," Sara Sue said. "Are you telling me that he arrested Smoke for murder before you even told him that Kennedy was dead?"

"Yes, ma'am."

"How could he do that? What I mean is how did he even know Kennedy was dead?"

"Yes ma'am, that's what Smoke asked and . . . I'll be

damned!" Pearlie said. "Bodine did it! He has to be the one who shot through the window. That's the only way he could have possibly known that Kennedy was dead. Uh, forgive me for the cussword, ma'am."

"No forgiveness is needed," Sara Sue said. "I think you are right. I believe Bodine is the one who killed Kennedy. Smoke is being falsely accused to protect Bodine."

There was a knock at the door and Pearlie waved Sara Sue and Thad to one side, then, drawing his gun, he jerked the door open.

"Oh!" the man in the hall said.

"You're the telegrapher, aren't you?"

"Yes, Lymon Cox," the man said.

"I'm sorry about this," Pearlie said, putting the gun away. "Do you have another telegram for us?"

"Yes, well, no. That is, not exactly. I've come to show you a telegram I just received that was meant for Mayor Kennedy. I thought it might be of some interest to you." He handed it to Pearlie.

MRS JENSEN IS OUR GUEST AS REQUESTED STOP WHEN WILL MONEY BE SENT STOP GALLAGHER

"Look at this, Miz Condon," Pearlie said, showing the telegram to Sara Sue. "At least we know that Miz Sally is still alive."

"Oh, thank God for that. I hate that she is a prisoner, but I am very happy to hear that she is alive."

"Does Smoke know about this?" Pearlie asked.

"No, I showed the telegram to the marshal, but he took it from me. I didn't get a chance to talk to Mr. Jensen. They have him locked in the cell in the back of the building. There's a door between the front of the building and the cell, so I didn't even get to see him."

"Mrs. Condon?" a male voice called from the hall. "It's Richard Blackwell. May I come in?"

"That's Wee's pa," Thad said.

"Yes, please do," Sara Sue replied.

Blackwell nodded toward Cox.

"Don't mind me, Mr. Blackwell. I'm just on my way out," Cox said.

Blackwell waited until Cox was gone before he spoke. "If it's all right with you, Mrs. Condon, I would like to shut the door. What I have to say to you is for the ears of those in this room only."

"Yes, of course you can close the door."

Blackwell closed the door before speaking again. "I'm sure you know that Mr. Jensen's status now is quite precarious. It is my understanding that Bodine intends to hold a trial to be conducted by Judge Rufus Gordon. In addition, he will put only his deputies and others that they select on the jury."

"But the defense attorney will have voir dire, won't he?" Sara Sue asked.

"Have what?" Sandra asked.

"Before we got into the cattle business, my husband was an attorney," Sara Sue said. "Voir dire is used to determine if any juror is biased and cannot deal with the issues fairly or if there is cause not to allow a juror to serve because of possible bias."

"Believe me, Mrs. Condon, the defense attorney will also belong to Bodine," Blackwell said. "There is no way Smoke Jensen can win this trial. Why else do you think they have built the gallows?"

"I hope you didn't come to cheer us up," Pearlie said. "If you did, you sure aren't doing a very good job of it."

"Well, no, I don't suppose I am. However, I do have one thing that, if we are lucky, might work."

"What do you have?"

Blackwell held up a key as a big smile spread across his face. "I have a key to the cell."

"What? How did you get that?"

"As it so happens, sir, I own the jail."

"You own the jail?" Pearlie asked, surprised by the comment. "I've never heard of a private citizen owning a public building like a jail."

"Well, until Bodine was appointed, we didn't have a city marshal, and thus, we had no reason to have a jail. Then we got a marshal, and I made one of my buildings that I had been using for storage available for the town to use as a jail. I hired a contractor to convert the building into a jail and leased it to the town. The contractor was working for me, so he made me a spare set of all the keys to the building, including to the cell, and gave the second set to Bodine. This is the key to the jail cell where they are keeping Mr. Jensen."

"All right!" Pearlie said, reaching happily for the key. "Now, all I've got to do is figure out how to use it."

"The best way would be to get the key to him," Sara Sue said. "But I don't know how we will be able to do it. You know he isn't going to let you see Smoke."

"I can get the key to him," Thad said. "I'm just a kid. The marshal would never suspect me of anything."

"Especially if I went with him," Lorena said.

"What would be your reason for going to see him?" Sara Sue asked.

"We're going to thank him for rescuing us," Lorena said.

"That won't work," Blackwell said. "The whole town now knows that it was Thad who managed to rescue you."

"All the more reason I think the marshal might be suspicious of you, Thad," Sara Sue said.

"That's why I should go as well," Lorena said. "He might suspect Thad if he is by himself, but not if I'm with him."

"Mrs. Condon, Mr. Blackwell, I think the girl is right.

I think the best chance Thad has of getting the key to Smoke would be if the girl is with him," Pearlie said.

"Pearlie, you do realize that you are putting my son's life in danger, don't you?" Sara Sue said.

"To say nothing of Lorena," Sandra added.

"Please, Ma, I want to do this," Thad said. "Isn't the whole reason Mr. Jensen is over here, and in trouble now, because of me?"

"Well, yes, but—"

"Please, Ma?"

"It will be all right, Mrs. Condon. I'll be with Thad, and Mr. Bodine would never suspect us if I'm with him," Lorena said.

"Lorena, your mother—"

"I trust Thad," Sandra said. "He got my daughter out of that awful place. I trust him to look after her now, as well."

"Ma?" Thad said again.

"All right, Thad, go ahead. God help me if anything goes wrong."

Thad's smile spread all across his face. "All right!" he said, reaching for the key. "Come on, Lorena. Let's do it!"

CHAPTER 33

When Thad and Lorena passed by the gallows, it was nearly completed, and at least half a dozen people were standing around, staring at it.

"If you folks have enjoyed watchin' this thing bein' built, just wait till we actual use it." Boney Walls, one of the deputies, put his fist beside his neck, then, making a gagging sound, jerked his head to one side. "Sometimes their eyes bulge out so far they pop right out of their heads and roll around on the ground like little balls," he said with an insane laugh.

"Oh, Thad," Lorena said, grabbing Thad's arm. "That's awful!"

"It ain't true, neither," Thad said.

"Well, I tell you what, boy. Why don't you just bring your girlfriend by at noon tomorrow and see for yourself," the deputy challenged with another laugh.

As they walked away from the gallows and headed toward the jail, Lorena tightened her squeeze on Thad's arm. "He called me your girlfriend."

Thad smiled. "Well, I reckon that's true, isn't it?"

When they reached the jail, Thad opened the door for her as they went inside.

Bodine looked up from his desk. "What do you two want?"

"Please, Marshal, could we see Mr. Jensen?" Lorena asked.

"What? Why on earth would you two want to see that murderer?"

"He saved our lives," Thad said. "And if he is going to be hung, we'd like to tell him good-bye."

"Hanged," Bodine corrected. "He isn't going to be *hung*, he is going to be *hanged*."

"Then, please, let us talk to him this one last time," Lorena said.

"I've put out the order to my deputies not to let anyone see him," Bodine said.

"Yes, sir, and I can understand that," Thad said. "You are afraid that someone might try and help him escape or something. But you are the marshal, so you can do anything you want. You can let us see him, if you want."

Bodine drummed his fingers on the desk for a moment, then he nodded. "Very well. I'll let you see him. I can't imagine that a couple children could do anything to help him escape."

"Thank you, Marshal," Lorena said with a sweet smile.

Bodine opened the door to the back of the building then led them to the cell. Smoke was lying on the cot with his hands laced behind his head.

"Jensen, I have granted the request of these two urchins to visit you," Bodine said.

"Thad, Lorena, it's nice of you to come visit me."

"Marshal, would you please open the door so I can give Mr. Jensen a hug?" Lorena asked.

"Now, what kind of marshal would I be if I allowed a child in the cell with a murderer?"

"Alleged murderer," Thad replied. "In our system of justice, a person is innocent until proven guilty."

Bodine smiled and clapped his hands quietly. "Very good, young man. I'm impressed."

"My pa is a lawyer," Thad replied, "and if he hadn't been shot, he would be here to defend Mr. Jensen."

"Yes, too bad he isn't. However, the court will provide a lawyer for him."

"If we can't give Mr. Jensen a hug, can we at least shake hands with him?" Lorena asked.

"All right. I don't see why not. Jensen, don't try anything like grabbing one of these innocent children and holding them in some ploy to give you leverage over the situation, because it won't work."

During the exchange, Smoke had noticed that Thad had winked at him. He wasn't certain what the wink was about, but it did put him on the alert.

"Good-bye, Mr. Jensen," Lorena said, sticking her hand through the bars. "Thank you for coming to rescue us."

"And thank you for coming to visit me," Smoke said.

Thad was next. "Good-bye, Mr. Jensen. And thank you for giving me my horse, Fire."

As Smoke took Thad's hand, he felt the key. "You take good care of that horse, now."

"I will."

"Bodine, thank you for allowing them to visit," Smoke said. "I was wondering if you would allow my friend, Pearlie, to visit."

"I'm afraid not," Bodine replied. "I wouldn't put it past the two of you to come with a bit of chicanery in an escape attempt. He can see you at your trial."

"We'll go now," Lorena said. "Thank you for letting us visit."

"I've got an idea, if you think the telegrapher will go along with it," Pearlie said.

"Mr. Cox is a good man." Blackwell had remained after Thad and Lorena left. "We have done a considerable amount of business together. I'm sure if your idea is feasible, he will be willing to do anything he can."

"Would you go see him with me?" Pearlie asked.

"Of course. I'd be glad to," Blackwell replied.

Just as Pearlie and Blackwell were about to leave Thad and Lorena returned. The smiles on their faces told of their success.

"Oh, I've been so worried about you two," Sandra said, greeting them.

"There was no problem," Thad said.

Pearlie smiled. "We don't have to worry about Smoke anymore. Now, let's take care of Miz Sally."

"How are you going to do that?" Sandra asked.

"By sending a telegram.

Cox smiled as he read the telegram. "Technically, this would be a violation, but under the circumstances, I think it is absolutely the right thing to do."

New York City

Gallagher smiled as he read the telegram. "Listen to this." He began to read the telegram aloud. "I am coming to New York with ten thousand dollars in cash. It is important that Mrs. Jensen be healthy and in good condition so that I may complete my business transaction. Wire me at Chicago Depot to tell me where we should meet. Kennedy."

"What do you think he means by business transaction?" Brockway asked.

"I think he has gone to see her husband and has made a deal to return her to him for cash," Gallagher said.

"Sure 'n it must be for a lot of money if he can bring ten

thousand dollars in cash to us," Brockway said. "Just how rich is the man, Jensen, anyway?"

"I believe he is very rich," Kelly said. "It is said that he is one of the biggest ranchers in all of Colorado."

"That's what you've read in one of those books, have you?" Gallagher asked.

"Aye, but it must be true, I'm thinkin', or the books would have no' been wrote."

"Haven't you ever heard, *don't believe everything you read*?" Gallagher asked.

"He must be rich, or where is the money comin' from? 'Tis too bad O'Leary was killed before the job was done. He's missin' out on his share," Kelly said.

"Why is it too bad? If he was still here, our share would come only to twenty-five hundred dollars apiece. But without him, it's thirty-three hundred dollars apiece," Brockway added with a laugh.

"There will be no shares, for we'll not be dividin' the money up," Gallagher said.

"'N would you be for tellin' me why we're doin' this if not for the money?" Brockway asked.

"For to rebuild the Irish Assembly," Gallagher said.

"Do you think we could really do that? I mean, look what happened to us the last time."

"That was because Kennedy was in charge then. He won't be in charge this time."

"You'll be in charge?" Brockway asked.

"Aye, I'll be in charge. Tell me, Brockway, would that be a problem for you?"

"No, no, 'twould be no problem at all. Sure 'n you'd be a hell of a lot better 'n Kennedy ever was."

"Kennedy wants to know where we should meet. Are you going to bring him here?" Kelly asked.

"Aye, we'll bring him here."

"Ian, are you sure you want to bring him here?" Brockway asked.

"I don't see why not."

"It's just that I don't really trust him all that much. He's the one that led us into the fight with the Five Points gang, then he left, sort of abandoned us, you might say. 'Tis thinkin', I am, that we might want to arrange a meeting somewhere else."

"Aye, perhaps you're right." Gallagher smiled. "All right. We will meet him somewhere else, 'n I know just where it can be."

Mule Gap

Smoke stuck his hand through the bars, placed the key into the keyhole, and was rewarded with a satisfying *click* as he turned it. Going back to the bunk, he took the blankets and pillow from the other bunk in the cell and wadded them up in a way that a quick, casual glance would suggest that someone was in the bed. It would survive only the most casual glance, but that's all he would need.

"Hey!" he shouted from inside the cell so the location of his voice would not be suspicious. "Hey, Marshal, would you please come in here? I've got something to tell you!" Moving quickly, he stepped up to the room door and waited.

"What the hell do you want?" The gruff voice belonged to Boney Walls. He stepped into the cell area.

"I want out," Smoke said from behind Walls.

Walls turned, "Wha—" and was caught on the chin by a hard uppercut. The deputy went down and out.

Smoke dragged him into the cell, then shut the cell door and locked it.

With Boney Walls's pistol in hand, Smoke opened the door and looked into the outer office. No one was there, and seeing his own pistol belt hanging from a hook, he strapped it on, then stepped outside.

Bodine was standing at the foot of the scaffold with Lute Cruthis, Boots Zimmerman, and Angus Delmer. At least half a dozen others were standing nearby, one of whom, an older man, was dressed in a suit.

"I want the trial over quickly, Your Honor," Bodine was saying to the man in the suit. "I intend to hang him by noon tomorrow."

"How can you say you are going to hang him, sir, if you don't know the results of the trial?" the judge asked.

"That's a good question, Bodine. I'd like to know the answer to that myself," Smoke said.

"What the hell?" Bodine shouted, shocked to see that Smoke Jensen was not only out of jail, but armed.

"Answer the judge," Smoke said.

"Perhaps the hanging won't be necessary." A confident smile appeared as Bodine turned to face Smoke.

Realizing there was about to be a gunfight, the others moved quickly to get out of the way. Their move left Smoke standing alone, facing Cruthis, Zimmerman, and Delmer.

And of course, standing with the deputies, was The Professor himself, Frank Bodine. "It looks to me as if we may have just wasted time and money building the scaffold." His draw was considerably faster than most gunmen who had tried to kill Smoke. He was able to bring his gun up to level.

Smoke drew and fired before Bodine was able to pull the trigger. The bullet hit the marshal right in the center of his chest, and he went down.

Keeping his gun ready, Smoke hurried over to look down at him.

"I should have killed you the same time I killed Kennedy," Bodine gasped.

"Did you hear that, Judge?" one of the witnesses asked.

"I heard it," Judge Gordon said.

Zimmerman pulled his gun and pointed it at Smoke.

"Look out!" the same witness shouted.

Smoke fired, and the deputy went down with a bullet hole in his forehead.

"Don't shoot! Don't shoot!" Cruthis said, holding his hands in the air.

Delmer looked as if he might try Smoke, but when he saw Cruthis with his hands in the air, he raised his hands, as well. "I ain't drawin'," said in a desperate tone of voice. "I ain't a-goin' to draw on you."

"I would say that is a wise move," Smoke said.

The townspeople who had moved so quickly to get out of the way of the gunfight came drifting back. A few looked down with morbid curiosity at the two bodies, but many of the others, emboldened by what Smoke had just done, took some initiative and placed Cruthis and Delmer under a citizen's arrest. Within a matter of minutes they joined Boney Walls in jail.

Word of what had transpired spread quickly through the town, and Pearlie, Blackwell, and Rafferty joined Smoke and the judge in the front of the jail.

"I will admit, gentlemen, that I am an alcoholic," Judge Gordon said. "but I am not a crook. There is no way, except under threat of death, that without a fair trial, I would have found Mr. Jensen guilty."

"The point is, Judge, you *were* under threat of death," Blackwell said.

"Indeed, I believe that I may well have been," Judge Gordon replied.

"What are we going to do with these three prisoners?" Rafferty asked. "We have no law, we have no mayor, and we have no city administration at all."

"I will authorize their internment here until Sheriff Sinclair can send a few deputies down to escort them up to

Rawlins for trial," Judge Gordon said. "A legitimate trial, I hasten to add."

As Smoke and Pearlie left the jail, they were met by the telegrapher.

"Apparently your idea is working," Cox said to Pearlie.

"What idea is that?" Smoke asked.

"I sent a telegram to Gallagher."

"A telegram?"

"Yes, sir," Cox said. "And I just got this one in return." He smiled. "It was sent to Mayor Kennedy, of course, since Gallagher believed the telegram he received had come from Kennedy." Cox showed Smoke the telegram he had just received.

MRS JENSENS HEALTH IS GOOD STOP
WE AWAIT YOUR VISIT AND THE
CONCLUSION OF OUR BUSINESS STOP
GALLAGHER

Smoke looked up from reading the telegram. "I have a couple telegrams I would like to send."

CHAPTER 34

The first telegram Smoke sent was to the railroad depot back in Big Rock, requesting that a private engine and car be made available to him, and that all track clearances be arranged from Big Rock to New York City. He emphasized in his telegram that it was imperative that he reach New York in the fastest time humanly possible.

Then he sent a telegram to Cal.

THE MAN BEHIND THE KIDNAPPING OF
SALLY IS DEAD STOP HAVE GOOD REASON
TO BELIEVE SHE WILL BE SAFE NEXT
SEVERAL DAYS STOP DO NOTHING TO
AGGRAVATE SITUATION UNTIL PEARLIE
AND I ARRIVE STOP WILL WIRE YOU FROM
CHICAGO STOP SMOKE

With that arranged, he returned to the hotel to meet with Sara Sue. Thad, Lorena, and Sandra were still in the room.

"Smoke, I have heard what has happened," Sara Sue said. "I'm so glad you are safe."

Smoke smiled at Thad and Lorena. "If it hadn't been for these two very brave young people, I would still be in jail and facing a very public hanging. Thad, I'd like to shake your hand again . . . this time without the key," he added with a chuckle.

Smiling broadly, Thad stuck his hand out to take Smoke's.

"Lorena, you asked to give me a hug, back in the jail. Does that offer still go?"

"Yes, sir," Lorena said, moving to him to give and accept an embrace.

"Sara Sue, Mrs. Coy . . ."

"Sandra," she corrected quickly.

"Sandra," Smoke said. "I hope you two ladies are aware of what fine children—no, not children—young man and young lady you have."

"We know," Sara Sue said, putting her arm around Thad. "Oh, I got a telegram from Sam while you were in . . . uh, while you were detained," Sara Sue said. "He is aware now that Thad is safe, and he also says that he is feeling well and is ready to get back to work."

"Good. I suggest that you withdraw your money from the bank now and pack your things. I've rented a private coach to take us back home."

"All right," Sara Sue replied. "By the way, Sandra and Lorena will be going back with us. I told Sandra that I was sure we could find a place for her to live and a good job."

"So I was told. The coach will easily take care of all of us."

"Mama, I want to tell Wee good-bye," Lorena said.

"I do too," Thad added.

The first person Lorena went to was Mrs. Blackwell.

"Hello, dear," Millicent said. "I want to thank you for how well you looked out for Wee when you were all in that awful place."

"Yes, ma'am, but the truth is, all of us looked out for each other. Even Wee had a job to do, and he did it well."

"I must say, he came back home no worse for wear. I was

so frightened that he would be traumàtized by it, but he seems just fine."

"Mrs. Blackwell, I've come to tell Wee good-bye."

"Yes, I thought as much. Your mother talked to Richard about it. We will certainly miss you, but not as much as Wee. Why don't you go see him?"

Wee was in the back of the Blackwell Emporium, sitting on the floor playing the game of pickup sticks. "Lorena, watch me get that one." He pointed to a yellow stick lying across two other sticks.

"Oh, that one will be hard."

"Not for me." With much concentration and his tongue sticking out of his mouth, Wee was able to press down on the back end of the stick and swing it around clear of the others without moving them.

"Oh, wonderful!" Lorena said, clapping her hands.

"You're going away, aren't you?" Wee said.

"Yes, honey, I am."

"Mama told me."

"I'm really going to miss you."

"Lorena, you know how I always told you that I was a big boy, and didn't want you to be hugging me?"

"Yes."

Wee stood up. "You can hug me now."

Lorena didn't do a very good job of hiding her tears as she and Thad walked back to the hotel. Thad reached out to take her hand in his.

Because there were six of them going back to Big Rock, Smoke hired a Concord coach and driver from the Northwest Stagecoach Company. Seven hours after they left Mule Gap, they stopped by Wiregrass Ranch to let Sara Sue and the others off. Sam came out to meet the coach, looking much better than he had the last time Smoke had seen him.

After a joyous embrace of his wife and son, he turned to his friend. "Smoke, there's no way I can ever thank you for rescuing my son."

"No need to thank me," Smoke said. "He did it himself."

"He rescued all of us," Lorena said proudly.

"You were kidnapped as well?"

"Yes, sir."

Sara Sue introduced Sandra and Lorena to Sam. "They will be staying with us until they can get resettled."

"Wonderful," Sam replied. "I look forward to their company.

"It's good to see you up and about, Sam, but now Pearlie and I must go," Smoke said.

"Must you leave so quickly?"

"He has to, Sam," Sara Sue said. "I'll tell you why."

With Sara Sue making his excuses for the quick turn-around, Smoke urged the driver to get them to Sugarloaf just long enough to get some fresh clothes, then on to the depot.

By the time Smoke and Pearlie reached the depot a Baldwin 4-4-2 engine, tender, private car, and caboose were sitting on a side track. Wisps of steam drifted away from the drive cylinders.

"We didn't know when you would get here, so we kept the steam up," Clyde Drake, the station manager said. "You're stocked up with food, and I've got three crews for you. That way there will be no need to stop and rest. As you pass each major point, the track will be cleared in front of you."

"What about the regular scheduled trains?" Smoke asked.

"Ha!" Drake said. "They're all excited about being part

of this. Everyone wants to see just how fast this trip can actually be made."

"How fast can the trip be made?" Smoke asked.

"I see no reason why we can't get you there in three days," Drake replied with a broad proud smile.

"Then let's go," Smoke said.

The chief engineer was Cephus Prouty, but he told Smoke to call him Doodle.

"I'm Smoke. He's Pearlie."

"Well, Smoke and Pearlie, if you'll climb aboard, we'll get underway."

New York City

Ryan, Doolin, McDougal, Keagan, and Quinn were sitting with Gallagher at a table in the back of Paddy's Pub. Like Gallagher, Kelly, and Brockway, the five men had been part of the original Irish Assembly.

"So, 'tis wantin' to put the Assembly together again, are you?" Ryan asked Gallagher.

"Aye. 'N if you five join, there'll be eight of us. That'll be a start, 'n 'tis my thinkin' that within a year we'll be back as big as we were before."

"It'll take a bit o' money to get started again," Doolin said. "'N have you thought of that, Ian Gallagher?"

Gallagher smiled. "Aye, I've thought of it. 'N would ten thousand dollars be enough, do you think?"

"Ten thousand dollars? 'N would you be for tellin' me how 'tis you'll be comin' up with ten thousand dollars?" Ryan asked.

"Warren Kennedy will be bringin' the money," Keagen said.

"Kennedy, himself who got us into a battle with the Five Pointers? M' brother was killed in that battle. 'N yer for tellin' us that we'll be workin' with Kennedy again? Thank you, no, but I've no wish to be workin' with the likes o' him."

Gallagher laughed. "I'm sayin' Kennedy is bringin' ten thousand dollars so he can take a woman that we're holdin' for him back to Wyoming." He smiled. "Only what he don't know is, there ain't neither one of 'em that'll be goin' back. Once Kennedy sees the woman 'n gives me the money, I intend to take care of both of 'em."

"Blimey," Quinn said. "You have the woman that Muldoon has been lookin' for?"

"Aye, all safe 'n secure," Gallagher said.

"Ten thousand dollars?" Doolin asked.

"Aye."

"The Assembly could be back on its feet with that much money. You can count me in," Doolin said.

"Me too," Ryan said.

"I'm in," Quinn added.

Keagan and McDougal added their assent as well.

When Gallagher returned to the fourth-floor walk-up on Third Avenue, Brockway was in the living room, and Kelly was in the small kitchen, cooking ham and potatoes.

"Did you meet with any o' the old lads?" Brockway asked.

"Aye. Ryan, Quinn, Doolin', McDougal 'n Keagan. They're in," Gallagher said. "They'll be with us when we meet Kennedy."

"Where are we goin' to meet him?" Kelly asked.

"I have the perfect place picked out," Gallagher replied.

Chicago

It was nine o'clock in the evening, thirty-two hours after leaving Big Rock, when the train rolled into Chicago's Central Depot in the middle of the city. Smoke had already been informed that it would take a couple hours to secure track clearance from Chicago to Cleveland, so he and Pearlie left the small train, which had been pulled onto a side track.

They accompanied Doodle to the Western Union office, Doodle to arrange for track clearance, and Smoke to send a message on to Cal.

"Are you here to tell me that you left Denver yesterday?" asked the telegrapher.

"Yes, sir, one o'clock yesterday afternoon," Doodle said. "Why, there were times when we were runnin' at sixty miles to the hour."

As Doodle continued arranging for track clearance, Smoke checked to see if there was a telegram for Warren Kennedy.

"Kennedy? I thought your name was Jensen," the telegrapher replied in surprise.

"I am Kennedy," Pearlie said quickly.

"Oh. Well, yes, sir, Mr. Kennedy, we've been holding it for you," the telegrapher said. He located the telegram and handed it to Pearlie.

MEET AT ABANDONED COTTAGES
BETWEEN 10TH AND 11TH AVENUES
ON 52ND STREET STOP ADVISE WHEN YOU
WILL BE THERE STOP
HAVE MONEY WITH YOU STOP

"Doodle, when do you think we'll reach New York?" Smoke asked after he read the telegram over Pearlie's shoulder.

"We'll be there by ten o'clock tomorrow morning," Doodle promised.

Unseen by the telegrapher, Smoke penned a telegram to Gallagher and handed it to Pearlie. He in turn took it to the telegrapher to send.

HAVE MRS JENSEN READY FOR TRAVEL AT
NOON TUESDAY STOP
I HAVE MONEY IN HAND STOP KENNEDY

Smoke then sent a telegram to Cal.

WILL BE AT GRAND CENTRAL DEPOT BY
TEN OCLOCK TUESDAY STOP SMOKE

CHAPTER 35

New York City

Sally was aware that some other men had joined Gallagher, Brockway, and Kelly. She had not yet seen any of the new men, but she had heard enough additional voices to imagine that the small living room must be quite crowded. This morning, the voices were much more animated. As she listened to determine if she could learn anything from the conversation, her mind whirled.

"Today at noon," Gallagher said.

"And are you sure he'll be there?" Brockway asked.

"Aye, the telegram came last night," Gallagher said.

"Does he have the money?"

That was not a familiar voice, so Sally realized the question had come from one of the men she had not yet met or even seen. *They are talking about money. Are they talking about Smoke? Has he come to New York to pay the ransom?*

"Kennedy will have the money," Gallagher said. "For he knows what will happen to him if he doesn't."

"Aye," one of the men replied. "But does he know what will happen to him even if he does have the money?"

A great deal of laughter followed that comment.

"Will you be meeting him by yourself?" Kelly asked.

"No. For one thing, I think 'tis good that we all go so that Kennedy can't be for pulling any tricks on us. 'N for another, ''is to show each of you that I'll not be for holding out on any of the money.''

They're talking about Kennedy. Would that Kennedy be Smoke's friend from Mule Gap? Sally wondered. *Why would Smoke be sending Kennedy with the money, instead of bringing it himself?*

"Ha! 'Tis betting I am, that when Kennedy asked us to snatch the woman, he had no idea we would be usin' the money to get the Irish Assembly goin' again," Kelly said.

"Aye, especially since the son of a bitch is the one to cause it to be destroyed in the first place," Gallagher said.

Kennedy is the one who arranged for me to be kidnapped? Yes, it would have to be him, Sally realized.

Kelly had told her that it was someone in Wyoming. She scolded herself for not realizing that earlier. After all, who else in Wyoming would not only know who she was, but also have a New York connection?

"Are we goin' to turn the woman over to him?" Again, the voice was from one of the men she had not yet seen.

"Oh, yeah, we'll turn her over to him, all right," Gallagher said.

"If he takes her back, and she goes back to her husband, what's to say *he* won't come after us?" Kelly asked.

"What do you mean, 'come after us'?" another of the new voices asked.

Gallagher laughed. "Don't be for paying Kelly any mind. He's been reading dime novels about the woman's husband 'n what a hero he is."

"But 'tis like I said, they would not be writing books about him if he wasn't like they say he is. Why, he once took on a whole gang of train robbers all by himself," Kelly insisted.

"Even if he is the hero you think he is, how is it he'll be

comin' for us? He has no idea where we are or even *who* we are," Gallagher said.

"I know Mrs. Jensen," Kelly said. "Do you think she won't be for tellin' him who we are and where we are?"

"How is she going to do that?" Gallagher asked.

"What do you mean?"

"Think about it, Kelly. If we aren't goin' to let Kennedy go back, how is the Jensen woman goin' to go back?"

"Well if she doesn't go back, what will we do with her?"

"What do you think we'll do with her?"

"Wait a minute. You told me the woman wouldn't be harmed."

Brockway laughed. "Do you know what I'm thinkin', Gallagher? I'm thinkin' Kelly has fallen for the Jensen woman. Tell us, Kelly, when you 'n the woman has been alone, have you been climbin' inter bed with 'er?"

"No, nothin' like that," Kelly replied resolutely. "I was just commentin' is all."

"Don't comment. Just listen," Gallagher said.

Although the special train had been granted clearance to come into Grand Central Terminal, the track that had been allocated was the most distant from the depot. As soon as the train stopped, Smoke and Pearlie stepped out of the private car, and Smoke walked up to the engine. Even at rest, it was alive with the sound of boiling water and vented steam.

Doodle was looking out of the cab window. "Sorry we're so far away, but this is the track they gave us," he called down.

"After being cooped up for so long, the walk will do us good," Smoke replied. "I want to express my thanks to you and the entire crew for getting us to New York so fast."

"It was a pleasure," Doodle said, smiling broadly. "For

the entire time I've been an engineer, I've always wanted to open 'er up 'n see just how fast I could go. Why, for a little stretch there, we were running almost seventy miles to the hour. I'm the one who should be thankin' you for the opportunity."

Smoke smiled back at him, and with a final wave he and Pearlie started the long walk past all the other trains to the terminal. Once outside, they took a cab to the Fifth Avenue Hotel.

When they reached the hotel, Smoke started toward the front desk with the intention of getting Cal's room number, but even before he reached the desk, he heard a familiar voice call out to him.

"Smoke!"

He turned to see Cal coming across the lobby toward him.

While the meeting between the two men would normally elicit a smile, the expression on Cal's face was one of worry and shame. He reached out to take Smoke's extended hand. "I'm sorry, Smoke. I was supposed to look after her and I failed. To be honest, I wasn't even sure you would be willing to shake my hand."

"Nonsense," Smoke said. "It happened. Now, we're going to get her back."

Cal shook hands with Pearlie then turned and motioned toward a uniformed police officer who was standing some distance back. "Mickey, come up here. I want you to meet my two best friends in the whole world. Smoke, Pearlie, this is Officer Mickey Muldoon. We've been working together. We were on his beat when Miz Sally was taken."

Cal explained how it happened.

"Officer Muldoon," Smoke started, but he was interrupted.

"Sure now, the lad, Cal 'n I are usin' first names between

us, 'n seein' as the two of you be his best friends, I'd like it if you'd be for callin' me Mickey."

"All right, Mickey. If this is your beat, I'm sure you're very familiar with it. The man who set up the kidnapping was someone I had considered to be a friend. His name was Warren Kennedy. He was from New York and—"

"Warren Kennedy is it?" Mickey said, interrupting. "I know the man. He was leader of a gang that called themselves the Irish Assembly, 'n 'twas an evil man he was, too."

"I found that out," Smoke said. "I'm ashamed to say, though, that he had me fooled for a long time."

"No shame to it, m' lad. 'Tis many a man Kennedy 'n his slick tongue had fooled."

"Apparently the man he was working with here in New York is named Gallagher," Smoke said. "Is that a name you can associate with Kennedy?"

"Aye, that would be Ian Gallagher. Some would say that the Irish Assembly is no more, 'n 'tis true, they are no longer the gang they once were. But there are still enough of them around to cause trouble, 'n Gallagher is one of them."

"Mickey, didn't you say that O'Leary was part of the Irish Assembly?" Cal asked.

"Aye, lad, that I did, 'n I was thinkin' there might be some connection. 'Tis glad I am that you brought me a name," Mickey said. "I think we can find him, 'n maybe get an idea as to where yer lady might be."

"No need to go looking for him," Smoke replied.

"What do you mean, we don't need to look for him?" Cal asked. "Have you got something else in mind?"

"If everything goes as we have it set up, he'll meet us at noon, and he'll have Sally with him."

"So, you'll be payin' the ransom, will you?" Mickey asked. "Well, I can't say as I'll be blamin' you. I would probably do the same thing if 'twas my loved one."

Smoke shook his head. "I'll not be paying the ransom."

"Askin' too much, is he?"

"Mickey, I just spent fifteen thousand dollars to rent a train to bring Pearlie and me here in record time. There's no such thing as *too much* money as far as my wife is concerned. I don't trust him to turn her over to me, even if I have the money in hand, so I have something else in mind. That's why I sent a telegram, asking him to meet us."

"And he agreed?" Cal asked.

"Yes. Apparently there are some abandoned cottages on 52nd Avenue between 10th and 11th Streets. Do you know the address, Mickey?"

"Aye . . . there is a whole row of deserted houses there, 'n 'tis a place frequented by brigands 'n hoodlums. 'Tis not a place for a decent citizen to be."

"I thought it might be something like that."

"Do you think, maybe, Gallagher might suspect Kennedy has something set up for him?" Pearlie asked.

"That could be the case," Smoke said. "Or, perhaps Mr. Gallagher has something planned for the late Mayor Kennedy."

Back at the apartment where Sally was being held, Kelly stepped into her bedroom then held his finger across his lips, signaling her to be quiet.

"Ever'one but Gallagher has gone to meet Kennedy," Kelly said. "Gallagher is downstairs 'n he sent me to bring you down. But if you do just what I tell you to do, I'm goin' to help you escape."

"Thank you, Mr. Kelly. That is a courageous thing for you to do."

Kelly opened the door and looked outside, then he turned back to her. "There is a fire escape on the back side of the buildin' that goes down to the alley. Once we get into the alley, follow me."

Sally nodded, and Kelly held his hand out toward her, holding her back as he made one final check.

"All right. There's nobody here. Let's go," Kelly said.

The two moved quickly through the living room and into the small kitchen. He lifted the window, then stepped through it onto the fire escape deck. He turned back toward Sally. "Come on," he beckoned.

She climbed through the window, as well, then followed him down the ladder. Kelly reached the ground first, and he stepped back to wait for Sally.

"Which way now?" she asked.

"Why don't you come this way?" Gallagher stepped out from behind a large trash bin, holding a pistol.

"Gallagher!" Kelly gasped.

"I knew you couldn't be trusted," Gallagher said. The sound of the gunshot was loud in the close confines of the alley.

"Mr. Kelly!" Sally called out in despair as she saw her would-be rescuer go down with a hole in his chest. He was dead within two more gasping breaths. "You killed him."

"That I did, lass, that I did. Now, would you please be for putting these on?" Gallagher tossed her a pair of manacles.

CHAPTER 36

With Mickey Muldoon leading the way, Smoke, Pearlie, and Cal rode the trolley car to within one block of where they were to meet with Gallagher. They stepped down from the car at about ten minutes to twelve.

"There you be, lads," Mickey said, pointing. "It's but one block that way, 'n we can't be for missing it. 'Tis one long building, all joined together. Two stories, they are, 'n mostly boarded up."

"You don't think Gallagher will be alone, do you, Smoke?" Muldoon asked.

"No, I don't. If he intended to meet us alone, he wouldn't have chosen the site of abandoned and boarded-up cottages."

"'Twould be my guess that he 'n whoever he has with him are already there," Muldoon said. "Come, we'll see what this is all about."

"Thanks, Mickey," Smoke said, "but this is as far as you go. We'll take it from here."

"But you will be for needin' me, seein' as I'm the only policeman."

"You would like to remain a member of the New York Police Department, wouldn't you?" Smoke asked.

"Aye, 'tis all I've ever known."

"Then trust me. You don't want to be with us."

"'N how, may I ask, will it be legal for you to arrest Gallagher and those who are with him?"

"I don't intend to arrest them," Smoke said.

"Then how will you—" Mickey started to ask, then he realized what Smoke was saying.

"Mickey, it's been good working with you," Cal said, putting his hand on the policeman's shoulder. "But you want no part of this. I'd advise you to take the next trolley out of here."

Mickey nodded, then he took Cal's hand. "Take care, m' friend. If Gallagher truly shows up, 'tis for sure 'n certain he won't be alone."

"Here comes another trolley," Pearlie said.

Cal stood with Smoke and Pearlie as Officer Mickey Muldoon, his new friend, stepped onto the car, then waved back at him as the driver snapped the reins at the horses.

"He's a good man," Cal said as the trolley moved quickly down the track.

"I've no doubt, otherwise you wouldn't have befriended him," Smoke said. "All right. What do you say we go get Sally back?"

At that very moment, less than one-quarter mile away were Gallagher and the six men who had come with him. His force had been decreased by one when he left Kelly in the alley behind his Third Street apartment.

"Brockway, you go up to the second floor of this apartment," Gallagher said, pointing to the one they were standing before. As he assigned each man, he pointed to three other apartments. "Doolin, you take that one, Quinn, that one, 'n Ryan, that one be yours." He also positioned McDougal and Keagan, leaving the bottom floor of the middle townhouse for himself.

"Why we doin' all this for one man?" Brockway asked.

"Sure now, Brockway, 'n you know Kennedy as well as any of us. Are you for thinkin' that he'll come here alone? He'll have some men with 'im, 'n it'll be his thought to kill us 'n take the woman back without payin' for her. He's not like us. He's not an honest man that can be trusted."

Despite the peril of her situation, at Gallagher's suggestion that Kennedy wasn't an honest man the way they were, Sally couldn't help but laugh out loud.

"'N would you be for tellin' me why 'tis you're laughin'?" Gallagher asked in a gruff voice.

"Never mind. I don't think you would understand," Sally said.

As the others took their positions, Gallagher kept Sally, who still had her hands manacled, close enough to him so he could keep an eye on her, or so he told the others. In truth, she was acting as his shield. If Kennedy really did want her alive, he would be careful where he shot for fear of hitting Sally.

With everyone in position, Gallagher stood with gun in hand, waiting for Kennedy to show.

"Hey, Gallagher," Brockway called down. "They's three men comin' this way from Tenth Street."

"What did I tell you? I tol' you he wouldn't be alone."

"That ain't Kennedy," Doolin called. "I don't know who they are."

"Look at that feller on the left," Brockway said. "He's the man that was with the woman the night we took 'er. He's also the one that kilt O'Leary, but I don't know who the other two are. They're not cops, I can tell you that. All three of 'em is dressed just alike 'im, 'n all of 'em is wearin' pistol belts."

"Smoke!" Sally said the name involuntarily, her excitement overcoming caution.

"Son of a bitch. I should have known Kennedy would be for tryin' somethin' like this," Gallagher said angrily.

"Brockway, you 'n the others hold your fire 'till they get real close. When you're sure you can't miss, start shootin'."

Sally moved into position so she could see through the window and that it was Smoke, Pearlie, and Cal approaching. How many times since she had married Smoke had she seen this very thing—Smoke, Pearlie, and Cal facing death together? Even though she knew that their situation and hers was precarious, she couldn't help but feel confident that rescue was at hand.

She waited until just before she thought that Brockway and the others would start shooting, then she yelled. "Smoke, look out! It's a trap!"

That forced the issue, and though the three approaching men were not yet within a very easy, can't-miss range, Gallagher's men had no alternative but to start shooting. They were hampered by the fact that none of the three approaching men were close enough for a sure shot, and also because the warning had caused the three men to split apart so that none offered an easy target.

Pearlie was able to take cover behind one of the denuded and dead trees that grew in the front of the buildings, while Cal hurried to a rock pillar that anchored one end of the rusting, iron stake fence. Smoke stood in place, gun in hand, looking at the building waiting for the first shot.

The first shot came from a second-story window right in the middle of the row of connected buildings. He returned fire and saw a man tumble from the window. He didn't move when he hit the ground.

Firing broke out in general then, with several shots coming from various positions within the old abandoned buildings. The firing was answered, shot for shot, as Pearlie and Cal were well positioned.

The only one still exposed, Smoke was anything but an easy target. He moved around, snapping shots back at the wisps of gun smoke that drifted from the windows. He saw a shooter appear in one of the windows, preparatory to taking a shot. Before the shooter could get off a round, Smoke fired, saw a little mist of blood fly from the shooter's head, and knew he had made a killing shot.

At almost the same time, Pearlie killed one, and Cal another. Smoke had no idea how many they were against, but while the shooting continued, the intensity of the shooting diminished as each of the ambushers were killed until finally, the shooting stopped.

"Brockway?" a voice called. "Ryan? Doolin, McDougal, Keagan, Quinn?"

There were no answers to the call.

Since *Gallagher* had not been one of the names shouted out, Smoke realized the caller was Gallagher and shouted, "They're all dead, Gallagher. You're all alone."

"Where is Kennedy?" Gallagher shouted back from the middle apartment.

Smoke knew it was the same apartment from which Sally had called her warning. For that reason, not one of them shot through that window. "Sally?" Smoke called.

"I'm all right, Smoke," Sally answered.

"Where is Kennedy?" Gallagher asked again.

"Kennedy is dead."

"Are you the one who killed him?"

"No. I planned to, but someone else killed him first. Send my wife out."

Although Smoke had not really expected any response to his demand, the door opened, and he saw Sally standing there. "Sally, can you come toward me?"

"No."

Almost as soon as she responded, Sally did start toward him, but it was easy to see that she wasn't moving of her own volition.

Bent over behind her in such a way, Gallagher offered nothing as a target. "I have a gun pressed up against your wife's back. Put the ten thousand dollars down in front of you, then all three of you drop your guns and walk away. If you don't do that, I'll kill the woman."

"Then what?" Smoke asked.

"What do you mean, 'then what?' If I kill her, she'll be dead."

"So will you," Smoke said.

"'N are you for tellin' me, that you'd be for riskin' yer own wife's life?" Gallagher asked.

"I can get another wife. You can't get another life."

Sally laughed. "Smoke, I can't believe you would say something like that."

"You could always bow to my brilliance," Smoke said.

"I guess I could, couldn't I? Here's to you, oh brilliant one," Sally replied. Then, not in any sudden move as if trying to escape, but even as she was still laughing, she made a deep bow.

Sally's unexpected move caught Gallagher completely by surprise, but he wasn't surprised long. A bullet from Smoke's gun hit him right between the eyes.

Sugarloaf Ranch

Smoke was standing on the ground in front of a magnificent black horse with a white face and three white stockings. This was the son of the Seven who had been killed. Technically, his name was *Seven Number Four*, but Smoke called him, as he had those before him, just *Seven*.

"Where is the sugar, Seven?" he asked.

Seven put his nose first to one shirt pocket then the other, then lifting his nose, he pushed Smoke's hat back. Smoke took off his hat and removed the lump of sugar he had concealed there.

"Ha!" Thad grinned from atop his horse. "You can't fool Seven. He's almost as smart as Fire."

"Almost, huh?" Smoke replied.

"But you can't blame Seven. He's still learning."

"Fire might be smart, but he isn't as handsome as Sir Charles." Lorena leaned forward in the saddle and patted her horse on its neck.

"I can't believe you named your horse Sir Charles," Thad teased. "He's probably so embarrassed by his name that it's a wonder he can even move."

"Really? Catch me." With a quick slap of her legs against the sides of Sir Charles, the horse burst forth like a cannon-ball.

Thad dashed out after them, his and Lorena's laughter filling the air.

"Cute kids," Sally said as she, Smoke, Pearlie, and Cal watched the two riders grow smaller in the distance.

"I wonder if they'll remember this when they are both in their seventies?" Cal asked.

"Why not?" Smoke replied. "They'll be able to remind each other."

Almost overnight, Dead Broke turns into a lawless
hotbed of angry out-of-work miners
and out-for-blood merchants. In desperation,
Mayor Nugget considers a few hairbrained schemes like
bringing in mail-order brides, building ice castles to
attract tourists, even planting other minerals in the mines
to fool investors. Dead Broke needs law and order, so
Nugget sends for top gun Mick MacMicking.
But a notorious gambler named Connor Boyle has other
plans—and with his band of hired guns will blow
Dead Broke off the map completely to get what he wants.

For this town to survive, Nugget, Mick, a drunken
lawman and a woman gambler will have to
put the dead back in Dead Broke . . . and some
cool-hand killers in the ground.

**National Bestselling Authors
William W. Johnstone
and J.A. Johnstone**

DEAD BROKE, COLORADO

First in a New Western Series!

On sale now, wherever Pinnacle Books are sold.

**JOHNSTONE COUNTRY.
WHERE DYING IS EASY AND LIVING IS HARD.**

Live Free. Read Hard.
**williamjohnstone.net
Visit us at kensingtonbooks.com**

1885

PROLOGUE

Allane Auchinleck was drunk that morning.

But then, most wastrels on This Side Of The Slope would have pointed out that Allane Auchinleck was seldom sober any morning, any afternoon, any evening. Any day of the year. Since he had seldom found enough gold in Colorado's towering Rocky Mountains to pay for good rye, he brewed his own whiskey. It wasn't fit to drink, other miners would agree, but it was whiskey. So they drank whatever Allane Auchinleck was willing to sell or, rarely, share.

Auchinleck charged a dollar a cup—Leadville prices, the other miners would protest, but they paid.

After all, it was whiskey.

And in these towering mountains, whiskey—like anything else a man could buy or steal in Denver, Durango, Silverton, or Colorado Springs—was hard to find.

Besides, Auchinleck usually was so far in his cups that he couldn't tell the difference between a nickel and a Morgan dollar. For most miners, one cup usually did the job. Actually, two sips fried the brains of many unaccustomed to a Scotsman's idea of what went into good liquor. Two cups, a few men had learned, could prove fatal. Auchinleck held the record, four cups in four hours—and still alive to tell the story.

Although, it should be pointed out that those who had witnessed that historic drunken evening, would swear on a stack of bibles—not that a Good Book could be found this high up—that Auchinleck's hair, from topknot to the tip of his long beard, wasn't as white, but had been much thicker, before he passed out, not to awaken for three days. That had been back in '79.

But then, Auchinleck was accustomed to forty-rod, and it was his recipe, his liquor, his cast-iron stomach and his soul, the latter of which he said he had sold to the devil, then got it back when Lucifer himself needed a shot of the Scotsman's brew.

On this particular glorious August evening, with the first snow falling at eleven thousand feet, Auchinleck was drinking with Sluagdach. Most of the miners had already started packing their mules and heading to lower, warmer, and much healthier elevations. Some would head south to thaw out and blow whatever they had accumulated in their pokes. Many would drift east to Denver, where the heartiest would find jobs swamping saloons or moving horse apples out of livery stables. Others would just call it quits as a miner and find an easier way to make a living.

But not Allane Auchinleck. "Mining is my life," he told Sluagdach, and topped off his cup with more of his swill.

"Aye," Sluagdach said. "And a mighty poor life it has been, Nugget."

Nugget had become Auchinleck's handle. There are some who say that the Scotsman earned that moniker because of his determination, certainly not for his lack of profitable results. More than likely, the moniker had stuck to the miner like stains of tobacco juice because Nugget was a whole lot easier to remember or say than Auchinleck.

That was the year Sluagdach came in as Auchinleck's partner. It made sense at the time (though Sluagdach was a touch more than just fairly inebriated) when such a partnership had been suggested in a tent near the headwaters of the Arkansas River.

They both came to America from Scotland, Auchinleck had pointed out. They could enter this deal as equals. Nugget still had his mule; Sluagdach had to eat his. Sluagdach had a new pickax, while Nugget had been the first to discover that Finnian Kuznetsov, that half-Irish, half-Russian gravel snatcher, had run into a she-bear with two cubs, and had not been able to raise his Sharps carbine in time. The she-bear won that fight, and the cubs enjoyed a fine breakfast, but Nugget had given the Russian mick a burial, and taken the shovel and pack, and a poke of silver, and Kuznetsov's boots and mink hat. Although he did not let his partner know, Nugget had also found the dead miner's mule (lucky critter, having fled while the she-bear and cubs enjoyed a breakfast of Kuznetsov), which is how Nugget brought a mule into the partnership, his own having been stolen by some thief, or had wandered off to parts unknown while its master slept off a drunk.

"I said," Sluagdach said, raising his voice after getting no response from his drunkard partner, "that a mighty poor life it . . . ." But the whiskey robbed his memory, as Nugget's whiskey often did.

"Who can be poor when he lives in this wild, fabulous country?" Nugget, whose tolerance for his special malt had not fogged his memory or limited vocabulary. "Look at these mountains. Feel this snow. God's country this is."

"God," Sluagdach said, "is welcome to it."

That's when Nugget, against his better judgment, reached into the ripped apart coat that he had also taken from the dearly departed dead miner, and pulled out the poke. By the time he realized what he was doing, the poke had flown out of Nugget's hand and landed at Sluagdach's feet.

The muleless miner stared at the leather pouch, reached between his legs—he did not recall sitting down, but that

Scotsman's liquor had a way of making men forget lots of things—and heard the grinding of rocks inside. It took him a few minutes for his eyes to focus and his brain to recall how to work the strings to open the little rawhide bag, and then saw a few chunks fall into the grass, damp with snow that hadn't started to stick.

No matter how drunk a miner got, he was never too far gone not to recognize good ore.

"Silver," he whispered, and looked across the campsite at his partner.

"That's how Leadville got started," Nugget heard himself saying.

"Where was his camp?"

After a heavy sigh, Nugget shook his head.

"Best I could tell," he explained, "he was on his way down the slope when 'em cubs et him."

"To file a claim." Sluagdach sounded sober all of a sudden.

Nugget felt his head bob in agreement.

One of the nuggets came to Sluagdach's right eye. Then it was lowered to his mouth, and his tongue tasted it, then it went inside his mouth where his gold upper molar and his rotted lower molar tested it. After removing the bit of ore, he stared at his partner.

"This'll assay anywhere from twenty-two to twenty-five ounces per ton."

No miner on This Side Of The Slope and hardly a professional metallurgist from Arizona to Colorado would doubt anything Sluagdach said. No one knew how he did it. But he had never been more than an ounce off his predictions. The Russian-Irishman had never made a fortune as a miner, but his good eye, his teeth, and his tongue knew what they saw, bit, and tasted.

Unable to think of anything to say, Nugget killed the bit of whiskey remaining in his cup, then belched.

"Where exactly did that ol' feller got et?" Sluagdach asked. His voice had an eerie quietness to it.

Nugget's head jerked in a vague northeasterly direction. Which he could blame on his drunkenness if Sluagdach remembered anything in the morning.

Finnian Kuznetsov had met his grisly end to a grizzly sow and her cubs about four miles southwest.

"Think this snow'll last?" Sluagdach asked.

"Nah." It was way too early, even at this altitude, and, well, twenty-two to twenty-five ounces per ton had to be worth the risk.

They set out early the next morning, finding the hole where Nugget had rolled Finnian Kuznetsov's remains and covered with pine needles and some rocks, which had been removed by some critter that had scattered bones and such all over the area. Then they backtracked over rough country, and around twelve thousand feet, they found the Irish Russian's camp.

Two months later, they had discovered . . .

"Not a thing," Sluagdach announced, although he had used practically every foul word that a good Scot knew to describe that particular thing.

By then, at that altitude, winter was coming in right quick like, and their supplies were all but out. This morning's breakfast had been piñon nuts and Nugget's whiskey. Sleet had pelted them that morning, and Sluagdach had slipped on an icy patch and almost broken his back, while Nugget's mule grew more cantankerous every minute.

"We'll have to come back next spring," Sluagdach said.

With a sad nod, Nugget went to his keg of whiskey, rocked

the oak a bit, and decided there was just enough for a final night of celebration—or mourning—for the two of them.

It was a drunk to remember. Sluagdach broke Nugget's record. Shattered it, would have been a more accurate description. Five cups. Five! While Nugget had to stop drinking— *his own whiskey*—after three.

It wasn't because he couldn't handle his wretched brew. It was because he now saw everything. He saw that Sluagdach would dissolve the partnership. Sluagdach would come back to these beasts of mountains and find the Russian mick's discovery. Sluagdach would go down in history. Allane "Nugget" Auchinleck would be forgotten.

Auchinleck. What a name. What a lie. He remembered way back when he was but a lad, living near the Firth of Clyde in the county of Ayrshire on Scotland's west coast of Scotland, and his grandfather, a fine man who had given Nugget his first taste of single malt when he was but four years old, had told him what the name Auchinleck meant.

"A place of field with flat stones," the old man had said.

It sounded glorious to a four-year-old pup of boy, but now he scoffed at it all. A place of field with flat stones. Oh, the stones were here all right, massive boulders of granite that held riches in them, but would never let those riches go. And flat?

He laughed, and tossed his empty cup toward the fire.

There was nothing flat on This Side Of The Slope.

That's when Allane Auchinleck decided it was time to kill himself.

He announced his intentions to Sluagdach, who laughed, agreeing that it was a fine, fine idea.

Sluagdach even laughed when Nugget withdrew a stick of dynamite in a box of dwindling supplies. Laughing? That swine of a Russian mick. No, no. Nugget had to correct his thinking. Sluagdach was a Scot. The Russian mick was

Finnian Kuznetsov, dead and et by a Colorado she-grizzly's cubs.

"I'll speak lovingly of you at your funeral," Sluagdach said, and he cackled even harder when Nugget began to cap and fuse the explosive.

It wasn't until Nugget lit the fuse by holding the stick over the fire that Sluagdach acted soberly.

For a man who should, if the Lord was indeed merciful, be dead already or at least passed out, Sluagdach moved like a man who really wanted not to be blown to bits.

He came charging like that she-bear must have charged old the Russian mick, and the next thing Nugget recalled was his ears ringing and the entire ground shaking. Somehow, Sluagdach had knocked the dynamite away, and it must have rolled down the hill toward that massive rock of immovable stone.

Nugget could not recall the explosion, but his ears were ringing, and he felt stones and bits of wood and more stones raining down upon him. They would cover him in his grave. Peace of earth. God rest this merry gentleman.

"You ignorant, crazy, drunken fool."

That was not, Nugget figured out eventually, the voice of St. Peter. He sat up, brushing off the dust, the grime, the mud, the sand, and looked into the eyes of his equally intoxicated fellow miner. His partner.

He didn't think anyone would call him sober, but he realized just how drunk—and how close to death, real death he had come.

"Oh . . . ," however, was about all Nugget could muster at that moment.

"Oh." His partner wiped his bloody nose, then crawled out of the rubble and staggered toward the smoking ruins of part of the camp they had made.

"Mule!" Nugget remembered.

The brays gave him some relief, and as smoke and dust

settled, he saw the animal through rocks and forests about three hundred yards away. It appeared that the tether had hooked like an anchor between some rocks and halted the beast's run for its life. Otherwise, the mule might be in Leadville by now.

Maybe even Omaha.

He started for the animal, but Sluagdach told him to stop. "Come up here!" his pard demanded.

Well, Nugget couldn't deny the man who had stopped him from killing himself. He climbed up the ridge, where he looked down into the smokiness.

He could smell the rotten egg stench of blown powder. And he could see what one stick of dynamite could do. It had created a chasm.

And unveiled a cave.

"Get us a light," Sluagdach said.

Somehow, the campfire still burned, and Nugget found a stick that would serve as a torch, so they walked, slipped, skidded, and slid down into the depression and toward the cave.

"Bear," Nugget remembered.

"If a silvertip was in there, it would be out by now," Sluagdach argued.

They stopped at the entrance, and Nugget held the torch into the opening.

The flame from the torch bounced off the left side of the cave. Slowly the two men staggered to that wall, and Nugget held the torch closer.

"The mother lode," Sluagdach said.

He didn't have to smell and taste the vein of silver to know that. What's more, when they moved fifty yards deeper into the cavern, the torch revealed something else. At first, Nugget thought it was an Egyptian mummy. He had seen an illustration in one of those newspapers he could not read.

But this wasn't a mummy. He held the torch higher,

praying that it would not go out. At least there was no wind here to blow it out.

"It's . . ." Nugget could not find the words.

"The biggest . . . chunk . . . of sil-ver . . . I ever . . . did . . . see."

I am dead, Nugget thought. Or I'm dreaming.

His partner stuck his dirty pointer finger in his mouth, getting it good and wet, then touched the gleaming mummy that was a statue of precious metal.

The biggest nugget Allane Auchinleck had ever seen. The biggest one anybody had ever seen.

Maybe he was dead after all.

Sluagdach brought his pointer finger, slobbery with his slobber, and rubbed it on the giant nugget. It was shaped like a diamond. A diamond made of pure silver.

Sluagdach then put his finger back in his mouth.

His eyes widened.

"It . . . I . . . I . . . aye . . . aye . . . It . . ."

That's when the wind, or something—maybe Sluagdach's giant gasps at air—blew out the torch.

And Sluagdach collapsed in front of the silver diamond.

Nugget never knew how he did it, but he found his pard's shoulders, then dragged him out into the fading light of the camp. The old man with a Midas tongue stared up. But his right hand gripped the coat above his breast, and the eyes did not blink.

"Your ticker," Nugget whispered.

Yes. The sight of that strike . . . it had been too much for a man, even a man who had downed five cups of that lethal brew.

That meant . . .

Nugget rose. "No partner." He ran back to the campfire, found a piece of timber, part of the suicidal destruction he had reaped, and stuck it in the coals till the end ignited. The wood must have been part pitch, because it blazed with a fury, and Nugget raced back down, past his dead pard, and into the cave where he held the blazing torch again.

It was no dream. No drunken hallucination. It was . . . real . . . silver . . . the strike of a lifetime.

He ran back, ready to mark his claim, and get his name onto a document that made this.

"All mine."

When he stepped outside, it was dark. He walked slowly, using the timber as his light, and stopped in front of the body of his poor, dead, pard.

"I won't forget you," he whispered to the unseeing corpse. And it a moment of generosity, he proclaimed.

"You're dead, and I was broke, but Colorado will remember us forever, because I'm naming this mine, and the town that'll grow up around it, Dead Broke. That's it." He felt relieved.

"Dead Broke, Colorado." He nodded. The flame seemed to reflect in the dead man's eyes, and maybe it was because of the light, but he thought Sluagdach nodded in agreement.

"Dead Broke, Colorado," he said.

"Because who would want to work and live in a place called Sluagdach Auchinleck?"

Visit our website at
KensingtonBooks.com
to sign up for our newsletters, read
more from your favorite authors, see
books by series, view reading group
guides, and more!

Become a Part of Our
Between the Chapters Book Club
Community and Join the Conversation